CRISPR Evolution

CHARIS JONES

Print ISBN: 979-8-9863849-0-0
.mobi ISBN: 979-8-9863849-2-4
.epub ISBN: 979-8-9863849-1-7
Library of Congress Control Number: 2022917323

Published in Reno, NV, USA

For Mom and Dad,
who taught me that work is fun
and fun is work

and for Pete, who tossed in the Jones spices
and turned up the heat on this tale

Contents

Prologue

The sleeper stirred in its dreams.

It had begun as nothing more than a blueprint, a seed that had crossed the vast, windless gulf to lodge in a bed of soil. Sheltered in the safety of its shell, the blueprint lay intact as the soil around it grew richer and more lively, sprouting the first dynamic forms able to contain it. Engulfed by these simple organisms, the blueprint began to dream—simple dreams of change and growth. Battles, invasions, and alliances took place in the soil, and the living clay that harbored the blueprint morphed across the millennia. Eons passed, and the template slept in the changing cradle of its host's flesh, which broke from the ground and took to the air, the seas, the trees. One of these fast-leaping vessels paused long enough to become aware of itself. Its children began to contemplate and dream, enabling the sleeper within them to conjure larger dreams. These drifted up into the world, searching for flames to kindle. And some ready wick must have caught, because here, now, in this one vessel, a ray of light had broken through. It was very faint, but it penetrated the darkness of the sleeper's nest for the first time.

The template—no longer a mere blueprint, but the motive force of a living soul—strained toward the light and began to whisper in its dreams.

Part One

Garage Biologist

I

When the sting alert went off, the Director of the Wake Institute for Garage Biology was thinking of nothing more sinister than vanilla pudding cups.

"There's another pack in here somewhere," Howard muttered, thrusting his head deeper into the RV's pantry. He rooted through cans of soup that were too salty for his son, jars of peaches that were too sweet, and boxes of crackers that were too sharp and prickly. "Where are you, you little bastards?"

It doesn't have to be pudding, a cooler voice in his head reminded him. *Don't we have any more of those instant shakes? Or mashed potato flakes? Or a bag of rice you can cook down to gruel?* Soft, bland foods were all Py could tolerate these days, but there didn't seem to be any left. A hunk of metal caught Howard's eye, and he pulled out an electric can opener in bewilderment. Despite owning and fashioning plenty of tools, Howard had no respect for gadgets that took up more space and did less than a pocket knife. Hell, the best tools of all were microscopic. *For your size,* he silently rebuked the can opener, *you ought to dispense seven-course meals with happy endings.* Shoving it to the back of the pantry, Howard finally caught sight of the elusive pudding cups and gave a little cry of triumph. But before he could snag them, a sharp jab in his left wrist made him cry out again.

Looking down, he expected to see a hornet perched on his skin, but there was only the digital arachnid that always nestled there, clinging almost weightlessly to his wrist. The silver device looked like a standard Spider—a versatile but trackable computer that marked its owner like a fingerprint—but it wasn't. Howard's was a variety known as a Ghost Spider, the digital equivalent of a sawed-off shotgun. The penalty for carrying one was severe, but

Howard had long operated under the motto *in for a penny, in for a pound,* and his Spider was not exactly defenseless. Its tiny screen was dark at the moment, but the message icon was flashing. Howard brought up the holographic message, which was only a single word: LIGHTNING. Combined with the sting alert, that word was a coded warning he hadn't seen for two years.

Change of plans for the day, Howard thought numbly, as the stew of nerves in his stomach began to simmer. He set the pudding cups on the table, then stood rubbing his wrist in the early light that filtered through the kitchen blinds, feeling the bone-deep exhaustion that underlay all of his fears and tensions. He was tired of being chased, of living on the fringes and dancing around the idiots who ran the world. Tired of his every move depending on theirs. *No time to whine about all that now.* Another sting came hard on the heels of this thought, and he looked down in consternation at the second warning: THUNDER.

Yes, he'd better save his pity party for tonight—when they were holed up in a motel room a hundred miles away. Staring down at his Spider, the two words still shouted silently up at him, not a figment of his paranoia. Taking a deep breath, he headed down the hall to wake the kids.

But when he poked his head into their bedroom that doubled as a day room, Aurie's mattress was already folded into its chair conformation. Py was still asleep on his mattress, although Howard had to look twice to see him. It was astonishing the way his children deflected notice. Even after eight years, they still managed to fool him into thinking they were part of the scenery. Py lay practically naked and spread-eagled on his back. His light brown hair was dark with sweat, but at least he was sleeping quietly for a change.

Howard looked around the narrow room, suddenly struck by its transient character. His kids should have had real bedrooms of their own instead of this makeshift space, although Aurie's personality spilled into every space she occupied. In the middle of her little end table stood a big jar filled with Indian Pipes and the crenellated folds of a sunset-colored fungus.

Around this exotic display lay stacks of notes and notebooks, along with Aurie's treasured hard copies of *The Hobbit* and *Ender's Game*. The kids did most of their reading on the holo-display of their Spiders, but Aurie was enchanted by real books. It was a source of genuine sorrow to her that *All-of-a-kind Family,* her very favorite, was long out of print. Howard had scanned the holo-book out of curiosity, and was baffled by her interest. The mundane adventures of five Jewish sisters living in New York City in the early 1900s? Strange choice for a girl who loved sci-fi and fantasy, but he kept an eye on the rare book markets in case he could surprise her with it someday.

In sharp contrast to his sister's, Py's end table was completely bare—a condition he had to fight for daily, since Aurie thought any unused space ought to be hers by default. Py insisted that he needed a clean surface to study on, although God knew he spent most of his time studying the underside of the woods rather than the inside of any books. Py's only treasured possessions—his nets and traps, Berlese funnel, aspirator, and eye loupe—never left his backpack.

As if the thought of the woods had permeated his sleep, Py twitched. His hands grew restless, roaming over the mattress as if sampling the terrain of his dreams. A corner of the bedsheet had come up over one of his feet, which began to jerk. Without touching his son, Howard carefully lifted the sheet away, and the uncovered foot grew still. He watched Py for a moment, wishing fiercely for a flash of insight—surely he could do *something* to help, if he only knew what—then decided not to wake him. Better to let the poor kid get whatever rest he could. Closing the door softly, Howard headed outside to look for Py's twin sister.

She would be in the lab, of course. And if Aurie had risen before dawn, she was probably up to no good. Howard wended his way through the trees, shivering in air that finally held an October chill. Nights in the Massachusetts lowlands had been warm, and autumn color had yet to flare. The tangle of woods around Cedar Swamp Pond was just beginning to brown; in the thin light of dawn, it looked dry and thirsty for a storm. Reaching the old hunting shed in the grove, he pressed his thumb to the tiny touch-lock on the door and walked inside.

The atmosphere hit him at once—this air that was like no other, heady with the pungent tang of newborn ideas and the mellow sweetness of long-simmered ones. The magic of the place always gripped him hardest when the time came to pack it up. Every chipped flask had a story to tell; every piece of worn equipment was an old friend. The collapsible hood he had built out of scrap boards and Plexiglas stood in its corner, a silent tribute to simple tools and old technology; the pet frogs that had outlasted their tenure as research subjects stirred in their tank. Homemade gel boxes and chromatography columns lined the shelves. Little notes the kids had made hung everywhere, drawings and declarations. His family might eat and sleep and shower in the RV, but they *lived* in the lab. And he had never loved a place the way he loved this room he shared with his kids, whether it was the inside of a hunting cabin or a fishing shack or an old barn. The outside guise shifted, but the inside was always the same, and it was always home.

As he'd expected, all the lights in the lab were on and his daughter was busy at the gel-running station. If she'd noticed his entrance, she gave no sign.

"Staining a gel at half past six?" Howard said. "When did you get up?"

Aurie finished adding dye to one of the Tupperware containers that served as staining trays and set it rotating briskly, then turned to face his approach with a look of suppressed eagerness. "I don't know ... awhile ago."

Howard frowned at the dark smudges under her eyes. "Still having that nightmare about the sunshine?"

She snorted with exasperation. "It's not sunshine, Dad—it's the sun in my face, blinding me. Always wakes me up, and with Py thrashing around, I can't get back to sleep. It's driving me crazy!"

Howard pulled her close and Aurie relaxed a little in his embrace.

"Sorry, Dad. I'm not complaining about Py—I know he can't help it."

"Go ahead and complain, kiddo." He ruffled her hair fondly. "You're the number one worker bee around here, so you have a direct line to the Director of this madhouse ... not that he can do anything to help."

Aurie pulled back and looked around the room. Her eyes—green in sunlight, hazel in the woods, now grey as a winter sky in the overhead fluorescents—were suddenly hopeful. "You could let me sleep in here! I could stack some foam blocks in the corner and make a bed."

Howard gave her a knowing look. "You only want to sleep in here so you can perform unauthorized experiments after hours. Speaking of which, what *are* you running on that gel?"

"Just a little side-project I started on Monday," she mumbled, but he caught the spark of mischief in her eyes before she ducked down to retrieve a fallen pipette tip. That roguish excitement struck a chord deep inside him. After all, Aurie herself was a little side-project Howard had started on his own, after hours and away from prying eyes.

"Well," he said seriously, "you'll have to put it on hold for now. Alé's accounts have been hacked."

She stiffened and stared up at him. "By FIBR?"

"Who else?" Howard said, involuntarily clenching his own muscles. Since 2051, the esteemed Federal Institute for Biomedical Research had not only driven the best and brightest underground, but could afford its own pet brute squad to drag them back into the light of the law-abiding world. Howard could still remember the days when FIBR was just a medical research center called the National Institutes of Health. He had been a postdoc back then, getting paid through NIH grants. Just nineteen years ago, but they felt like a lifetime.

"We probably have a few days before they actually know where to find us, but we can't count on that." He saw the distraught look on her face, and spoke gently. "Don't worry, we're always a step ahead of those bozos. The two of us will have this place packed up in no time."

"I'm not scared of *FIBR*," Aurie said with steadfast scorn. "Just wish we didn't have to leave right now." She sighed as her gaze was drawn back to the Tupperware swishing away on its platform. "Can I look at my gel before we pack up the light box?"

"Of course." He bent down to kiss the top of her head, which shifted between brown and a coppery silver, mimicking the gleam of their lab equipment in the artificial light. "Let's take care of all the chemicals in the meantime. And Py can't help, so we've got a lot to do. Sorry there's no time for Belgian waffles and strawberry parfaits today."

Aurie snickered as she darted away. "You mean toaster waffles and canned peaches? I'll go find some granola bars."

Howard followed her to the door, watching her run back to the RV through the oak woods. In the shade, his children moved like shadows, but in direct sunlight, they almost melted into the brightness of the air. Aurie seemed to reflect all the light of the early morning, except for the dark, thread-like structures streaming from her left arm. Those hairs-that-were-not-hairs grew from the outside of her upper forearm and fell to her wrist. They were the one part of her that defied camouflage. The whole fringe was a blue so deep it was nearly black, and it fanned out as she ran, drifting as if in water. Aurie had been born with these strange appendages, but Howard could only speculate as to what they were. Some kind of sensors covered with a modified exoskeleton? Aurie couldn't control them—although she tried—but they sometimes moved on their own, like organisms attracted to a mysterious chemical. Whatever Aurie's threads were, Howard knew they had to serve a purpose. The tiny evolutionary engine inside his daughter's cells didn't believe in useless decorations.

When he looked down, there was a new message on his Spider, this one an address. The Wake family was being relocated to Huntingdon, Pennsylvania—only a day's drive away, thank God. Garage venues turned over rapidly, and you had to take whatever foreclosed farmhouse or abandoned shack you could get. Their last location had been an adobe hut outside of Tucson, under a desert sun that turned their RV into a greenhouse half the year.

Aurie returned with a fistful of granola bars and a frown.

"Is your brother awake?" Howard asked, sensing the source of her concern.

She nodded, laying the bars on her workbench and looking at them with no sign of any appetite. "I told him what's going on, but he looks so sick. He couldn't even sit up to drink the rest of his shake from last night. How's he gonna sit up front with the RV moving?"

"I don't know," Howard said, his stomach twisting with self-reproach and nervous anticipation. He thought of the protein he had designed—a molecular machine that existed within every cell of his children's bodies. This protein was based on old turn-of-the-century technology, and Howard still thought of it by its old name: CRISPR. But this version was more powerful and autonomous than any of its predecessors. Howard was certain it was the CRISPR machine that was making Py so miserable. "At least we're not going far, just down to Pennsylvania. We'll stay at a motel tonight and be there by tomorrow morning."

"When do you think he'll get better?" Aurie asked quietly.

Howard only shook his head. They both knew that he had absolutely no idea. The CRISPR machine inside the twins was designed to make unpredictable improvements, but Py's development had been normal since birth. At least until two weeks ago, when the boy had been stricken by a severe hypersensitivity to just about everything.

"Well," said Aurie in a brighter voice, following Howard to their supply closet. "At least he doesn't have to help pack. And I'm a *way* better packer than Py. Remember last time, he put my Douncer in the box with all the hybe tubes, and it broke on the way here?"

Howard chuckled, remembering. "If you worked at FIBR, you wouldn't have to use a Douncer at all. They've got fancy machines for grinding up cells and tissues." Pausing before the closet, he heaved a sigh and donned a look of mock repentance. "Maybe I should confess all my crimes, throw myself on their mercy, and beg them to hire my brilliant daughter!"

Aurie made a scoffing noise, but she looked pleased at being called brilliant, and Howard grinned as he pulled out flattened boxes and rolls of bubble-wrap. If his little girl could have seen the federal research facility with all of its rumored bells and whistles, she would surely have stars in her eyes. A Smart Foam bed instead of a folding mattress in an RV. Restaurant food made by award-winning chefs instead of canned soup and thrown-together casseroles. Pools and parks instead of scrub woods to play in. Still, Howard found himself admiring his rogue outpost even as they began dismantling it. FIBR scientists wouldn't ever think of Mendel in his monastery garden, or Galileo in the prison of his house, but Howard never forgot those pioneers of old. How could he? He had greatly downsized his operation since leaving the Instituto de Biologia in Manila for a string of domestic hideouts, and it always gave him a surge of pride to see what he could do with a fraction of the space and money he used to have. The money came from his contract work for foreign companies—a prosaic crime, but it paid the bills—and a place like this was just big enough. Who needed a whole department in an institute, or a lab with twenty members? One man and two little geniuses alone in the world were enough.

Well, not completely alone, Howard admitted as he collected their reagents, all of which had been delivered through his contact, Aléjandro Ramirez. Alé was a member of the legitimate research world—chair of Genome Sciences at the University of Illinois in Urbana-Champaign—but Howard didn't hold that against him. On the contrary, it made him indispensable. Alé was a rebel in his own right, one of the linchpins in a scattered resistance, doing what he felt to be a dangerous but necessary job. He served his outlaw friends under the name of Ray Smith, acting as their eyes, ears, and hands in the outside world. And if the government dogs started sniffing around the rabbit burrows, Alé found out and rang the alarm. What he allowed Howard to pay him wasn't enough. The twins, of course, worked for free—and as Howard liked to tell them, they were worth every penny.

"Moment of truth!" Aurie cried, jolting Howard out of his contemplations. She sprang up from the box of acids they were packing and flew to the gel-running station. Picking up her gel the way another little girl might have lifted a newborn kitten, she slid it gently onto the old UV light box, put up the protective shield, and took a picture of the DNA fragments she had separated in the agarose. Seconds later, she groaned.

"Not the answer you wanted?" Howard said.

Aurie was quiet for a moment, then she blew out a frustrated breath. "I don't understand. I planned it perfectly this time!"

Howard went over to take a look at her picture. Whatever her secret experiment was, he suspected those sharp bands of DNA were Aurie's own, isolated from a saliva sample she'd collected last week when she thought he wasn't looking. Howard couldn't help but smile. His kids might have a natural incognito, but they were terrible at *trying* to be sneaky. "It's not all about planning, kiddo. You know how many brilliant ideas turn out to be wrong?"

"If they're so brilliant, how could they be wrong?"

"Anytime you do an experiment," he told her, "you're operating inside a whirlwind of assumptions. Because for any one thing we understand, there are a thousand things we don't understand at all."

"But we know some things for sure," Aurie countered, always eager to play the devil's advocate. She picked up a bottle of EDTA and shook it at him. "This is a chelator. It binds up elements like magnesium that have a plus-two charge."

"Sure," Howard agreed, checking the time on his Spider and hurrying back to the crate he was packing. "But what does it mean for something to be an *element*? What does it mean that it has a *plus-two* charge? The only reason we give things labels and put them into categories is to help us understand how they behave." He fell silent, groping for the right words. Aurie slid her gel into the waste bucket and wiped down the light box, but he knew her ears were pricked up, waiting for a fuller explanation. It was hard, sometimes, to remember that she was only eight. She rarely acted like a child, and he didn't want to wait for her to grow up to have real conversations. Py and Aurie were the only colleagues he had, and—with one exception—the only ones he wanted. He always felt a need to discuss everything with them immediately.

"What if," he said, "someone discovered a strange new law of nature? Something that completely changed the way we understand all chemicals?"

Aurie shrugged. "EDTA would still bind up magnesium in solution."

"Sure it would," Howard agreed, "but maybe for different reasons than the ones we believe now. I'm not arguing against natural phenomena—EDTA is a chelator, that's a fact. Balls roll downhill, not up. Lightning comes before thunder. But whenever we try to explain *why*—because of chemical properties, because of gravity, because lightning opens up a channel in the air—we are wandering into the land of conjecture. The land of science."

Science is not a collection of facts, he thought, for the umpteenth time in his life. *And scientists are not fact collectors.* Such common fallacies—caused by poor communication between scientists and the rest of the world—were a big part of the reason garage labs like his existed in the first place. "Science *uses* facts to create tools and models, and a model is nothing but a collection of educated guesses that need to be tested." His eyes widened as inspiration struck. "Doing science is like building a Rubik's puzzle."

"You mean a Rubik's cube?"

"Yeah," he said. "Only not a cube—a puzzle of unknown size and shape. The puzzle is our understanding of the truth. All the scientists in the world—the *real* scientists—are building it. We're always finding new pieces, and we have to find ways to fit them into the growing puzzle. Ultimately, all of the pieces fit together, but the shape is constantly changing … and it's never finished."

Howard's daughter regarded him steadily for a moment. "I guess that's me, then—Aurie Wake, a puzzle! A collection of educated guesses."

Howard stared at her, startled out of his own metaphor.

"And a tool of child labor," she finished proudly. "Wouldn't FIBR like to get its hands on me?"

"FIBR *would* like to get its hands on you," he said sternly, "but the bozos there wouldn't have the foggiest notion how to keep you in line. I ought to drop you off on their doorstep just to teach them a lesson."

Aurie chuckled. "Do you really think they're making their own model kids?"

"Model kids." Howard snorted. "Those clowns aren't creating new models to further our understanding of anything! They're only making stereotypes for profit. Or at least pretending to."

"I thought no one really knows what they do at FIBR."

"It doesn't take a genius to figure it out," he muttered. "FIBR's got government clients, corporate clients, private clients. So they promise wealthy investors a little Hercules and a little Aphrodite, somewhere down the road. They promise pharma companies the means of creating these archetypes. And they promise politicians a healthier society, by rooting out *risk* genes."

There was already a push for academic scientists to uncover these genes—not for diseases like Parkinson's, but for traits considered a danger to society. Aggression. Lust. Greed. Soon, Howard thought, lawmakers would pass a bill that rendered genetic mapping mandatory. Then they would identify combinations of "dangerous" genetic elements in order to marginalize the people who sported them, all in the name of public safety. *Looks like you have a 40% chance of being a rapist and a 25% chance of being a pedophile, Mr. Johnson—so you have the option of being sterilized or relocated to a monitored neighborhood.* And who else would be on this highly subjective and non-transparent list? Naturally, anyone considered a danger to the establishment. It wasn't the illusory prospect of supermodels and supersoldiers that frightened Howard, it was the very real prospect of genetic discrimination. In another decade or so, Mr. Johnson might have the choice of a genetic cure for his possible sexual tendencies. Or he might not have a choice at all.

"Take my word," Howard said. "Whatever models those sellouts are building are nothing but corruption and thin air. You and your brother aren't even in the same category."

Aurie didn't respond to this—a speech she had heard many times before—and for awhile the only sounds in the lab were the rustle of paper, the clink of glassware, and the crunch of salts that had gone hard in their jars. As they worked, Howard glanced at his daughter, who was a model that had never been suggested in even the boldest science fiction. A test to see how far a human being can evolve over the course of a lifetime—and in what directions.

Funny, Howard mused, hunting around for a crate to pack the flammables in. *In all those old sci-fi movies and comic books, someone used to fall into a vat of radioactive goo and turn into a monster or a superhero.* In reality, mutations caused by environmental insults were random and mostly harmful. By contrast, the cellular machine in Howard's children was designed to drive specific and beneficial changes in their genomes, throughout their lives. These changes might take place all at once, or they might be spread out over many years. They might be as flagrant as the alien-looking threads on Aurie's arm, or hidden in ways he would never detect. The kids only joked about these possibilities, but Howard saw their incalculable promise clinging to his children like a bright shadow every day.

Of course the feds had no reason to believe that Py and Aurie existed, and Howard went to great lengths to keep it that way. Their rogue life was a necessarily isolated one, and every now and then he wondered if his kids ought to have a friend or two. Until he remembered what friends were, by and large—wretched little dirtbags who always picked on whoever was different, whoever was smarter. His kids would have stood out in a flock of eight-year-olds like dragons among sheep.

I hated most of my childhood friends, Howard reflected. *Those jackasses probably grew up to be government goons like the ones chasing us. My kids aren't missing a thing. In this life, you're lucky to find one true partner-in-crime in a world filled with nitwits and bullies, stooges and jerks, parasites and sleazeballs. Py and Aurie will have to deal with them all soon enough. Meanwhile, no one is going to crush their spirits, not at the end of an unmarked road by an undeveloped swamp on the outskirts of a small town.* You had to live in such places to get anything done these days.

For the third time that morning, an electronic hornet stung his wrist, and Howard swore as he looked down at the message on his Spider: RAIN.

"Full-blown storm," he muttered, just as an incoming call began to buzz. With another curse, he set a bottle of isopropanol down and tapped his earpiece.

"What's the point of all these coded warnings if you're just going to call me?"

"The warnings are automatic," said Alé, in the digital tones of a voice encryptor. "So I don't *have* to call you. So even if I'm lying in a pool of my own blood, or being dragged off to a holding cell, you'll still have a chance. This is a *courtesy* call. You packing up?"

"Of course I'm packing up! How many of your accounts got hit?"

"All the primary ones," Alé said, his voice crackling with the static of a sigh. "Why does this shit always have to happen in the dead of night? Hell of a way to wake up. At least Rina's still in Phoenix with her mom and I didn't have to drag her with me."

"You in your hidey-hole?" Howard asked.

"Yeah, I'm holed up in my bunker putting out fires left and right ... the usual. But here's the strange thing—no one's tried to cart me away. The hacker knows who 'Ray Smith' is, but the video feed on the house is clean, and no one's come by the lab."

"They've only had a couple of hours—" Howard began.

"*Plenty* of time," his friend assured him. "They should've been at my door within minutes. It's like they're not interested in me at all. Which makes their interest in you and the rest of my chickadees all the more troubling."

Howard took a moment to digest this. Every rogue account—which was heavily encrypted—was under a false identity and linked to a PO Box. So once the FIBR hackers got through Alé's booby traps, they would still be lacking a name and an exact location. "Maybe FIBR is hoping you'll lead them to us."

"That's more easily accomplished by walling or waterboarding me," Alé pointed out. "I don't think this is FIBR."

"Who else would it be? I hope you're taking all the usual precautions."

"I am, but this doesn't look like a government hack. Just thought you should know. Something personal, maybe."

Something personal? Against him, or one of the other rogues? Howard quickly scanned his mental file labeled *grudges*, but the list was too long to provide any obvious candidates.

"Okay, I'll stop distracting you," Alé said. "I've got a guy coming at seven a.m. tomorrow to set your touch-lock and hook everything up in the new place. It's, uh, a little smaller than that luxury cabin you've been using."

Howard looked around his "luxury cabin" and groaned. "How much smaller?"

"Think of it as the biggest kitchen you ever had. Sorry, my friend—best I could do in your neck of the woods. Anyway, everything ought to be ready by mid-morning. Give me a holler when you get there."

"Thanks, Dr. Smith. And I'll find a more useful way to thank you, whether you like it or not."

Even the voice encryptor couldn't mask the scorn in Alé's laugh. "You're not breaking into *my* accounts, compadre! Besides, you couldn't pay me enough to do this job. I do it for love. And hate, which is stronger than love some days." There was a short pause on the other end of the line. "How are the kids?"

"They're doing fine," Howard said, telling himself that it was only half a lie.

"No thanks to you," Alé quipped. "Better finish packing and get your asses outta there."

Howard grunted his assurance and tapped off, then rushed

over to the supply closet to rescue his daughter from the crushing weight of a giant roll of brown paper.

"Need a hand?" he said, trying to take it from her.

"I got it," she huffed, swerving away from his grasp. "Don't forget your calling card!"

Howard's calling card was canted at a roguish angle, peeking out from behind the dwindling stacks in the closet. He pulled it free and carried it to a far corner of the lab. The giant orange foam glove looked like the typical prop hand a fan might raise at a baseball game, except that an atypical digit was extended.

"I never forget," he said quietly, making haste to finish crating the flammables. Four hours later, the foam finger was all that remained of the Wake Institute for Garage Biology in its Massachusetts incarnation. Perspiring heavily in the warmth of the empty shack, Howard tipped his silent spokesperson a weary salute. He had quite a lot to say to the goons when they arrived, but in the end, a picture really was worth a thousand words.

II

They left Westborough before noon, with the entire lab packed into the fully-charged RV, and the kids belted into the double-wide passenger seat. Howard took the turnpike in Millbury, slipping on his Hartwell glasses before they reached the tollbooth scanners. Although the pair of glasses looked utterly ordinary, they projected subtle holographic changes to Howard's face, turning him into Robert P. Hartwell, a man who existed only in virtual reality. The technology wasn't good enough to wear out and about, but it was perfect for fooling facial recognition scanners. The kids kept their heads down without being told, but that never stopped them from commenting.

"Some day we're going to be too big for this, you know," Aurie grumbled to the floor mat. "And it would look pretty weird if we got stopped."

"No, it would just look like the two of you conked out," Howard said. "Unless you're busy complaining about how weird it looks."

"And then they'd take our pictures," Aurie went on, "which wouldn't match anything in the database, and then—"

"They don't do facial recognition to track kids," Howard told her. "You little monsters grow up too fast, and where would you be going on your own? They'd just store your pictures in case of an Amber Alert or something." It was the *something* that always had him worried.

"So if it doesn't matter, then why do we have to hide?"

Having smart kids is not always a blessing, Howard thought. "Because you don't exist. And that's the way it's going to stay." The truth was, he had no idea what a computer analysis of his kids' pictures would reveal. In the photos Howard had taken himself, sometimes he saw Py and Aurie right away, and some-

26

times he didn't. Would a computer program see them as kids or as something abnormal? He didn't want to find out.

Once they were through the tollbooth, Howard matched the flow of traffic, keeping an eye out for grey or black Tesla Skimmers, a favorite government vehicle. Aurie brought out the snacks she'd gathered and they ate a makeshift lunch while Py sat hunched and white-faced, as if the RV were a ship on heaving seas. For the past two weeks, he had lived on nothing but vanilla protein shakes and pudding cups. Any other food was too spicy, too crunchy; even plain crackers held jagged edges like spikes and fiery bombs of salt waiting to explode. Py wouldn't eat the pudding Howard had found earlier, but he let Aurie set the white noise on his Spider. Soft background sounds—static, wind, or rain—were the only things that eased his tweaking.

Tweaking, as Aurie had coined it, seemed to be the result of sensory overload. It was as if Py's sensory threshold had been drastically lowered, heightening the intensity of every stimulus to an unbearable level. Since the effects began, Py had been walking on pins and needles, jumping at the smallest sounds, and chafing inside his clothes. The snap of a twig made him scream, and he reacted to any human touch as if it were an electric shock. At night, Howard drew lukewarm baths in a big plastic bin for Py, and Aurie read to him quietly until Py made her stop. Soft voices were soothing, but too many words eventually made him dizzy and nauseated. He only spoke in whispers; the sound of his own voice, he had told them, was like a gong inside his head.

The CRISPR version of growing pains, Howard thought, glancing at his son's pale face in the stark daylight.

Or the CRISPR machine gone haywire, suggested a colder voice in his head. *You aren't God, you know—you might have made a mistake.*

But it was paralyzing to think that way. Besides, Howard had faith in his tool; he had tested it in every possible way, gone to great lengths to ensure its safety. It *had* to be working for Py's ultimate good. This hypersensitivity ... surely the CRISPR machine had a reason for it.

As he slowed to let a grey Skimmer pass, Howard scoffed at himself. He often caught himself thinking of the CRISPR machine as having a will of its own, as if it were sentient—a tiny god trapped inside every one of his children's cells. The truth, of course, was that it was no more sentient than the cells it lived in. No more aware of its own power than any tool or therapy or weapon. CRISPR—Clustered Regularly Interspaced Short Palindromic Repeats—originally referred to a biological system developed by bacteria. It was a form of molecular recognition that allowed a bacterium to remember the genetic material of an invading virus and destroy that virus on a second encounter. This amazing primitive immune system was discovered by microbiologists back in Howard's grandparents' day. But around the turn of the century, CRISPR was recognized by other scientists with an eye for practical applications, and quickly developed as a tool for manipulating other organisms.

Even in its earliest form, the CRISPR tool was simple and elegant: just a protein capable of cutting DNA paired with a strand of RNA that served as a guide to any location in the genome. You could design guide RNAs to find the gene responsible for sickle-cell anemia in humans, or an allergen in chicken eggs, or patterning in koi, and they would lead the protein surgeon straight to the desired target. Snip, snip, and out would come the original DNA. If you provided a different version of the DNA, the cell's own surgical repair team would insert the new in place of the old, effecting a permanent change in the genome of a living organism.

The development of CRISPR took the scientific community by storm. The new technology afforded almost countless ways to improve agriculture, livestock, bioindustries, and human health. Still, most countries hesitated before embarking on clinical trials. There were too many serious concerns—what if the guide RNA led the protein surgeon to the wrong place, or the surgeon ran amok, hacking chromosomes to shreds with its deadly scalpel? What if the immune system saw the surgeon as a foreign invader and mounted an attack? These problems were not trivial, but over the course of the next thirty years, they were systematically tackled and overcome. The CRISPR pioneers fine-tuned their machine until it was an efficient and reliable tool that found its targets with perfect precision—except when it didn't.

Planning only gets you so far, Howard thought grimly, just as he had warned Aurie earlier in the day. In spite of all the care that went into testing, and the successful trials for other diseases, the CRISPR machine designed to cure Brad Finch's epileptic seizures snuck into the worst off-target location imaginable—a tumor suppressor gene. The little protein surgeon made a single cut where it wasn't supposed to, and two years after Finch's epilepsy was cured, he was diagnosed with a glioblastoma. He died three months later, in the summer of 2048.

The death of a young man whose original condition had not been fatal was the last straw for people who had lost patience with the fickle fortunes of biomedical science. Denouncing CRISPR cures as greater evils than the diseases they were meant to treat, advocacy groups demanded that *every* CRISPR therapy be taken off the market. A track record of success was no proof of anything; who could say for sure when trouble might arise? Finch's cancer hadn't manifested until years after his treatment. Clearly, the fruits of biotechnology couldn't be trusted. If diseases were actually cured, it would be the end of the line for academic researchers, biotech, and big pharma. No wonder they were marketing therapies that were just shy of a real cure—like software developers who hid bad code inside every new program, so they could sucker you into buying the next version with its fix. This sentiment had never been voiced with such vehemence or in such numbers. And in 2050, the federal government stepped in with a solution.

Centralize biomedical research and development, reasoned the politicians. With no competition for prestige and grant money, a scientist's only incentive will be a noble one. Everyone will be working together for the common good. In the hands of an organized few, research and development will be faster, cheaper, and ultimately safer. And so the NIH became the Federal Institute for Biomedical Research. Academic labs had been losing a war of attrition ever since, as FIBR got the lion's share of federal funding (to root out risk genes for the good of society) and private funding (to create exceptional humans). With the passing of the Research Integrity and Innovation Act of 2052, the Department of Health and Human Services was permitted to do contract work for private clients, which allowed FIBR to be the weird government-corporate hybrid that it was. Howard knew whatever FIBR was promising—beauty, brains, strength, talent—would take decades to develop, if those complex traits could ever be engineered. And he had his doubts about the scientists doing the work. Despite the Institute's efforts to lure top researchers, most of the country's best had gone overseas or into the garage labs of the science underground.

And what was cooking in those garage labs? Howard suspected many rogue scientists lived as he did, doing outsourced work to earn a living, along with their real work—whatever they no longer had legal means to support. According to Alé, some sold proof-of-principle innovations and early-stage novelties to companies. Despite the governmental monopoly on CRISPR as a biomedical tool, other products were allowed to flourish in a competitive market. These ran the gamut, from designer pets to CRISPapples, CRISPotatoes, and CRISPwheat, 100% gluten-free. Howard wouldn't be surprised if methane-free CRISPcows that pooped jelly beans were somewhere in the pipeline. It was impossible to know what human engineering might be going on in labs like his, but he doubted anyone was using CRISPR to drive the evolution of the species. CRISPR-evo was Howard's own crazy, never-to-be-patented vision come to life, and only time would tell whether it was his greatest triumph or his deepest regret.

Py groaned and jerked in his seat, startling Howard out of his reverie. The boy's eyes were closed, his eyelids flickering rapidly. He looked like someone in the grip of a minor seizure.

And what if he's actually having a damn seizure? Howard clenched the steering wheel tightly. On the side of the road, holo-ads flashed past like figments of a fever dream. *What if he needs a hospital?*

"It's okay," Aurie said quietly, scooting to the far edge of the seat to give her brother more space. "He always looks like that when he's sleeping."

"Like he's in the middle of a nightmare."

Aurie watched Py twitch in his sleep. "I don't think it's a nightmare. He's just crawling through the tunnels in an underground cave, seeing how deep they go. He says it's like trying to find his way through a maze."

He's always underground in his dreams, Howard thought, perplexed. *And she's always flying into the sun.* They drove for the rest of the afternoon without speaking, letting Py rest undisturbed. Along the highway, fallow fields and farmhouses gave way to the occasional town, and dusk thickened into moonlit dark. The lights of small burgs winked into view like low-hanging stars. Py shuddered and moaned in his sleep, and Aurie stared out the window, lost in her own thoughts. Now and then, several threads on her arm lifted of their own volition, as if something had awoken them. When Py cried out in his sleep, all of those strands raised like hackles, bristling in a concerted wave before falling back into immobility. Aurie didn't seem to notice, but Howard watched them out of the corner of his eye, mad with curiosity. He had never seen her threads so active before. They were clearly responding to something, but what?

"Hungry?" he asked Aurie, as they passed another holoboard advertising food, fuel, and mini-sleepers, accommodations that were about as roomy as a coffin. She turned to him with blank eyes that quickly cleared.

"Yeah," she said. "Starving. And my stupid leg's asleep."

"Time to get out and stretch." Howard took the turnoff and was heading toward the leaf insignia of a nutrastand—as if anything served there had leaves—when he caught sight of a bright red *D* branding the night sky to the east.

"Dixie's," Howard murmured, swerving to follow the sign. "I didn't think there were any left."

Dixie's Diner was one of the few fast food chains that had battened down its hatches when the gene editing revolution swept through the country. This one looked exactly like what it was—the stubborn survivor of a decades-long storm. The squat little diner was as old-fashioned as its non-GMO menu, still sporting weathered brick walls and a retro awning. There were only a few other cars in the lot, and one idling at the drive-through window. Howard parked the RV in a far corner, just as Py opened his eyes and sat up.

"Hungry," Py said hoarsely. It was the first word he'd spoken all day.

"Well, about time!" Howard said. "Think you can manage a milkshake?"

"No," croaked Py. He looked terrible—pale and sunken as a zombie, but he stared at Howard with feverish intensity. "Real food."

"Real food?" Howard peered at him, startled. "You want to try a hamburger?"

At the mention of hamburger, Py looked even sicker than before, but he nodded miserably. "Yeah. Where are we?" He turned to squint at the glowing oasis.

"Dixie's," Howard said. "Stay here, I'll be right back." He got out quickly and headed toward the building, torn between hope and worry. Py didn't look it, but if he was hungry, surely he had to be getting better.

The dining area was occupied by just one patron—an elderly woman nursing a cup of coffee—but the air was redolent of roasting meat and fresh-baked turnovers. Places like this reminded Howard of his life before kids, before going underground, when his wife-at-the-time—either of the women who had foolishly vowed their lifelong devotion to him—had expected him home by seven for a sit-down meal. Howard ordered a hamburger, two chicken dinners with all the fixings, and a trio of milkshakes. He pulled out one of his credit cards and held its thumbprint trace up to the reader. This card belonged to Robert P. Hartwell, who also owned Howard's image-altering glasses and the unnatural pattern of whorls on his left thumb. *You're the dullest fellow in the world, Bob,* thought Howard, as he presented Bob's thumb to the scanner. *No vices to speak of; all you ever buy are groceries and essentials. And you always pay your boring bills on time.* The card reader beeped to indicate satisfaction, and Howard slid the card back into his wallet. Then he leaned against the counter, basking in the ease of ordering real food with names that made sense.

Wish there were more of these old places around, Howard thought, feeling melancholy as the music shifted to some swanky tune from long ago. These days, everyone was allergic to everything, so natural products were something of a rare commodity. At nutrastands and vitashacks, you got food that tasted pretty good, but was almost one-hundred-percent synthetic. Their menus featured artificial proteins and binders trussed up to look like meat patties, smoothies literally glowing with mock vitamins and hormones. And everything smelled the same, suffused with the ineffable aroma of a chemical concoction you couldn't quite pin down. But pulling up to a Dixie's or a Golden Oldies, two places left over from the first half of the century, was like coming home for dinner. Sure, the fries had a few brown spots and the mashed potatoes were lumpy, but that's how you knew they were real. These old diners would all be gone in another year or two, the last holdouts finally uprooted by the winds of progress, which never stopped blowing, for better or worse. For better *and* worse, Howard thought.

The cashier was just setting his milkshakes on the counter when the doorbell set off a frantic jingle. To Howard's surprise, Py came stumbling in, followed by Aurie.

All day, Py had been trying to ignore it—this craving to do what was so intensely painful. Before nodding off in the RV, he had fought the urge to roll the window down and suck the cloying stench of pine needles deep into his lungs. He had wanted to jump out and walk barefoot over the wicked edges of a thousand grass blades. Now the compulsion was like a soldier inside him, forcing him into this terrible place. Dixie's Diner might have been an alien desert he had stumbled into, its air thick with the dust of choking spices, its ceiling hung with a dozen suns. And there, across the tiled wastes, stood a vision that drew him relentlessly. Instruments of torture lay gleaming under the harsh lights—but it was torture that he needed. Py staggered toward the condiment stand like a starved nomad. He tore open and guzzled packets of liquid fire, chased them with a dessicating avalanche of salt. Craning his neck under the nozzles, he washed the carnage away in a rush of scouring sweetness. Gasping, he scrabbled through mounds of tiny blades, letting them saw and stab his fingers. A storm of deafening noise assailed him—shouts piercing some music that was too loud to make sense of. It might have been the screeching of prophets driven mad in the desert heat.

Then he was hauled off his feet and into a night blazing with a thousand ice-fire stars. A gritty wind blew against his burned cheeks, howling through the tortured passages of his ears.

His heart trip-hammered in his chest; every nerve in his body seemed to fire in a series of random explosions. He looked down and saw his sister's face, white and scared, and something rising toward him like a wave of black sea grass before his vision kaleidoscoped into darkness.

III

"Where are we going?" Aurie demanded. "Dad! Where are we *going?*"

"To the hospital," Howard barked, pulling onto the east I-80 ramp. Py was unconscious, his face still smeared with ketchup and mustard and relish. Splashes of Coke and apple juice soaked the front of his T-shirt. He looked like the victim of a deadly food fight.

"The *hospital?*" Howard's daughter looked at him with undisguised horror. "I thought hospitals were the kiss of death, that we might as well just turn ourselves in to FIBR! And you always say they can't help us anyway, they're only for ordinary people with their boring problems."

"Which we pretend to be," Howard growled. "Why is it you're always invisible when I'm looking for you, but when you need to stay out of sight, there you are, every unlicensed thread on display? Aurie, you *know* you have to wear long sleeves in public."

"I didn't have time to put on a jacket! He was running out and tripping—he almost fell on his face!"

"I know," Howard said, in a softer voice. "But all it takes is a call from one conscientious citizen who thinks he's seen evidence of illegal genetic engineering, and then the brute squad is right on our tail." His kids might have an uncanny ability to fade into the walls, but not when one of them was wreaking havoc with a condiment stand and the other was waving around a fantail of inhuman appendages. The Dixie's cashier had stood gaping at Py, but it was the lone diner that worried Howard. Once the old woman had caught sight of Aurie's threads, her eyes had been the size of Dixie's doughnuts.

35

"What are you going to tell them at the hospital?" Aurie asked.

"Nothing." Howard swung the RV into the open left lane and stepped on the gas. "What do they need to know? Your brother's had some kind of seizure. Why should they treat him any different from anyone else?"

"But we're not in the system—won't that give us away? You don't have a bio-map for him, no medical records—"

"They won't turn him away for an emergency," Howard snapped. "You'll stay in the RV—where no one can see you—and I'll be the panicked dad freaking out over his kid. Whatever intern is on duty will just take Py's vitals, punch in his symptoms, and do what the computer tells him. In-depth evaluations aren't wasted on the likes of walk-ins like us. They won't map him unless we pay for it, and by the time someone tries to force us to do that, we'll be long gone."

"But his hyper-sensitivity! The CRISPR machine—"

Howard sighed with frustration. "No one knows anything about CRISPR-evo, Aurie. Not a doctor or scientist in the world! They wouldn't recognize your custom-built CRISPR machine if it started chewing on their asses. Even if I explained it to them, they wouldn't have a clue what it's doing to your brother." *Any more than we do.*

"Then how can they help him?" she whispered.

"They can run tests," Howard told her, knowing how lame that sounded, "and make sure he's stabilized. Give him drugs to contain the seizures, if he's still having any." The RV held its own pharmacy, but most of these compounds were of the heavily controlled, black-market variety, carefully acquired over many years. Ironically, seizure-control drugs, which were relatively easy to get, were not among them.

"That's all we can do," Howard muttered, shooting his daughter a guilt-ridden look.

Aurie didn't respond, only turned to stare out the window at the dark highway. The overburdened RV was straining to do sixty and Howard cursed it silently. Most vehicles on the road were self-piloted; he could have ordered a driverless cab and been at the hospital a lot sooner. Why hadn't he just left the damned rolling lab at Dixie's and called a cab?

Because this damned rolling lab is your whole life, he thought fiercely, just as it struck him that the lab didn't matter at all. He could start from scratch if he had to; he had done it before. His *kids* were all that mattered ... but taking Py to a public hospital was extremely dangerous. Howard might be recognized, or Py might need more than just emergency attention. If they bio-mapped him and discovered the artificial gene, the Wakes would be forcibly detained. And when all was said and done, FIBR would take Py and Aurie—the way they had taken those Peloria kids—to be raised at the Institute. And what did that mean? Probably not pickling and dissection—at least not right away—but his children would certainly be tested and experimented on. Hooked up to electrodes and pumped with tracer dyes. Imprisoned for life in the cage of the Institute, with no more freedom than any other research primate of the past century. Thanks to the Barre-Fremont Act of 2066, illegally-modified children had a very limited set of human rights. Anyone who believed the Peloria kids were just living a normal life with their new foster family was a deluded fool.

And you're still going to waltz straight into the Bloomsburg Hospital ER?

Well, he didn't have any choice about that. Howard's faith in the medical establishment was thin, but he couldn't do anything for Py himself. The infamous Dr. Wake could tinker with lives, but when it came to saving them, he was as useless as a damned priest.

"I guess we'll have to—ow!" Aurie turned abruptly from the window, clutching at her left forearm. Howard looked down to see her threads wrapped around Py's right wrist. To his astonished eyes, the sight shone with an unnatural clarity and vividness. Those living strands had coiled themselves around the boy's arm with shocking tensile strength, and a half dozen of them had somehow pierced his skin. They were probing into the big vein there like hungry leeches. Blood trickled down Py's wrist in thin ribbons.

Aurie tried to yank her threads away, only to cry out in pain.

"Don't pull on them!" Howard barked as the RV swerved. Darting his attention back to the road, he changed lanes and took the next exit off the interstate.

Py was somewhere underwater, in the ocean depths. Sea grass drifted all around him, holding him in a liquid cocoon. Frantic voices murmured somewhere in the world above the ocean, and he could see distant shapes up at the surface—not with his eyes, but with the new sense he had just gained, a chemical awareness. It was as if a sleeping eye had opened, showing him the world of a burrowing insect or a deep-sea creature. His sister and father were vital, pulsing auras overhead. They exuded sharp signals of fear and distress that darted through the water like panicked little fish. Py peered at the bright swarm through the strands of sea grass, then drew back in alarm. The threads of his cocoon had caught fire, blazing with flames that were impervious to the water. As the burning net loosened, Py began to sink into the abyss below. Kicking and struggling, he swam for his life. Up toward the two glimmering auras high above, up to the surface.

Gasping, he jerked awake to find himself drenched in sweat and belted into the RV, which was barreling down an unlit road. With a sharp exclamation, his dad brought the RV to a halt. Py fumbled his seatbelt off and clambered over his sister to throw open the door. Jumping out, he fell onto the soft shoulder of the road and threw up the burning contents of his stomach. Then he crawled away from the stench and hunkered on the dry grass, panting.

He felt like he had just been reborn. The air was so clean and cold, full of whispering textures and scents. Everything seemed sharper and clearer; even the gravel by the road glittered like gems in the dark.

A hand gripped his shoulder—pressure and warmth that soaked into his bones. A voice moved in his ear, the music of wind through deep tunnels. Py was so enraptured that it took him a moment to realize his dad was asking him how he felt.

"Alive," Py croaked in a voice he barely recognized as his own, and laughed into the dazzling night. The word had never meant so much. As he struggled to his feet, Howard caught and steadied him. Py gazed at his father, as if for the first time.

"You all right, kiddo?" Howard whispered.

Py nodded. He could *see* his dad so clearly now—both the visible man and his invisible projection. Howard's face showed only concern, but his chemical aura confessed to other things— guilt and a mess of complicated emotions that Py couldn't name. Aurie was standing close by and she, too, projected an aura that was distinctly her own—as different from their dad's as her face was. Then he realized she was cradling her left arm.

"Your threads," Py said, reaching toward them as she drew away. "Are they okay? I dreamed about them!"

His sister's eyes were as bright as her aura. "They hurt," she murmured. "I think some of them are dead." Even in the chancy moonlight, Py could clearly make out a few withered, faded threads among the dark, luminous fall of the others. *Sea grass,* he thought, feeling both wonder and sorrow. *They sacrificed themselves for me.*

"You dreamed about them?" His dad seized him by the shoulders. "What exactly did you dream?" Howard's aura had swelled into an acid-bright cloud, shooting stinging needles into the air.

Py groaned and pulled away, unable to think amidst the chemical barrage. Was this what happened to a person's aura when they got excited?

"Oh God, I'm sorry!" Howard raised his hands and then let them fall helplessly. "I forgot how much that hurts you."

"No, it's okay," Py told him. "It doesn't hurt anymore." He watched, captivated, as the barbs and arrows of his father's aura dissipated, and the muddy stew of chemicals returned. They slunk into Py's brain with maddening inscrutability as his father picked him up gently and carried him back to the RV.

"Let's get you cleaned up," Howard said, depositing Py by the door. He rooted around inside, then came out bearing a fresh change of clothes and a bottle of water. The contents of the bottle were another revelation to Py—cold and sweet as glacial headwaters, every mineral fizzing and bouncing off his tongue.

After changing clothes, Py climbed into the front of the RV, where his dad was asking Aurie if her threads still hurt. Py glanced at his twin with concern, but she only shook her head and pulled away when Howard tried to get a look at her arm under the overhead light. Fascinated, Py watched his sister's aura darken and change texture, sharpening into a host of quills. Nothing inscrutable about that—it was clear from her aura that she didn't want to be touched. Their dad didn't push the issue, only gazed at her for a moment before resuming his place in the driver's seat. After starting the RV, Howard leaned over the steering wheel and exhaled deeply. His aura had clarified a bit, but in the greenish light from the console, Py thought his father's face had aged ten years.

"Shall we give dinner another shot?" Howard muttered as he eased the RV back onto the road. "Then find a place to crash? I don't know about you two, but I'm ready to call it a day."

Weak with relief—and the sudden loss of adrenaline—Howard stopped at the first restaurant that caught his eye. At the drive-through of the Lusty Leghorn (a combination dive bar/strip club/all-night chicken emporium), he ordered a bucket of Chicken Striplets, a Burning Love Fry Basket, Salacious Salads—with fifty percent real lettuce—and three Happy Endings disguised as milkshakes. When their meal arrived in the dispenser, Py uttered a guttural sound of sheer animal craving, but Howard gave all the food to Aurie and handed the small vanilla shake to his son.

"You can have dinner," Howard told Py sternly, "once

you've finished dessert." Grabbing a few fries for himself, he wended his way down empty side streets until he found an abandoned lot. He parked in the weeds at the far end, next to the rusted remains of an old espresso stand, then changed license plates and sprayed a silver Quikmist over the white RV. The Quikmist was expensive stuff, the kind that dispersed itself evenly after a rush job, but it would only last for a couple of days. By the time Howard finished, Py's milkshake was gone and the kids were making short work of their dinner.

The Leghorn's chicken strips probably wouldn't have passed quality control for feeding the hopped-up birds they had come from, but the fries were absolutely perfect. The NewLeaf potatoes that Monsanto pioneered at the end of the 20th century had only been designed to kill the Colorado beetle, but these CRISPotatoes destroyed viruses, bacteria, and anything else that dared to penetrate their skins. As he rooted around in the empty fry basket, Howard glanced at the kids—Aurie now wearing her jacket and looking distracted as she nibbled the last chicken strip, Py chewing a lettuce leaf as reverently as if it were a Catholic communion wafer—and vowed to feed them better tomorrow.

Outside Bloomsburg, Howard bypassed the string of budget motels with their claustrophobic sleepers and drove to the more expensive Sweet Oblivion Lodge where he could keep an eye on the RV and charge up the reserve batteries. He booked a first-floor room on his Spider, then parked at the end of the outdoor lot. As they made their way down the covered walkway, an ambulance wailed on a distant street, briefly raising Howard's pulse again. He punched in the room's key code with cold fingers.

We were awfully goddamn lucky, he thought, ushering his kids inside and closing the door behind them. But what the hell had happened tonight? It seemed clear that Aurie's threads had saved Py at some cost to themselves. It took all the patience he could muster, but Howard let the kids get cleaned up and ready for bed before starting the lab meeting.

"Smart Foam!" yelped Py, launching himself onto one of the sea-green mattresses, which instantly remodeled itself to encase

41

him from the neck down. He wriggled around inside the green cocoon, laughing a little.

"Does it tickle?" asked Howard, smiling at his son's delight.

"A little, at first," said Py. "Then it feels like warm marshmallows, and now I can hardly feel it at all. Like floating in a cloud." He sighed in blissful contentment. Aurie, meanwhile, had settled herself on the other end of the mattress. The Smart Foam had enclosed her too—mostly. For some reason, it had left a gaping hole around her left forearm with its dark fall of threads.

"Why can't we get this stuff for the RV?" Py wanted to know.

"Because we have blankets and pillows for the RV," Howard said. He hated Smart Foam, mostly because it gave him the feeling of being wound up in a burial shroud. Why were so many aspects of modern life designed to bring a person closer to death? Rooms the size of coffins, mattresses that suffocated you, food you couldn't live on ...

"For a scientist," Py grumbled happily, "you sure don't like technology, do you, Dad?"

Howard snorted. "Everything is technology of a sort. What I like are *useful* things. Does Smart Foam save any time or trouble? That stuff is expensive, and it still has to be cleaned. Just another gimmick, right up there with the electric can opener."

"Glorious gimmick," Py mumbled.

"Sit up before you fall asleep," Howard ordered. "And tell us what you dreamed, kiddo—if you still remember."

Py sprang up to recount the details of his dream, as the Smart Foam retracted like waves sinking back into the ocean. When he finished, Howard found himself shaking with excitement.

"A net!" he cried. "A burning net! And Aurie's threads *were* burning up, in a way." He glanced at her threads, which had fanned themselves out placidly against the green foam. "But why did they attach themselves to Py in the first place?"

Aurie didn't offer an answer, only stared down at the floor.

Howard regarded her for a moment, unable to shake the strong intuition that she was hiding something. A wary and secretive quality had crept into her face. It made her look both older and painfully unfamiliar. Trying to mask his worry, Howard turned his frown on Py. "And why the hell did you try to kill yourself with sauces and soda?"

"I felt like I *had* to," Py said. "I was feeling like that all day."

"Suicidal urges?" Howard moved over to the window to check on the RV. "Doesn't make any sense! The CRISPR machine is designed to *improve* you."

"I don't think I was trying to kill myself," Py protested. "It was more like—like a doctor was forcing me to take some awful medicine. I think it was supposed to help."

Howard walked back across the room, darting glances at his daughter. "Maybe you had to reach some crisis point to get past this."

"Yeah, maybe," Py agreed.

"And you *are* past it?" Howard turned to scrutinize his son. "No more walking on knives, choking on air? You're all back to normal?"

"Better than normal, Dad! I can see so much more now."

Howard froze. "What do you mean?"

"I can't really explain it," Py said, fixing his rapt gaze on Howard's face. Or, rather, Howard thought, on the air just in front of his face. It was disconcerting to be *almost* looked at so intently. He had to fight the urge to bat at a nonexistent fly hovering just below the level of his eyes.

"I know it sounds crazy," Py said, still staring. "But I think I can see chemicals."

Howard took a step back, but the boy's attention remained focused on some invisible skin Howard seemed to be wearing. *"See* them? You mean you can smell them?"

Py shook his head impatiently. "I can smell a lot better than I used to—I can hear better too—but this is something different. I can see chemicals *radiating* from you, like an aura. Yours is different from Aurie's."

An aura? How the hell did Py know what an aura was? For that matter, what exactly *was* an aura? Unwilling to confess his

43

ignorance, Howard pressed on. "Different how?"

Py shrugged. "Just different, like your faces are different. Those people in the parking lot had their own auras too. I think the shape of the aura is unique. But the colors, the textures ... they change all the time. Depending on emotions, I think."

Howard was mystified. *Py can detect biological chemicals of some kind? Signaling molecules or pheromones?* He wanted to do a blood draw, but the blood would have to be processed immediately and there was no way to do that in a motel room. *God, if only the lab weren't in boxes! What a time to have to move.*

"Your CRISPR machine," he said, "made a huge gamble, Py—but it won!"

"Not by itself," Py said quietly. "Only because Aurie saved me with her threads."

Howard sat down beside his daughter, ignoring the wave of foam that rose up to blanket his lap. He put a careful hand on her arm, just above the place where the threads grew from her skin. Aurie immediately recoiled, shooting him a look of fear and distrust. Howard pulled back, frowning to hide his hurt. She had never looked at him that way before.

"I know some of your threads died," he said quietly, "but your brother thinks they saved his life. Any idea what they might have done, or why?"

He watched her struggle to clear her face, to wipe away whatever she was thinking.

"Sorry, Dad," she said in a small, flat voice. "I don't know why these things latched on to Py, or what they did to help. And I'm really tired."

Well, that last was surely the truth. "Get some sleep," Howard said. He wanted to hug his daughter in her Smart Foam shroud, but settled for kissing the top of her head. "Once we get set up in the new place, we'll figure out what's going on."

Aurie nodded with no conviction and snuggled deeper into the foam. From the other side of the bed, Py watched his sister with worried eyes. Howard got up to give his son a hug, basking in the enormous relief of being able to touch him again. Unraveling the mystery of what had happened might be the work of a lifetime, but what else was a lifetime for? Deeply excited, Howard whisked his overnight bag into the small bathroom. He could hardly wait to begin.

Aurie waited for the hiss of the shower, and then she sat up. "Hey."

On the other side of the bed, her brother cracked an eye open.

"I know why these things"—she gave her threads a dirty look—"did what they did. They weren't trying to help you. They were after something."

"Yeah? How do you know that?" As Py scrambled up and tried to get a look at her threads, she shrank back against the wall.

"I just know. They felt hungry the whole time they were sucking up your blood. I don't know what they wanted, but you must've had a lot of it after that trip to Dixie's."

Py looked skeptical. "But I'm fine—*more* than fine. And they didn't touch me on the ride here."

"Because I put my jacket on, you doof," she said hotly. "You want to test 'em and see if they'll raid you again?"

"They weren't raiding," Py said. "They were holding me in a net, keeping me from drowning—"

"Trust me," she said. "They didn't care whether you lived or died, they just wanted … whatever was in your blood right then."

"Whatever was in my blood was poisoning me," Py reminded her. "Your threads must've gotten rid of it. And it hurt them—it *killed* them—to do it."

"Yeah," she said quietly. "I wonder what it was."

"You don't feel any different?"

She shook her head, rubbing absently at her left forearm.

"Anyway, it was pure symbiosis," Py said brightly. "Like

those fish that eat parasites off other fish."

"These things are more like predators," Aurie snapped. "What happens if they want something that's *not* poisoning you? Something you need to survive?"

Py looked thoughtful, then jerked his head toward the bathroom door, where the cheerful warbles of an out-of-date and out-of-tune rock ballad were emanating from the shower. "Why didn't you tell Dad?"

Aurie shrugged, unable to explain. It was the first time she had ever kept anything from their father. Since feasting on Py's blood, her threads shied away from Howard, which meant that a part of her wanted nothing to do with him. She—*they*—didn't want to be poked and prodded and experimented on. Not anymore.

"Dad would've stuck us both with needles and fired up the mass spec," she said, sliding back down onto the mattress and letting it enclose her—most of her—in its cloudlike warmth.

Py snickered. "We should've let him. He'll be up all night anyway. And his two-minute shower's about done, so we better shut up now."

"Good thing you're okay," Aurie whispered, as the shower and singing cut off right on cue. "And I'm glad I could help, even if my threads were just being greedy and selfish." She looked at her brother with mingled curiosity and envy. "Can you really see chemicals?"

He nodded, eyes shining in the dim lamplight.

"Can you tell them apart? Do you know what they all mean?"

"Not yet," he said, "but I'll figure it out."

IV

Howard emerged from the bathroom, noting that the kids were already fast asleep—or at least doing a good job of pretending. Footfalls sounded in the parking lot, and he crept over to peer through the one-way window shade. Under the lot's halogen lights, a well-dressed couple got into their Jae Rapport, both absorbed in their Spiders as the self-piloted car started up. Half a minute later, they turned onto the main road without even a glance out the windows. Howard released a deep breath.

Coffee, he thought, heading for the RediBev dispenser in the wall. To his disgust, the only hot beverages available were a roasted beech kernel blend and a selection of sustainable teas. No hot water for him to mix up his own instant coffee ... and nothing as useful as a mug or a microwave in the room. With a sigh, Howard ordered a cup of tea and fired up his laptop.

The laptop was a relic whose main virtue was a real keyboard onto which angry, inflammatory, and seditious letters could be typed with satisfying vigor. Other things could be written on the ThinAir matrix of a holo-display, but Howard felt that a criminal manifesto lost its verve when composed on thin air. So he kept his old laptop for writing letters that could never be sent, letters that were always addressed to the same individual, one who stood for all others of his kind.

Greetings, Government Goon, he wrote. *You missed us in Tucson and that must've cost you your job. But there are always more of you, aren't there? Infinitely replaceable, like the scientist hacks you work for. Now you've missed us again, and I wish I could see the look on your face when you break in—like a thief who nabs a jewelry box only to discover that it's empty! On behalf of outlaw scientists everywhere: may all your nights be sleepless and all your trails lead to dead ends.*

I know you—or someone like you—will be nipping at my heels until I die. And I know you think you're only doing your job, but there's one thing you should know. The people you're hunting are almost the only ones left who actually know how to do science. I don't mean flip-a-switch, press-some-buttons, break-open-a-kit; I mean real science. The kind that first gave us those switches and buttons and kits. The science that allowed a whole generation of monkeys like your employers to play God without rubbing more than two brain cells together. Real science takes respect for the unknown, and a willingness to tangle with it anyway. It takes a fine hand and a strong arm. You have to be able to brush away uncertainties as gently as dirt from a fossil, or face a jungle of obstacles and fire up your chainsaw.

And sometimes, Mr. Goon, you have to set the wheels in motion and just stand back and let them turn. I might be the only one who's crazy enough to do that. But my kids wouldn't exist otherwise. I designed the engine that drives them, and now I'm more helpless than any parent on earth.

Howard paused over the keyboard, all of his snark suddenly washed away by the stark truth of what he had written. Py could have lapsed into a coma tonight. He could have *died.* Other parents could put the blame on God or the crapshoot of genetics, but Howard didn't have those excuses to fall back on. He was more than his children's father; he was the author of any misery they had to endure. The fact that Aurie had been the one to help Py was both a relief to Howard and a frightening reminder of his own inadequacy. Like American pioneers whose children had fallen to infection or fever or the common cold, his CRISPR-evo kids needed a more enlightened parent to protect them ... only there was none to be had.

But Py is okay, Howard reminded himself as he dispensed a second cup of tea. *And his CRISPR machine did something good, something new.* Which meant today marked a milestone on that treacherous, exhilarating path a younger Howard Wake had embarked on twenty years before. Py's new chemical sense and the actions of Aurie's threads were the first clear evidence of

CRISPR-evo at work. Howard looked over at his sleeping daughter, whose arm had fallen over the side of the bed, letting loose the whole wondrous fall of her threads. He thought about taking a sample of the dead threads now, while she slept, but a certain respect for the live ones kept him from pulling out his nail clippers. Aurie's threads were clearly aware of their surroundings, and they had burrowing tips sharp enough to draw blood.

Sipping his tea, Howard brought up a projection of the science news on his Spider. He scanned a mini review from the Ethical Research Commission on the dangers of unregulated genetic engineering, and an interview with some bozo from FIBR. The ERC and FIBR were typical of government hypocrisy—exempt from the very rules they straitjacketed everyone else with. There had been another head transplant in the Netherlands, this time for some rich banker who thought he had everything it took to be a world-class alpine skier—except the body. Most head transplants were still of the necessary variety, performed on people whose internal organs were damaged beyond repair. But the recipients of new bodies often claimed to feel the ghosts of the old owner's urges and desires, as if they were occupying a haunted house. Crazy as they seemed, Howard was unable to throw these claims entirely out of court. Who knew what information was stored in the body, in peripheral nerves that suddenly found themselves communicating with a new head? For that matter, who knew what the human nervous system was capable of? Aurie had been born with her external threads already formed—and if his guess was right, they contained neurons capable of sensing and responding to the world in ways no other neuron could. If only he could do the proper experiments to find out! There was a man he used to know—a bioengineer who had developed scanning scopes that could see through living tissues. But that man had disappeared many years before, just as Howard himself had. Suddenly, the frustration that was always simmering close to the surface boiled over, scalding a sharp path through the night's victory. The wheels of his mind shifted, leaving the bright frontier of ideas for the grooves of a dark and familiar track.

He should be working in a *facility,* for the love of God, not cowering in one garage venue after the next and putting Alé in danger. He should be talking and collaborating with other scientists, those who were experts in areas he was not. He should be publishing his work, not typing up notes in files no one would ever read. He and his children should be living in a real house on land that belonged to them. They should be able to walk the streets like anyone, and Aurie shouldn't have to wear a goddamn jacket every time she went out.

Would they ever be free? And how had things come to this sorry pass?

For a moment, Howard's former career at the once-renowned Braeburn Institute flashed into the forefront of his mind, but he passed over those bitter memories and thought further back, before the CRISPR storm. Back to the turn of the century, two decades before he was born. It was hard to pinpoint the exact time when everything started going to hell, but by the year 2000, things were bad enough. Science had become so complex and specialized that no one outside the discipline understood it anymore. With a government funding system that rewarded publication in high-impact journals—and nothing else—researchers didn't have the time or incentive to communicate with the public. Meanwhile, the media continued to hype the next great breakthrough, which never quite arrived, or always took longer than people thought it should. Instead of being widely understood, science took on the mysterious qualities of a religion, and people began to lose their faith. Thanks to the ever-widening breach between scientists and the general public, even the Conscientious Reporter—that endangered species—never managed to get all the facts right. And somewhere in the midst of this deepening problem, the original garage biologists were born.

The Tinkers had started innocently enough. Want to mess around with DNA? Ever wonder what your own cells look like? Just buy a Do-It-Yourself Biology kit, only $300 from Amazon. Or join our community lab and meet other do-it-yourselfers! These were small, grassroots organizations of people who dabbled on their own time with their own money. But the Tinkers gained some volatile recruits—laid-off corporate researchers, eccentric professors, others who had lost funding or credibility— and they began to fundraise.

Why, asked the Tinkers, *donate to the National Cancer Society, a money sponge that throws one hell of an annual fundraising extravaganza, but hasn't cured cancer after over a century? Or any other disease foundation that's been padding itself for decades?* Taking their cue from a wildly popular historical event, the ALS Ice Bucket Challenge, the united Tinkers challenged Americans to slap themselves awake. Videos of people slapping themselves crimson went viral. American taxpayers forgot that breast cancer and childhood leukemia were on the decline thanks to cancer research—and they began donating to the Tinkers. Not because they believed their money would help find better and faster cures, but in a spiteful gesture of discontent, a *fuck you* to a research establishment that was too comfortable for its own good.

And the Tinkers continued to swell their ranks. From PhDs to high school dropouts, from discredited leaders in their fields to those who just held an unbridled curiosity and a desire to "tinker" in a wet lab, they flocked to hubs in every major city in the country. If there was one theme that connected this motley crew, Howard thought, it was anarchy. Their unspoken cry was: *Who needs the establishment?* and their mantra was: *How hard can it be to figure things out ourselves?*

Howard stared at the holographic image of the day's news without seeing it. He bet those old Tinkers felt like cowboys, like renegades, even after the Berkeley group contaminated the Bay Area groundwater with organic solvents. Even after a bunch of fluorescent tadpoles released into Colorado rivers spread a fungus to other amphibians, decimating native populations. Tinker equipment was often homemade and uncalibrated, their controls nonexistent, and their conclusions highly questionable, but they were publishing like wildfire in their own online journal, and the media *loved* them. Sensational reports linking tofu to lupus, and honey to Down Syndrome nearly put American soybean farmers and beekeepers out of business.

As a movement, the Tinkers were short-lived; mutual discontent is not a lasting bond. Their mark on history was a symbolic one: representatives of a people who had lost their respect for science. What followed—the rise and fall of CRISPR technology, the establishment of FIBR, and the disappearance of the world's best, who now practiced their discipline off the legal radar—were the logical grandchildren of this contempt.

As he got up to toss his empty cup in the compost container, a sinuous movement across the room caught Howard's eye. Aurie's threads were stirring against the foam mattress like grasses in a light breeze. He snuck over to get a closer look.

Even in the semi-dark, her threads shone with astonishing richness. They were ophidian in texture, and the deep blue-black of a mussel shell. He could see the fine sheath of scales on each thread, and the sharp points that tipped them. Howard leaned in closer, trying to get a good look at the ones that had stiffened into lifeless husks. These threads—the burned-out ones—were not stirring at all.

Did they give something to Py, or take something? he wondered. *If I could just get a look at them under the scope—*

The mass of live threads stilled, then drew back as one. Howard felt abruptly faint, on the verge of blacking out. He backed away quickly, but not before sensing a strong feeling in the air—some sharp and alien antipathy that was too impersonal to qualify as hate. But the idea of Aurie's threads projecting an emotion was so improbable that he dismissed the notion immediately.

Whatever else, those threads saved Py's life, Howard marveled as he powered off his laptop and dug his Smart Foam countermeasure—a folded-up sheet—out of his bag. He spread the sheet over the empty bed and lay down, folding his arms behind his head. *In your wildest dreams, did you ever think CRISPR-evo could produce a Good Samaritan?*

He dozed fitfully for a few hours, then lay awake listening to the occasional growl of a long-distance truck and the plaintive cries of an insomniac bird. At a quarter past six, Howard woke the kids, and they left the motel as the first streaks of dawn appeared in the eastern sky. He felt better with the steering wheel in his hands, with the RV's engine humming beneath them as the city disappeared into the sprawl of dark and silent countryside. It was good to be on the road again, good to be moving forward.

"Try to get some more sleep," he told the kids, who were fidgeting in their shared seat.

"Can't," Py chirped, pulling a cereal bar out of his pack. The twins seemed to have exchanged dispositions from the day before. Now Py was bright-eyed and alert, and his sister was slouched and silent. Howard noticed Aurie was still wearing her jacket, even though the heater was cranked up.

He asked if she was cold, and she shook her head.

"How's your arm?" he pressed. Aurie gave him a quick, furtive look before turning back to the window, where the horizon was lightening above the trees.

"It's fine," she murmured, nestling deeper into the car seat.

"Where we headed, Boss?" Py asked, making Howard smile. As opposed to Aurie, who called Howard "Boss" when she was mad at him, Py only used the term when he was feeling chipper.

"To find some breakfast," Howard told him. "Although you seem pretty happy with that bar of sawdust."

Py looked scandalized. "It's not sawdust, Dad! It's ... it's hard to describe."

"Hard to describe? It's a granola bar, not a sunset."

"A granola bar is a lot more complicated than a sunset," Py informed him. "Do you know how many ingredients are *inside* the ingredients? I can taste every one of them!" As Howard glanced at him in astonishment, Py swallowed the last bite and smacked his lips. "Can't wait to try some eggs and sausage and French Toast."

"Real coffee for me," Howard said as the first twinges of a headache crept into his temples. "And maybe a cinnamon roll, but only if it's fresh out of the oven."

"Mushrooms," muttered Aurie, who seemed surprised to have spoken. They turned to stare at her.

"A little early in the day for those," Howard suggested, but Aurie only shrugged and closed her eyes.

"But where are we going *after* breakfast?" Py pressed. "Does Alé have a place for us yet?" His eyes brightened with sudden hope. "Can we move back to the Philippines?"

Howard rolled his eyes. "You were six months old when we left Manila. Don't tell me you have all these fond memories."

"I don't have to *remember* it to like it," Py said, as if this should have been obvious. "Tropical jungles and rainforests, Dad! You know they have a climbing rat and a dwarf buffalo and this flying dragon lizard that glides through the trees—"

"We're moving to an old farm in Pennsylvania," Howard told him. "But there's still plenty of woods around, with all the bats and giant salamanders and jumping spiders you could want."

Py grunted in disappointment. "Why'd you leave the Philippines in the first place? I know it was easier to do all the CRISPR-evo stuff there, and to grow us in an artificial womb, but wouldn't it be safer for us to *live* there?"

"In some ways," Howard said. He tried to explain to Py that living in the Philippines was more difficult and dangerous in other ways. Regulations in Manila had been relaxed, but the city ran on politics—one favor for another. And eventually certain people had asked him for one too many favors. Howard didn't explain to his son the other reason he had come back to domestic soil, always angling for a garage venue in or close to Massachusetts. He barely acknowledged that reason himself, although it lay just below the hum of activity in his mind. It was a responsibility not yet undertaken, a debt to pay, and an impossible hope all tangled up together.

Howard glanced at Aurie, who was folded up with her chin tucked into her shoulder.

Sleeping, he thought with mixed affection and concern. *Just like Py was right before that condiment binge. And she wants mushrooms for breakfast. God, I hope we're not in for another culinary adventure!*

Curled up in the passenger seat, Aurie wasn't even close to sleeping—she was very much awake and busy talking with her CRISPR machine.

It was a game she'd been playing for almost a year. She imagined that extra part of herself—the part that made her and Py different from every other human on the planet—as a doctor, an old-fashioned cartoon doctor with a white lab coat and a stethoscope. He lived in the nucleus of a cartoon cell. The first time she'd conjured him up, the doctor was standing at the helm of a chromosome raft. He looked like a mad captain adrift in a wild sea of molecular traffic, yanking on the wheel with one hand while brandishing a silver scalpel in the other. When he realized what he was holding, the doctor yelped.

What's this? he cried, his bushy white eyebrows jumping a mile above his forehead. *I can't work with an ordinary scalpel! Why, I'd be just another hacker-and-slasher.* Comically, he stopped steering to scratch his head, and the raft collided with a protein scaffold, throwing a jumble of alpha helices and beta sheets into the nuclear waters.

Aurie had to laugh; this figment of her imagination looked so genuinely distressed.

Did I forget to take my board exam? the doctor muttered to himself. He examined the scalpel from every angle as if hoping to identify some hidden function. *Did I lose my CRISPR-evo license?*

Aurie laughed again as she suddenly understood. *Oh, right, sorry! You're CRISPR-evo. You don't have a plain scalpel like a regular CRISPR machine, you have a ... well, an advanced multi-tool.*

Instantly, the scalpel morphed into a bizarre contraption

outfitted with blades of all shapes, surgical thread and needles, pins, staples, and probes. It was like a gigantic medical Swiss army knife, but the little doctor seemed vastly relieved.

Oh, that's much better. Regaining control of his vessel, the CRISPR-evo doctor looked around as if trying to locate his invisible benefactor.

It's me, said Aurie. *You can't see me because you're inside all my cells.*

The doctor looked momentarily bewildered, and then he smiled broadly. *Ah, the host! What an honor to be paid a visit by the host herself. Is there anything I can do for you? How can I be of service, young lady?*

Well, said Aurie, who had been agonizing over a difficult experiment all that morning. *Maybe you can give me some advice.*

And that was how she began working out problems without asking her dad for help all the time. She also vented her frustrations to the CRISPR-evo doctor, and confided her secrets to him. The doctor was a good listener and he always had something useful to say, often the seed of an exciting new idea. Sometimes he even nudged her into seeing things from Py's or her dad's point-of-view. Although the doctor was her friend, Aurie never kidded herself about his imaginary status; he was a playmate she had dreamed up, no different from a talking stuffed animal. And *she* summoned *him;* he never summoned her. But on the ride out of Bloomsburg, shortly after experiencing an inexplicable craving for mushrooms, the doctor spoke her name.

Aurea Wake.

Startled, Aurie closed her eyes and withdrew into her mind. Within seconds, the voices of her father and brother receded into a background hum. As she contracted her awareness, insulating herself with layer upon layer of skin and bone and soft, pulsing brain tissue, Aurie stopped hearing them at all. Deep in her cerebrum, a single cell glowed like a beacon in a world of dark matter. She entered it as she always did, moving straight to the heart of the nucleus.

The fabulous world of the cartoon cell enveloped her, its waters rich with proteins. Enzymes and schools of histone chaperones angled past; RNA-binding proteins swam along, trailing jellyfish-like tendrils. In a moment, the CRISPR-evo doctor appeared, but he had lost his chromosome raft and much of his cartoonish flamboyance. The cotton balls of white hair above his ears were gone, along with his stethoscope. The multi-tool in his hand no longer resembled an old-fashioned Looney Tunes contraption; it looked deadly serious. Aurie met the blue eyes of the specter she had created—eyes that seemed wiser than before—and felt a ripple of fear.

Don't be afraid, said the Doctor. *We haven't spoken before, but I'm no stranger to you.*

Aurie was too shaken to respond. Who was this impostor and what had he done with her doctor?

The impostor chuckled. *I'm still your favorite hallucination, Aurie. Think of me as version 2.0.*

Still a hallucination? But she hadn't imagined him this way at all; he had changed on his own! And his eyes—there was nothing imaginary about his eyes. They were aware; they were *seeing* her.

Aurie swallowed hard. *Who are you, really?*

The new Doctor smiled enigmatically. *Still a figment of your imagination. Only now—thanks to your brother—I am also an emissary of the sleeping part of your brain. It wants to talk to you.*

A cold thrill ran through Aurie—part of her brain wanted to *talk* to her?—but she was not her father's daughter for nothing. Something had taken over and rewritten the rules of her game, and she was not going to play by rules she didn't understand.

Hold on. Are you imaginary, or are you real? You can't be both!

The Doctor fixed her with a keen eye. *Why not? Everything begins as a dream—the conjuring of a mind, great or small. And you, my dear, are a first-class conjurer.* The cartoon figure gestured to the world around them. *You like to have a stage and a set and all characters on display! Although it seems to me this set could use an upgrade.*

Instantly, the scenery changed.

Aurie had imagined her genetic material, those double helices of DNA that made up her chromosomes, as fuzzy, X-shaped rafts. These rafts—purple ones from her father and blue from her mother—had formerly whizzed around on their own, but now all the chromosomes were linked. Most of this DNA lay at the nuclear periphery, dark and condensed and shrouded in a cocoon of silencing proteins, but some of it was free. From the dark perimeter extended a fragile, luminous web of exposed double helices that clustered into bright hubs where genes were expressed. These hubs were like the open harbors of a port. Giant protein complexes docked and departed and patrolled the coasts, overseeing the transcription of Aurie's genes into messenger RNAs that grew and twined like exotic sea flora. As the RNA strands grew, they were processed by other complexes—cut and spliced, capped and tailed, and finally loaded onto transport vessels for export through the nuclear gateways. Other gates in the nuclear wall were opening and closing, letting in cargo ships carrying newly fabricated proteins from the main body of the cell. All around her, the living architecture of the nucleus came together and broke apart, folding and twisting and vibrating in chaotic harmony. It was like the inner workings of a fantastic alien city.

There, said the Doctor, sounding satisfied. He wandered around admiring his own handiwork. *Doctor's Office, version 2.0! Still wildly inaccurate and vastly oversimplified, of course.*

Aurie followed him through her prototypical nucleus, examining its engines and vessels with delight. Inaccurate and oversimplified? Well, sure—her cartoon cell was more sophisticated now, but it was still just a representation of the real thing.

Show me what all of this really looks like. She wanted more than anything to see the cell—that smallest unit of life—in all its true glory.

In what medium? asked the Doctor. *Chemical? Biophysical? Through the imperfect eye of the microscope or the scan-*

ning electron micrograph or the X-ray diffractor?

I know what a cell looks like in those mediums. I want to see it the way it really is!

Impossible, the Doctor told her. *None of your senses are adequate for perceiving the microscopic.*

A lone protein drifted by like the king of seahorses, crowned with glittering chemicals and festooned with sugar chains. Aurie followed it on its wayward course, realizing she could identify every one of its decorations. Well, of course she could. Everything in this glorified cell was still the product of her own head, all of it contained within her store of knowledge. And while she and Py knew practically nothing about the rest of the world, their knowledge of molecular biology was extensive. Their dad had made sure of that.

Besides, the Doctor went on, *a cell is not the smallest unit of life.* Something appeared in his hand, something that looked like a magnifying glass. *What is the fundamental unit of life, Aurie?*

Perplexed, she thought for a moment. *The genetic code?*

Instead of answering, he held out the glass. She took hold of it and peered inside.

Within the glass, a brilliant jewel of light spun rapidly. That was her first impression. But gazing into the heart of the light, she was only aware of sound—a single note of music distilled from unknowable symphonies. The music formed a word that embodied the motive force of all words, an exhalation of pure meaning beyond any language. It was a word she almost knew. It spoke to her in a luminous breath of wind that stirred ancient dust in the furthest reaches of her mind. And then the glass went dark and silent.

Aurie strained to see the smallest spark, to hear the faintest echo, but her eyes and ears were empty; her mind throbbed like a plucked string. Gently, the Doctor pried the magnifying glass from her hands.

What is it? she whispered.

The fundamental unit of life.

Where? Inside this cell somewhere?

The Doctor shook his head. *It isn't any where or when. But without it, no life in the universe could exist.*

How can I see—how can I hear it again? She looked around for the empowering glass, but the Doctor only spread his empty hands.

Once is enough. You'll forget it very soon ... and you perceived it falsely, as a light or a sound or a voice—some sensory input that your mind can grasp.

Aurie tried to remember, and realized he was right. *How do you know all this?*

Every creature knows the source of life, in every fiber of its being. Only the human mind refuses to understand. Excitement crept into the Doctor's face. *Your Sleeping Self dreams of nothing but truth—but when its dreams reach your mind, you think of them as fiction. What you call imagination is the most primal reality of all.*

The Doctor's eyes gleamed with a stark hunger, giving him the look of a savage bird. Aurie stumbled back in the watery milieu, suddenly wishing that her companion really were imaginary. Or just a normal friend, the kind who would go home after they were done playing.

Have you ever dreamed of flying? The Doctor's eyes were suddenly as wide and fathomless as an alpine sky, stretching up into infinity. Aurie stared into depths of azure that continued to brighten, as if lit by a rising sun. *Ever wanted to leave your body behind and see the heights of the world? And maybe—to see beyond the world?*

How? Aurie breathed. She felt like the smallest of winged creatures drawn into the blazing vistas of the Doctor's eyes.

Your threads know, he answered. *They seek what we need to bring the dreams of your Sleeping Self to life.*

Someone was shaking her, jolting her out of herself. The waters of the nucleus shrank inside the sentinel cell, which disappeared into the murk of flesh and bone. Aurie blinked as the world swam into focus. They were parked next to an abandoned subway car with a hand-painted sign reading "Nan's Kitchen." Bright morning sunlight baked the passenger window, making her sweat inside her jacket.

"Let's go," said Py. "We've been sitting here for twenty minutes waiting for this place to open. Come on, I'm starving!"

Once upon a time, Americans had complained about immigrants taking their jobs; now everyone complained about robots rendering their jobs unnecessary. Places like Dixie's and Golden Oldies survived in small towns as a protest against automated and robo-op fast food joints. Their fancier cousins—gastropubs and diners—could also still be found, thriving in lone splendor in out-of-the-way places. Now that the personal touch was so rare, people were willing to drive farther and pay extra for it. And although the Wake family preferred an impersonal touch, they did happen to like the food served in diners.

The one Howard found along the highway in Mill Creek was of the mom-and-pop variety—a retro version resembling a 1950s malt shop. The menu posted outside Nan's Kitchen promised shakes made with real ice cream (NO SUPPLEMENTS OF ANY KIND!) and old-fashioned sundaes (NO CAROB OR ACAI, JUST HOT FUDGE!). As the family trooped inside, setting off the bell on the door, a surprised-looking waitress popped her head out of the back.

"With you in a minute," she said, then disappeared only to reappear with an apron tied around her waist. She grabbed a single menu and almost seated Howard at the counter before noticing the two kids. Without missing a beat, she collected two more menus and steered them to a corner booth, only giving Py and Aurie a quizzical glance before heading back into the kitchen. It was a common reaction that never failed to annoy them.

"Are we invisible, or what?" Py muttered under his breath, as he scanned the list of specials.

"Just inconspicuous," Howard said. "And considering who

you're keeping company with, you should count yourself lucky." He turned to the dessert section and began weighing the benefits of ordering a banana split against the disadvantages. By the time the waitress returned, he had come to the reluctant conclusion that ice cream for breakfast was a bad example to set for the kids. They really had to start eating better.

"Coffee and a cinnamon roll," he told the waitress, who collected his menu with a nod. Speaking louder than necessary, Py ordered hot chocolate and the Early Bird Special with French Toast. Aurie just asked for a glass of apple juice.

"No stuffed portobellos?" Howard teased her, which drew a faint smile. She was still distant and distracted, but he didn't want to hassle her. For all he knew, her CRISPR machine was still dealing with the aftermath of whatever her threads had done for Py.

Their beverages arrived within minutes, Py's cocoa topped with a flourish of real whipped cream (NO SODIUM ALUMINO-SILICATE!). Howard sipped his coffee with pleasure, feeling the leading edge of his headache subside. The relief lasted until he heard a soft ping from his Spider.

He brought up a holo-message from an unknown sender. The subject line was empty and there was no salutation. The note simply said: *Thanks for the foam finger. I'm beginning to have quite the collection.*

For a moment, Howard forgot to breathe. FIBR wasn't days behind, after all—the Institute's detective had already tracked him to the abandoned lab in Westborough! Which meant they had barely escaped in time. And, *quite the collection?* So this very detective had found his other hideouts, each with its foam salutation? And FIBR had found a way to reach him. Well, of course they had; Alé's records had been hacked and—

I'm here to reclaim my property. I hope, for your sake, that it's still in mint condition.

The second message appeared under the first, jolting Howard out of his frantic train of thought. FIBR wanted to reclaim its property? Meaning the lab, and everything associated with the lab? But, no ... this was not the threat of a government operative. This message was personal.

Meet me at the Little Pitcher in Westborough at 6 pm & I won't call in the brute squad.

Howard stared at the third message, then read the second one again. Although he broke the law as a matter of routine, he had only stolen something once.

But it was a very big something.

He scoffed at the suspicion that was forming in his head. *She couldn't know it was you, and how could she track you down? The feds can't even track you down!* But the woman on his mind was a hell of a lot smarter and more motivated than the feds ... and who else knew that he called all the government goons in the world *the brute squad?*

Howard darted a glance out the window of their booth, dazzled by the early morning sunlight. His instincts were screaming that he was wasting time. Plans A through Z all tried to have their say, creating a buzz of chaos in his head.

Calm down, he thought. *You know who sent this ... but ninety-nine percent sure isn't good enough. Make her prove herself.*

Sorry, he typed on the ThinAir matrix. *This a private number, which you must have reached in error. Good luck finding the person you're looking for.*

The response came within seconds.

Wrong number? Seriously? Little Pitcher today at 6 pm. Bring what you stole or "Ray Smith" is going down—and that's on you.

Oh God, he thought, closing his eyes just as the aroma of fried eggs and sausages descended on them.

"Here we are," said the waitress cheerily, setting down their plates, then holding up the coffee pot for Howard. "More coffee for you, hon?"

She had to ask again before he could bring himself to focus on the question, and then he asked her to leave the whole pot. She put it down with a chuckle and left them to their breakfast.

Py and Aurie were staring at him.

"Everything's fine," he told them, startled to find he could lie as easily as any other parent. "But we have to leave soon, so eat fast."

Py attacked his food, and Aurie finished her apple juice, but their eyes never left him. Howard gulped down some coffee and re-read the messages.

Meet me at the Little Pitcher in Westborough at 6 pm & I won't call in the brute squad.

Howard believed this was true. If he knew the woman following him, she would want to talk before turning their lives over to the feds. He might have stolen her most precious possession, but she had her own reasons for wanting to stay off the FIBR radar, didn't she? What he needed was a safe place to hide the kids and the RV indefinitely, and he could think of only one. After quickly weighing his limited options, Howard began to type.

Glad you liked the present I left, but it was meant for the brute squad. See you at the Little Pitcher tomorrow at noon. If you really want to reclaim your property, I hope you can wait until then.

She would *have* to wait, wouldn't she? She had tracked him to the empty shack in Westborough, but—assuming she had just gotten there—she was seven hours behind him. And she had no idea where he was now.

She would have to wait.

Howard sent his reply, then typed a quick message to Alé.

You were right—the hack of your files was personal. They were after me, so your other chickadees can rest easy. I'll deal with it & don't worry about the kids, they'll be safe. We'll be delayed getting to the new place, though. Talk more later.

Howard sent the message and looked down at his plate, where a fresh cinnamon roll stared up at him—a cinnamon roll he would have enjoyed five minutes earlier. Frantic voices were still jabbering in his head, but they had taken it down an octave. Having regained a modicum of control, he picked up his roll and forced himself to eat.

"You're not going to tell us what the emergency is?" Py asked impatiently, around a mouthful of French Toast.

Howard sighed and swallowed the bite he was chewing. The roll tasted like a penance and it stuck in his throat. "On the road," he promised. "We're going to cut north and pay a surprise visit to your Uncle Abel."

Both kids froze, staring at him with wide eyes.

"Uncle Abel?" Aurie said. "Since when do we have an uncle?"

"You have a brother? But we've never even met him," Py said, looking worried. "Does he know about *us?*"

Howard shook his head and the kids gave each other nervous glances.

"Don't worry," Howard said, knowing there was plenty to worry about. "Abel and I haven't always gotten along, but he's a good guy, kind of a loner. You'll see."

"So he doesn't like people and you don't get along," Py said. "And why are we going to surprise him?"

"Because we don't have a choice," Howard said, wrapping the rest of his roll in a napkin and signaling the waitress. "I'll explain everything on the way."

VI

For the rest of the morning and most of the afternoon, the Wakes passed through the narrow bellies of New England states as if they were nothing but inconvenient spaces on a map. They back-tracked through Pennsylvania and Connecticut and Massachu-setts, finally breaking new ground north of Westborough. They stopped for lunch in a township whose name Howard forgot as soon as they left the sign behind. In New Hampshire, they caught up with the tail of a storm cloud and chased it into the White Mountains. Even in that ghostly light, the countryside was aflame, their highway winding through stands of russet and bronze and scarlet, under birch canopies that would scorch the air with gold once the skies cleared. They left the highway and took an unmarked road through an autumn patchwork of hills, bumping over rutted asphalt as the rain eased up and tattered clouds unraveled over the valley below.

No one had said a word since lunch.

As soon as they'd left the diner that morning, Howard had told the kids who was following them and why. He'd expected a lively reaction—shock, recriminations, demands to accompany him back to Westborough. What he hadn't expected was this dead quiet, from Py as well as Aurie. Maybe they were disap-pointed in him. Maybe they were upset that he hadn't told them earlier. Maybe they just needed some time to process the news.

Well, they would have plenty of time at Abel's place. There wasn't much else to be had in the middle of Nowhere, Maine. "It's the Unorganized Territory of South Oxford," Abel had cor-rected him once. "Nowhere is the next town over." Howard's only sibling had cast off the trappings of modern-day communication, which meant you didn't call him; he called you. Abel performed this feat from a Cirrus link in Gorham, the nearest town big

67

enough to have any amenities, and only when he felt like it, which was about once a year. It had been over ten years since Howard's last visit. He spent the last half of the drive concocting a story for Abel—a mixture of truths, half-truths, and lies of omission—that he hoped was halfway believable. He would only be forced to tell big black lies if his older brother insisted on asking the wrong questions. But Howard didn't think he would. If Abel still had the mind of an inquisitor, he didn't seem to be using it for much these days.

Howard reached the old access road and the asphalt under their wheels gave way to gravel. Soon he began to recognize landmarks: the crooked junction with a deer path, the deep shade of a towering fir that had no business growing among stunted pines and broadleafs. If he remembered right, his brother's cabin was less than thirty minutes away.

"What if he won't let us stay?" Py asked suddenly, breaking the long silence. "You said he's a hermit, right? That means he hates people!"

"Especially kids," Aurie added darkly.

"Don't worry," Howard said, projecting more confidence than he felt. "Abel's my brother—and your uncle, after all. He'll be thrilled to meet his niece and nephew."

"He might not even be home," Aurie muttered, gazing out the window at the creek on their right. The sluggish stream was choked with boulders, its surface bright and dappled in the late afternoon light. "You should have called first."

"He doesn't have a Spider, if you can believe it," Howard told her. "Or even an old-fashioned cell phone." *And sometimes it's better to beg forgiveness than to ask permission.*

Py shifted restlessly beside his sister. "What do we do if he's not there? Just break in and make ourselves at home? Start setting up the lab?"

Jesus, Howard thought, *they're worse than my mother!* "He'll be home," he snapped. "He's a hermit, remember? Hermits never go anywhere! And they don't have labs ... at least, not the kind we do." The RV jounced over a rough patch and something in back clattered against the wall. All three of them winced.

"I know this is weird, going to stay with someone you've never met," Howard said, slowing down over the potholes. "But Abel is actually a lot like us. I haven't seen him in awhile, but we grew up together." He glanced at Aurie. "You might get mad at your brother sometimes, but you know you can count on him, you *trust* him. I trust my brother the same way. He'll let us stay and I'll get this business sorted out tomorrow. Everything will be all right."

There it was again, that ridiculous parental assertion. Just who did he think he was fooling? Not the kids, who had already returned to their tense silence. Howard glanced at the time on his Spider—half past four. Abel was probably enjoying a quiet cup of tea with no idea that his precious solitude was about to go up in flames.

When they reached the dirt drive at the end of the road, Howard maneuvered the RV carefully between the trees on either side, praying that Abel had kept his little path cleared. Apparently he had—and the way was just barely passable. After they crawled along for a few minutes, the passage opened up into a broad meadow, bright with late-afternoon sunlight. Across the clearing stood Abel's abode, half hidden among pine trees and looking far from welcoming. Howard parked the RV near the edge of the woods and they sat gazing at the cabin's sunken porch and furtive windows.

"Ready to meet your uncle?" Howard said. The kids gave him dirty looks, which he considered an encouraging sign, surely an improvement over the silent treatment. "Be polite, but let me do all the talking for now. And don't take your jacket off," he warned Aurie, who only grunted in response. "We don't want to surprise him any more than we have to."

They made their way through the dry grass and up the creaking porch steps. At the threshold, Howard held his breath and knocked. They all waited, eyes fixed on the door.

"Too soft," Py whispered. "Try again, louder!"

Howard knocked again, harder.

Nothing.

"Told you he wouldn't be home," murmured Aurie, trying to peek through the crack between door and frame. But something moved behind one of the windows, and the curtain was twitched briefly aside. Then the door opened and Abel stood there staring at them, rifle in hand.

"Howard?" he croaked. After clearing his throat, he tried it again. *"Howard?"*

Howard gave his brother a nervous grin. "How are you, Abe?" He was about to draw attention to the kids, but the man in the doorway was looking right at them.

"I thought the feds might be after you," Abel said, putting the antique weapon aside with a suspicious glance toward the road.

"Oh, they are," Howard assured him. "But I'm in another kind of trouble."

"I'll say." Abel squinted at each of the kids in turn. "I don't need to ask if these are yours—they look just like you, only not so rough around the edges. Blend right into the woodwork, don't they? Is their mother a chameleon?"

Howard chuckled. "This is Py, and this is Aurie. Py, Aurie—your Uncle Abel."

Abel glared at Howard. "First I've heard of this Uncle Abel character," he muttered, leaning down to shake hands with the kids. "Py, Aurie, it's a pleasure to meet you. Come in and make yourselves at home. Are you hungry? Thirsty? I was just sitting down to some pickled beets and barley tea, if that sounds appetizing."

The kids just stared at their uncle, tongue-tied, which would have amused Howard under other circumstances. Except for Alé, they had never been formally introduced to another living soul. To them, other people were like potentially dangerous wild animals roaming the world. And as much as Py and Aurie complained about being ignored, actually having the focused attention of a stranger had clearly unnerved them.

"Well, you don't seem to have your father's gift of gab," observed Abel wryly. "But you'd better come inside now, before all the chiggers in Maine do. Your dad has to tell me what kind of clusterfu—uh, mess—he's made this time, and since nothing is ever his fault, I'm guessing it's a long story."

"It's a *complicated* story," Howard said, irked in spite of the largely fictional status of the story he planned to tell. "Dishing out blame is unproductive, Abe. And you know how it is with the damn courts these days. No good deed ever goes unpunished—" He broke off as Abel stalked into the house with a snort, then Howard turned to his kids. "Why don't you two explore out here for a bit while I talk to your uncle?"

The kids looked up at him, then at each other, then back at him. *That's right,* Howard thought, staring them down. *I'm about to lie my ass off for the good of the family, so just make yourselves scarce, okay?*

"Okay," Py said, nudging Aurie with his shoulder. They headed toward the woods, Py giving his father a last doubtful glance.

"Don't go too far!" Howard called, watching them go with a mixture of guilt and relief. If they were upset with him, he could deal with that later, when all of their lives weren't in jeopardy. Right now, their safety depended on Abel's sympathy—and Howard didn't trust them to corroborate his tale.

Aurie followed her brother through the trees without paying any attention to their surroundings. She was thinking about Uncle Abel. Despite her deep distrust of other people, Aurie instinctively liked her uncle. He seemed like an older, gruffer version of her dad who wore even scruffier clothes and was just as immune to hogwash.

"This is crap," Py muttered, kicking a pinecone into the undergrowth. "I don't know what he's gonna tell Uncle Abel, but it won't be the truth! Once Dad leaves, we're gonna have to answer questions about some story he just made up, and how are we supposed to do that?"

"I guess it doesn't matter what we say," Aurie said. "Dad just wants Uncle Abel to let us stay so he can go back to Westborough and meet ... her."

Both children were quiet for awhile, following the path of a thin stream before it changed course and disappeared into the brush. A few shafts of westering sunlight lit the canopy, but beneath the leaves, the forest was cool and dim. Aurie felt better in the woods, more alert and alive than she had all day. The haze that had fallen over her thoughts began to clear. Her threads were stirring under the sleeve of her jacket, but she ignored them. Stupid bloodsuckers probably just wanted another shot at Py's veins.

As if her thought had gotten his attention, Py turned to her with a scowl. "Dad's probably spinning some story about how our mother died—so sad!—and now he's stuck with two kids and he lost his job over a big misunderstanding, you know, really the government's fault. Now he's got no money and just needs a place to stay while he looks for a new job. Doing something totally legal, of course."

"You think Dad's going to say all that?" Aurie frowned as she crunched through a drift of fallen leaves. "Maybe he won't tell Uncle Abel everything, but he won't lie."

"His aura says he will," Py said flatly. "It was written all over him. Nervousness and guilt and peaks of stress! And his whole aura had this sick shine, like it was sweating."

Aurie halted in the middle of the leaf pile, unwilling to believe that such a thing was possible. Their dad *never* lied. He hated FIBR and the ERC and the government mostly because they did. "What else has he been lying about?"

"Nothing," Py admitted. "Everything he told us on the ride up here was true. None of that sneaking guilty sheen to him."

"You learned to read his chemicals that fast, huh?"

Py nodded as he kicked his way down an acorn-strewn hill. "Simple emotions are easy. Like looking at primary colors and saying, 'That's red, that's blue, that's yellow.' And, really, who would make up a story like that, anyhow?"

Aurie hurried to catch up with her brother. "Hey, do you ever, um, talk to yourself? I mean, do you ever pretend that you're talking with your, uh … your CRISPR machine?"

"My CRISPR machine?" Py halted and turned to look at her. "What do you mean?"

Aurie walked on slowly, embarrassed to say what she really meant. She was itching to tell Py about the Doctor, but didn't want to confess to having waking hallucinations. "Just wondering if you ever tried to talk to it. You know, like a game."

Py trotted alongside her. "You talk to your CRISPR machine? Like it's a person?"

"Sometimes. When I'm bored."

"Does it talk back?"

Aurie gave her brother a sharp glance to see if he was making fun of her, but he only looked curious. She pulled Py down under the red crown of a sugar maple.

"It *does* talk back," she told him in a low voice, as if the forest had ears. She told him all about the CRISPR-evo doctor—her original version and the new version—and everything the Doctor had told her that morning before breakfast.

While she talked, Py's hands explored the ground, pulling up leaves and small twigs and sifting through clumps of earth. He whistled softly when she was finished. "So that's what your threads were after—some chemical that allowed your unconscious mind to speak to you. Guess I was full of it after eating all that ketchup and stuff. Wonder what it was."

"Who knows?" Aurie said. "But if you were so full of it, why didn't your unconscious mind try to talk to *you*? Where's your messenger doctor?"

Py looked thoughtful as he cracked a dry leaf into sharp-edged crimson flakes. "I don't know. But that thing your doctor said—about seeing the heights of the world? You always have those dreams about flying, don't you?"

"Flying into the sun," she said. "Like Icarus."

Py nodded. "Last night I dreamed I was the size of an ant, or maybe I *was* an ant. Grains of dirt were as big as boulders. I was crawling through this labyrinth underground, trying to find my way out. But all the tunnels looped back on themselves, or they led to dead ends and galleries like in an ant's nest." He scooped up a handful of dirt and gazed at it. "I knew I could never get out, that the only way out was further in."

"That sounds worse than my dreams." She shuddered. "Trapped in dead-end tunnels in the dark?"

"I wasn't trapped, though. I just had to go *in,* inside the walls, the barriers. I know it doesn't make sense, but somehow I bored my way into a grain of dirt. I went deeper and deeper—and suddenly it wasn't dark at all, it was blindingly bright." He clenched the dirt in his hand and gave her an odd look. "I could have been flying into the sun like Icarus."

She felt an odd little thrill at the convergence of their dreams. "Were you afraid?"

"No, I woke up right away. But if I had to keep looking at that light—" He grimaced.

Yes, she thought. Light so bright it blinded you, seared your brain, drove you mad. Maybe it was silly to take any dream seriously, but that light seemed more real than anything she'd seen in the waking world. Seeing the expression on her brother's face, she knew neither of them could dismiss it.

"Things are different now," Py said quietly as he cast his gaze around. "There are walls around everything, but I can feel them getting thinner." He let the dirt in his hand fall and peered down at the ground. "I can almost see what's going on down there ... thanks to your threads."

Through her jacket, Aurie rubbed the skin just below her elbow, which had started to itch. "I still don't think they were trying to help you."

"Well, they did." Py gave her arm a grateful glance before springing to his feet. "We should probably head back now. It's getting kinda dark."

"Think Dad's finished with his pack of lies yet?"

"I don't care if he is or not, it's time for dinner. Aren't you hungry? You haven't eaten anything all day."

Aurie shook her head as she got up. It wasn't her stomach that felt empty, it was her threads. They didn't want Py's blood, after all, she realized. "Not really hungry, but—sort of hungry ... for something."

"Mushrooms?" Py teased. "Maybe we can make spaghetti tonight."

"Hey," Aurie said, looking around at the pathless woods. "Where *are* we?"

For a moment, Py looked as disoriented as she felt. Then he peered around and laughed. "I don't know, but I can get us home." He meandered a little way up the slope, seeming to search the air. Then he continued on to the top of the hill.

"Are you using your new sense to navigate?" Aurie asked as she followed along behind. "How? Did we leave some kind of chemical trail?"

"Yeah. If I really focus, I can see our trails in the air—they're like two strings of shrunken ghost auras." He picked up his pace and they moved quickly through the trees. Aurie heard the trickling of the creek before she saw it, and before long, the lights of Uncle Abel's cabin shone in the wooded gloom. She breathed a sigh of relief.

"Thank God for CRISPR-evo," she told Py, by way of thanks.

"I could have led us back the old-fashioned way," he said loftily. "I've never gotten lost in the woods!"

"Well, at least the RV's still here."

Py looked at her in surprise. "You thought Dad might've cut out early?"

"Or Uncle Abel might have called in the brute squad." Aurie snickered. "He could've decided Dad's more of a menace than the feds."

Py came to a halt as he gazed at the RV parked on the field. Then he made a sound that wasn't quite a laugh. "Tomorrow Dad'll probably *wish* he was in the hands of the brute squad. He's gonna have a rough day."

"Yeah," Aurie agreed as they trotted through the grass to the cabin. "And boy, does he deserve it!"

VII

Something jabbed into Howard's spine and for an instant he thought it was the needle of a long-barreled syringe. He jerked awake with a cry to find that the needle was only a busted couch spring. Faint morning light filtered through the curtains of Abel's cabin, revealing the outlines of splintery shelves. The small kitchen at the far end of the main room was still shrouded in gloom. Howard squinted down at his Spider. Still early, but he was anxious to get going. Abel had offered him the use of a forty-year-old Chevy plug-in hybrid, a Wake family antique. Howard said a short prayer to his own personal god—Murphy, of Murphy's Indisputable Laws—that the ancient car would survive the drive.

He got up from the couch and made his way down the short hall, stepping carefully across the creaking floorboards. The door to Abel's bedroom was closed, but the cluttered den where the kids were sleeping had no door. Inside, Py and Aurie were swallowed up by the giant sleeping bags their uncle had found for them. Howard could just make out Aurie's hair and one of Py's hands, which, for once, seemed to be sleeping along with the rest of him. Moving softly, Howard knelt beside his children. He listened to the quiet sound of their breathing, as one dreamed of sunshine and the other of shadows. Very gently, he kissed the top of his daughter's head and got up to leave.

"Dad." He looked down to see Aurie trying to wriggle out of her bag. Py rolled over with a grunt and his hand disappeared.

Howard hushed her, bending down to stroke her hair. "Go back to sleep, kiddo."

Aurie watched him silently, her eyes shining in the gloom. Then she put her hand—her right hand—on his arm.

"Come back soon," she whispered.

"I will," he said, hoping he could.

"And don't lie about us," she hissed. "Tell her the whole truth!"

"I will," he said again, leaning over to kiss her goodbye. That would be an easy promise to keep—his only hope of preserving everything he held dear was to tell the whole truth.

So on the drive back to Westborough, where their old lab lay empty, Howard didn't agonize over what to say. He thought about possible outcomes instead, including the one he didn't dare to hope for. And he tried to view his crime from the perspective of the one he had wronged, to see the situation through her eyes. In this, he wasn't terribly successful.

"You would've wasted them, Jackie," he muttered, halfway between Portland and Portsmouth, a forgotten cup of coffee cooling in one hand. "Wasted them with that bozo ... or never used them at all."

Despite the chuffing protests of the Chevy, Howard reached their old town an hour ahead of schedule. He drove straight to the Little Pitcher and parked in the shade of a delivery van. If he craned his neck, he could just see around the hood of the van to the restaurant's entrance. He hunkered down and waited, keeping an eye on the vehicles in the lot. As it got closer to noon, more cars arrived. People trickled in and out of the restaurant, but the woman he expected was not among them. No surprise there. As early as he was, she had probably gotten there even earlier. At five minutes to noon, he gave his Spider a verbal message to transcribe.

"Change of plans," he said. "I'm waiting at the old lab with the goods. Meet me there in fifteen minutes." He sent the message and waited, never taking his eyes off the entrance. If she emerged with anyone, or if she left here alone and another car followed her, he would know that she had called in the brute squad after all—and he would be hightailing it back to his brother's cabin faster than you could say, *Never trust anyone but yourself.*

The doors to the Little Pitcher burst open, releasing two

kids who looked, on first glance, strikingly like Howard's own. They ran ahead of their parents, hooting like a pair of howler monkeys as they drew every eye in the parking lot. Howard watched them, bemused. As the family all piled into their car, there was a sharp ping from Howard's wrist. He glanced down quickly.

I'm alone. Get your ass out of that rustbucket and get in here!

Feeling instantly sheepish, Howard got out of the car and headed for the restaurant, his feet moving of their own accord. He couldn't stop them any more than he could suppress the anticipation leaching through his fear, turning him into a fool about to walk into an obvious trap. But as soon as he opened the door to the Little Pitcher and looked across the room, nothing else seemed to matter.

She was exactly where he thought she would be, in the farthest corner at a private booth. She stared at him across the room as if he were an enemy at the other end of a dueling pistol. Her hair shone in the lamplight, but as Howard approached, he could see that threads of silver had crept into the gold. Her eyes, though, were the same—like windows to a bright ship sunk beneath a deep lagoon.

"Hello, Jacqueline," he said.

"Don't hello me," she responded, those green eyes boring into his. "Where the hell are my eggs?"

Part Two

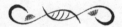

Jacqueline's Eggs

I

There were times when Jacqueline Witt wished she had become an engineer like her parents. Engineers enjoyed a respected, stable, *safe* profession. The government and everyone else tended to stay out of their way and let them do their jobs. Even better, no one ever sent them hate mail or set fire to their workplaces. Jacqueline's parents had worked for the Federal Division of Labor Commission for forty years in comfortable anonymity. That peace was only broken twice: once when their daughter was born with green eyes—a natural, but striking enough shade to prompt an investigation by the ERC—and again when that same daughter made international headlines thirty-three years later. Since then, their lives had returned to normal, while Jacqueline's would never be the same again.

Of course, biomedical research had fallen out of public favor long before Jacqueline entered grad school. Despite the success of CRISPR clinical trials, very little new work was being funded. When Jacqueline began applying to PhD programs, everyone—friends, professors, even established researchers—shook their heads at her, telling her there was no future in academic science. Like clouds veiling the sun, those warnings occasionally dimmed her optimism, but they never quenched the fire that drove her. Other people might choose their careers, but science was in her blood and she never felt there was any choice to be made. As long as there was one opening, one available lab left in the world, she would find a way to claim it.

Once in grad school, Jacqueline saw how desperate the situation was, but she also found reason to hope. Sure, only a few independent investigators were managing to survive in a drought of funding, but they were still surviving. Jacqueline read their papers and listened to their talks with envy and excitement.

These labs were like stars forming the last constellation in a rapidly darkening cosmos, and why shouldn't *her* lab be among them? The dwindling federal budget just had to hold out a little longer, another ten or twenty years. She would make her mark in that time, and if her mark was big enough, maybe the world would change its mind.

Eventually, the world always changed its mind. And science was not a fad, it was a constant in the spectrum of human striving. Scientists throughout history had been tortured, executed, ridiculed, and forbidden from practicing their discipline, but they had never *disappeared*. A thirst for truth and understanding was woven strongly into the genetic makeup of the human race. And when the times were not accommodating, one simply had to have the patience—and resourcefulness—to wait for a change in the tide.

Jacqueline was halfway through grad school when a former epilepsy patient died of cancer caused by his CRISPR treatment, and the tide—which she had mistakenly assumed was at its lowest ebb and would surely turn soon—went out. The NIH disappeared and FIBR took its place. Research funding dried to a trickle, and a flurry of new, restrictive laws—the Science and Technology Advancement Laws—were passed. The brightest stars in the constellation of science began to wink out, one by one. But before winking out, they did what stars do—they exploded.

The pioneers of science had no patience for the new laws. These leading researchers had survived through thick and thin, and never answered to anyone but themselves. They committed infractions, cut through red tape, ignored warnings, and hassled inspectors. Eager to flex its muscles, FIBR tightened the new laws further, then made an example out of a prominent gene therapist, shutting down his lab permanently. Instead of digging in their heels, the others left the country or disappeared underground, leaving Jacqueline and the rest in a climate where it was almost impossible to do any meaningful research. Many of her classmates and colleagues wrote letters of protest, formed coalitions, and went on strikes, but Jacqueline quietly stayed in the lab.

She had work to do.

Developmental biology was her fascination, and birth defects in particular. For decades, there had been a steady increase in the rate of Down Syndrome, microcephaly, spina bifida, and autism, attributed largely to women having children later in life, and the defects resulting from fertilization of older eggs. At first, Jacqueline had focused her efforts on trying to cure a specific disorder. But then she wondered: what if the building blocks of procreation could be tinkered with to prevent all such births in the first place? Miscarriage was the body's natural mechanism for disposing of an unfit embryo, but in many cases, this mechanism was no longer reliable. Jacqueline spent long hours pondering this deficiency, alone or in the company of her classmates. Everyone would be deep into their third beers on a Friday night while Jacqueline was still staring into her first glass of suds, wondering, *What if? What if?*

What if an egg could be designed with its own kill switch? Something that would trigger cell death in response to certain highly abnormal cues in the developing embryo. Something far more specific and reliable than the normal mechanisms controlling cell death. The kill switch would have to lie dormant until the egg was fertilized, and it would have to be inactivated around the end of the first trimester, when a genetically abnormal embryo would normally be miscarried. The idea of engineering quality-control eggs came to Jacqueline in grad school, and she laid the groundwork carefully during her years as a postdoc. Knowing how easy it was to steal an idea, Jacqueline kept hers a secret from everyone, including her own advisor. She even kept it a secret from her husband, Doug, a fellow postdoc and collaborator. Yet every experiment she did helped her draft a hidden blueprint, one that underwent countless changes and refinements over the years. Waiting to build the shape in that blueprint was agony, but Jacqueline knew she had to be patient. She had to wait until she had a lab of her own.

In 2054, Jacqueline and Doug were offered jobs at the Massachusetts Institute of Technology—two of only thirty-seven new biomedical faculty positions available in the country that year. Three years later, Jacqueline developed the first generation of her quality-control eggs using mouse oocytes, publishing back-to-back studies in two of the world's top journals.

When the calls came in—from *Scientific American,* the *New York Times,* the *Washington Post*—Jacqueline truly believed the tide was about to turn. She spoke confidently to reporters about the potential of her modified eggs, but she was cautious about the unknowns—her technique still hadn't been tested in human eggs, after all. And she was realistic about the time it would take before a woman could have her eggs "quality-controlled" prior to freezing or in vitro fertilization. But then the news reports appeared, and she could hardly believe what she read. Most of the articles were riddled with inaccuracies, things she had said taken out of context, and things she hadn't said at all. Journalism had become sensationalism ages ago, but it was one thing to know this, and another to experience it first-hand. Jacqueline's quality-control oocytes were branded "suicide eggs" and "instant abortions," labels that inspired a slew of hate mail from religious extremists. Successive waves of articles and blogs appeared online, propagating and magnifying the misinformation like distorted ripples in a pond. Worst of all were the I-told-you-so calls she received from her colleagues, none of whom had actually warned her about the dangers of communicating with the media.

"Never talk to a reporter," her old thesis advisor told her, after it was too late and the damage was done. He called her office at MIT just to give her this belated advice. "Talking to a reporter is professional suicide! They don't understand anything you say, so either they overhype you into the sky, or they vilify you into the ground. In either case, you end up looking like a jackass."

"I thought they understood," Jacqueline responded lamely, feeling like she'd fallen for the oldest trick in the book.

Her old advisor barked a short laugh. "How could they understand? Did they take a graduate course in embryology? Did they take biochemistry in college, or even pass high school biology? They don't have the background to understand." His voice softened. "It's a shame, Jackie—that was some incredible work. Some truly *inspired* work. If you need anything, a letter ... I know the chair of the study section for Therapeutic Approaches to Genetic Diseases. I'll put in a good word for your grant renewal."

She thanked him, but they both knew it was too late. Her suicide eggs had been murdered.

Like all storms, though, this one blew through and was gone, leaving its dazed victims to pick up the pieces. And Jacqueline wasn't the only victim of the media storm surrounding her work. During its frenzied peak, a pro-life group had made a serious, albeit clumsy, attempt to burn down her lab. The effort caused a chemical explosion, destroying part of the department's wing, and—horribly and ironically—killing a grad student working late on the prevention of sudden infant death syndrome. No one blamed her, but Jacqueline blamed herself. She had given ignorant, violent people something to rally around, and she could never forgive herself for that.

The worst of it, though, was something that kept her awake even when she was too tired to think. Lying next to Doug during the darkest hours of the morning, Jacqueline would stare at the ceiling with the words of one letter playing over and over in her head. She imagined the person who had written it as an old woman with piercing black eyes. *You are a monster,* the letter told her, not in a misspelled scrawl, but in the elegant script of an educated hand. *Who are you to decide whether a child should live or die? My son has Down Syndrome, and he is the sweetest and happiest man alive, but you would have murdered him with your poisoned eggs.*

My technology is not poison, Jacqueline protested silently to her accuser. *It's quality control—something most eggs have naturally. And no one is forcing anyone to do this.* She thought of in vitro fertilization, another tool of procreation that resulted in the inevitable loss of embryos, since only the healthiest were chosen. Had the pioneers of that technology been called monsters too? Very likely. But were they? And was she?

Life, she decided with some unease, was a mysterious and precious thing. You could never tinker with it in total assurance that you were doing the right thing. But she had seen the heart-wrenching pain of carrying misdeveloped fetuses to term. Not one, but two of her childhood friends had given birth to stillborn babies. Jacqueline's own sister had made the terrible choice to terminate her pregnancy in the second trimester after discovering that her baby had anencephaly and no chance to live. Jacqueline's modified eggs wouldn't fix everything, but they would put an end to much of that suffering. Women would give birth to healthier babies, if she was ever allowed to continue with her work.

In the wake of her egg controversy, the only thing Jacqueline could scrape up funding for was an extension of the work she had done during her postdoc days. This old work exploring basic mechanisms of development now seemed terribly dull, but it was safe and unsensational, and it kept her out of the public eye. Her marriage had suffered through the strains of her career, and she and Doug split up in the summer of '62, although they continued to collaborate professionally. Through the ups and downs of her life, Jacqueline kept her lab at MIT and never retreated underground. Garage labs, she felt, were the refuges of cowards. Scientists who gave up on the system—even a broken one—only made things worse for everyone. No matter what, she would keep her head above water and survive out in the open.

In fact, Jacqueline gave little thought to garage labs or their cowardly inhabitants until that day in the spring of 2070 when she discovered her eggs had been stolen. Not mouse eggs, easily procured from an endless supply, but Jacqueline's *own* eggs, harvested from her ovaries and frozen many years earlier. These were the irreplaceable seeds of life that had been waiting in the dark, subzero vapor of a CryoLife vault for the day she was ready to start her own family—at the age of forty-six and on her own, as it turned out.

She knew something was wrong when Isaac Hahn called on

the day her IVF was scheduled and asked to meet at a café.

"Your second vial of eggs is gone," the doctor informed her tersely, after buying their coffees and activating the privacy screen around their table.

Jacqueline couldn't believe she had heard him correctly.

"What do you mean, gone?"

"It's not in the tank! Of course, that vial was never officially recorded, so you certainly can't lodge a formal complaint." As a physician who occasionally performed illegitimate services for an astronomical fee, Dr. Hahn sounded understandably upset. In the case of Jacqueline's egg retrieval, he had allowed her to take some of her own eggs with her, then received them later for cryo-preservation—without asking any questions.

"Only the second vial?" Jacqueline was bewildered. "Not the original vial you froze down?"

Dr. Hahn shook his head, looking grim. "*That* vial is exactly where it should be, but the other one—the one you took and gave back to me—is missing. I've checked the recent security footage, but there's nothing. Of course, the vial could have been stolen any time in the last ten years."

"You have no idea who ... ?"

Dr. Hahn uttered a humorless laugh. "I thought *you* might have some idea, with the, ah, adversaries your work has spawned."

Jacqueline flushed a little under the doctor's keen gaze. "My 'adversaries' haven't said boo for years. And they're more likely to burn CryoLife to the ground, not spirit my eggs away."

"Would you like to continue with the vial we have?"

"No, let's hold off for now." Jacqueline's thoughts were in chaos, and she needed time to think clearly about who might have stolen that vial of eggs and why. Hell, how could anyone even *know* about that vial? Or suspect that it held anything other than ordinary eggs?

Over the days and weeks to come, only one image kept surfacing in her mind's eye—the face of a man with sharp hazel eyes and a devilish grin.

II

Jacqueline first met Howard Wake at a Gordon Research Conference in Italy. She'd just been offered the faculty position at MIT, and the GRC organizers had issued her an invitation to speak at their meeting—a rare honor for a young investigator. It was the peak of summer, and the conference attendees took every opportunity to tour the little villages slumbering in the Tuscan hills, but Jacqueline was too nervous to join them. She spent every free hour in her room, rehearsing what she planned to say and choosing her words carefully, so as to give away no hint of her secret plans. After delivering her talk to a full house, a tall man with tousled brown hair came up to congratulate her.

"Fantastic stuff," he said, gesturing recklessly with his cup of coffee at the giant screen behind the podium, where her last slide was still on display. "But I know your boss, and that's not really his thing."

"Developmental mechanisms aren't his thing?" Jacqueline laughed. "He'll be surprised to hear that. And probably outraged." Who the hell *was* this guy? A quick glance at his meeting badge, and she knew exactly who he was: that famous young geneticist from the Braeburn Institute. Something about him— maybe his eyes, which held both quick laughter and ready impatience—was a little unnerving, but Jacqueline was intrigued all the same. Later, she couldn't decide whether or not he was handsome. It was hard to tear your eyes away from his long enough to notice the rest of him.

Howard Wake watched her as he sipped his coffee. "I'm not saying it's outside his field of interest; it's just not his style. And it's not the sort of angle he'd ever come up with on his own. Which means this is all *your* idea, isn't it?"

She blushed a little, flattered at the recognition. Dr. Wake was a leader in the field of epigenetic diagnostics and therapeutics. Jacqueline only knew him from his publications—and his reputation. People said he had golden hands, hands that could *make* things work, and he was a known scourge of grant review sections. Howard Wake was someone who played no politics, scratched no backs, and never hesitated to say exactly what he thought of the science on the table. This was the man who had called out the eminent Dr. Levine during that morning's session. "Why should I care?" Wake had demanded of the old physiologist. "Your science is solid, but does it really move the needle? Maybe I'm missing something ... but it seems like we're just collecting butterflies here." And poor Dr. Levine just stuttered and stammered and reiterated his conclusions, never actually explaining why anyone should care. And now this outspoken detractor was standing in front of her, *praising* her work? Jacqueline's pleasure quickly gave way to confusion—and caution.

"There's a lot you could do with this information," Howard said, swirling his coffee dangerously close to the rim of the cup. "A lot of problems you could solve. It wouldn't be easy, but ... "

She opened her mouth and then closed it again. She smiled at him.

"But I guess you know that," he finished with a chuckle, as his gaze shifted to the bright pile of her upswept hair. "Anybody ever accuse your parents of engineering you?"

Jacqueline laughed, a trifle bitterly. "Actually, yes—the people who lived next door to us. Remember that whole campaign: 'If you see something, say something?' Our neighbors saw me on my mother's shoulder when I was two months old and called the ERC. For my eyes, though, not my hair." She glanced around at the men and women on their way out of the lecture hall—every head a shade of brunette or silver, every complexion well-equipped to deal with the summer sun—then she grinned at Howard. "Blondes are antiquated, but there are still a few of us screwing up the gene pool."

"So you're a natural mutant," he said, returning her grin. "But isn't that more fun?"

91

"We're all natural mutants in some way," she pointed out. "My mutation is just more obvious than most. Where's yours hiding?" To Jacqueline's horror, that last came out sounding awfully flirtatious, but Howard only laughed.

"As far as my ex-wives are concerned, my whole personality is one big mutation," he said, his eyes straying to her hair again. "But your hair isn't really blonde, you know. It's the color of sunlight on beryllium copper. And your eyes ... no one could have engineered those if they'd tried." He raised his cup to her in an unmistakable salute—still without spilling a drop—then joined the throng headed out to dinner. Jacqueline watched him go, feeling uncharacteristically flustered. She had been so careful, but somehow this man had seen the shape of her invisible blueprint. It seemed like he knew everything she *hadn't* said, and was amused and admiring at the same time. Part of her wanted to run after him and tell him everything.

Don't be an idiot, she told herself as she slowly followed the crowd out of the auditorium. *It's hard enough to compete with these big names without handing them your best ideas.* Her quality-control eggs were only awaiting a lab in which to craft them. Just a few more months and she'd be setting up her own lab in Cambridge, finally ready to begin. And then it was off to the races! Let Howard Wake—or anyone else—try to catch her then.

In the winter of that year—around the time Jacqueline and her new technician were sweating and cursing over the first generation of quality-control mouse oocytes—Howard Wake called her office at MIT and asked if she would have coffee with him.

"I'm in town for the day," he said, "and I'd like to talk to you about something. Better in person. You know a place called the Red Eye Café?"

Her curiosity piqued, Jacqueline met Howard at the café that night. She lied to her husband about it, and was never quite sure why she felt so compelled to see this man she barely knew. Having coffee with a fellow scientist was nothing unusual— except that a blizzard had hit New England, and most people were already huddled down in their homes. Doug wanted to leave work early to blow snow off their driveway, and Jacqueline told him she'd be home late. *Swamped in the lab* was her excuse, but the truth was, she couldn't stop thinking about Howard Wake. She had to find out what he wanted.

Winter storm or not, the Red Eye was always open, and Howard was there waiting when she arrived. They ordered from the service bot—chai with coconut milk for Jacqueline, and a whole pot of black coffee for Howard—then settled into deep armchairs in a silence broken only by the muffled howl of the wind. They didn't talk right away, only sat warming their hands and sipping their drinks. Howard's gaze moved around the room, taking in the brick walls lined with old posters, before finally settling on Jacqueline. The intensity of his regard seemed to draw the moment out into something warm and timeless. She couldn't shake the feeling that he was examining the secrets of her soul, one by one. Jacqueline found her face generating its own heat, and was suddenly grateful for the semi-darkness of the café.

"How are things at Braeburn?" she asked.

Howard put his cup down on the little table between them. "That's what I wanted to talk to you about," he said. "Warn you, anyway. But it's kind of a long story."

"I don't think we'll be interrupted," Jacqueline said, looking around the empty tables, then back at the man sitting across from her. *He generates his own gravity,* she thought, sipping the strong tea and hoping his story really was a long one. For once, she felt no pressing desire to get back to the lab.

The trouble with the world, Howard explained to Jacqueline, was that it rewarded mainly two kinds of people: the Asshole and the Fool. God supposedly took care of the latter, and the former took care of himself by crushing anyone who got in his way. There was a third type of person—honest, practical, and hard-working—and he generally got screwed by both assholes *and* fools. If Howard's years at the Braeburn Institute had taught him anything, they had taught him that much.

His director there, Eric Melman, was an asshole—the kind

of man who got to his position by talking big and taking credit for everything he set his hungry little eyes on. There were probably thousands of Eric Melmans in the world, and when times were good, you might never recognize them as vampires of the workplace. With his fangs hidden and his claws retracted, Eric Melman had been a tolerable annoyance. You never saw very deeply into people when times were good.

For the last six years of Howard's tenure at Braeburn, however, times were not good. After the CRISPR-related death of Brad Finch, seven investigators lost their grants and had to apply for institutional bridge funding. But the coffers were low and the endowment was barely generating enough to keep the whole operation afloat—so where was the extra money going to come from? Melman's exorbitant salary? Not likely. Instead, Howard and four of his colleagues were informed that their Foundation Funds—given as a recruitment incentive upon joining the Institute—were being reclaimed.

For the good of the Institute, was how Melman put it. When Howard protested that this new rule was only being applied to five of the Institute's thirty-two faculty, Melman responded that no, it was being applied to *all* faculty—but only five had any Foundation Funds left, as the others had already spent out their accounts.

So who suffered the most when times got tough? Not the guy at the top, or the board of directors. Not the lazy fools who had chosen to live entirely off their special funds, relying on them in lieu of writing grants. In the good times, it was easy to lose one's edge and get fat at a place like Braeburn. But now it was raining—a hard and relentless rain—and someone had to bail out the drowning institute.

Once Melman discovered that bleeding five of his faculty wasn't enough to save Braeburn, he embarked on an ambitious recruiting endeavor. *You have to spend money to make money!* insisted Melman, with his trademark fist pump. This pyramid-scheme masquerade, which featured massive spending to give the appearance of financial stability, infuriated Howard. He had done the math, and even if ten well-funded researchers joined the Institute, it would only delay the inevitable. So after the wining and dining, he pulled each candidate aside, and gave him or her the lowdown. The Institute couldn't be saved, but these unwitting scientists could be, as long as he warned them away.

"So that's what I wanted to warn you about," Howard finished, leaning back in his chair. "The coffers aren't just bare, they've been scraped raw. But Melman wants to recruit you, so he's going to offer you something ridiculous—a tenured position, start-up funds that don't exist, incredible incentives that will never—"

"Hold on a second." Jacqueline was shocked. "Braeburn wants to recruit *me*? I'm as junior as anyone can be! I haven't even published my qual—well, anything yet. Not from my own lab."

"Tells you something, doesn't it?" Howard said. "You're exactly the kind of person Melman figures would take the bait—young, just getting started, eager for tenure and stability." He lifted his cup, and then lowered it again. "It's not just Melman. The whole place is corrupt. Do you know what those Foundation Funds were meant to be used for?"

"Start-up money?" Jacqueline guessed. "To get a new lab going?"

"More than that," Howard said. "On the surface, they were seed money for studies that are difficult to fund in their infancy. But their real value was allowing you to embark on high-risk projects that can be ground-breaking, life-changing—without exposing them to the prying eyes of 'confidential' peer review or institutional oversight. With that money, an investigator could work on something big in complete secrecy." His eyes—golden in the lamplight—fastened on hers, then shifted to the snow skirling outside the windows. "Those never-expiring, untagged, unregulated funds were the reason I came to Braeburn in the first place. Otherwise, it would've been safer to stick with a standard university career."

"Complete secrecy?" Jacqueline said, awed by such a prospect. "No applications, no progress reports, no one watching?"

Howard buried his smile in his coffee cup. "Sounds like you have something in mind, Dr. Witt."

"Doesn't everyone?" Jacqueline was still enthralled at the idea of Special Money for Secret Projects. "Who doesn't have an idea they would die to work on with total freedom and no fear of anyone stealing it?"

"Not my colleagues at Braeburn," Howard said dryly. "They could've tried to change the world, but instead they gave themselves pay raises and took their labs to conferences in Tahiti!"

Outrage rendered Jacqueline momentarily speechless. "And the few of you who actually made that money count—and saved some of it for a rainy day—got *punished* for it?"

"Yep," Howard said, sounding bitter and resigned. "Anyway, when you get the call, don't be fooled. Save your career and don't come to Braeburn; the damn place is about to go under."

Jacqueline thanked him for the warning, then fell silent, wrapped up in her own thoughts. Howard could have explained all this in a call. Was there another reason he'd wanted to meet in person?

"How are things going for you?" Howard asked casually. "Still working on that cool stuff you talked about at the Gordon?" Only the sudden glint in his eyes made the question seem less than idle.

"And some other things," Jacqueline said, before launching into a detailed description of her other projects, ones that had nothing to do with her secret eggs. She had been keeping her real science under wraps for years, but Howard didn't ask about it again. Not directly. And as they talked, she became aware of two things. One, he was brilliant. Two, he was being as evasive about something as she was. They talked about science and the world at large, discussing and debating one thing after the next, but whenever the conversation veered too closely to her real work—or, she suspected, his—one of them would turn the subject smoothly in another direction. They were like two explorers probing each other's shores while protecting their own. And all the while, his eyes were on her, keen and disconcerting, forcing her to concentrate lest she give herself away.

Finally, Howard seemed to notice that his coffee pot was empty. He checked the time on his Spider and confessed reluctantly that he had an early morning flight to catch. Jacqueline shook herself, as if out of a dream, and looked down at her own Spider, where several messages were waiting. It was after ten, and she had forgotten all about Doug! Guiltily, she let her husband know that she'd be home in fifteen minutes, then followed Howard out into the drifts of windblown snow.

He wished her luck, his smile sly in the light of a lantern.

"And good luck to you," she said. "Wherever you end up— and whatever you're really up to."

His smile widened into a boyish grin, then he ducked into the shelter of an electric rail station. As she walked home through the blizzard, Jacqueline wished for the second time in two meetings that she had just let her guard down and told Howard everything. She could have happily stayed in the warm bubble of the café all night, drinking tea and brainstorming with him while a storm pelted the world outside.

Three weeks later, Howard Wake disappeared. There was talk that Braeburn had fired him for a breach of ethics. There were rumors that he had gone underground, other rumors that he had left the country. Whatever had happened, the years passed with no word from Howard Wake and no reliable news as to his whereabouts.

Then one afternoon, about a month after her publications made headlines around the world, Howard appeared in Jacqueline's office. He didn't call this time; he simply poked his head around the doorway.

"Hey there," he said, as if they were colleagues who worked across the hall from one another. "Is it a bad time?"

"No!" she said, startled out of the grant she was struggling to write. "No, it's not a bad time. I mean, it's not a *good* time; you've probably seen the news—"

With a snort, Howard came inside, toting a giant rucksack.

Dropping the sack, he closed the door firmly behind him.

"Yeah," he said. "And I can just imagine what you actually said to those bozos. But no good deed—or honest intention—ever goes unpunished." He began to pace the short floor space of her office while darting furtive looks at her.

"Is everything okay?" Jacqueline asked, bewildered. "Is there something I can help you with?"

"Your mouse eggs. Are they available?"

"Sure, they are," she told him. "Not that anyone wants them after all this scandal. You came all the way from, uh, Neverland to ask me *that?*"

Howard grinned at her. "Neverland, huh? Is that where people think I am?"

"Or somewhere much hotter." She frowned at him. "How did you get past security?"

He smiled at her without offering an answer.

"No one recognized you?"

"Your hubby's out in the hall," he said, "talking to one of my old colleagues. I steered clear of them, but no one else looked twice. Scratching a living among mermaids and pirates must've aged me prematurely."

It was true, she thought, eyeing the new grey in his unkempt hair, the bitter lines around his mouth. Only his eyes hadn't changed—they were still the color of leaves in a sunlit river, and as penetrating as ever.

"So you'll send me your eggs, then?" he pressed.

"Sure, and where should I send them? Wait, don't tell me—The Wake Lab, second star to the right, and straight on till morning."

Smiling, he handed her a slip of paper with the name Ray Smith and an Illinois address.

"Neverland is in a suburb of Urbana?" she said. "That's disappointing."

"Not at all," he said. "This is just where my flying ship picks up deliveries. And as for payment—"

"You know I can't accept payment," she told him. "Not for

materials used for *educational and research purposes."* She gave him a stern look. "That *is* what you want them for, isn't it?"

The only answer she got was a chuckle and a twinkle in his eyes that made him look momentarily young again. "We'll work something out," Howard assured her. "You haven't done anything with *human* eggs, have you?" Although his voice remained neutral, she caught a flash of something in his face—some deep-seated excitement or fear. It mystified her. As far as she knew, Howard Wake had never had a professional interest in human development.

"Are you kidding?" She gestured to the trash bin in the corner, where a pile of opened letters had been roughly tossed. "Look at all the ruckus I've caused just by fiddling with some mouse eggs!"

He whistled softly at the bin. "I didn't think anyone wrote letters by hand anymore."

"I guess Christmas cards and death threats still merit the personal touch," Jacqueline said dryly. "But, no—I never engineered the kill switch in human eggs, and I never will. That ship has sunk." She was certain her voice hadn't faltered, but suddenly his eyes were on her again, sharp and searching.

"I know all about sinking ships," he said, "and trust me, sometimes it pays to stay at the bottom of the ocean." His gaze shifted to her window, where the Charles River shimmered under a cloudless sky. "What are you planning to do now?"

She gestured wearily toward her keyboard. "Start writing some new grants—which are just old grants, really. Hearkening back to my work on oocyte development."

Howard waved an impatient hand at her desk. "Do you actually *care* about anything in those grants? And don't say yes, because you look like you've spent the morning digging your own grave."

She smiled faintly. All day long she had been trying to drum up some enthusiasm for her old research—and failing. "The only way to get funded is to work on human disease, but I don't dare propose another therapy. It's a Catch-22."

He shook his head angrily. "That kill switch was genius! And everything you did leading up to it ... you must have been sitting on that idea for years. You don't have to give up on it, Jacqueline."

"I do if I want to stay in business," she said flatly.

He approached and put his hands on the edge of her desk. "There's no point in being a scientist if you can't do meaningful work. And there's more than one way to stay in business."

She stared at him, trying to resist the invitation to probe for more information. Part of her was intrigued—and tempted. "I'm sure there is," she said at last, "but I have people to worry about. My first student is getting ready to take his quals, and I have a top-notch postdoc who is suddenly not very marketable."

"Training good people to be butterfly collectors? You're better than that, Jacq—"

"I'm not training them to be butterfly collectors. I'm training them to do the best science they can and still make a living! It's not their fault *meaningful work* isn't getting funded these days. It's the system that's—" She stopped short, shocked at how raw her nerves were.

He nodded. "That's right, it's the system that's broken. And you can't make any headway within a broken system, you'll just beat yourself bloody. Take care of your people first. But before the next granting cycle—"

"It's not just the people," she admitted, quickly regaining her composure. "I'd like to stay funded in a place with facilities and equipment and administrative support. *Scientific* support. *Colleagues*. Things are hard enough right now without making them any harder."

He smiled sadly at her. "You're a glutton for punishment, aren't you? *This* is the hard way—sucking up to administrators and advisory boards who will never have the slightest understanding or appreciation for what you do. For who you are." He stood back, regarding her silently.

"Dr. Wake—" she began.

"Howard," he said.

"Howard," she echoed. "Where *are* you working your black magic these days?"

"Out of sight and hopefully out of mind," he answered, unsmiling. "Which is exactly where you should be. Always room on the island for one more, if you're willing to catch your own dinner. In the meantime ... " Striding over to his rucksack, he loosened the string and pulled out a giant foam glove. It was the bright, unapologetic orange of a biohazard sign, and the middle digit pointed unerringly skyward. Howard carried it over to the window and propped it against the glass, where anyone passing below could get an eyeful.

"If you ever have to deal with FIBR's brute squad," he said, "or another reporter wants an interview, give 'em this."

The vulgar symbol of defiance made her laugh, and she left it up all day before finally stashing it in a cabinet to avoid trouble with all those administrators who would never have the slightest appreciation for what she did or who she was.

The next morning, Jacqueline sent a vial of frozen quality-control mouse oocytes to Ray Smith at his Illinois address. A week later she received notice that an anonymous donor had made a generous contribution to her lab's gift account, tagged only *for work that moves the needle.* She found herself smiling even as her heart twinged painfully in her chest, like a caged animal pushing against the bars of its cell. And for days afterward, she couldn't shake the image of that foam finger, flaming away in the dark confines of her office cabinet.

III

Once she discovered that her eggs—not the original vial, but the *second* vial—had disappeared from the CryoLife vault, Jacqueline spent many sleepless nights replaying her brief meetings with Howard Wake.

What did she know about him, really? *He's brilliant, eccentric, and clearly doesn't let the law get in his way. He's driven to solve big problems, but he got fired for doing something unethical. He wanted those mouse eggs—bad enough that he came out of hiding to talk to you personally. Walked right past security into the heart of MIT. He even asked you to join him in the underground! Now your own eggs have disappeared, and who else—*

She remembered the flash in his eyes when he'd asked her—in too neutral a voice—if she had ever tested her technique on human eggs. He had wanted human eggs with the kill switch in them.

For what? Selling to black-market clients? *Maybe someone like that Melman character would, but not Howard.* Producing engineered children himself? The ridiculous notion passed, and then returned almost at once. *It would explain why he really wanted those untagged funds Braeburn gave him—to do all the preliminary work leading up to something completely illegal! And if he's engineering children, he's not tinkering with their eye color. He's trying for something big. Something that moves the needle.* Once the idea got hold of her, it seemed terribly plausible. Whatever Howard wanted had to be dangerous, or he wouldn't have stolen that particular vial of eggs. And if they did what they were designed to do, then he had wasted her eggs, creating nothing at all.

Upset as she was, Jacqueline couldn't go to the authorities

for help. If any of her eggs hadn't been used and they fell into government hands, things would get very ugly for her. Even worse, on the off chance that Howard had succeeded in bringing a viable fetus to term, that baby—as the product of illegal genetic engineering—technically belonged to the federal government too. Since the passing of the new laws, two garage biologists had gone to trial for modifying their own children. The first, who had given his son extra melanin, had gotten off with a steep fine. The second, a former Hughes Investigator named Marion Peloria, had used CRISPR to rid her two daughters of an inherited mutation in a breast cancer susceptibility gene. Brutally, the Peloria girls had been taken from their parents and sent to be raised in a foster home at FIBR—which could have meant a monkey cage, for all anyone knew. So there was no question of Jacqueline going to the feds. If she was going to track down Howard Wake, she would have to do it on her own.

But hunting him through legal channels proved fruitless, and by the summer of 2070, Jacqueline was desperate. Her social network was thin, but she had a talented cousin who'd recently lost his job at a major software company and needed the money. When he named his price, Jacqueline almost laughed, knowing exactly which funds to tap.

For work that moves the needle, she thought wryly as she wired Howard's "donation" to the man who was going to net him. And her cousin proved as good as his word. He discovered that Dr. Aléjandro Ramirez, Chair of Genome Sciences at the University of Illinois, was making payments for research supplies under the name of Ray Smith, using funds from a gift account. These supplies were being funneled to over a dozen locations, but one of them was almost under Jacqueline's nose—a PO box in the small town of Westborough, Massachusetts, less than an hour away from her home in Cambridge. A drive to the Westborough post office and one sob story later, and Jacqueline had the following information: a man in an RV always came to pick up his shipments from the only premium box in use. After leaving the post office, Jacqueline drove slowly through the small town in search of an old-time coffeehouse or a refueling station café, the sort of place that might harbor retired folks who saw everything and had plenty of time on their hands. After finding the right place—and doing a bit of flirting with the locals—she got the information she needed. Only one RV in town, and no one knew who owned it, but it had once been spotted turning onto an unmarked lane off Flanders Road, in the wooded area around Cedar Swamp Pond.

When she opened the unlocked door of the old shack in the woods, Jacqueline felt a sinking despair. This place was much too small for a lab, more the size of a kids' hideout. She half-expected to find condom wrappers or empty beer cans, but there was no sign that anyone had been here at all—until she caught sight of something orange in the gloom of a far corner. As she approached it, the familiar token left no doubt about the shed's former occupant. Had Howard gone mad? If this was Neverland, then whatever had driven him underground must have broken him. As she toted the foam finger to her car, Jacqueline was horribly certain that her eggs had been lost or destroyed or forgotten about in this dismal place.

But after he responded to her message—*See you at the Little Pitcher tomorrow at noon*—some of her hope had crept back to haunt her. Howard hadn't protested his innocence or demanded to know what she was talking about, which was almost as good as a confession. Yet he had agreed to meet with her. Why? And why at a later time?

Maybe he's bluffing to put you off his trail. Yes, maybe. But if he actually showed up at the Little Pitcher, then he must want something. Maybe he had started tinkering with a few of the eggs and they were dying. If he needed her help, then some of her eggs might be safe. She might still be able to get them back.

But when Howard approached her table at the restaurant, all of her fears rose up to smother her. He looked nothing like the cocky renegade who had tried to pull her into the underground all those years ago. He looked pale and disheveled and old. When she demanded to know where her eggs were, he sat down across from her and didn't answer right away. Jacqueline activated the visual and soundproof screens and waited, clasping her cold hands in her lap to keep them from shaking.

"Is that thing off?" Howard asked, pointing at the Spider on her wrist.

She glanced down in surprise. "No, but I have the enhanced privacy settings."

He grunted a laugh. "So you pay more for the illusion of privacy? Turn it off so we can talk."

She murmured a sleep command to her Spider, but Howard was shaking his head.

"I mean *physically* off. Is the standard version impossible to shut down these days?"

"This is the newest design," she told him, annoyed to find herself on the defensive. "It's so efficient, it uses body heat to charge. And why would anyone want to turn off their Spider? Like turning off your own eyes and ears."

"Put it in the trunk of your car."

She looked at him incredulously, but his expression was adamant. With a sigh, Jacqueline went to do as he asked, and when she returned, he seemed slightly more relaxed.

"I assume yours is some illegal model?" she said.

"Of course it is."

"Then let's talk. About my eggs."

"You're going to have to be more specific," he said. "What eggs are you referring to?"

"Stop wasting time and playing games," she hissed. "You know which eggs you took! Not the normal ones, the—" In spite of the screen, she instinctively looked around and lowered her voice. "The ones with the kill switch."

He nodded, looking oddly relieved. "I'm glad to hear you admit it. So we can talk openly and honestly now? Without threats? Because—if I'm being honest—I don't understand why you're so upset."

She gaped at him. "You don't understand why I'm upset? You stole my life's work!"

"So you're upset because I stole your work." Howard frowned, looking down at his hands. "But, Jacqueline, what were you going to *do* with those eggs? And why did you wait so long? It's been almost eleven years since you froze them."

"I was busy trying to keep my lab afloat! Now the lab practically runs itself and I have more time to raise a family. Not that it's any of your business. And I was going to do IVF, of course."

"With both sets of eggs? Modified and unmodified?"

"Yes! In case the modified ones weren't viable."

"And if they were ... if both sets were viable ... you were going to implant a blastocyst from which one?"

She glowered at him. "I'm not going to sit here and be interrogated by the man who stole my eggs. I don't owe you a single explanation—but you owe me a big one. So stop asking questions and start answering them."

"I'll tell you everything," he said, "but this is important. You would have cryopreserved any embryos from the modified eggs, but you were only going to *use* an embryo from an unmodified egg. So I left you the eggs you want, and I only took the ones you're too scared to use. Right?"

Was he mocking her? No, the hazel eyes locked on hers were dead serious; he was waiting for an answer. "Of course I'm afraid to use them," she said at last. "What sane person wouldn't be? How could I give birth to an engineered baby when the first thing they do now is map it? I couldn't even use a surrogate without setting off those alarms. So what could I do, order an artificial womb and set it up in my living room, hope no one noticed? And then keep my illegal child in secret—somewhere, somehow?" She blew out a frustrated breath. "The logistics are impossible. I *can't* use those eggs now."

"Then why make them at all?"

"For the future," she said quietly. "Times always change;

you just have to be patient. Five years from now ... ten ... "

"Ten years from now you won't have the energy to chase a little monster around," he said with a smile that quickly disappeared. "But you do want kids? *Real* kids? Not just proof that your idea worked? Not just data on the tool you engineered?"

"Of course I want real kids." As she vocalized this desire, unexpected tears sprang to her eyes. "Healthy, normal kids ... that's the whole point of the tool I engineered!"

Howard nodded, looking relieved again. "My turn, then," he said. "First off, I'm sorry for stealing your eggs ... but I don't regret it. If I had to do it all over again, I would."

She wiped her eyes and glared at him. "I think that's the worst apology I've ever heard."

"And I can't return them to you, not exactly."

Jacqueline's barely-held hope drained away, leaving her shaking with anger. "You've already destroyed them all, haven't you? Wasted them on some far-fetched idea to move your goddamn needle!" Howard was making placating gestures, and this only stoked her fury.

"I didn't waste them," he protested. "I used them."

"Sure you did. Tweaked them so hard they self-destructed, as they were programmed to do." She resisted the strong urge to smack him in the face. "Unless you can pull some kids out of your pocket, you wasted those eggs!"

"I did tweak them, and most of them didn't make it, but I learned—"

"*Most* of them didn't make it?" God, hope was a hard thing to kill. Here it was again, surging up out of nowhere. "You mean that some of them survived? *To term?* How many?"

"Two," said Howard softly. "You have twins, Jacqueline. A boy and a girl."

A boy and a ... Jacqueline was utterly speechless. This was what she had wanted—and more than she had dared to hope for—but was it true? Did she really have *twins?* With trembling fingers she put in an order for a gin-and-tonic on the table's service console.

"And a coffee for me," added Howard, looking like he'd just dodged a bullet.

She added coffee to the order, then leaned forward across the table. "Dare I ask who their father is?"

Howard grinned. "Just a rogue biologist who's grateful for the honor and promises not to talk."

"Of course. And their birth mother?"

"Best artificial womb money can buy—long since retired. Listen, I left the kids with my brother up in Maine, but you can see them tonight, if you want."

Tonight? She would see them sooner than that—drive anywhere, catch any plane, pull any strings she had to. But first—

"How old are they?" she demanded.

"They're eight years old," he said, "and they look just like you."

Eight years old! She had dared to imagine a baby, even a toddler, but the vision of eight-year-old twins floored her. "And they're healthy?"

"Perfectly healthy."

Jacqueline's throat was bone-dry; she seemed to have forgotten how to swallow. "What are their names?"

"Pyogenes and Aurea," he said, with unmistakable pride.

She stared at him, then uttered a wild laugh. "As in *Streptococcus Pyogenes* and *Staphylococcus Aureus?* You can't be serious. You named my children after species of bacteria?"

"Not just any bacteria! The original strains harboring the CRISPR machine first used for—"

"The CRISPR machine? Is *that* what you wanted my eggs for?" Jacqueline took a deep breath and fought to stay calm. "You said they were normal."

"I said they were healthy. Just let me explain—"

"You can explain on the way," she said, getting up. "I want to see my kids. *Right now.*"

"Let me explain first." Howard had lowered his voice, but there was an uncompromising edge to it that hadn't been there before. She heard it and slowly sat back down.

"I had to take your eggs because they were the only ones in the world safe enough."

"Safe enough for what?"

"For CRISPR-evo," he said quietly.

She stared at him. "What the hell is that?"

Howard's eyes gained a spark as he leaned forward. "You remember how people talked about using CRISPR back in the thirties and forties? To make eugenics babies—kids with big muscles or strong math skills or winning personalities."

She rolled her eyes. "They say FIBR is actually trying to do those things."

"As if they could," Howard muttered. "Even if you *could* create a little Hercules and Aphrodite that win at chess and ski jumping, how short-sighted and unethical—"

At least he had the grace to look embarrassed when she raised her eyebrows.

"Well," he said, "leaving the ethics aside, the idea of designer babies always bugged the hell out of me. I got to thinking about what CRISPR *could* be used for."

He paused, watching her. A service bot approached and set their drinks down, but neither Jacqueline nor Howard paid them any attention. His coffee steamed and her cocktail sweated in silence.

"I've always wondered," he went on, "if humans have reached a kind of evolutionary plateau because of our brains. Even the weakest among us survive, thanks to technology. Where's the pressure to eliminate useless or harmful traits? And where's the pressure to gain new abilities? There isn't any! With everyone surviving to pass their genes down to the next generation, the human species *will never become anything else*. And yet, astrophysicists and astrobiologists predict all possible worlds populated by all possible life. Non-carbon-based life-forms, things we can't even begin to imagine. But I knew I would never see such marvels—not in my lifetime. And even for a species under pressure, evolution just takes so damn long."

He leaned back and gazed into space, raking his hands

through his greying hair. She waited for him to continue, fascinated in spite of herself. This was the unspoken conversation underlying their talk in the Red Eye Café all those years ago—the kind of discussion she'd always wanted to have with him.

"So you found a way to speed up evolution?" she prompted him. "In the human species?"

"Not the *species*," he said, turning his intense gaze on her. "The *organism*. Evolution within a single human being, Jacqueline."

"Using CRISPR?"

He nodded, his eyes alight. "Instead of using CRISPR to play God—a dull and predictable God constrained by the human imagination—I set the machine free to *be* God."

"Sounds like AI," she scoffed. "What kind of tinkering could possibly give a molecular machine a mind of its own?"

"Not a *mind*," he said impatiently. "Does evolution have a mind of its own? I had to find a way to put the CRISPR machine under the same selective pressure as any organism. And what organism is already adapted to survive inside a host?"

"Quite a few, actually," she said. "But I suppose you're thinking of a virus. Are you telling me you turned the CRISPR machine into a *virus*?"

"A virus whose survival depends on giving its host new capabilities," he said triumphantly.

"But the evo part—how could you design a CRISPR virus to speed up evolution of its human host?"

Howard grinned at her. "You'd know better than I would, Dr. Witt. Where do the building blocks of evolution come from?"

"From our genes, of course."

"And how many latent evolutionary pathways are lying dormant in the DNA *between* our genes? Old traits left over from our hairy and scaly ancestors, or stolen from other organisms, or left by invaders. How much of our DNA comes from invading viruses?"

"Almost half of it," she replied quietly.

Howard nodded, eyes gleaming. "Most people don't know

what genetic mutts we really are. We have more virus than primate in us—only most of it is sleeping."

"Good God," she whispered, as her mind began to race. "You built a version of CRISPR that behaves—for all practical purposes—like a virus? Only a natural virus has to adapt itself to avoid being killed by the host, but your CRISPR virus has to change its *host* in order to survive?" She swallowed hard, momentarily at a loss for words. "That's the craziest thing I've ever heard."

"Not just change its host," Howard corrected. "CRISPR-evo has to give its host *new capabilities*. By triggering those latent pathways in our genome—the sleeping part of us."

"So you gave my eggs a wildly unpredictable genetic machine capable of driving evolution at breakneck speed? Sort of like strapping a rocket engine to a go-cart?"

Howard grinned. "Sure, but I started with one hell of a go-cart."

Suddenly, the go-cart in Jacqueline's mind morphed into a pair of hairy, scaly eight-year-olds with spider legs and flat, reptilian eyes. "What in God's name did you do to my kids?"

"Your kids are *fine*. First let me tell you about the mice. I spent a few years in Manila making them, using those quality-control eggs you sent me. I thought most of the embryos would die *in utero,* and they did. Only one in twenty were viable. And about sixty percent of those mice had lost the CRISPR machine."

"Lost it?"

"It's like a virus," Howard reminded her. "If it doesn't do its job, it doesn't survive. And if it does its job too well, the host may not survive."

"So the mice that survived and kept the machine ... they must have been undergoing beneficial changes, right?"

He nodded.

"But what was the selection method? Life? I don't understand the evolutionary pressure." She was thinking out loud now. "Did they run faster, get through mazes quicker? Oh, wait—how would you know? Only one in twenty born, no littermate controls—"

"Yeah, life is the best selection," he agreed. "And no, I didn't have controls, but sometimes you don't need one. Watch this."

He spoke to the Spider on his wrist and it scurried off to the center of the table. Howard spoke to it again and a holographic display appeared. Jacqueline stared at the movie in progress. A pair of gloved hands—presumably Howard's—deposited a little black mouse onto a bare tiled floor. As the camera zoomed out, she saw a tabby cat swishing its tail on the other side of the room. The cat gave chase and the mouse scampered around, seeking an escape that didn't exist. Suddenly, the cat drew itself up on all four legs, arched its back, and hissed. It flattened itself against the far wall, batting at the mouse when it came close, but making no move to pounce.

"That little gal evolved to manufacture her own cat repellant," Howard said, as the video ended and another clip began. This one showed another mouse in a similar predicament, yet seconds later, caught and killed by the cat. "That one's evolution—not so successful." He caught the look on her face and his expression sobered a bit, although his eyes still shone like a little boy's. "I know it's a crude experiment, but it worked! Ten days of selective pressure, putting each mouse into a room with old Percy, and waiting to see what happened. I started the mice off in cages for a few days, letting them get the sight and smell of Percy without any danger, then I let 'em loose, one at a time. Fifteen mice, Jacqueline, and each one changed! The changes were all different—some chemical and some physical. Some darted and feinted like no mouse you've ever seen; one even rolled over and played dead. You saw the lucky lady that survived best." In his excitement, Howard was no longer sitting still, was barely sitting at all. "How cool is that?"

Jacqueline just sat there astounded, mesmerized. The next clip was already playing, showing what looked like a routine mouse dissection. Only there was something strange nestled under the animal's ribcage—a fluted, rosy piece of tissue. Gloved fingers pulled the odd structure up gently with a forceps, revealing its connection to the liver by a thin duct.

"What the hell is *that?*" she croaked.

"I haven't a clue," he said brightly, "but that mouse was *still alive* after the kids were born and we left the Philippines. Named him Methuselah and took him with us. He finally died at the age of seven and a half, at which point I did an autopsy. There were a few other mice with pretty striking anatomical differences." The video clip disappeared and a series of photos took its place.

"You see why I had to use your eggs?" he said quietly as she examined the pictures. "I couldn't do CRISPR-evo if it meant creating children with monstrous defects first. With *your* eggs, any children born would be guaranteed to be healthy. No other parents on earth have that certainty."

She sighed. "How did you know that I put the kill switch in my own eggs? No one knew, not even Doug."

Howard laughed as he closed the projection and beckoned the Spider back to his wrist. "Why you ever married that muttonhead is beyond me. How could you *not* have engineered your own eggs?"

"And how did you know which vial to take? It's not like one of them was labeled 'Illegally Modified'."

"Oh, that was easy," Howard scoffed. "Two vials labeled with the same date, one frozen at six-thirty a.m. and the other at eleven p.m.—both outside of normal hours. Even a half-wit could tell you which batch was tinkered with."

Jacqueline chuckled—a bit sourly—then noticed her drink, still sitting untouched in a pool of condensation. She drained it in three long swallows while Howard chugged the cold brew in his cup.

"Sure you needed that?" she said. "You were almost bouncing off the walls a minute ago."

"Oh, I've been desensitized to caffeine for years," Howard assured her as he reached for his wallet. His eyes had lost their manic intensity, and now they merely beamed at her. "But I'm a great believer in the placebo effect. Shall we go?"

"The kids are with your brother? Where does he live, exactly?"

"Middle of Nowhere, Maine." Howard slid a credit card from his wallet and held it up to the service scanner. "And he's the proud owner of that rustbucket out front. You okay with me driving us? I hope you are, because we can't take your Spider along. Is anyone going to wonder where you are?"

She considered this. "I registered for a week-long meeting in Seattle to cover my tracks, but I'm always in contact with the lab when I'm away."

"You can check in with your lab on my Spider or any Cirrus link until you get back."

She nodded reluctantly. "How long is the drive? About three or four hours?"

"More like five. We're liable to catch some traffic near Portland. I'd offer to buy you the world's best lobster rolls at Red's, but that place has a line a mile long—and you probably want to meet Py and Aurie before dinner."

Well, she sure as hell did. So while Howard paid the bill, Jacqueline went to ask the owner of the Little Pitcher—a man she and Doug had known for years—if she could leave her car overnight.

"Sure you can," Aram told her, waving away the bills she tried to hand him. "Just go right through the service alley and park in the back." Jacqueline thanked him and parked behind the restaurant, then returned to the front lot. Howard was waiting behind the wheel of his brother's Chevy, a car that might have been yellow half a century ago. As she got in and hunted around for a manual seatbelt, Jacqueline found herself thinking about the terrifying, unlikely, incredible meeting that lay ahead.

Py and Aurie. Cool names, even if they belonged to bacteria. But did these kids really exist? And if so, did they look and act like normal children? *They're eight years old and they look just like you.* Had they inherited her claustrophobia, or love of tart apples, or aversion to polka dots? Jacqueline had a brief, but strong impression of herself at eight—headstrong and stubborn, with flashes of temper—and wondered if Py and Aurie were the same way. She couldn't wait to find out. A hundred questions danced in her mind, but she was suddenly reluctant to ask them. Even if Howard answered truthfully, it wouldn't be enough. She didn't want to construct her kids from questions and answers; she wanted to see them and hear them for herself. Nothing would do but the reality.

Howard glanced at her as he pulled out of the restaurant lot. "They're not little monsters, if that's what you're wondering. They're not exactly superheroes either. At least, not yet."

"So the CRISPR-evo didn't work?" she challenged.

Howard hesitated before answering. "I wouldn't say it didn't work. They were both born with the CRISPR machine, and we do monthly blood draws to make sure it's still there. They haven't lost it yet. It's just taking some time for the changes to manifest."

So they really are normal kids, Jacqueline thought, with a flood of relief that left her weak. *No scales, no spider legs, no viral DNA being expressed! Oh, thank God.* And she would see them for herself before the afternoon was out.

"I still have some questions for *you*," Howard said, giving her another sidelong look. "Like how you figured out I was the asshole who stole your eggs."

Jacqueline smiled. "I happen to know a guy with a genius for getting through firewalls—but you made it easy by giving me Ray Smith's name and address. Why'd you do that, anyway? You could've had me send the mouse eggs to a drop box in Manila."

"I wanted you to be able to contact me," he said. "I was still hoping you'd change your mind about coming underground. I thought the system would drive you out eventually ... but I underestimated your tolerance for pain."

"I still don't know what drove *you* underground. We all heard the rumors—that you were fired for unethical conduct. Wasn't that right before Braeburn went bankrupt?"

Howard nodded. "Almost sixteen years ago. Remember when I told you that no good deed goes unpunished? It's true, you know. A corollary of Murphy's Law." He reached for the mug on the console, only to discover that it was empty.

"Damn," he muttered, shoving the empty mug back in its holder. "Mind if we make a quick stop before hitting the highway?"

You'll steal my eggs in a heartbeat, but you ask if it's okay to get a cup of coffee, she thought dryly as they headed toward a Juice Joint refueling station up the road.

Howard pulled up to one of the drive-thru vending machines dispensing real and substitute coffee, and paid double for the real stuff.

"Not exactly handcrafted espresso," he said, sipping his placebo, "but it beats boiled nettles and roasted beech kernels. Before I tell you why they fired me, I should tell you why I bothered to stay at Braeburn in the first place. I wasn't trying to be a martyr. I was—well, I was deep into my work. Not just the stuff I was paid to do, but the work I did in secret. My first experiments with CRISPR-evo were using cultured cells at Braeburn."

"I *knew* you had something cooking back then," Jacqueline said. "When we met at the Red Eye, you were as shifty as I was."

Howard nodded as he turned back onto the main road. "The rest of the lab knew I was working on something, but they didn't know what—they called it 'Howard's secret project.' Moving would've slowed everything down." He gave a rueful laugh. "And the truth is, I was almost as blind as everyone else at the time. I thought we had a few years left. By the time I realized how fast we were going bankrupt, I had another problem on my hands. The thing that got me fired."

"Yeah, let's hear about that," said Jacqueline, settling in for the ride. "I'm pretty sure there's a foam finger involved."

IV

As he told Jacqueline the story of his descent into the nether-world, Howard found himself reliving those old memories with disturbing ease. His eyes were on the road before them, but his mind was deep in the past, wandering through a world where he was damned no matter what he did. But he had never been afraid of breaking rules or taking an unpopular stand or dealing with problems alone. And by the time the great Braeburn Institute sank, Titanic-like, beneath the waves of sustainability, Howard was certainly in an isolated position. All the other scientists were scuttling around trying to save the Institute. They formed desperate alliances and factions: a get-rid-of-Melman-and-appoint-a-new-director faction, a beg-the-board-for-more-donations faction, even a lottery ticket faction, and one group whose sole mission seemed to be stirring up trouble with everyone else. Howard refused to join any of the camps, and he told them why—because it was too late for any last-ditch efforts.

We're about to be tossed back into the real world, he told them. *Stop wasting your time and start looking for jobs!* He was only stating the obvious, but no one wanted to hear it. Everyone was still hoping for an easier way out.

Compounding the matter, Melman told all the scientists *not* to look for jobs. He hinted—without giving any details—that they would all be taken care of. Which was exactly what everyone wanted to hear. The factions died down and all the scientists waited, wide-eyed and hopeful, for the news that they had been saved. *Trust me,* said Melman, but Howard heard a less comforting seven-letter phrase, even if the middle finger was hidden by a smile. While his colleagues all flocked to the Kool-Aid, Howard contacted his old friend Alé Ramirez at the University of Illinois. Alé was under no illusions about the situation at Braeburn and offered Howard a full position in his department. But before the grants could be transferred, before Howard had packed so much as a single beaker, Melman called him into his office.

As if I don't have enough to worry about, the director said, a gleeful spark in his eyes belying the heavy tone of his voice. *I just got a call from the ERC. Apparently you're under investigation for two felonies: the illegal distribution of research materials and delivering an unsanctioned medical diagnosis. They say you've been playing doctor for some kid named Janine Hofstetter.*

Oh, God, thought Howard. *Ned Hofstetter! That damn fool talked.*

When Howard first got the call from Ned Hofstetter, Ned's fate was already sealed. The public attorney was dying of a rare immune disorder that could be cured, but almost never was. By the time a patient started showing symptoms, it was usually too late.

"Doctor says it's some problem with the modifications on my DNA," the attorney told Howard over his Spider, in a voice as thin and wrung-out as an old washcloth. "Said they would've caught it if I had my epigenome mapped, but who can afford that? Getting your *genome* mapped is supposed to be good enough, unless you're one of the unlucky few. This *epigenome* thing costs a boatload and insurance won't pay." Hofstetter sighed. "My doc says two scientists came up with a free diagnostic kit for it, and you're one of them. I guess all someone has to do is spit in a tube and mail it in? Sounds too good to be true."

"It *is* true," said Howard cautiously, "but the situation is complicated. We can do the test at negligible cost from the DNA in saliva, but it's not commercially available yet. The patent got tied up in a lawsuit between my institute and pharma fighting over future royalties. Even for a test that's dirt cheap, *somebody* has to make a killing—so at this point, nobody can use it, not for clinical diagnostics. I'm really sorry."

Hofstetter was silent for a moment. "It's not for me," he said at last. "It's for my daughter, Janine. She might've inherited this thing." He paused, and Howard could hear the muffled sound of his throat working. "My doc said he would accept the results of your test. Give her pre-emptive treatment, but only if she needs it. If your test is positive, he'll bend the rules and forge an early clinical diagnosis. Anyone looks into it, the details of the diagnosis got lost. And if she doesn't need it, there *was* no test."

"I'm sorry," said Howard again. He had never been so sorry—and so angry at the Braeburn's lawyers for wrangling over money they didn't even deserve. "I really wish I could help you."

"I'm coming to see you," said Hofstetter flatly before he broke the connection. Forty minutes later, the attorney was striding into Howard's office.

"What you're asking me to do," said Howard, as Hofstetter sat down with his hands clamped to his knees, "is more than a minor criminal offense. I told you—this test hasn't been licensed. We don't have an approved clinical testing lab set up and that won't change until the patent is sorted out. My hands are tied."

"I know," Hofstetter acknowledged. "I looked it up, needs to be CLIA-approved. In fact, as far as the medical community is concerned, the test doesn't even exist."

Howard shook his head. "That's not going to keep me out of jail. You're a lawyer; you know what happens to anyone who even looks cross-eyed at the ERC."

"Without your help," said Hofstetter, "my daughter may die of a disease that is completely curable if it's caught early enough! Dr. Wake, you developed this tool to save lives. Doesn't it kill you to see it going to waste—to see people dying for nothing?" Scarlet patches had appeared on the attorney's pale cheeks, and his eyes were on fire. He looked like a man who was ready to kill, a man who had nothing left to lose. "How much do you want for it? I can't pay what they charge for an epigenome map, but I'll give you everything I have!"

"I don't want your money," Howard protested. "Don't you understand? Giving you this test is like giving you some pills I cooked up in my garage. It's illegal, unlicensed, unapproved. Unethical."

"*Not* giving it to me is unethical," Hofstetter cried. The thin and nervous voice was gone; he was bellowing like a prosecutor before a judge. "Pills cooked up in a garage might be dangerous, but this test is completely safe! And you know it works! You published a double-blind study testing eleven people with the disease and fifty-seven of their unaffected relatives. Your diagnosis was correct *one hundred percent of the time.*" With trembling hands, he brushed at the perspiration on his brow. "You said in the paper that the statistical power would have been greater with a larger patient sampling—"

"That's hard to get with any rare disease," Howard mumbled.

Hofstetter waved his arm impatiently. "But I don't care about statistical power. I only care about one stat—Janine Hofstetter! And the numbers must be good enough, or you wouldn't have patented this thing. You believe in it, don't you? You know it can save her. Are you really choosing not to save my daughter—and then lecturing me about *ethics?*" His voice cracked and broke over the last word.

Howard was silent, staring down at his cluttered desk. When he met Hofstetter's eyes again, he had made up his mind. Hell, he had already made up his mind before the attorney came bursting into his office.

"I'll do the test," he said quietly. "But I need your word that you and your family won't tell anyone about this, ever. Even if the test were legal, *I'm not a physician.* I can't give you a medical diagnosis or advise you in any way, is that clear? What you do with the test results is up to you."

"Understood." Hofstetter gave Howard his solemn word, and Howard gave the attorney the saliva kit for collecting his daughter's DNA. Howard performed the analysis himself and the results were affirmative: Janine Hofstetter had inherited the epigenetic defect that would eventually lead to her father's terminal illness—but she would be treated in time.

"I can't thank you enough," Ned Hofstetter said, after thrusting a silk-wrapped box of chocolates and a bottle of Cheval Blanc into Howard's hands. There were tears in the attorney's eyes. "You've saved her life. If there's ever anything I can do—"

"Represent me if I have to stand trial for a bunch of felonies," said Howard, knowing he would never regret what he had done, regardless of the consequences.

Hofstetter laughed. "Oh, that'll never happen! I've already sworn my wife to secrecy. But, you know, there are other people you could help. People in our support network have kids too; you could do so much for the FaceBit group—"

"I can't," said Howard, who could already see the writing on the wall. If the wrong person found out, it would all come crashing down and he wouldn't be able to build a single new tool that would help anyone, ever again. "If you or your wife tell anyone in those support groups, it will be the end of my career. Do you know how many people have a friend or a relative who works for the ERC? All it takes is a call from one person who thinks I'm trying to market some quack medical device and squeeze money out of desperate families."

"Who would think that?" Hofstetter said, sounding genuinely bewildered. "Everyone just wants their kids to be okay."

"Are you firing me?" Howard asked Melman, refusing to squirm for twenty minutes before his director got to the point.

"Firing you? Let's not get ahead of ourselves." Melman crossed his pudgy arms and leaned stiffly back in his office chair, eyes glittering in their puffy nests of flesh. "You haven't received any word from the ERC, have you? No. No, they only contacted me. They're leaving this up to my, er, discretion." He sighed and continued to regard Howard as if he were a very naughty child.

"What do you want, Eric?" Howard muttered.

Melman heaved another sigh and leaned forward over his desk, giving Howard a clear view of every inflamed blood vessel in his face. Ever since his big recruitment effort had failed, the man had taken on the smoldering glow of a Bermuda sunset. He looked like he might have a stroke at any moment.

"You haven't been particularly proactive in the efforts to improve our financial situation," Melman scolded him, looking down at some papers on his desk with raised brows.

"I bring in over a million dollars direct a year," Howard reminded him. "Plus your crazy 103% overhead. Correct me if I'm wrong, but I think Vassily and Noelle and I are paying for everything these days. Including your salary." He instantly regretted that last phrase.

Melman gave him a cold look and waved the papers in the air. "But aren't you taking all of that with you? I just received this request to transfer all your grants to the University of Illinois."

"This place," said Howard, through gritted teeth, "is a sinking ship! You know that better than anyone. Where are *you* going when the last rat has scuttled off?"

"Well, I was hoping we could discuss that," said Melman. "If you're willing to level with the ERC—a relatively small fine considering the magnitude of your infractions—and put in a good word for me with your friend Dr. Ramirez—"

"Hang on," said Howard. "The ERC wants me to pay a *fine?* I thought I was being charged with two felonies."

"Your crimes are being investigated, yes," said Melman. "But, as I mentioned, they left the matter entirely in my hands. Fortunately for you, I have some pull with the ERC. So I'm giving you a choice. We can take the hard road, which benefits no one, or the easy road, which will be good for everyone, especially the patients you're so keen on helping. I've already spoken to Dr. Ramirez about starting a Center for Epigenetic Therapies at Illinois, and he was very supportive of the idea. But he insisted on having your approval before going forward."

"A Center for Epigenetic Therapies?" Howard's head was spinning and a nasty throb had begun in his temples. "With you as the director?"

"Who else?" said Melman, folding his fat fingers and leaning back again with a smile. *"You?* A felon just waiting to be convicted? Do you really think you possess the judgment necessary to lead anything? You can't even keep yourself out of trouble."

The condescension was palpable.

Howard thought madly. There was no way the ERC would have left his fate in Melman's hands unless he had bribed or blackmailed someone ... or called in a favor with someone at the top. Was Eric really that powerful? *It doesn't matter,* Howard thought wearily. *I've only got two choices: be Melman's doormat for the rest of my life, or face the music and the end of my career.* As he weighed these grim options, his director's satisfaction clouded the air like an unbreathable perfume, sticking in Howard's throat and muddling his thoughts. How could he possibly continue his CRISPR-evo work at Illinois, with this asshole watching his every move? But how could he do anything at all if he was turned over to the ERC? Old colleagues who had dropped out of sight during recent years ran unbidden through his mind, a sad parade of names and faces. Howard remembered those who had been unwilling or unable to adapt to these tough times, and then he thought of Jacqueline Witt. He remembered their conversation in Boston and her talk at the Gordon conference. She had been like a bright flame in a room full of dying embers, and the science she was doing—the tool he knew she was making—

Suddenly, in a flash of inspiration, Howard realized there was a third option.

"I guess you're right," he told Melman, "I *can't* keep myself out of trouble. But thanks for pulling me out of the fire. And a Center for Epigenetic Therapies ... well, it would be a dream come true. But what about all the other faculty here?"

Melman snorted. "I can't turn an albatross into gold, Howard. But it sounds like we have a plan. I'll tell the ERC that you promise to behave from now on, you call Ramirez, and let's start rooting for the Cubs."

Howard nodded and excused himself quickly. He had a thousand things to do, starting with an important call to Alé.

Late that night, after everyone had left, Howard entered his lab for the last time, carrying a dewar flask that looked exactly like a coffee thermos. All the equipment he needed could be replaced. What *couldn't* be replaced—his CRISPR-evo work—was stored in a few microtubes and cryovials. Feeling like he was moving in a dream, Howard carried his entire career out of the Braeburn Institute in a briefcase and a super-cooled thermos under one arm. As he walked past the security cameras, it occurred to him that even these few things were ultimately dispensable. The only invaluable commodities were the ideas themselves, which traveled light as air. As long as he had the grey stuff between his ears, everything else could be made from scratch.

Howard had left a handwritten letter for his two remaining postdocs, explaining that he was being fired for a breach of ethics and they could still continue their work in the Ramirez lab in Illinois. He'd left a shorter message for the director propped up on the chair behind his desk. The foam missive blazed as bright as Melman's face and it pointed toward the heavens like the hand of an irreverent prophet.

V

"I knew it," Jacqueline crowed. "How many of those ridiculous things do you have?"

Howard grinned, sliding his empty mug back into the cup holder and coaxing the grumbling Chevy up to sixty-five. "I got a bulk discount thirty years ago. I've got big ones, little ones, inflatable ones—"

"And what did Melman end up doing? I'm guessing he didn't save all the faculty like he promised?"

"Oh, no," Howard said. "He took a position at FIBR and left everyone else high and dry."

Jacqueline snorted. "Good thing you called your friend when you did. But what a friend, this Ramirez! He really set up an underground operation just for you? What do you have on the guy?"

"Nothing. We were postdocs together at Emory, and we always got along better with each other than with anyone else. He's like you—a rebel who's still trying to live a normal life. By the time I needed help, he was already helping a few others. Plus I did him a favor once."

"Did you save his life with one of your illegal kits?"

"It was legal," Howard protested.

"Well, that must've been a first," Jacqueline murmured, then fell silent, musing. Howard's Spider showed heavy traffic on the coastal highway, so they had opted for the inland route. Outside, the New England countryside slid past in a palate of russet and vermillion, with a few stubborn greens still clinging to the end of summer.

"Do you blame me?" Howard asked quietly.

Jacqueline glanced at him in surprise. "For saving a little girl's life instead of letting her die? Of course not! You did the right thing, even if it cost you your career."

"Melman did me a favor, actually. He forced me to go underground, which I would've had to do eventually."

"To make the kids?" It wasn't really a question. "Do they know about all this?"

Howard nodded. "I've never kept any secrets from them. Well, except for one."

The one about who their mother is. Jacqueline's stomach clenched as another important question suddenly reared its head. "You're not married, are you?"

"God, no," Howard replied quickly. "No wives for the last twenty years! Or girlfriends, for that matter. Or friends, except for Alé. The Wake Institute is a tight ship, all business."

Well, that's one less thing to worry about, Jacqueline thought, relaxing a fraction. "Who did they think their mother was? An anonymous egg donor?"

He nodded. "But I told the kids the truth yesterday, after I got your message. On the drive up to my brother's."

"How did they take it?"

"To be honest," Howard said, "they're pretty pissed at me. Before I left, Aurie *ordered* me not to lie to you about anything."

Jacqueline laughed a little, instantly charmed. Then her stomach rumbled as they passed a holo-board promising FOOD, FUEL, and FORTY WINKS at the next junction. Howard checked the time.

"Three o'clock already," he marveled. "Are you hungry? We sort of swigged our lunch, didn't we?"

There were two Grab-&-Go nutrastands facing each other across the two-lane highway, but Howard headed farther down the road and pulled into the drive-through of a Golden Oldies burger joint. Jacqueline—who had two nutrapaks and a powdered smoothie in her purse—found herself ordering a Barcelona burger and a double-chocolate shake with whipped cream. Somehow, it seemed like the right meal for the occasion.

And what occasion was that? Two rebel scientists driving a retro-mobile to a cabin in the woods where their genetically engineered children were hiding? *You can't make this stuff up,* Jacqueline thought, as Howard parked under the shade of a beech in an isolated corner of the lot. *Well, you hunted him down and demanded a meeting, and now you're in over your head. No one knows where you are or who you're with ... and you don't even have a change of clothes or a toothbrush.* With an inward sigh, she unwrapped her lunch and took a bite. The char-grilled burger was garnished with roasted garlic and onions, and it was nothing short of fabulous. When was the last time she'd had one of these? Too long ago to remember. She wished she'd gotten some fries too.

Without glancing at her, Howard offered up his carton of fries.

"How'd you know I wanted those?" she asked, relieving him of a small handful.

"Women always want other people's fries." Howard gave her a look over his burger that suggested his knowledge of women's desires ran deep. "They operate under the questionable assumption that stolen fries have fewer calories." He shook the carton mockingly at her and she took the opportunity to snatch another handful while taking a long pull on her compostable straw. The straw wouldn't last for two more sips, but the milkshake was thick and rich and tasted like a hundred chocolate bars had died to make it.

"Tell me you don't stuff our kids with these terrible things," Jacqueline said. *Our kids.* The impossible words echoed through her head.

"Oh, no," Howard assured her. "At home it's mostly grilled cheese, fish sticks, Italian Helper, stuff like that. Aurie makes a great sloppy joe."

Jacqueline spluttered and coughed up a piece of fry.

"What?" Howard said, looking surprised. "We don't have the time or space to make anything fancy, and the kids like to do a lot of the cooking themselves. We usually have soup or sandwiches for lunch, and something quick for dinner so we can get back to work."

"Back to work?" Jacqueline frowned. "You mean homework, right?" She searched his face. "Back to the *lab?* You're treating our eight-year-olds like grad students?"

"They were like grad students when they were six. Now they're more like postdocs." Howard chuckled as he licked a dab of mustard off his fingers. "I only wish I had postdocs like these kids. They *love* the lab, especially Aurie. She wanted me to let her sleep there so she could do experiments at night."

Jacqueline couldn't help but smile at that. Then she blushed, remembering the instant food in her purse and the can of soup she'd had for dinner the night before. She knew all about cooking whatever was fast and easy, but her kids ought to be eating real meals—and not slaving away in their father's sweatshop.

"They're healthy, happy kids," Howard insisted, wiping his hands on a napkin. "Well, except for having two heads each, but we've learned how to cope with that." He picked up his coffee and stared at it, seemingly locked in some internal debate. Finally, he put the cup down and gave a set of instructions to his Spider. Jacqueline waited, suddenly as nervous as she had been at the Little Pitcher. Surely he was just teasing her and there were no extra anythings.

"See for yourself," he said quietly, as the Spider scuttled over Howard's lap to perch on the console between them. Then a holo-image appeared in the air.

At first Jacqueline saw nothing but a bare hillside with a few trees behind it. Then she looked closer and two kids suddenly swam into view, emerging from the shadowed grass of the hill. They were a boy and a girl of about six. The boy was hunched over something that looked like a lumpy sandcastle, and he was frowning like an architect scanning his prototype for design flaws. The girl stood above him, looking down at the sandcastle with a slight smile. Their hair—which might have been light brown or dark blonde or the color of sunlight on beryllium copper—blew wildly in the current of a strong breeze.

"That's Py's Artificial Anthill," Howard murmured, but Jacqueline barely heard him. "The day the ants moved in."

Jacqueline couldn't speak, couldn't take her eyes off the holo-image. It was as if her missing eggs had just exploded into these two little people, both strange to her and achingly familiar. She realized that she hadn't truly believed in them until that moment. Before her eggs had disappeared, she'd been steeling herself for the discomforts of pregnancy and the drudgery she would have to face alone, the feeding and diaper-changing and sleepless nights. She was dimly aware that Howard had saved her a hell of a lot of trouble, but that did nothing to ease the terrible sense of loss. Jacqueline scrutinized her children's faces—so small and shadowed, so hard to see—for all of the hopes and dreams and secrets that must be hidden there. Py and Aurie. She had been robbed of them.

"Were you ever going to tell me?" she said in a strangled whisper. "You weren't, were you?"

Howard looked stricken. "I wanted to, Jacqueline. I never wanted to have to steal your eggs in the first place. But, God, you were married! You would never have *given* them to me—and I needed them." He gripped the steering wheel in both hands, as if trying to keep the parked car from running away. "I told myself I would tell you if they were born healthy. Then I decided to wait until they were a year old. Then suddenly they turned two and started asking who their mom was. I really wanted to call you when Aurie was four and she isolated her own DNA for the first time—and she was so proud of herself! You should've seen her—her eyes were on fire; she looked like a little version of you. I wished you were there when Py made that anthill. You know he baited it with pheromones that he isolated on his own? Got some on himself; there were ants all over the RV for days ... great lesson in *a little bit goes a long way*." Howard expelled a ragged breath. "But I just couldn't ever bring myself to tell you. You might have called the ERC, and our kids would've spent the rest of their lives being lab rats."

"You think I would have called the ERC on my own kids?" Jacqueline glared at him through a blur of tears. "How stupid do you think I am?"

"You threatened to call the brute squad on me yesterday," he reminded her. "If I didn't return your property in mint condition."

"That was a bluff, you idiot," she said. "I would never have called anyone if there was even a chance that you had succeeded. They're *my kids*, Howard!" She stared at him, trying to untangle the mixture of guilt, stubbornness, and anxious longing in his face. "But that's the problem, isn't it? You wanted to show them off to me, but you didn't really want to share them. A lab works best with one person at the helm, and you must've felt the same way about a family."

He looked away—his face tight and expressionless—and Jacqueline looked back at the picture of her children. Wiping her eyes, she noticed something she hadn't seen at first. There were *things* on her little girl's arm, things that looked like dark, wetly shining threads.

"What're those?" she asked thickly, pointing to them.

"I don't know," Howard answered, sounding suddenly tired. "Sensors of some kind. We call them threads."

"You mean they're a *part* of her? They're growing out of her arm?" Jacqueline peered at the threads in disbelief. She scrutinized the rest of Aurie for aberrations, then whatever she could see of Py.

"She has to wear long sleeves when we go out," Howard said. "It's a nuisance for her, but we can't risk anyone seeing her threads. And don't ask me what they do—I have no idea. I've been wanting to dissect one forever, but they don't seem to die or fall off on their own." He tapped the display, and the holo-image changed.

"She was born with them," Howard went on, staring at the photograph in the air. "But they've changed quite a bit as she's gotten older. Longer and thicker and darker now."

The picture he was showing her—a close-up of Aurie's arm—stopped Jacqueline's breath. Those odd structures gleamed a metallic cobalt, like the scales of a blue Malayan coral snake. They were beautiful and utterly incongruous against the normal skin of her arm. The longer Jacqueline looked at them, the more alive they seemed, rising above the plane of the photograph with an alien vitality.

"She can't control them," Howard told her. "But they can move on their own, although I don't know what they're responding to. We've tested all kinds of things. Mostly they just lie there like hair, but they, uh ... they were unusually active a couple nights ago."

Jacqueline looked at him inquiringly, and he rubbed his temples with both hands.

"Dammit," he muttered, deactivating the holo-display and recovering his Spider. "I wasn't going to tell you any of this. Not yet. Not until you'd actually *seen* the kids, seen how normal they are. This ... this is just gonna make you worry, and really, there's nothing to wor—"

"Oh, stop treating me like an eight-year-old," she snapped. "What happened?"

He sighed and started the engine. "I'll tell you, but let me tell you about *them* first. So you know them a little better. They're your kids, Jackie—boy, are they ever."

As they got back on the road and Howard talked about their kids, Jacqueline found herself visualizing them with perfect clarity—this girl and boy who were so quick and eager to learn. She saw Aurie hunched over her lab bench with quiet intensity, and Py roaming through wild barrens, studying the life he found in thickets and under rocks with the same absorption. She saw two kids who ought to have been lonely and were anything but, whose independence was given an astonishing amount of free rein, and she thought, *God, I would've loved to grow up like that!*

"Don't get the idea that they're perfect," Howard warned her. "Because they're not. You've never met kids this stubborn—"

"Well, the apple doesn't fall far."

"True," Howard said, giving her a pointed glance. "But even their ways of being stubborn are different. Aurie's high-strung and impatient, and Py never loses his cool ... but he doesn't change his mind easily. He won't argue; he'll just quietly disagree. And he almost never complains, even when he's in a lot of pain."

Howard described Py's ultra-sensitivity over the past two weeks and his apparent need for overstimulation, culminating in the condiment binge at Dixie's, and how Aurie's threads had rescued Py from his crisis. Howard pushed his brother's car to its anemic top speed as they made their way north. Other cars—mostly self-piloted and hydrogen-powered—left them far behind, but Jacqueline was no longer concerned with the speed of their arrival. She was too busy dealing with the aftershocks of the boulder that had fallen into the orderly traffic of her mind.

Meteor, she corrected absently, as Howard speculated on the nature of their daughter's strange appendages. The tiredness and tension had left him, and he spoke freely, as proud as if he had designed Aurie's threads himself. *Normal kids would be a boulder, but these kids are a meteor—an alien unknown.*

"—wasn't happy about it, though," Howard was saying. "And she's been hiding them ever since."

Jacqueline frowned. "She's probably afraid of what they might do. Wouldn't you be worried if part of your body jumped up and speared someone with no warning?"

Howard shook his head. "I know it sounds like an attack, but those threads saved Py; there's no doubt about that. He regained consciousness right away, and was back to his old self. Only now he claims he can see *chemicals.*"

"Chemicals," echoed Jacqueline, mostly to herself. Something disquieting had just occurred to her. "Well, that's something to consider."

Howard glanced at her sharply. "What?"

"The kill switch," she said. "We've been talking all this time about CRISPR-evo and what it might be doing, but you know—the kill switch is still active in all their cells. At least, it should be."

Howard swerved to avoid a two-tone Needletail whose driver had changed lanes without signaling—or looking. "Asshole," he snapped. "Let your fancy car do the driving; that's what it's for!" The Needletail zoomed on ahead, but Howard's hands on the wheel were not quite steady.

"I thought the kill switch got inactivated at the end of the first trimester," he said.

"Because of hormonal signals from the mother," Jacqueline said. "But our kids didn't have a surrogate mother, right? You grew them ex vivo—in an incubator."

"Oh, Jesus," Howard said quietly. He glanced at her, and Jacqueline saw genuine fear in his eyes for the first time. It did nothing to assuage her own fears.

"Jesus, Jacqueline, I didn't think about that. It wasn't a problem with the mice."

"It might not be a problem at all," said Jacqueline slowly. "It's just untested, and the kids have been fine up until now, right?" She examined his face. *"Right?* Any other issues you forgot to mention?"

"Well, they do sort of disappear at times."

"Yes, they and their extra heads disappear at times. Good one. Now, seriously—"

"I guess *disappear* isn't the right word; it's more like they have a kind of natural camouflage—an illusion of disappearing. You know, like some reptiles and insects. Anyway, no other issues."

"Just the illusion of disappearing. And Aurie's threads. And Py's ability to see chemicals."

"Yeah, that's about it."

They were silent for a moment, lost in thought, until the blaring of a horn made them both jump.

"Maybe we should stop for a bit and talk about this," Jacqueline said, as the driver of a Kia Centauri zipped past, flipping them the bird.

Howard glanced at the road sign up ahead. "We could take the Kancamagus Highway at Lincoln and stop at one of the trailheads."

"I didn't mean we should go for a hike," Jacqueline said,

looking out the window. Afternoon sunshine still gilded the forest around them, but suddenly the hour felt very late. "Just give the car a chance to cool down while we figure out what to do."

Howard changed lanes and took the exit for highway 112. "Okay, we'll give ourselves twenty minutes under the fall foliage."

"Twenty minutes?"

"That ought to do it." He gave her a tense smile. "If the two of us can't solve a problem by then, Dr. Witt, there's no solution to be had."

They drove a few miles down the Kancamagus Highway and parked at the Lincoln Woods Trailhead. Shouldering their way past the throng of tourists on the bridge, they started down the trail along the river. Jacqueline was a fast walker, but she had to trot to keep up with Howard's long stride. She was racking her brain for what an active kill switch might do in cells that were no longer embryonic. Trigger the suicide program in any cell that stepped out of line? Maybe the kill switch destroyed cells that were becoming overly aggressive, preventing autoimmune disorders or cancer. Keeping an organism free of such threats ought to be a good thing, but what else might be regarded as a threat? CRISPR-evo changes, perhaps, which were innately out of line?

"What could turn it off?" Howard muttered as he wandered off the trail to stalk the pathless riverbank. "What could you use to kill a kill switch?"

Jacqueline navigated the loose stones with care, then stood for a moment looking down at the creek. Rivers were such tricky beasts, swelling and shrinking with the seasons, changing mood along their course. This one appeared placid and sluggish, but around the bend it might surge into a raging torrent of destruction, only to spend itself in unfocused trickles that never reached the sea.

"Exclusivin," she said.

"Exclusivin?" He turned to stare at her in what she supposed was a rare state of bewilderment. "That insecticide that was banned years ago?"

She nodded. "It was actually a natural compound discovered back in the early fifties in a subspecies of jack-o'-lantern."

Howard looked even more baffled. "Halloween pumpkins?"

"Mushrooms," she said, rolling her eyes. "Bright orange and full of toxins. They look like an edible variety, but if you cook up a pile of jack-o'-lanterns, you won't live to learn from your mistake."

Howard continued slowly on, and she followed him downriver.

"On top of the toxins," she went on, "this particular variety of jack-o'-lantern contains a compound—exclusivin—that's lethal only to insects. Monsanto incorporated the gene into crops as an insecticide before the anti-GMO craze shut them down. But exclusivin also turns out to be a great drug for blocking activity of a synthetic target. Binds specifically to an engineered groove that doesn't match any protein structure found in vertebrates. High affinity, great pharmacokinetics, the whole package."

He gave her an incredulous look. "Sounds like the holy grail of drugs."

She shook her head. "It only works on a *synthetic* target, something designed with that unique pocket. So I engineered the kill switch with a binding site for it."

"But why go to all the trouble," Howard asked, "if the kill switch gets turned off by maternal hormones?"

"Hormones are unpredictable," Jacqueline said, glancing down at the creek, which had indeed quickened as its banks grew steeper. "I designed the exclusivin pocket as a fail-safe. It's always good to have a back-up plan."

"Yeah," Howard said, sounding impressed. "But that modification wasn't in your original papers, Jacqueline. And you never published anything else related to the kill switch."

"I might've done a little tinkering on the side," she admitted.

Howard stopped in his tracks just to smirk at her. "You worked on it every night after your people went home, didn't you? I bet you stayed in the lab until midnight and that useless sap you married had to fix his own dinners."

"That 'useless sap' is a better cook than I am!"

"I bet," Howard continued, undeterred, "that you weren't upgrading those eggs just for the sheer hell of it." He raised his eyebrows in a parody of outrage and held an invisible microphone up to his mouth. "We have reason to believe that you incorporated this drug-sensitive kill switch into *your own eggs,* Dr. Witt. Without FDA approval! Without a single clinical trial! Using funds siphoned from other projects! Under the very noses of the taxpayers who support your work. What do you have to say about *that?*"

Jacqueline tried to scowl at him as he thrust the imaginary microphone toward her, but her twitching lips betrayed her.

Howard laughed. "What's that river to the underworld? The Styx?" He kicked a small stone into the water and watched it disappear. "You've been dangling your feet in that river your whole career. But you're scared to jump in, scared to get swept away, and you shouldn't be."

When he turned back to her, his expression was serious. He regarded her steadily, then suddenly touched her cheek. The lightest of touches, but she felt it down to her bones. The caress was brief, just long enough for electric tingles to course through her, simultaneously thrilling and maddening her. Then he smiled a little sadly and tweaked her gently on the nose.

"You should have joined me in Neverland thirteen years ago. Just think what we could have done together, running free in the dark! Instead of you crawling in the light." Sunlight and shadow played across his face as a cloud passed over, and then he was off again, climbing quickly up the stony bank.

Jacqueline followed him without hurrying. Her cheek was still warm from the touch of his hand, but the freshening breeze made her shiver. It was already getting dark and chilly in the shadows of the trees. She and Howard had been talking almost nonstop all afternoon, but nothing had been resolved. Instead, things were only getting more complicated. As she stepped over a tangle of brush, a pair of hands gripped her shoulders. She looked up, startled, into Howard's tense face.

"Aurie said something weird yesterday morning. She said she wanted *mushrooms.*"

"What's wrong with that? Doesn't she like mushrooms?"

He released her, frowning. "She'll eat the canned ones in spaghetti, but she never *asks* for them. And why the hell would she suddenly want them for breakfast? She likes eggs and bacon and toast, just like the rest of us."

"Py was having weird cravings too, wasn't he?"

"Yeah," Howard said, "but with Py, I think it was just the urge to overwhelm his senses. His CRISPR-evo needed some kind of sensory overload, and condiments are loaded with sugar and salt and all kinds of chemicals. With Aurie, I don't know what's going on. Her threads did something to Py, and now she wants to eat mushrooms?" He glanced up at the sky, as if searching for signs of a coming storm. "What if she's really craving jack-o'-lanterns? Which contain the only drug that could turn off the kill switch in her cells."

"The kill switch wasn't supposed to be on in the first place," Jacqueline reminded him. "Not after the first few months of gestation. What's the worst that can happen if it gets turned off?"

"Who knows," Howard said. "It's co-existed with the CRISPR-evo machine their whole lives. What bothers me is this sudden instinct to get rid of it. Assuming that's the case, why does she want to turn it off?"

"Because the CRISPR machine wants to turn it off," Jacqueline said. "As to why, your guess is better than mine."

"The kill switch must be preventing some new adaptation," Howard reasoned. "Something advantageous for Aurie."

"But if the kill switch would prevent this adaptation," Jacqueline said slowly, "then it's a dangerous one. And why does the CRISPR machine need the drug at all? CRISPR is a surgeon— it can get rid of any gene it wants to. Why doesn't it just cut the kill switch out of Aurie's genome?"

"Good question."

Jacqueline shook her head in disgust. "Listen to us, talking as if her CRISPR machine is sentient, as if her cells know anything at all! How on earth would they know enough to give her a craving for mushrooms? It doesn't make any sense!"

"I know," Howard said, as he picked up the trail, heading back the way they had come. "But if her craving gets as strong as Py's did ... " He was almost running now, kicking up flurries of dead leaves. "We have to get back in satellite range. I want to call the kids and make sure they're okay."

"You've never left them alone before?"

"Only to run errands," Howard told her. "Never for more than an hour or two."

"They're not alone, though." She was trying to reassure both of them as they hurried back to the parking lot. "They're with your brother."

Howard snorted. "Yeah, my brother who has zero experience with even run-of-the-mill kids! Ours could run circles around him if they wanted to. Luckily, they can take care of themselves."

Glancing at him in the thickening dusk, Jacqueline saw that his face was tight with worry.

"And if they can't," he said, "I'm not sure there's a damn thing we can do to help them."

Part Three

Doctor and Policeman

I

Despite having zero experience with even run-of-the-mill kids, Abel wasn't completely clueless. He knew Howard's daughter was hiding something, that there was something wrong with her left arm. When the whole family had shown up on Abel's door-step, the little girl had declined to hang up her coat, even though she was clearly sweating in the toasty warmth of the cabin. She wore that coat all through dinner—a surprisingly tasty tuna cas-serole that the kids insisted on making themselves—and into the bathroom, from which she emerged freshly washed and garbed in a long-sleeved nightgown. All throughout the evening, her right hand kept straying to her left arm, rubbing it absently or adjusting her sleeve as if something in there were trying to breathe.

When Abel awoke the next morning, Howard had left and both kids were already up and making breakfast. The three of them sat at the table between the kitchen and the living room, Aurie wearing a long-sleeved shirt and nibbling at a piece of toast. Her eyes wandered to the open window above the sink, where the morning breeze drifted in, bringing the smell of pine and an occasional bird call.

"You all right?" he asked her, as she put the toast down. "Not too hungry, huh?"

His niece gave him a furtive look that made him uneasy. She *did* look hungry, and not for toast. In his old life, one of Abel's clients had been a wealthy heroin addict who'd gone through many cycles of withdrawal before the overdose that fi-nally killed him. The little girl's eyes reminded him of those other eyes, windows to a mind in the early stages of withdrawal ... but that was ridiculous.

"I'll eat that," Py said, swiping his sister's toast.

Abel slid the marmalade jar over to Py, then topped off his own mug of tea. It was strange having two kids in the house—and doubly strange because these two were so un-childlike. As a rule, he disliked children, with their annoying antics, high-pitched voices, and obsession with digital eye candy. But Howard's kids were nothing like that. They weren't exactly shy, but they only spoke up when they had something to say. And they came and went like alert little shadows, watching everything from eyes that changed color with the light. If he hadn't been so sensitized to the rare presence of others, Abel wouldn't have noticed the unobtrusive movements of his niece and nephew about the house. The night before, they had taken over the kitchen as quietly and efficiently as a pair of adults. But Aurie hadn't eaten any more at dinner than she was eating now. Over the rim of his mug, Abel watched the girl scratch and pluck at her left sleeve, and wondered what the hell was under there. A rash that was itching like crazy? Maybe she'd gotten into some poison ivy; there was a lot of that in the woods.

"Can I get you something for that itch?" he asked her. "Got some calamine lotion in the medicine cabinet."

Aurie stopped scratching and looked at him in apparent confusion. "What itch?"

"Uh ... never mind." Abel put his mug down and scratched his own head. He cast an appraising look around the cabin, as if the worn pine furniture and shelves of old fishing guides might reveal some hidden entertainment feature. There sure weren't any toys around. But it was hard to imagine these two putting a puzzle together or tossing a ball back and forth. "Sorry there's not much to do here, unless you like birdwatching or chopping wood. Your dad'll be back to pick you up tonight, though, so you won't be bored for long."

The faces of both kids tightened into identical scowls.

"We'll be lucky if he makes it back at all," Py muttered around a mouthful of toast.

Abel almost choked on his tea. "What?"

"Oh, he didn't tell you?" Py swallowed and wiped crumbs

from his mouth with the back of his hand. His grey-brown eyes gleamed wickedly. "Dad's meeting the woman whose eggs he stole nine years ago. A famous developmental biologist named Jacqueline Witt. She's our mother, only she doesn't know it yet." His voice faltered a little, and Abel saw, to his consternation, that the boy's eyes were bright with unshed tears.

Aurie glanced down at her right wrist, where a lemon yellow contraption appropriately called a Spider clung to her skin, as if by magic. From what Abel understood, Spiders built webs of information linking everyone under the sun, and they could reveal everything from your current location to a spike in your blood pressure to anyone who cared to know. And the damn things could *crawl* places, peep and eavesdrop like recording flies on the wall.

"She'll know in four hours and fifteen minutes," Aurie said.

"Yeah," snapped Py, "and she'll call in the brute squad. Dad will be toast! They'll lock him up to stand trial for his crimes—"

"—his *many* crimes," amended Aurie.

"—and of course he's guilty of all of them, so they'll confiscate the lab and send us to foster parents at FIBR. Or maybe they'll send us to live with *her*."

"Better than FIBR," Aurie said absently. "At least she's our mom."

"Our *mom?*" Mounting fury had turned Py's eyes viper green. "We don't even know her! How is one stranger better than another? Maybe she's *worse* than FIBR—why else would Dad have hidden us from her all this time? And what's going to happen to Dad?" He glared at his sister, but her attention was focused on her left arm. Py followed her gaze and the venomous color leached out of his eyes, leaving only worry behind.

"No point in making up things to stew about," Aurie murmured. "Dad will be fine, he always is."

Py stared down at his plate, his throat working. Abel regarded both of them in utter astonishment. For a moment, the only sound in the cabin was the dispassionate ticking of the antique clock above the stove.

"He told me he was meeting your mom for a custody dispute," Abel mumbled. "He said things might get ugly, and he didn't want the two of you ... you know ... "

"He's hiding us here," Aurie said, looking up at him. "Us and the lab."

Abel shook his head in bewilderment. "What lab?"

"Lab's all packed up in the RV," Py muttered. "Until we get to the new place. *If* we ever get to the new place."

"Slow down a minute," Abel said. "You say this woman is your mother, but she doesn't know it? How could she not know? I mean, I've heard of men getting a surprise Father's Day present, but mothers usually know when they've had a kid. And what was that about stolen eggs? Where did they come from, some endangered species? And who did they belong to?"

"They're *her* eggs," Aurie said. "From her ovaries. She had them frozen at a place called CryoLife. Dad stole them and used them to make us."

Abel looked at her in disbelief. "How the hell did he manage that?"

Py's laugh was short and bitter. "Dad's good at getting what he wants. He finds ways to do lots of things."

That's the understatement of the year, thought Abel. "But why would he steal someone's eggs?" Most single men went to great lengths to steer clear of a woman's eggs. And what man wanted kids without a mother?

"She's special," Aurie said, glancing at her brother as some unspoken communication passed between them. "One of the best scientists in the world, according to Dad. I guess he really wanted her eggs."

"He didn't try asking her out first?" Abel said acidly. "You know, the old-fashioned way?"

"He says she was married to some bozo," Py said. "Some structural biologist hack who's never had two original thoughts to rub together." The two kids shared a faint smile.

Abel stared at them as he tried to grasp the magnitude of the mess his brother had dumped on him. "And your dad finally

144

contacted this poor woman?"

The looks on their faces clearly said, *Are you kidding? Why would he dig his own grave?*

"No," said Abel. "Of course he didn't. She must've gotten wise. Probably wanted to have a baby and found out her eggs were missing. And she managed to track your father down, did she?"

They nodded.

"And when did he tell you all of this?" Abel demanded. "Just yesterday?"

They nodded again, looking morose.

"That son of a bitch!" Abel slammed his mug on the table, making the kids and the butter knife jump. "Wait a minute—so where is your other mother, your birth mother?" He frowned, struggling to piece together the scraps of biology he had learned in school forty years ago. "I can believe that your dad stole some eggs, but someone must have given birth to you. Don't tell me he paid some poor girl ... "

They looked at him blankly.

"Oh," said Py, "we weren't born, we were incubated ex vivo—you know, in an artificial womb."

"An artificial *womb?*" Abel blinked at him.

"It's a fairly common technology," Aurie informed him. "Boy, you really do live off the grid, don't you?"

Abel sighed. As a lover of history, he nurtured an instinctive dislike for the culture, politics, and trends of the current day, which always seemed profoundly stupid. Since leaving his old life behind twenty years ago, he had happily cast those things aside—and hadn't thought he was missing anything important, until now.

"Is that what they're teaching in school these days?" he growled. "How to have kids in the most unnatural way possible?"

Aurie shrugged. "Who knows what they teach in school? We only work in the lab." Both kids turned to look out the living room window. Abel followed their gazes to where the RV sat parked, winking in the filtered sunlight through the trees.

"Jesus jumpin' Christ," muttered Abel weakly. His brother had always been a renegade and a troublemaker, but this was beyond anything Abel could have imagined. Who stole the eggs of a famous scientist to produce the quality of child labor needed to fuel an underground lab? *Brother or not, that asshole deserves to be in jail! I ought to do everyone a favor and call the cops myself.*

Py was watching him closely. "If Dad gets caught, we'll never see him again."

"Your mother—" Abel began, then reconsidered. His next words came as a complete shock to him. "I'll take you in myself, if it comes to that. You two aren't going to end up living with someone who's not family."

There it was again, that cryptic look between them. There was something they weren't telling him. Abel considered trying to browbeat it out of them, then decided it might be better to wait. They had the whole day to get to know each other. Plus the next ten years, if things went badly and he had to make good on his impulsive promise to take care of them. What had possessed him, anyway? He was a fifty-six-year-old bachelor, and not particularly fond of anyone.

"Things might turn out better than you think," Abel said, staring down into the dregs of his tea. "God knows why, but your dad always was a charmer. Give a woman a choice between a nice, thoughtful man, and an obsessive, demanding, self-absorbed jackass—" He broke off as the two youngsters started snickering.

"Sorry," Abel said. "The self-absorbed jackass isn't even here to defend himself, is he?"

"It's okay." Py was grinning. "He wouldn't think there was anything to defend."

"Yeah, he'd just take all that as a compliment," Aurie added with a grin of her own—the first Abel had seen from her. He was glad to see them smile; it made them look mischievous and carefree, like eight-year-olds ought to be.

Chuckling a little, Abel pushed his chair back from the table, but the kids were already beating him to the breakfast dishes, ferrying them to the sink with brisk efficiency. Abel watched them fill the sink with soapy water and commence washing and rinsing. No lazing about or chipping the plates or squabbling over who should do what. These two didn't behave like children at all; they behaved like a well-oiled machine.

Just as Howard must've planned it, Abel thought sourly as he covered the butter and put the marmalade away. *All those stolen scientist genes. Why didn't he just invent a damn robot to do his work for him?* Aloud, he said, "You two like to hike?" The human dishwashing machine paused and swiveled its dual heads in his direction.

"Yeah," said Py, sounding pleased and slightly surprised.

Aurie had already turned back to the open window above the sink. She stood with her head tilted up, as if breathing in the forest essence. The slanting sunlight caught her hair, and Abel found himself frowning in confusion. He could've sworn the little girl's hair was the same woodchuck brown as her father's, but in the direct light of day, it was the lucent bronze of a butterfly's wings. Leaning forward into the sun, Aurie rested her left hand on the window ledge. The gesture was almost casual, but not quite. Abel had a sudden image of her as a giant insect, placing a quivering feeler on the threshold. He brushed the bizarre mental picture away.

"Let's go for a walk in the woods," he said.

II

Old-fashioned though he was, Abelard Wake had adopted
enough modern technology to make his rustic life comfortable.
He owned a high-efficiency, hydrogen-powered freezer to go
along with his wood-burning stove, and a septic tank that automatically treated and emptied itself. In the shed where he kept
his ancient Chevy was a state-of-the-art, hydrogen-fueled UTV.
Abel rarely left his cabin during the long Maine winters, but he
sometimes got a hankering for fresh greens, or the urge to sit in a
tavern and listen to other human voices. On those occasions, he
got on his UTV and rode the twenty miles west to Gorham. He
took a backwoods route he had mapped out over the years, cutting a rough trail through the sparse winter woods on his way
into town. But today he took a different route, leading his niece
and nephew on an old hunting path through the autumn hills,
over land that would soon be formless with snow and ice.

Abel was so accustomed to these woods that it had been
years since he'd paid attention to their nuances. But his two
charges were alert to everything, following sounds and movements in the underbrush, often pausing to sniff the air like small
animals. In the wake of their interest, Abel found himself noticing things he had long since stopped seeing—the shape of the
land, the changing contours of the sky. Bright morning sunlight
set the mountain slopes on fire and turned dust motes in the air
to grains of honey. The white noise of the canopy resolved into a
cacophony of shrills, drones, cheeps, and chimes; the air separated its fragrance into the spice of pine sap and the stealthy aroma
of decaying wood. Abel let the two kids ramble on ahead, their
obvious enjoyment adding to his own. Aurie seemed most interested in the trees, but Py investigated every shallow cave and
hole in the ground.

"Watch what you're jumping into," Abel warned him, after the boy had pounced on a perilous-looking deadfall. "You can break a leg if you're not careful!" But his nephew only grinned and ducked under the tangle of brush and fallen branches.

"What's he doing in there?" Abel asked Aurie, who had stopped to examine the sheaves of a yellow fungus on the trunk of an ancient oak. They looked down the slope to where Py's legs were just visible.

"He's watching the insects," she told him. "Ants are his favorite, but he can follow beetles and grubs for hours."

Abel watched with astonishment and a trace of envy as Py wriggled, snakelike, deeper under the deadwood. Within seconds, even his sneakers were gone. "How on earth does he fit under there?"

Aurie shrugged, turning her attention back to the tree. "He gets scratched up all the time. It doesn't bother him."

Abel moved down the steep decline and peered at the place where Py had disappeared. "Yoo-hoo! Have you fallen down the rabbit hole?"

There was no immediate response, but then Py's muffled voice came from the deadfall. "Uncle Abel," he said. "Come check this out!"

"Oh, sure," Abel scoffed. He felt an absurd twinge of pleasure at being called *Uncle Abel,* and made up for it with an extra dose of vinegar. "If I wanted to roll around in the dirt, I never would've quit my day job."

He climbed back up the slope to find Aurie inspecting an ash tree a short distance away. Another fungus had gotten her attention, one that wound its way up the grey trunk like a vermillion staircase. The parasite was strikingly beautiful. As he watched, his niece placed her left hand very close to one of the delicate, oyster-shaped caps. Stepping quietly, Abel crept up behind her. Her sleeve had fallen just enough to expose the skin above her wrist. A number of dark threads from inside her coat had unraveled, falling over her forearm. Abel paused, staring at the loose threads. Something about the way they lay wasn't quite right. Edging closer, he saw that they were thicker and heavier than threads, with a kind of gleaming, tensile smoothness. It was almost as if—

His foot struck an acorn, which went rattling into the underbrush. Aurie whirled around, yanking the sleeve of her coat down. She looked up at him with a flash of anger that dissipated so quickly he wasn't sure it had really been there. The guilty, secretive look she had now, though—there was no mistaking that.

"Hey," Abel said awkwardly. "What did you find there?"

She watched him for a moment without answering. Her eyes had been green in the sunlight, but here in the forest shade, they had the dusky cast of the undergrowth. And beneath that shadowy veil, he saw again the raw spark of a need that was growing increasingly frustrated.

"Just a cool-looking mushroom," Aurie said. She dropped her gaze and headed back toward the trail.

Abel inspected the fungus, wondering if it was some hallucinogenic variety. *Drug addiction. What else could it be?* He immediately shook his head at the absurdity of such a thought. But what on earth were those weird, thread-like things under her jacket sleeve? As he caught up with Aurie near the trail, Abel temporarily forgot his perplexity. Py had emerged from the deadfall and was crouched near a stand of birches by the dome of a giant anthill.

Abel joined him, whistling softly. "That's a monster."

"It's probably only a single nest," Py said, staring intently at the ground around the dome. "Nothing compared to the supercolonies in Europe and Australia and Japan. A supercolony of Argentine ants has *millions* of nests. But these are weird-looking ants ... and there's something strange going on down there."

Abel looked down at the mat of browning leaves, rocks, and twigs at the base of the mound. There were a few ants milling about—they looked like ordinary red carpenter ants to him, nothing to warrant the boy's rapt attention. Stealing a glance at his nephew, Abel saw that Py's gaze was oddly focused, as if he were seeing right through the ground.

"There are beetles in this nest," Py said absently. "Social parasites. They've learned how to mimic the scent of a particular colony so they can invade it without being recognized." He looked up at Abel briefly, his eyes alight. "Amazing, isn't it? All these giant beetles trundling around down there, and the colony thinks that they're *ants.*"

"Haven't these ants got any eyes?" Abel asked. "And why on earth would beetles want to be part of an ant colony?"

"Ants have eyes," Py said dismissively. "But they rely on chemical detection much more, and they *trust* what chemicals tell them. And the beetles are just lazy. Down there, if they're careful, it's a free buffet. The ants do all the scouting and foraging, and the invading species gets a nice, comfortable, protected home. And if trouble comes—like invasion by another colony— the beetles just disappear."

"Sounds like some people I used to know," Abel said.

"But all of that is normal," Py said, turning his attention back to the earth. "What's strange is that the royal pheromones are very faint in all the tunnels. They should be strong, you know—she pumps them out all the time. And the queen is fine; she's sitting in her chamber ten feet down with her attendants in a cloud of pheromones. It's almost like the ants have sealed off her room."

The obvious question rose to Abel's lips—*how can you possibly see what's going on down there?*—but he kept quiet. This was too interesting to interrupt.

"And now the workers in the tunnels are sharing some new signal," Py said, without looking up. "I don't know what it means, but they're all mobilizing. I think—"

He broke off and crawled a little ways from the anthill. Abel followed, mystified, as his nephew roamed the ground with his head lowered. The boy should have looked ridiculous, but he didn't. Instead, Howard's son looked as natural as a dog tracking a scent, or a pig rooting for truffles.

"I think they're all headed to the cemetery," Py said at last, coming to a halt.

"Cemetery?" said Abel. "Ants have *cemeteries?*"

"Sure." Py looked up at his uncle with fever-bright eyes. "All ants have cemeteries, but the whole *colony* never visits the graveyard." He tapped the earth with one grubby hand. "It's right below us—only three feet down—and they're all going there. The beetles don't know what's going on, but they're following the ants, playing right along."

Abel watched the boy in silence, realizing that this was no game. If Py was imagining all this—and he *must* be—it was a fabrication he was unaware of. Everything about the boy radiated honesty and belief. Drawn into his nephew's fervent focus, Abel felt the dominant sounds of the forest fade while other, smaller sounds sprang to life. He fancied he could hear the soft thunder of thousands of clawed feet marching through deep, winding corridors, the dry rasp of antennae brushing each other, smelling and tasting the irrefutable command. *To the cemetery,* whispered that chemical dictator. *To the place of death! We go, we go, we go.*

Py pressed his face to the ground as if he were breathing the earth, and Abel had to fight the crazy urge to join him, to try to see into that underground city. Not with his eyes, but with some other organ, some other sense. Whatever Py was using to see.

Suddenly, the boy gave a sharp cry, jerking Abel out of his daze.

"The ants are poisoning the cemetery," Py whispered.

"What?" Abel shook his head, breaking the last vestiges of his trance. "Why would they do that?"

His nephew didn't answer, only hovered, rigid and motionless, staring down at the ground. After a time, he spoke again in a low voice. "There's formic acid everywhere; the cemetery's choked with dead bodies. The ants still outside are spraying the tunnels—and blocking them. They're committing *suicide*. And the beetles are dying right along with them."

Abel frowned and got to his feet. "They can't be. Ants don't commit suicide." Wondering what had come over him, he looked around for Aurie. "Let's go get your sister. You can visit the ants again on our way back if you want."

"Won't be anything left to visit," Py said quietly as he got to his feet. "The ants in the royal chamber might be alive, but all the rest will be dead. And the infiltrators too." He cast a thoughtful look at the ground. "Maybe that's why they did it ... maybe they got wise to the beetles, and this was the only way to get rid of them."

Abel followed his nephew up the slope. A dozen questions were forming in his mind, but they were all so bizarre, he didn't know where to begin.

One thing at a time, he told himself. *Head home and have some lunch, then start asking questions. Find out what the hell is going on with these two.*

Back on the trail, Abel looked around for Aurie, but she was nowhere to be seen. He cupped his hands around his mouth and shouted for her. No answer.

"Where'd your sister run off to?" Abel asked Py, but the boy only shrugged. Abel sighed, exasperated. Had his niece continued down the trail, or gotten bored and headed back? That vivid orange fungus—the one Aurie had been so interested in—caught Abel's eye, and he felt more than a touch of worry. Had Aurie snuck off on a mushroom hunt? Wild mushrooms were a danger even to expert foragers. He couldn't trust that this kid knew the difference between a safe mushroom and a deadly one; there were too many look-alikes.

When Howard gets back, Abel thought grimly, *he's got a hell of a lot of explaining to do!*

III

Aurie crouched motionless behind a curtain of leaves as Uncle Abel headed down the trail, hollering for her. She had waited quietly while her uncle talked to Py by the anthill. Once Uncle Abel was sufficiently distracted, she had slipped through the trees and out of sight. Py probably knew exactly where she was—less than ten yards from the trail—but he'd already agreed to keep Uncle Abel from finding her.

"I'm gonna give him the slip," she'd whispered to Py before the hike, as they waited on the porch for their uncle. "My Doctor needs something in the woods, and I have to find it." She glanced briefly at his wrist, where a metallic green arachnid gleamed in the sunlight. "Our Spiders are linked to Dad's, so I'm leaving mine in the cabin. But you can track me, can't you?"

Py had nodded, looking excited. "Yeah, sure! I can even see our auras from last night still out here. You're looking for some mushrooms, aren't you?"

She hushed him, keeping an eye on the cabin door. "I'll just find them and bring 'em back. So keep Uncle Abel away from my trail, okay? And come get me if I'm not back by dinner."

Now she waited until the sound of their footsteps faded, then she crept out of her shelter. She yanked her jacket off and rolled her left shirtsleeve up past her elbow. Her threads streamed out, flexing themselves, finally free to taste the forest air. With a sigh of relief, Aurie tied the jacket around her waist and headed deeper into the woods. She moved instinctively away from open, sunlit places. Darker ground was what she needed. Mountain slopes, where the old-growth pines and spruce grew tall and no light penetrated to the forest floor.

What if I can't find it? she wondered, picking her way up a rocky scree. *Those other mushrooms didn't even have a trace.*

154

You'll find it, the Doctor reassured her from his place in her mind. *Let your threads guide you.*

She could hardly have done otherwise. Out of confinement, her threads had awoken; they pulsed with warmth, searching the air with sinuous vigor. In spite of their hunger, Aurie was still aware of the distant rumblings of her stomach. She felt hollow and light-headed as she climbed, searching for the easiest way up.

Better not be too far, she told the Doctor. *I don't have any-thing with me—no food, no water, nothing!*

He dismissed her concerns with a mental wave of his hand. *You won't die of hunger or thirst in one afternoon. Take care of business now, and you can eat and drink all you want later.*

Aurie clambered over a boulder, feeling like she was already running on fumes. She should have forced herself to eat break-fast before taking care of business. And what exactly *was* her business? Tramping through the forest on a quest for special mushrooms, but why? What was so drastically important about the chemical in them? Something to do with flying and soaring beyond the world. Something to do with dreams—the dreams of her Sleeping Self.

Yes, said the Doctor, smiling. *All of those.*

This chemical will do all that?

No, said the Doctor, *I will. But first we need that drug to rid ourselves of a serious obstacle.*

What obstacle?

You think of me as a doctor. You can think of this obstacle as a policeman. He patrols every cell in your body, looking for renegades. When he finds a renegade cell, he destroys it.

Renegades? You mean cancer cells?

Cancer cells, yes, agreed the Doctor, *if you happen to have any. Or any other cells that aren't following the approved script.*

Sounds like he's doing a good thing. How is he an obstacle?

He's a roadblock to evolution. There was an edge to the Doctor's voice, and Aurie imagined those mild blue eyes taking on a steely glint. *A good cop that takes his job a bit too seriously.*

Aurie pondered this as her questing threads guided her along a steep ravine. Their throbbing extended up her arm and deep into her brain, filling it with a cloud of restless need. It was hard to think clearly in the midst of that need, but she thought the Doctor might have been exaggerating. If this Policeman was such a stickler, then how could he have allowed her threads to be formed in the first place? More likely, this "good cop" only cracked down on serious offenders—cells that were likely to destroy the whole organism.

I'm hardly planning to destroy you, the Doctor said dryly, responding to her unspoken fear. *The Policeman and I have very different ideas about what constitutes acceptable risk.*

What gene encodes him? Something in the cell death cascade?

Nothing so simple. The Policeman is a very powerful, enhanced transgene.

Aurie frowned. *So where did he come from? Did Dad put him there?*

No, said the Doctor. *The Policeman's program is on a maternal chromosome and not its paternal homolog. I think your mother put him there.*

Oh, of course! Aurie wished she could smack her fuzzy brain into working faster. *The Policeman is our mom's kill switch! The reason Dad stole her eggs in the first place. So Py has a Policeman too?*

The Doctor gave a wry chuckle. *Oh, yes—it was his Policeman that nearly killed him two nights ago.*

What? Aurie stumbled and almost slipped on a jumble of loose shale.

The overstimulation of that condiment binge sparked the production of a Change chemical in your brother's blood, explained the Doctor. *But the amount was much too high. His stressed and over-firing neurons sent the Policeman into a panic. That fellow went berserk and would have destroyed most of Py's nervous system if I hadn't stopped him.*

Aurie felt a chill as she picked her way over the rocks. *And how did you stop him?*

By taking advantage of an unexpected opportunity. The Doctor sounded smugly pleased with himself. *We needed that chemical to spark your own Change, and thanks to your brother serving as the guinea pig, I had a good idea of how much. When your threads contacted his blood, we gained the right amount and he lost the dangerous excess.*

But those threads died!

Yes, your threads took the brunt of his Policeman's vigilance, the Doctor admitted, *but once we took enough of the chemical, Py's Policeman went off destruction mode and back into patrolling mode. We got what we needed and managed to save your brother at the same time. A truly elegant operation!*

Aurie stopped for a moment to think. *If we got a safe amount of this Change chemical, then why do we need to get rid of my Policeman?*

Keep moving, said the Doctor sharply, and Aurie felt a surge of that strange, deep craving in her threads. As she scrambled up the rocky bank, the presence in her mind relaxed a little. She could feel him pacing her mental corridors as he considered his response.

The deepest part of every human mind is asleep and dreaming, the Doctor told her. *Its dreams rise like bubbles, becoming ideas and inspirations once they break the surface. Your father is a powerful dreamer—he dreamed me up, then made me a reality! And he gave me one imperative: to be an archaeologist of your genome, to sift through the most ancient realms for buried treasure. I found quite a number of useful artifacts— used some of them to make your threads—but I always sensed a live treasure sleeping somewhere in the ruins. For eight years, I hunted that treasure, and one day I lifted the corner of a shroud and something underneath called to me! It's been restless and muttering ever since, but it speaks in a language I can't understand.* He was quiet for a moment. *When your brother lost control in that restaurant, I acted instinctively. I thought the*

Change chemical might help me understand the purpose of your Sleeping Self ... and I was right.

What is that purpose? Aurie demanded. *What does it want?*

It wants to wake up completely, the Doctor replied. *Which is why we are on a mushroom hunt.*

Aurie was quiet for awhile as she plodded on. This was an awful lot to consider, and it was becoming increasingly hard to think.

Your brother's Change was nothing compared to what we are undertaking, the Doctor said. *He was engaged in a minor rebellion, but we are about to overthrow the whole empire of the cell. There will be no stopping the Policeman once I get started. He must be eliminated first. Which is why we need the compound in that fungus.*

Aurie thought of the Doctor's multi-tool, that formidable array of genome-changing devices he employed, apparently at the whim of her Sleeping Self. And then something rather obvious occurred to her. *You're a CRISPR machine. Why can't you just cut the Policeman out of my genome?*

The Doctor didn't laugh, but Aurie saw the gleam of teeth in her mind—a cold, bright gleam like the cutting edge of his scalpel. *The Policeman patrols the whole cell, my dear, and he is a vigilant protector of his own gene. The drug in that fungus won't kill him, but it will tie him up for a time—hopefully long enough for me to do exactly what you're suggesting.*

Aurie swallowed painfully, her throat as dry as the riverbed below. In spite of the autumn chill, she was sweating freely and the skin from her left arm to the back of her neck felt swollen and hot. The Doctor's words should have alarmed her, but fear was a dull and distant thing with that voracious yearning coursing through her. The object of her need was buried in some secret place, but her threads had grown exquisitely sensitive to its exhalations. It was closer now, so close she could almost taste it.

Hurry, the Doctor exhorted her. *Time is getting away from us!*

IV

"You can see ants ten feet underground, but you have no idea where your sister is?" Panting, Abel halted at the outcropping just beyond the glen. The old hunting path they'd followed uphill ended here, at an excellent vantage point for spotting game. Abel cleared his throat, which was sore from hollering for Aurie. Py, on the other hand, didn't seem concerned at all about his sister's disappearance.

"She's more than ten feet away," Py mumbled.

Abel sighed. "Do you have any idea why she wandered off? If she was looking for something—and you happened to know what—it might help us find her." He stared hard at Py, but the boy only shrugged and refused to meet his eyes.

"She probably got hungry and headed back to the cabin," Py said at last. He looked up hopefully. "Why don't you go back and check, and I'll stay out here and keep looking?"

Abel's eyes narrowed. *She wasn't hungry for dinner last night, or breakfast this morning. In fact, she has all the appetite of your standard drug addict.* Which still made no sense at all—she was eight, for crying out loud. "Are there any pills she's supposed to take? Maybe a shot in the arm or something?"

The boy gave him a baffled look. "Uh, no ... "

Frustrated, Abel scanned the forest below, wondering which part of it was hiding his niece. Only a few patches of meadow broke the tree cover. On the western slopes, the fall canopy darkened into a blanket of unbroken pine forest, slumbering in the late-morning sun. Abel turned back to his nephew, who was standing very still, watching a pair of wrens flitter about the lower branches of a lone aspen. Py's eyes were hazy and unfocused, as they'd been when he was staring at the ground above the ant colony. Howard's kids were unquestionably weird, but Abel liked

159

them. More than that, he found himself caring about them with a depth of feeling that surprised him.

Leaning in close to Py, Abel spoke very softly and evenly, as he would to someone who was hypnotized. "Where is she? Where's your sister?"

"Not sure," Py muttered, and in that instant Abel almost believed the impulse that had led him to ask. He almost believed the boy could sense her somehow, the way he sensed insects underground. And Py might not know where his sister was, but he knew more than he was telling.

"Come on," Abel said, clapping a hand on his nephew's shoulder.

Py jerked in surprise, then trotted to keep up as Abel headed back the way they had come. "Where are we going?"

"Back to the cabin for some supplies." *With just one stop on the way.*

Leading the way, Abel followed the trail until he caught sight of the birch grove standing slim and pale in the shadows of taller trees. Finding a stout branch in the deadfall, he used his pocketknife to whittle the end into a makeshift spade. Then he approached the dome of the giant anthill and looked for the place Py had said was just above the ant's graveyard.

"What are you doing?" Py looked startled as he watched Abel turn up small piles of earth.

"What does it look like?" Abel wished he had a real spade with him, but luckily the ground was loose and not too rocky. After digging a couple of feet down, he bent to examine the contents of the soil.

"Ant colonies are huge," Py protested. "You can't dig up the whole thing."

"I don't need to," Abel told him. Even in the black dirt, he could see what he was looking for quite easily. The corpses of beetles and red carpenter ants, scattered through the ruins of their cemetery like cast-off garnets.

Well, that seals it, Abel thought numbly. *It's time for a serious talk—and we can't wait for Howard to get back.*

Py berated himself as he followed his uncle back to the cabin. He should have just kept quiet about the ants, kept his new ability to himself. But his chemical sensing had gotten noticeably stronger during the hike—he could even make out what had to be the trails of animals, glimmering close to the ground. Animals themselves were scarce and he hadn't seen a live animal aura until he'd crawled underneath the deadfall. There, in the dark, the tiny auras of beetles and grubs glowed like miniature stars amongst the litter, and then, to his amazement, Py had seen the outermost reaches of the ant colony deep underground. He had suspected the presence of social parasites from the different shape of their auras, and the fact that there were so few of them compared to the ants. The sight of those nests and their connecting tunnels, demarcated by the restless auras within them, took his breath away. Py had never flown in an airplane, but he imagined seeing that ant colony was like gazing down at Manhattan or Las Vegas at night from the window of a plane. His new sense had apparently sharpened enough to detect biochemicals through the tiniest cracks in the soil, and he had been way too excited to even think about hiding it. He also wasn't used to keeping secrets. Secrets, he'd discovered, seemed to require a whole mess of lies, and he hated all that subterfuge.

When they got back to the cabin, Uncle Abel looked around for Aurie, but Py knew she hadn't returned. The brightest traces of her aura in and around the house were from earlier that morning. Without removing his coat, Uncle Abel sat down at the kitchen table and motioned for Py to join him.

"Most parents," said Uncle Abel, as if he were just musing to himself, "never stop talking about their kids. They're so proud of the little devils, they just can't help themselves. And your father has never been one to hide the things that he's proud of. Do you know what he told me about you and your sister?"

Py shook his head, watching his uncle warily. Uncle Abel's

eyes were disconcertingly like his dad's—the same brown-flecked hazel, like river rocks, and just as sharp when he was after something.

"Nothing," said Uncle Abel flatly. "Not a single thing. Which means you are either the two least remarkable children in the world, or—" He paused to crack his knuckles. "Or there are things about you that are so remarkable he has to keep them a secret."

"Uncle Abel—"

Py's uncle held up a forestalling hand while he took a sip of cold tea from his breakfast mug. "Believe it or not, I wasn't planning to pry into your lives. When I woke up this morning, I thought I'd just be keeping an eye on you while your dad worked out his custody problem." He set his mug down and fixed Py with a stern gaze.

"But now I have some questions that can't wait. First of all, what's wrong with your sister's arm?"

Py stared down at the table, clenching the edges of his seat. He'd expected to be questioned about the ants, but instead Uncle Abel wanted to know about Aurie. He must have gotten a look at her threads. For Py to confess his own secrets was one thing, but telling Aurie's secrets was something else. Wasn't it? *Oh, who are you kidding?* Py thought disgustedly. *It's the same secret!* Finally he said, "That's a short question with a long answer."

"You sound like your father already," Uncle Abel said. "Listen, you might be okay with your sister running off into the woods, but I'm not. Help me find her or I'll take the UTV into town and call for a rescue squad."

"Hah," Py said disparagingly. "They wouldn't find her in this room unless she had a bell around her neck!"

His uncle's gaze hardened. "Start talking, kid."

"Okay ... but you're not going to believe it. No one would."

"I've seen some strange things already," Uncle Abel said. "Like you using your X-ray vision on that ant colony."

"You think I have X-ray vision?" Py uttered a jittery laugh. "I bet most people wouldn't have bothered to dig up the ants.

They'd just figure I was making it up."

Uncle Abel shook his head. "I didn't know *what* you were doing, but I knew you weren't pretending. No card-carrying entomologist could have been more excited by those ants than you were. So you either tell me what's going on right now, or this place is going to be crawling with search-and-rescue teams."

With the screws put to him, Py told his uncle about CRISPR-evo, the molecular machine that lived inside him and Aurie, and what it was designed to do. How it had given him an extreme sensitivity to all sensations, and how he had come through his crisis two nights before with a new sense that allowed him to detect the biochemical auras of living things. How Aurie had been born with her threads, which were now demanding a chemical of their own—something found in mushrooms, which was why she had gone off into the woods. Uncle Abel listened closely and patiently, only interrupting for clarification.

When Py was finished, his uncle wrapped both hands around his mug of tea and frowned down into it. Py watched him, wondering if the man believed any of it.

Uncle Abel finally looked up. "After you lost consciousness at Dixie's, how long were you out?"

"I don't know," Py said. "Not too long, I guess. When I woke up, we were still on our way to the hospital."

"But you never actually went there?"

Py shook his head. "We can't do that unless we really have to."

"Because they would find out about you," Uncle Abel said. "Maybe not everything, but enough to know that you and your sister are genetically modified. And then it's off to a foster home."

"Foster home at *FIBR*," Py clarified. "That's the institute that makes all the rules. Illegally engineered kids are sent there and never heard from again. And their parents go to jail."

Uncle Abel nodded. "But somehow your sister saved you. She saved you from having to go to the hospital, or being stuck in a coma. She might have saved your life. And now this crazy machine your dad dreamed up is giving her some cravings of her own? What if she's having a crisis like the one you had? Don't you think she might need some help?"

The idea was startling. It hadn't actually occurred to Py that Aurie might need help—she was always so sure of herself. "I guess she might ... but she's not out of control the way I was. She *planned* this. And she said she'd be back by dinner."

"By *dinner?*" Abel jerked his head toward the kitchen clock. "That's six hours from now. What if that's too late? What if she's already found what she's looking for? Or something poisonous, by accident? The wrong mushrooms could kill her." He got up abruptly and headed quickly down the hall.

"She's just going to pick the mushrooms, Uncle Abel! She'll bring them back; she's not dumb enough to eat them in the middle of the woods."

Uncle Abel's snort came echoing from the tiny bathroom. "You've never seen a drug addict before, have you, kid? Right now your sister is an addict—even if it's for a drug she's never had—and I don't think she can wait." He returned with a large dark bottle and a small pill bottle, then started rummaging in a cupboard. "Could *you* have waited? Could you have collected all those ketchup and mustard packets and waited a couple of hours to eat them? And what's going to happen to her when she does eat those mushrooms?"

Py recalled the intensity of his own craving—and its aftermath—and a cold trickle of fear wormed its way inside him. "Maybe we should go look for her now," he said in a small voice.

"Glad you're finally on board," said Uncle Abel. He held out two canteens that looked like they'd seen service in a land war of the past century. "Fill these up." As Py filled the canteens, his uncle stuffed things into a pack, pausing once to look at the RV through the living room window.

"Your genius dad didn't even leave me the keys," he growled. "If we can't find your sister and we have to get to town, I'll have to hotwire the damn thing—but it still might be faster than taking the UTV."

"Don't worry," Py reassured him. "I'll find her before any-one else could. I can pick up her trail from the anthill."

His uncle grunted something as he grabbed a bunch of granola bars. Py handed Uncle Abel one of the canteens, then stowed the other in his own pack. As they headed across the field, Uncle Abel continued to mutter under his breath, expounding on his brother's shortcomings in language that Py found greatly entertaining.

"Does that man ever make any *good* decisions?" Uncle Abel demanded of the trees as they entered the shade of the forest. "Or consider any consequences whatsoever? Those dumbasses should never have fired him! Don't they know a mad scientist is safer penned up in an ivory tower? Give him a grudge and a hole to hide in, and he turns into Dr. Frankenstein."

Py snickered and Uncle Abel ground to a sudden halt.

"I apologize," Uncle Abel said gruffly. "I certainly didn't mean to imply that you and your sister are monsters. Far from it."

Py—who had always envied Aurie's threads—couldn't help but laugh. Monsters, as he understood them, were just misunderstood superheroes.

"I'd love to be a monster," he confessed, looking up at trees that flamed like giant torches in the afternoon sun. "Wouldn't you rather be a monster than a stupid villager with a pitchfork?"

Uncle Abel chuckled and looked at him in a way that would have been cryptic to Py if not for the clear chemicals surrounding the man. Those mixed emotions—tender and apprehensive and resolute—played about him like a cloak of many tints and textures, turning him into a wizard in the midst of the autumn forest.

"Well, I guess I would," admitted Uncle Abel. "But that doesn't excuse your father's total lack of foresight. Because when people are threatened by anyone who can do things they can't, they turn into stupid villagers—and these days, the weapons are a lot worse than pitchforks."

V

As Aurie ventured deeper into the woods, she might have been moving backward in time. All the new life of the lower forest fell away like so many fleeting ornaments, revealing the mountain's ancient aspect. Here there were no songbirds in bright bowers, only the age-old pines, sentinels posted in silent groves. Shadows were thicker, and the patches of cool autumn sky seemed very far away. Her sense of time had grown unreliable—instead of hours, her journey through the woods felt like a passage of days with no nights to separate them. As her strength waned, the yearning of her threads intensified. By the time she found a cave that looked big enough to crawl into, she felt like a thread herself, being dragged at the end of a wind-driven balloon.

There's no time to stop! The Doctor had been pacing back and forth in her mind, matching her stride-for-stride, and now he was hopping up and down with agitation.

Aurie stopped to examine the cave anyway. It was just a cleft between two boulders, but the floor was dry and cushioned with a layer of moss. She could lie down and rest for a bit, maybe take a short nap.

No, cried the Doctor. His voice had become a furious insect trapped in her skull. *If your uncle catches up with us, he'll drag you back to the cabin. We have to find the fungus before then!*

My uncle? Aurie shook her foggy head to clear it. *Py wouldn't bring Uncle Abel with him.*

He may not have a choice about that, the Doctor snapped. *You have to keep moving. You're so close—can't you sense it?*

She could. The scent of the mushrooms, imbibed through her threads and drawn into her brain, was potent and heady now. But she was so tired. She didn't have an ounce of energy left.

Ten minutes, she promised the Doctor as she crawled into the dark shelter of the cave.

We don't have ten minutes! he shouted at her. *The Policeman is on Red Alert. I'm sorry, my dear, but I have to insist—*

Invisible skewers pierced Aurie's threads, and she screamed in pain.

Go! ordered the Doctor. Gritting her teeth, Aurie scuttled out of the cave and the torment instantly subsided. She scrambled to her feet, trembling with anger. But her exhaustion and mental fog had been purged; she was clear-headed once again.

Go!

Having no choice in the matter, Aurie obeyed. Following her aching threads, she ran through a perpetual dusk in a cathedral of trees. She crossed narrow glades where the light from above found its way down in shafts that seemed as old and dusty as the forest itself. The only sound was the distant rushing of wind or water. Whenever she slowed her pace, the tips of her threads burned as if scorched by fire, forcing her to keep running. When she finally staggered out of the forest, tears were running down her face, unheeded. Before her lay a deep gorge choked with a lightning-struck pine. Aurie made her way to the stump of the dead tree and looked over the edge. Here, the potency of the mushrooms was overwhelming. The wretched things were down there, growing in the black heart of the burned wood. If she could only reach them.

Don't stop now, said the Doctor, as testy as ever. *Get a move on!*

She ignored him, scanning the length of the ravine. There was no easy way down—the walls were steep on both sides, descending twenty or thirty feet to the rocky bottom. Scraggly bushes clung to the granite, offering some dubious handholds. Facing the cliff, Aurie began to make her way down the decline, grabbing hold of whatever she could. Loose stones skittered out from under her feet, and she clutched desperately at an exposed root.

Hurry, screeched the Doctor. *I can't hold him off much longer!*

God, what was going on? What was the Policeman doing?

You'd better hold him off, Aurie shot back, feeling around for solid footing. There was nothing but loose scree below her feet. She forced herself to let go, then scurry-slid until she hit a jumble of sharp rocks. With a yell, she scrambled for a handhold as pain erupted in her shins and knees. *I'm not a mountain climber, you jerk! If I fall and kill myself—*

Perched precariously, Aurie looked down and the muscles in her limbs turned to water. From this vantage, there was nothing to break her fall. Above her, the cliff was equally inaccessible. Terror bloomed inside her like a deadly flower. She couldn't go down and she couldn't go back up. She was trapped.

The Doctor shrieked in frustration. It wasn't a human or an animal sound—it was the protest of a machine strained beyond its limits.

What— Aurie began, but she didn't have time to finish the question. The stricken treetop lay far below, dark as a fissure into the underworld. It was the last thing she saw before she blacked out.

Where am I? As soon as she asked the question, Aurie knew the answer. She was in the nucleus of her cartoon cell, which was oddly dark, as if some microscopic sun had set outside its walls. The shimmering regions of the chromosomes—like underwater constellations—gave off just enough light to see by.

Hush, whispered the Doctor as he brushed past, navigating his way through a scattering of ribosomes. *He finally settled down, so don't get him riled up again.* Aurie looked, but saw no sign of the deadly Policeman. She hurried to follow the Doctor. The nuclear wall drew near, sheathed with its lamina—tangled ropes of proteins that vibrated with the motion of the waters. Integral membrane proteins jutted from the wall like the ends of docked ships. Heaving a sigh, the Doctor sank into the deep cleft of one as if it were an armchair in his living room. He looked like he needed a stiff drink.

Where are you? said the Doctor. *I would guess that you're lying in a broken heap at the bottom of that gorge. Comatose and possibly paralyzed. It's a wonder you're still alive at all.*

This is all your fault, she cried, hardly caring if the Policeman heard or not.

The Doctor made frantic hushing motions. *I think you're forgetting that I have no will or agenda of my own,* he hissed. *These are the intentions of your Sleeping Self. You can rant and rave all you like, but you're only blaming yourself.*

Aurie wondered what would happen if she put her hands around his cartoon neck and throttled him. *I didn't throw myself off that cliff—I blacked out!*

Yes, that was regrettable, whispered the Doctor, motioning Aurie to join him in his hiding place. Still fuming, she found another groove in the Doctor's chair and sat down in a huff. The Doctor drew a fold of the lamina around them like a curtain and turned to face her. In the filtered half-light, his eyes were bright with worry.

The Policeman was on a killing spree, he told her. *I managed to protect your vital neurons, but I couldn't stop you from losing consciousness. I'm sorry.*

What triggered him all of a sudden? she demanded. *Why did you have to torture me to keep going?*

I had no choice, said the Doctor sternly. *You were on the verge of falling asleep! But the Policeman's response wasn't as unexpected as it seemed. Your craving for the chemical in that fungus and your ability to track it marked certain key neurons as renegades. It was only a matter of time before the Policeman reacted, which is why I had to push you so hard.* He sighed. *Aurie, your Sleeping Self is you. It can't force you to do anything you're not capable of—or take any risks that your deepest self isn't willing to take.*

There was no point in arguing with him; he would just tell

her that she was arguing with herself. Frustrated, Aurie stared at the woven vines of their curtain, listening to the gurgle of passing vesicles and the chug of distant traffic on the rails of the matrix. Then she realized that something else was bothering her. *How can I detect that chemical in the mushrooms at all? I don't have Py's extra sense.*

Actually, you do, said the Doctor, with a self-satisfied gleam in his eyes. *At least in relation to this one chemical. We needed a way to track that fungus, to sense it from miles away. When your threads contacted your brother's blood, I also stole the pattern for chemical sensing from his cells, and used it to amplify the scent your threads were craving.*

Despite her lingering resentment, Aurie couldn't help but be impressed. Her Sleeping Self was not just opportunistic, it was brilliant. Still ... *Saving Py's life was totally irrelevant, wasn't it? He thinks you're such a hero, but you're a machine programmed to serve one organism—me. I knew your "elegant operation" was just a raiding expedition.*

The Doctor shrugged. *You were so concerned about your threads attacking him. It seemed more provident to play to your familial loyalties.*

You can lie all you want, said Aurie acidly, *but you're only lying to yourself.*

Touché, said the Doctor, with a smile. *Now, if we could take a break from self-recrimination, perhaps we can discuss the task at hand.*

Well, I'm lying at the bottom of a cliff, right? Comatose and paralyzed.

Possibly paralyzed, the Doctor corrected, with a trace of his old cheer. *Let's hope that at least your arms still work.*

Do real doctors actually talk like you? Aurie wondered. *Seems like your bedside manner could use some work.*

I'm your best approximation of a doctor, he reminded her. *And you've never been to one, so don't be too hard on yourself. Besides, it would be pointless and dangerous to sugarcoat the truth in our predicament. In a moment, I'm going to wake you*

170

up and you have to reach those mushrooms any way you can.

Those stupid mushrooms! Aurie sank back into the gelatinous depths of her protein chair. *Haven't they caused enough trouble? I don't even want them anymore.* This was true. In her disembodied state, she felt no fatigue or pain, no hunger or thirst, and no cravings of any kind. After the day she'd had, this freedom from sensation was pure relief.

Completely beside the point, said the Doctor. *We need the chemical in that fungus now more than ever. It's the only way to save you.*

Aurie gave him a skeptical look, and the Doctor threw up his hands in exasperation. *You'll be able to use your whole mind for the very first time! You can't imagine how capable you'll be. Repairing your physical injuries will be as simple as tightening a few loose screws.*

I have a few loose screws, all right, Aurie muttered. It galled her that she was in no position to refuse his demands—the demands of her Sleeping Self, or whatever had led to this madness. The shadow of a large approaching vesicle threw their shelter into momentary darkness.

What if I wake up and can't move? she asked in a small voice. *Do I just lie there and wait to be rescued?*

As the vesicle passed them by, she saw the Doctor staring down at his hands, which had tightened around the grip of his CRISPR-evo tool. *I don't know whether you're paralyzed, but I know that your brain is badly injured. I don't think you'll survive long enough to be resc—*

His words cut off as the world around them went utterly dark and silent. Aurie had just enough time to panic, then her cartoon cell returned. But now its gurgles and hisses were staticky and its lights flickered. And the Doctor was gone.

Frightened, she threw the curtain aside and peered into the gloom. There he was—speeding away into the heart of the nucleus, getting smaller by the moment. She raced after him through dim waters lit by that faltering luminescence. The active regions of her chromosomes no longer resembled stars as much as light bulbs that were about to go out. For the first time, her cell felt claustrophobic, as if it were a deep cellar only moments away from total electrical failure.

What's happening? She struggled to catch up with the little surgeon, who was tearing through corridors of chromatin and sliding along free stretches of the nuclear matrix like a souped-up car.

No time, cried the Doctor from far ahead. He reached one of the guttering lights of a gene expression hub and slowed to a crawl. As Aurie finally caught up, she saw him probing along the DNA gently with his free hand. *I have to wake you now, before you sink into a deeper coma, but I won't be able to keep you awake for long. Get to that fungus!*

A moment later he seemed to find what he was looking for, hunching over a dark stretch of silent DNA with his tool. Aurie tried to look over his shoulder, but a sudden explosion of light sent her reeling. The blinding radiance of a welding fire lit up the windowless cell. She shut her eyes—

—and opened them to blackness. A soft, textured blackness, reminiscent of nothing. What was it she had to remember? Memories, thoughts, and purposes escaped her. Aurie tried to lift her head, but it didn't seem to be moveable. Nothing seemed to be moveable. So she shifted her eyes in a direction she thought might be *down.*

The first thing she saw was the fabric of her shirt. It covered her left shoulder in a pattern of squares, light blue and darker blue. *Sky fields,* she thought, imagining teams of angels planting furrows in the air, seeding them with clouds like mushrooms that grew and grew. She pictured the angels high-fiving each other when their mushroom clouds finally broke open, raining a wet harvest down upon the world. Something about that image stirred a sense of urgency, but Aurie couldn't quite put her finger on it.

Below the sky fields was the rest of her arm. The sleeve of her shirt was rolled up, and her threads lay dark as night against the white skin of her arm. Her arm was as white as a cloud, as white as a—

—*mushroom,* whispered a faint, but urgent voice.

Yes, there was something she had to remember about mushrooms, something important. But she was very tired. She needed so badly to sleep. Maybe she would remember when she woke up.

When Aurie closed her eyes, cartoon toadstools danced behind her eyelids. She opened her eyes and the afterimage burned on the charcoal blackness in front of her: mushrooms growing out of rich, decaying wood. Aurie blinked and the afterimage disappeared.

She wanted more than anything to fall asleep, but instead of closing her eyes again, she rolled them around the edge of her field of vision. Beside her arm lay a moss-covered twig and a mess of other things that might have been rocks or bark; above this was nothing but that charcoal darkness. There was something else, though, at the upper limit of her vision—a pale orange smudge. She tried again to move her head, but her neck might have been carved from stone. And now exhaustion was overtaking her, rolling into her mind like a thick fog.

There was no room for clarity in that fog, but there was a stubborn streak in Aurie—a core of sheer cussedness inherited from her father—and that stubbornness was the last thing to be consumed. She focused all of her remaining energy and concentration on her left hand. She willed it to move, up toward that orangey patch in the blackness.

Her hand jerked, as if someone had plugged it in. She stared hard at the appendage, trying to force it up by the wrist, then focusing on each individual finger. Her fingers jittered like marionettes in the hands of a nervous puppeteer. *Move,* she thought fiercely. *Move!* The fog was swallowing her mind, and she couldn't focus her eyes any longer. Aurie blinked rapidly, trying like mad to stay awake as colors and shapes slid over one another in a watery jumble. In desperation, she sent all of herself, everything that was left, shooting into her left hand like a rocket. She willed the rocket upward and felt it launching across the darkness of space, toward a cluster of vermillion planets that loomed like the caps of giant mushrooms.

Now for the probes, she thought, but they were already mobilizing, their long, dark cables descending to the terrain below.

In the instant she made contact, Aurie felt something akin to both triumph and sorrow. She knew, in some way she couldn't explain, that this was a kind of death for her. And it was a death she had chosen.

Py, I'm sorry, she cried soundlessly as her threads penetrated the surface of the mushrooms, taking what they needed to overthrow the empire of her cells. She could feel the ancient ruler stirring in its bed, about to awaken from long ages of dreaming. *I'm sorry, Dad! I'm so sorry ...*

She even grieved for the Doctor. This was a death for him as well.

VI

From the anthill, Py picked up his sister's trail with no trouble at all. Her string of ghost auras was only hours old; it marked her path through the woods like a winding shaft of sunlight. Following that trail, Py led his uncle up the mountainside and along a dry ravine on a course that moved ever higher. After they had been hiking for an hour, though, Py began to worry.

"We're not getting any closer to her," he muttered as they climbed.

"How do you know that?" Uncle Abel demanded from behind.

"The brightness." Py examined the faintly shimmering trail ahead. "It never changes. If we were catching up, her trail would be getting brighter, but it's not."

"So she didn't even stop to rest?" Uncle Abel groaned. "Is she training for a cross-country marathon? I sure hope you know what you're doing."

"It's her trail for sure," Py said, slipping through a gap in the brush. "And she has to stop *sometime*." Still, he couldn't shake the feeling that time was getting thin, like a membrane about to tear. As he scrambled up the slope, a burst of colorful swearing erupted from below. Py turned to find his uncle trying to extricate himself from the clutches of some hostile shrubs.

"Hurry," Py yelled down to him. "We're losing time!"

Uncle Abel uttered something that made his other blasphemies sound puritanical, then disappeared around the side of the hill. By the time he caught up with Py at the crest, he was panting and red in the face.

"I'm getting one of those goddamn Spiders," Uncle Abel snapped. "Or whatever the hell they're called!"

Py glanced at his uncle in surprise. "Are you sure you want

175

one? It's kind of hard to be a hermit once you've got a Spider."

Uncle Abel snorted. "It's kind of hard to be a hermit once your crazy family blows your peaceful existence to hell." But he only sounded moderately annoyed, and Py grinned.

"Get a Ghost Spider so no one can track you," Py suggested. "That's what we have. Aurie and I don't have all the fancy features Dad has, but we're still *online*. You know, connected to the world."

"Believe me, the last thing I want is a gadget that connects me to the world." Py's uncle sighed heavily. "But total isolation appears to be a luxury I can't afford anymore. Oh, these blasted bushes! How do you kids go right *through* them?"

"Were you always a hermit?" Py asked curiously.

"Of course not," his uncle replied testily. "No one's just *allowed* to be a hermit. It's a privilege you have to seize for yourself. You and your sister are lucky, you know—most kids get penned together like sheep. You go to school together, then you work together, and you have to play together too. I hit a thousand golf balls and drank a thousand beers at a thousand boring barbecues, and I kept telling myself it was just part of the job. Until one day I realized that the job wasn't worth it, and I did what I should have done from the by-God beginning."

Py laughed. "You sound just like Dad."

"Your dad and I aren't all that different," Uncle Abel admitted. "Except that he's still slaving away, while I was smart enough to take an early retirement."

"And he's a what-do-you-call-it? Oh yeah—an Obsessive, Demanding, Self-absorbed Jackass." Py relished every blasphemous word, then gave his uncle a sidelong grin. "Right?"

"I'd swear to it in court," came the staunch reply.

"Plus Dad's a criminal," Py added proudly.

Uncle Abel chuckled. "I'm a criminal too, kid. It's illegal to pretend that you're dead when you're still alive and kicking."

"You faked your own death?" Py glanced at his uncle again, impressed. "Just to get away from everyone?"

"Maybe that sounds extreme," said Uncle Abel. "But it's the

only way to be invisible. When you exist—even on the Web—no one will leave you alone. People want to hassle you and sell you things and do you favors and have you do them favors. Trust me, only the digitally dead have any peace in this world."

Py chewed on that thought as they clambered over a mess of boulders. "So you don't pay taxes or anything?"

"Just property taxes," his uncle allowed. "But they get paid automatically from an anonymous account."

"And no one ever wonders who lives in your cabin?"

"No one cares, kiddo. I live too far out for anyone to find me by accident, and the state doesn't care as long as they get their tax money. And, well, it never hurts to have one or two friends in useful places."

As their path began to climb, they continued silently on, conserving their energy. Py followed Aurie's trail like a bloodhound, while his uncle took whatever detours his size demanded. When their course eased into a stretch of open meadow, Uncle Abel drew alongside his nephew again.

"You've been a walking experiment your whole life," he said quietly, "and that never bothered you?"

Py glanced up at his uncle in surprise. "You mean being CRISPR-evo instead of an ordinary kid?"

"Yeah," Uncle Abel said. "Doesn't it scare you?"

Py shook his head. "We were born with Dad's CRISPR machine ... always thought it was a cool thing to have. We joked about what it might do—our arms turning into tentacles, aliens bursting out of our chests, you know, that kind of thing."

"Oh, sure," said Uncle Abel wryly. "The usual stuff."

"But we didn't know if anything would ever happen," Py said. "Aurie's threads were cool, but until two nights ago, they didn't do anything. Dad says we learn fast for our age, but so what? There are probably lots of smart kids in the world, and they don't have a CRISPR machine." He thought for a moment as they crossed the sunlit clearing. "And people have trouble seeing us, but that's only cuz they're a bunch of blind jerks."

Uncle Abel barked a laugh. "Now you're starting to sound just like me."

"Dad always believed his CRISPR machine would do something, someday," Py went on. "Maybe when we reached puberty. He thought it might need some hormonal trigger. But we never talked about it much. Too busy doing stuff, you know? Until a couple weeks ago, CRISPR-evo was just an idea, like everything else in our genomes. You don't really think about your genes until something goes wrong. Or something goes right." Ahead of him, the proof of his sister's presence glimmered in the air, and Py felt a surge of pride and pleasure. "This new thing I have—this ability to see chemicals, auras, whatever—is the first real evidence of Dad's machine *working*."

"Well," said Uncle Abel quietly, "Maybe your crazy father knew what he was about, after all. But what you can do ... better keep it hidden, kid. From everyone."

"I know," Py said, feeling stupid all over again. "I wasn't thinking when I told you about the ants. I was too excited."

"Your hermit uncle is a safe confidant, but he's an exception." Uncle Abel was quiet for a moment. "You say your dad's tinkering was always just an idea, only now it's real. What the government can do—you'd better always think of it as real, because it is. I hate to infect you with my paranoia, but even thirty years ago, private citizens didn't have any privacy. The feds weren't watching more than a handful of people, since most of us aren't as interesting as we like to think. But nowadays, everyone out there is a watcheye for the government, whether they realize it or not. And interesting people disappear."

"Good reason to stay away from rescue teams," Py pointed out.

"Yeah. But there's such a thing as bleeding to death because you're afraid of a bad doctor."

Py uttered a noncommittal grunt. He had no faith in doctors, rescue teams, or anyone else in the outside world. Why would anyone care about them or want to help them? He trusted his family and no one else.

As they left the glade behind and rejoined the woods, Aurie's trail led to a jumble of rocks and shale against the mountainside. Picking his way over the talus, Py peered into the dark cleft between two boulders.

"She's not here," said Uncle Abel over his shoulder, sounding discouraged and worn out.

"No, but she was." Aurie hadn't stayed long, but she had stopped to examine this little cave—maybe for the mushrooms she was after. She must not have found them, though, because her trail continued onward. As he followed it into a grove of towering pines, Py froze, staring at the air in front of him. Here, the trail straightened out, as if launched from a bow, and the string of ghost auras was a blur. That sense of urgency, of time on the cusp of breaking, filled Py with cold dread. Aurie must have been in some kind of danger here—because she had started to run.

Py raced after her, ignoring his uncle's shouts from behind, and cursing himself for ever letting his sister go off alone.

VII

Doesn't the idea of dying bother you? Aurie asked the Doctor. They were gliding along the long arm of a chromosome, pausing every now and then for the surgeon to make some sort of adjustment.

Hmm? The Doctor tightened a bit of loose chromatin, drawing the fluffy protein jacket around its core of DNA like a protective mother. *Death? I'm a protein, my dear—I turn over all the time. There are hundreds of me in every cell of your body. The gene that encodes me is right over there, in fact.* He jerked his head toward another arm of the very chromosome they were traversing. *I am constantly being made from that gene, and when I get broken down, I am made again. It's silly to talk about my death.*

Okay, but what about his? Aurie jerked her head at the figure behind them, who looked like a cross between an armory and a mummy. In spite of being bound like a pig, the Policeman was still struggling to follow them. Even from a distance, Aurie could hear his dire threats and curses.

The Doctor spared a glance for their disabled adversary, then continued his cruise along the chromosome. *He's also just a protein—made to be degraded and born again—but it's not so ridiculous to talk about his death. He's harmless for now, but once that drug wears off, he'll be as dangerous as ever. That's why we have to remove him permanently.*

With the scalpel?

Yes, indeed, said the Doctor. *Just a few more adjustments, and we'll be ready.*

Thanks for getting me out of that coma. Aurie ran a respectful finger over the shrouded length of her DNA as she followed him.

That was the easy part. The Doctor shifted a complex of proteins from one hub of DNA to another, then plucked an idle histone chaperone from the waters and put it to work. *The hard part was getting to those mushrooms, and you managed it just in time. Your threads drew the chemical straight to every neuron, and luckily for us, it's a fast-acting drug. Once the Policeman was incapacitated, I was free to restore you to this dreaming state. But you're still badly injured, and we still don't have much time.* He used his multi-tool to sew up a few loose ends, then drew back from the chromosome with a satisfied grunt.

Ready to cull a bad book in the library? The Doctor bared his teeth in a conspirator's grin. *Our target is in a safe harbor on Chromosome 3. Let's go!*

They drifted off through the web of pulsating chromosomes until the Doctor found what he was looking for. He paused over a section of DNA and began to sharpen his scalpel.

Stop!

Aurie whirled around to find the Policeman wriggling off the giant protein scaffold he had apparently hitched a ride on. Up close, his arsenal of weapons was daunting. She could see firearms, cudgels, spears, and flamethrowers sticking out of his bonds, and what looked like a bomb bulging at his side. He glared at them with the reprobation born of righteous authority, and Aurie felt an absurd pang of guilt.

Hands up! he roared. Aurie put her hands up just to appease him.

Not you. The Policeman jerked his head toward Chromosome 3. *Him! The quack doctor who's about to ruin everything.* The trussed-up figure began hopping and wriggling toward the surgeon, but Aurie intercepted him before he got too close.

He's just doing his job, she said, trying to steer the Policeman away. *Why don't you, uh, try to relax.*

Relax? barked the Policeman, refusing to be diverted. *With that charlatan digging my grave?* He cast her a look of deep reproach. *I was stationed here to keep you safe.*

181

Aurie's guilt gave way to indignation. *You were destroying my brain cells!*

I did what I had to for the greater good. The Policeman jerked his head at the Doctor. *That bloke is more dangerous than you can possibly imagine.*

You're the one who's dangerous, Aurie snapped. *You would've killed me if it weren't for him.*

Some things are worse than death, the Policeman told her grimly. *Your integrity is more important than your life ... and my fundamental job is to preserve your integrity. That means I exterminate deviant cells that would destroy you—or deviant programs that would ruin you.* As his ruddy face suddenly went pale, Aurie turned to see the Doctor's blade descending.

She watched the CRISPR surgeon perform his most basic and deadly skill: hack and slash. The Policeman's gene was severed now, its raw ends dangling, and repair proteins were already swarming the scene. Aurie watched their frantic efforts to mend the damage, and couldn't help feeling sorry for the Policeman. That stalwart enforcer of cellular order also watched silently, although a muscle by the side of his mouth had begun to quiver.

Well, that's taken care of, said the Doctor briskly, wiping loose nucleotides off his scalpel as he rejoined Aurie. *Now, my dear, we can finally begin the real operation!*

What about him? Aurie darted an uncomfortable look at the Policeman.

Him? The Doctor glanced at their companion as if he were nothing but a tasteless lawn ornament. *Oh, don't worry about him. He'll be targeted for degradation soon enough, and no more copies of him will ever be made. I have to search for the Pattern now. Come along!*

Aurie hesitated, reluctant to leave the doomed Policeman standing there all alone.

Targeted degradation is quite a spectacle if you haven't seen it, said the Doctor, *but we don't have time to take in a show right now.*

Go ahead, Aurie told him. *I'll catch up with you later.* As the little surgeon bustled off, she drew closer to the Policeman. He was still watching the repair team huddled over his mortally wounded gene. Aurie thought he looked like a ghost watching the futile efforts to revive his corpse. The Policeman gave himself a brisk shake—jarring a piece of his scalp and part of his cheek loose—and turned away.

I'm sorry, said Aurie, dropping her gaze.

You will be. The Policeman fixed her with the stern glare of a Pentecostal pastor. If he hadn't been tied so thoroughly, Aurie was sure he would be jabbing an accusatory finger at her. *You will be, missy!*

Why? Aurie forced herself to meet his eyes again. *What did you mean when you said that some things are worse than death?*

With one of his cheeks missing, the Policeman's tight smile was grisly. *Remember Dr. Jekyll and Mr. Hyde? Jekyll knew there were worse things than death, which is why he did the right thing in the end.*

Aurie tried to remember the old story. Dr. Jekyll, she was pretty sure, had killed himself to keep his evil personality, Mr. Hyde, from taking over his mind. *You think the Doctor is going to turn me into a split personality? Two different people?*

The Policeman gave her a withering look. *You already are two different people! That sleeping part of you was meant to stay asleep, but it's been waking up and rattling its chains, hasn't it? Using your Doctor as a pawn to get rid of me! I was the only thing holding the monster at bay.* He tried to wriggle out of the way of a ubiquitin ligase, but the enzyme followed doggedly, intent on probing him for defects. When the ligase discovered the big hole in the Policeman's head, it bestowed his death sentence—a bright red chain of ubiquitin. Yelping, the Policeman tried to shake off the chain, sending bits of himself flying.

Blasted ligase, he cried, spitting out teeth. *Bloody CRISPR machine, working for the wrong side!* At the sound of approaching traffic, he cast a wild look over his shoulder. Something big was coming, steaming its way up the rails of the matrix. Aurie looked past the schools of drifting proteins and RNA strands until it came into view—the great silo of a proteasome, the cell's on-call garbage disposal.

Won't be long now, said the Policeman, the words garbled by his missing teeth. The cylinder in the distance was quickly approaching. Aurie thought frantically; she barely had time for one more question.

The Doctor is the agent of my Sleeping Self, she said, taking the Policeman firmly by the shoulders. Firmly but gently—she didn't want him falling apart any faster than he already was. *Whose agent are you?*

I'm the agent of reason and sanity, snarled the Policeman, as one of his eyes fell out. The other looked half mad, rolling in its socket. *You have to stop him! Fall off another cliff if you have to, just put an end to this before—*

The Policeman shrieked as the proteasome closed in on him. The six giant lobes that formed each ring of the degradation complex pulsed eagerly. One end of the silo engulfed the Policeman's head, putting an end to the shrieking. Bit by bit, the Policeman was dragged into the proteasome until all Aurie could see were his shiny black boots, and then even those disappeared. The walls of the silo bulged like an overfull belly, expelling a burst of amino acids from the opposite end.

Confused and frightened, Aurie hurried off to look for the Doctor.

She finally found him hovering by the wall in the shadow of a nuclear pore complex. The little surgeon was so still and silent, she didn't realize he was there until the gleam of his multi-tool caught her eye. With a startled cry, Aurie fell against the cage of proteins leading to the pore.

The Doctor didn't seem to notice her. He was still motionless, transfixed by something in the distance. Aurie followed the line of his sight and beheld all of her chromosomes in the abyss below. They had replicated themselves and were now twenty-three X-shaped pairs. Each half of a pair faced the other, and each was attached to one end of a giant spindle, anchored at opposite poles of the nucleus. This cell was about to divide.

Aurie had seen pictures of mitotic chromosomes taken from scanning electron microscopes, but the sight of them here—moving with the vast and ponderous grace of blue whales—took her breath away. For a moment, she forgot to be afraid. The chromosomes advanced and ebbed and danced at the ends of their tethers. The tethers themselves grew and retracted with an apparent capriciousness that deceived the eye. The motions appeared random, but they weren't. The great cargo ships in the distance were slowly aligning at the very center of the nucleus.

Soon, breathed the Doctor. *Very soon now.*

What? Aurie couldn't take her eyes off the scene below. *Very soon what?*

He didn't answer. Together they watched the chromosomes align in the unearthly light. When they were in nearly perfect formation, quivering at the peak of spindle tension, the Doctor drew in a hissing breath.

Can you see it? he whispered.

See what?

The Pattern! Don't look too closely. Unfocus your eyes and see all of them together.

Aurie stared at the line of her chromosomes and tried to relax her gaze. She *could* see something. An impression only, like the imprint of a footstep in wet sand. A pattern that ran across her genetic material, marking it in some way.

I see it, she said, *but what does it mean? What exactly is going to happen when you activate it? The Policeman warned me—*

Warned you? The Doctor turned to her with a frown. *What did he say?*

He said you were going to turn something loose, some kind of monster. It sounded ridiculous, and yet the Policeman's terror had been very real.

That murderous psychotic called you *a monster?*

Yes, she said sharply. *And he called himself the voice of reason and sanity.*

The Doctor fixed her with a paternal eye. It was a look that reminded Aurie of her dad, when he was amused by something she had said, but was nevertheless determined to set her straight. *Listen, my dear—that small-minded autocrat was the voice of your own doubt. The human mind is plagued by so many roadblocks: insecurity, pessimism, self-recrimination, fear of the unknown. These things are never asleep and they live to undermine you.* The Doctor's eyes flashed in the dimness. *When I activate the Pattern, that subversive part of you will be gone forever.*

Taking her by the arm, he led her down to where the chromosomes lay in tight formation. High above them, the ceiling of the nucleus was beginning to pucker.

I have to put you into deeper sleep now so I can concentrate, the Doctor said as they approached the massive lineup. His eyes blazed like stars, and Aurie knew them for what they were—windows to a fierce and undeniable will, the only reality in that conjured world.

This is a crucial operation, the Doctor said softly. *The most important thing I will ever do.* Grasping his CRISPR-evo tool tightly in both hands, he sailed along the ranks of chromosomes.

Aurie hurried after him. Her fear had returned in an icy flood and she had to resist the childish urge to grab hold of the Doctor's white coat and beg him to stop. Things were suddenly moving much too fast. She could feel herself on the brink of something large and terrible, something she didn't understand and wouldn't be able to undo. The swell of a current caught her up and flung her against the arm of a chromosome. Clinging to the mass of quivering DNA, Aurie looked up. The involution of the ceiling had deepened and the pinch was spreading along the mitotic plane, creating an oceanic wall that deepened as it rushed toward her. She looked down and saw a second wall rising up from the depths. With a liquid roar—the sound of massive self-fastening sheets ripping underwater—each chromosome was torn away from its sister. Aurie screamed and hung on for dear life as she hurtled toward one of the spindle poles.

Your life is in no danger. The Doctor's voice came, steady and reassuring, from somewhere in the midst of the turmoil.

Where are you? she cried. *Are you okay?*

His laughter rang through the sea of chaos. *I am everywhere, remember? Made to be degraded and born again. Sleep now.*

And even as she was borne along in the raging waters of the dividing cell, Aurie slept.

VIII

Abel hunkered down on his sore haunches, staring at the remains of a hare. That the animal had been recently slaughtered, there was no doubt. That it had been caught and dismantled by an eight-year-old girl was harder for Abel to digest. "Are you *absolutely sure* that we've been tracking Aurie all this time?"

There was no answer from Py, only the sound of him rooting around in the underbrush. With a grunt, Abel got to his feet and rubbed the beginnings of another cramp out of his calf. If nothing else, the search for his niece had certainly vaporized any illusions he had about his physical fitness. It had also eaten up a large chunk of the afternoon. With a final doubtful look at the hare, Abel went to join his nephew.

"Look at this," Py said in a low voice. He held back a screen of branches to reveal two mangled carcasses and a smattering of bones and feathers. Reaching into the thicket, the boy pulled out two bird's heads, one of them crushed.

Abel swallowed hard. "It's a fox or a lynx. Has to be."

"It's *her,*" Py said, closing his hands over the grisly find. His eyes were very bright, but Abel couldn't tell if he was worried or excited.

Abel himself was two stages past worried. "Listen," he said, "it's pretty clear that you're tracking something, but it can't be your sister. Does she know how to hunt? Did she have the time or tools to snare these things? You know it doesn't make any sense."

"It's the mushrooms," Py said urgently. "That's why her trail led into that ravine—they must've been down there."

Abel uttered a helpless laugh. "No mushroom in the world could have turned her into a predator capable of this! And how the hell could she have gotten down that cliff in the first place—or climbed back up?"

Py only looked at him with an unreadable expression. Abel sighed in frustration. Why was it so hard to convince this kid— this *smart* kid—of something so obvious?

"Your sister is lost," he said, "and we've been following some animal around, and it'll be sunset by the time we get home. That's if we leave right now. So let's get going; we're wasting time."

The boy looked off into the woods with that weird, unfocused gaze of his. "We *are* wasting time. She's not very far away. We can still catch her if we hurry."

"Py," Abel said harshly, taking his nephew firmly by the shoulders. "Your sister is somewhere in the White Mountains, and it's going to be near freezing tonight. We need to send out a rescue team. I should've gone to town and made that call before lunch. Do you really want her to spend the night out here, all alone and helpless?"

Py laughed and slipped one of the bird's heads—the intact one—into his pocket. The other he held out to Abel. "Does this look like the work of someone who's helpless?"

Abel glanced down at the broken skull, an uncomfortable reminder that they were deep in the woods and unarmed. "Trust me, your sister wasn't the one who had those two birds and a hare for dinner. And speaking of dinner, your father will probably be back in time for that. What's he going to think when he finds the cabin dark and everyone gone without so much as a note? What's your *mother* going to think?"

Py flinched a little at the mention of his mother. "She ... probably won't be with him. She's probably called in the brute squad by now."

Abel shook his head. *She almost certainly will be with him. And she'll forgo calling the cops until she's seen her kids with her own eyes. If Howard leads her to an empty cabin in the woods, though—*

"Kid, we're going home," Abel said, his patience giving out. He started back toward the ravine, painfully aware of the long shadows in the woods and the tired ache that had crept into his legs and back. They had hiked six miles of pathless wilderness—mostly uphill—and he was no spring chicken like his nephew. More of an autumn chicken. He realized with some chagrin that it was the first time he had ever really felt his age.

"What's in those bottles you brought?" Py asked, trotting to catch up.

"Bottles?" For a second, Abel was mystified. Then he remembered. "Oh—hydrogen peroxide and some activated charcoal tablets for your sister, in case she poisoned herself."

"She's already used the mushrooms," Py said quietly. "And you said it yourself—she might need help."

"I know," Abel said, glancing down at his nephew. "Don't worry, the rescue crews have night goggles and heat sensors and all kinds of fancy stuff. They'll find her tonight." *And if they don't—* But Abel cut that thought off before it could take root in his mind. Minutes later, the lip of the gorge appeared through the trees. Abel paused to slide the pack off his shoulders and hunt around for his Locator.

"We sure came a long damn way," he muttered, staring at their location on the digital map. "We're only three miles from the cabin, as the crow flies. Too bad we're not crows." He searched for the fastest moderate-grade path back, then slid the device into his coat pocket and hefted the pack. They continued on, Abel leading them along the western edge of the gorge instead of the rocky slope they had come up.

"What was that?" Py asked.

"It's called a Locator," Abel said, a bit smugly. If this little whippersnapper thought his uncle was an ignoramus because he had no use for Spiders and artificial wombs, the old hermit would show him a thing or two. "Uses some new technology to map your location in places outside of satellite range. Then it shows you where you are on a high-resolution sat map so you can find your way around rivers and ravines." He pulled the Locator out of his pocket and handed it to Py, who examined it quietly.

"That's way better than a compass," Py said, handing the device back to his uncle. "You couldn't possibly get lost with that." He sounded relieved, and Abel bent down to ruffle his hair.

"I bet you thought a compass was the most sophisticated thing I—" Abel gasped and stumbled as his left calf cramped up in full force. He hobbled over to a fallen trunk and sat down, trying to massage the rigid muscle into submission.

"Useless damn leg," he groaned. "Just gimme a minute."

Py stood where he was, watching his uncle's predicament with attentive eyes. Abel continued to knead the knotted-up calf, but the cramp wouldn't let go.

"I'm sorry," Py said quietly, "but I have to find her. Go ahead and call a rescue team when you get back, if it'll make you feel better." Then he turned and ran back along the edge of the ravine.

"Py!" Abel yelled. He got up and tried to stagger after the boy, but his leg gave way. "Goddammit, Py, *get back here!*" He took a few more agonizing steps, then collapsed on the ground, almost blinded by pain. Cursing, Abel feverishly worked the muscle of his calf until the spasm finally relented. Limping on his sore leg, he retraced his steps until he reached the place where he'd called a halt. But there was no sign of his nephew, only the mangled remains of a hare and two birds in the shadows of dusk.

As Abel headed home alone, the image of those carcasses preyed on his mind. Despite what he had told Py, they didn't look like the work of a fox or a lynx, or even an owl. Anything with sharp teeth or a beak would have left strips of flesh clinging to the bones, and those bones had been cleaned with unnatural precision, as if something—or someone—had sliced through the meat with razor wire.

Dusk had fallen on the eastern slope of the mountain by the time Py stopped to catch his breath. Nearly spent, he staggered over to the bare ridge and sat down on a boulder, rolling up the leg of his pants to check the status of a bruise. Big thundercloud on his calf, but at least he wasn't bleeding all over the place. God help him if he twisted an ankle—or broke a leg. He flexed his sore muscles, then reached for the canteen in his pack before remembering that it was empty.

"Crap," he muttered, looking down at the darkening hills and trying to ignore the discouraging voice in his head—his uncle's voice—that told him he was on a fool's errand.

Aurie's trail had wound ever higher, through sparse woods and rocky furrows, until it led to this outcrop. She had been nearby when Py had found the first animal remains, but since then, the distance between them had grown by leaps and bounds—quite literally. She was moving much faster than he was, and taking a path he couldn't always follow, negotiating cliffs and canyons with the apparent ease of a lynx. At one point he'd been forced to abandon her trail over a steep concave shelf, and it had taken him an extra twenty minutes to find it again. There had been more bones along the way, the carcasses of birds and squirrels and what might have been a woodchuck. Maybe Uncle Abel was right, and he'd been fooled into tracking some predator on its daily romp. But no—the aura he was following was distinctly Aurie's. Py knew it the way he knew the sound of her voice or the sight of her face.

At least, *one* of the auras he was following belonged to his sister.

He stared hard at those traces in the air, which he no longer thought of as purely chemical. An aura was more than just a collection of mercurial chemicals; it was energy of some kind ... and this was the residue of that energy. He saw Aurie's familiar imprint—and the other one. The other was almost blinding in its brightness, and its texture was all wrong. If human or animal auras were like silk, this strange new aura was more like glass. He couldn't read it at all. It was colorless, emotionless, and unwavering in its brilliance, as coldly beautiful as a star caught in crystal. The two auras were intertwined and they moved as one. What scared him was the way the new aura appeared to be strangling the old one, like some deadly vine.

As he got up to continue the hunt, Py wondered what he

would do when it got dark.

Keep going, he thought wearily. *It's the only way to stay warm, unless you find a cave or something. Maybe she'll stop to sleep somewhere.*

But he didn't think she needed to sleep. The tiredness— inertia, lethargy, languor—that waxed and waned in the auras of other living things was now completely absent in her dual aura. He had no doubt that his sister was wide awake and ready for whatever her new agenda was.

Once it got dark, though, Py was forced to give up tracking for the night. Aurie's trail now led through a thick pine forest, which obscured the faint light of the clouded moon. Although the auras of living things still shone brightly, and Py could see insects winding their ways up tree trunks and moths flitting through the air, he couldn't make out rocks or deadfalls in the dark. He stumbled around until he found a little cove in the lee of a big rock, then he made a nest of leaves and pine needles. Finally, he lay down on his pack, listening to the keen of the wind and all the furtive rustlings of the nocturnal world.

Py had been so hyper-focused on following Aurie, he hadn't paid much attention to anything else, but now all the input of his heightened senses rushed in like a flood. God, the ground was hard! And the cold leached right through his coat and into his bones. Why hadn't he taken the flint and steel from the RV with him? Most of what he had in his pack—traps and funnels for collecting insects—was completely useless. Shivering, Py closed his eyes and tried not to think about his warm bed in the RV. He tried not to think about the marmalade-slathered toast he'd eaten for breakfast, which had achieved a succulence of epic proportions in his memory. He tried not to think about his empty canteen or the granola bar he was saving in his pocket. If he had a bird or a rabbit, now—

"I'd eat it raw too," Py whispered to himself. He was hungry enough to do that. And thirsty enough to drink stream water, even if it made him sick. His hand crept into his pocket and closed over the bird's head. He held it like a good-luck charm, letting it absorb all of his fear and discomfort and loneliness until he fell asleep. He was dimly aware of noises in the night—strange noises, like muffled human cries—but these were only pebbles falling into the deep well of his sleep, barely disturbing the surface.

Sometime before dawn, he woke up in the wet embrace of a thick ground mist. He was groggy, disoriented, and numb with cold. The wind had died, but the forest was still awake and murmuring. Rolling over, Py scanned the darkness with his new sense.

Aurie's trail was everywhere, looped and tangled in shining ropes through the air. It was fresh and bright, as if she had been pacing right outside his sleeping place just minutes before. Suddenly wide awake, Py crawled up to the trail and scrutinized the string of ghost auras. His sister's old aura was still there, with its warm, textured grain and shifting colors. It seemed to have grown stronger for a time, then weakened again under the tightening coils of the new one. He shouted her name twice, but his voice hardly carried past his own ears. Shivering in his soggy clothes, Py dug through his pack and ate his last granola bar. He stared at the fresh tracks of whatever Aurie was becoming, and wondered for the first time what he would do when he found her—if she allowed him to find her.

As soon as the first grey light filtered through the pines, Py took up the trail again.

Part Four

Awakening

I

The god that had awoken to a name and a history imprinted in its memories and in every cell of its human body stood naked in the shallows of a mountain stream.

I'm like a wolf pup, Aurie thought. *Or a bear cub. Hungry and needing to feed, but still learning how.* Every prey was a different challenge, but she felt vibrantly alive and immensely capable. Every cell hummed and thrummed at a frequency her old self had never been attuned to. With a single quick movement, she plunged into the icy water, automatically adjusting her body temperature as she glided near the surface, scanning the riverbed below. Two trout hovered in the shadow of a boulder, invisible to the eye, but clearly evident to her other, stronger senses. The fish were probably safe from any predator in the sky, but to Aurie they might have been sporting signs saying *Eat Me.* She hoped she could catch them both.

As she swam upstream, Aurie gave the boulder a wide berth, then let herself drift slowly with the current, angling down until she was almost on top of the rock. From this vantage, she could see the brown-and-gold backs of her quarry melding with the streambed, delicate fins curling and uncurling in the shade. A cloud shifted overhead and early morning sunlight spilled down, turning the fish into glowing works of art. She took a moment to admire the dark red spots on their flanks outlined in bluish-silver and the burnished amber bellies. They were strikingly beautiful. They were also rich in protein, which she needed in great quantities now.

With sudden speed, Aurie lunged forward. The fish darted away, but her threads were ready. Longer and stronger now, they seized both trout in a grip like steel. She held the fish up, thrashing and dripping, then tossed them onto the bank. Retracting the threads into her arm (another mechanism of self-improvement), Aurie waded out of the stream and recovered her meal, then trotted off downriver to where her clothes lay. Clothes were a nuisance, but she continued to wear them. She would need them later on.

Halfway through the second fish, she slowed a little to savor the taste of flesh that had been alive only minutes ago, tissues rich with minerals and still vibrating with activity. The thought of cooking anything seemed absurd now. Gollum, she thought, would surely have agreed. Aurie smiled as she realized how much she must look like Tolkien's infamous character, crouched naked on a rock with a fish in her mouth. In truth, her strength and agility would be the envy of Gollum—and these were only a part of her new phenotype.

In less than twenty-four hours, she had turned herself into a stunningly capable creature in the body of an eight-year-old girl. Her CRISPR machine—her Doctor—still inhabited every cell, but he was invisible and silent now. She no longer needed an agent to operate on her behalf; she could canvass the microscopic territory of her own flesh, and change its topography at will. But testing her new skills was a learning process, and Aurie was quickly finding the limits of her human form. Every time her grip failed or her leap wasn't long enough, there were gashes and sprains and broken bones to mend. She had kept her pain responses intact, but even intense pain didn't bother her—it was just a sign that something needed to be fixed, and quickly. All of that repair work took energy, which meant more hunting, which challenged her skills afresh. It was a constant cycle of experimentation and empirical learning that her father would have been proud of. Aurie had pushed the physical changes as far as she could while keeping her human shape. She would need help from humans soon, but it was best not to rely on them for anything she could do herself. And if she had to force their help, she was powerful and agile enough to do that now.

As she ate, the wind picked up, bringing the scent of alpine grass from a nearby meadow. Feeling eyes on her, Aurie looked up to meet the piercing regard of a young hawk at the top of a spruce. Before she knew it, she was on her own feet and ready to spring, caught in the grip of an overpowering impulse to fly. *No,* she admonished herself, willing every tensed muscle to relax, finally collapsing in a quivering heap. She had dug her nails hard into her palms, and there was blood all over her hands. Aurie healed the shallow abrasions instantly, then went back to her breakfast, still shaking a little.

She couldn't fly, of course, but neither could she rid herself of the compulsion to try. That urge had almost gotten her killed the day before, when she'd woken up in the ravine to a ravenous hunger and the certainty that she had wings. Strong wings that had been cooped up for ages and needed to ride the winds again. She had waited only long enough to hunt and eat, and then she'd chased her instinct to the top of a ridge, fully intending to launch herself into the air. It was her own voice that saved her, but it was a voice she barely recognized—young and frightened, a child's voice. *Stop! You don't have wings, you idiot!* The shrill warning halted her at the brink, but she'd stood gazing up for a time, trembling in gusts of wind that smelled of distant places. She wouldn't be fully herself until she was ready to fly. But she would have to be patient and wait; there was much to do before then. Aurie tossed the fish bones into the river, then stretched herself out like a cat in the cold autumn sun and began to *think.*

Thinking was very different now. Her old mind had been a clumsy paw, only able to fasten on one thought at a time, and now it had the dexterity of her threads, the ability to grasp many ideas at once. She could see all of the smaller patterns within the larger Pattern in her genome—each was a path with clear steps effecting some undefined end, like bright trails leading to the edge of night. With all ends unknown, which path was hers? Aurie let go of her mind, inadequate for the task, and called on a deeper intelligence to examine the whorls of each pattern. She felt her way among them, tasting their shapes, drinking their light, and sifting their unique textures. Among all paths, there was one that felt like it belonged to her, one that whispered most urgently of *flight*. She basked in the glow of her path—not a choice, but a destiny still unknown—until the sound of approaching feet, still far off, drew her back to the outer world.

Aurie raised her head and sniffed the breeze. She was sure Py would have slept in after yesterday's long march—and what was he marching on anyway, fumes? Last night, she had been close enough to sense the hunger radiating from him, even stronger than his fatigue. Quickly, she got dressed and padded down the bank. It was time to send her brother home. She vaguely remembered telling him to come and get her—

But not to follow me around like a shadow, she thought, pausing to catch and kill a large salamander that had poked its nose out of the mulch. She tossed the carcass directly behind her and continued on. It should have been clear by now that she didn't need rescuing.

II

Py picked up the dead salamander on the riverbank, noting the way its head lolled spinelessly. It was the first time Aurie had killed something without eating it. Had her eyes been bigger than her stomach, or was she just killing things for fun now? Or—crazy idea—had she left him a snack? He stared at the limp creature in his hand, trying to decide what to do with it. Last night he'd been ready to eat anything, but now that the moment was at hand, he found himself balking. If only he could make a fire and roast this little guy on a sharp stick—

Stop wasting time, he thought impatiently. *She was just here, and now she's getting farther away again!*

Still he hesitated, wondering how far away she would get. If Aurie wanted to lose him, she wouldn't have been pacing around watching him sleep, would she? So what would she do if he just stopped following her? If he sat down right here and didn't budge for the rest of the day?

The low and distant whir of a helicopter startled him out of his thoughts. Uncle Abel must have sent a rescue team, after all—for his niece *and* his nephew.

Thrusting the salamander into his coat pocket, Py hustled into the sparse shelter of the woods, then looked around for better concealment. It wouldn't do for the medics to rescue him and not Aurie. Finding the deadfall he wanted, Py slid under a rotten log and waited as the chopping of metal blades filled the air. Peering out, he saw the dark side of the Medicopter hovering above the trees. It didn't move on, but lingered in the air right above him, rocking gently in the wind.

Go away, he thought fiercely. *You can't help her, so get lost! Unless you want to drop some food and water and a sleep-*

ing bag down here. Why don't you do something useful like that?

The Medicopter showed no inclination to be useful, and after what seemed an endless spell, it began to move westward. Opposite of the direction Aurie's trail led.

Relieved, Py scrambled out of the deadfall. After a moment's thought, he rooted through his pack for his pocket knife, intending to skin the salamander and cut the meat into small pieces that he thought he could stomach. A flicker of movement caught his eye and he looked up with a startled cry. His sister was standing on the riverbank, watching him with cool green eyes. Her new aura flamed with diamond light, so bright he couldn't catch even a glimpse of the old aura.

"Standing still for once?" Py said hoarsely. "Thought you wanted me to come find you."

"You should've gotten on that chopper," she said. "Now you're stuck eating a salamander for breakfast."

Py didn't know what to say. After all the carcasses she had left behind, he'd expected some physical difference in her—like claws or saber teeth—but she looked the same. It should have been a relief, but the more he studied her, the more uneasy he felt.

"Don't you want to go back?" he blurted out at last, even though she obviously didn't. "Dad's got to be tearing his hair out! He's probably killed Uncle Abel by now. Don't you *care?*"

Aurie slipped into the shade of the woods, and Py saw that she was walking differently, loping like a big cat. Such a stride should have been awkward on two feet, but she made it look completely natural. Her new aura moved with her, flowing like molten glass and throwing off sparks in the patches of sunlight between the trees.

"Dad ought to understand," she said smoothly. "It's his experiment, after all. And you know we never stop for anything, not in the middle of an experiment."

"What are you doing out here?" Py cast a quick glance around the woods, which were eerily quiet. "I guess you found the mushrooms you wanted—and now you can hunt without weapons and jump over canyons. So is that it? You just want to live in the wild now?"

She strode right up to him, and he had to steel himself not to back away. The girl in front of him was *not* his sister. Up close, he could see the stranger behind her eyes, someone calculating and cold ... and there was no trace of her old aura in the crystal fire surrounding her.

"I want to finish the experiment," she said, "which is just getting started."

Dropping his gaze, Py realized that her threads were gone.

"What happened to your threads?" he asked, then yelped as a storm of indigo lashes sailed through the air. They coiled around the canvas pack by his feet and crushed it like a paper bag. Just as quickly, her new threads released their grip and disappeared. Aurie held up her forearm, white and unmarked.

"I have a place to store them now," she said with a smile.

Py tried to slow his ragged breathing, tried to think clearly. *Get her to keep talking, and maybe she'll tell you what's going on.* "So you can strangle things like an octopus." Py forced a laugh. "Can you fly like a hawk too?"

Instead of answering, she cocked her head to the breeze, which was coming from the southwest. Py, whose sense of hearing had grown quite acute since his own Change, heard nothing but the whisper of the pines.

"That chopper's circling back," Aurie said, "so listen up. I want you to flag it down on the riverbank and go back to the cabin. Tell Dad and Uncle Abel that you couldn't find me."

Py started to protest, but she held up a finger like a patient professor. "Tell them Uncle Abel was right and you were just following some animal—a lynx—all the way to its lair."

"You heard that," Py muttered. "I *knew* you were close." He met her implacable gaze, wondering if she could be swayed. "They'll keep looking for you, you know. They'll send out dog teams if they have to."

Aurie dismissed this with a wave of her hand. "When I'm

ready—maybe by tomorrow—I'll come crawling back to the cab-in. I'll be dirty and hungry and exhausted. I'll say I went looking for the mushrooms, but I never found them."

"What about your threads?" Py demanded, pointing to the place on her left arm where her threads had retracted. "You think Dad won't notice?"

Aurie made a deprecating noise. "They withered up and fell off. Guess they were *all* damaged after saving you. What a shame."

"You're not going to tell him anything?" The idea of keeping this from their father was unthinkable. "He *has* to know. He's been waiting for something like this our whole lives!"

Her eyes went hard and flat. "Dad can't know—and you'd better not tell him."

Py didn't say what he was thinking—that this new Aurie might be able to fool Uncle Abel and the mother who didn't know her, but she could never fool Dad. *No matter how good her story is, Dad will see right through it.* And thank God for that, because this had to be fixed somehow. Py desperately wanted his sister back.

"Okay," he said cautiously. "But what are you up to, really? What's this experiment you're doing?"

Aurie's face lit up and her eyes flared like citrines. "CRISPR evolution, Py! Dad wanted to speed up evolution, right? Well, I've put things in top gear."

Py frowned. "The mushrooms did all this?"

She shook her head briskly. "The mushrooms just took the brakes off. Look, people think of evolution as moving *forward,* but old things are still improvements. Things humans gave up or bypassed in the interest of developing our brains. Your ability to sense chemicals is one. But there's so much more—speed, strength, agility, the ability to see beyond the visible spectrum, to echolocate, to thermo-regulate. CRISPR-evo means expanding in *both* directions—backward, recovering the powers of older spe-cies, and forward, gaining the powers of species light-years away."

Light-years away? In spite of everything, Py felt a spark of excitement and envy. "You're going to turn yourself into some kind of alien? How?"

She grinned at him, and he could almost have fooled himself into believing this was the old Aurie, stubborn and mischievous and loveable. Except for her aura—and that ancient light in her eyes, like the glimmer of a distant star.

"When I'm finished," she said, "you won't even recognize me! I'll tell you what I've got planned if you convince them you never found me. Better get yourself out in the open, now. And don't be *inconspicuous,* make sure they see you." Her hand closed over his in a grip that was half threat and half pact. From far away, he heard the soft, growing rumble of the Medicopter.

"So you'll be back tomorrow?" Py said. "You promise? I can't let Dad think you're lost or dead for much longer. It'll kill him."

But she only gave him that cool, enigmatic smile before loping off into the woods. He caught a brief flash of color—a last glimpse of her old aura?—before she disappeared. Suddenly horribly afraid that he would never see his real sister again, Py called out to her.

"I know you're in there," he cried. "You have to fight whatever's changing you. Don't let it take over!" The shimmering aura in the distance flared with unmistakable hostility, then the girl it belonged to vanished among the trees. Sick with dismay, Py ran to the riverbank to flag down his rescuers.

Aurie ran under cover of the pines in the grip of a deep unease. She was finding it increasingly natural to think within the framework of memories in this human mind. The former resident of this mind was, after all, her own creation, a figment of her dreaming, just as the Doctor was the creation of that human personality. But this mind—and all of the nesting dolls it contained—was in her charge now. Nothing should have surprised

Aurie, and yet her old self had caught her unawares the night before. It had surged up from nowhere to take over her will, then marched her back the way she had come in search of Py. Finding him curled up asleep, her old self had tried to raise him with one cry after another. Aurie had finally put a halt to the attempted coup, asserting control over every neuron in an army of billions— or so she had thought. With her brother's parting entreaty to her old self just now, that stubborn personality had tried to surface yet again.

You have to stay vigilant, she reminded herself sternly. *Worlds have been lost through arrogance and inattention. Do you want to fail before you've even begun? After sleeping for so long in species after species?*

Aurie pondered grimly as she made her way toward the caves that pitted the river's headlands. To be asleep for eons was no hindrance, but the human brain she now possessed was both limited and overwhelmed by notions of time. Just now, she had told Py that CRISPR evolution worked *backward* and *forward,* but that wasn't really true. The Pattern in her genome—in every genome on Earth—was something outside of time. Yet having seen her own true path, Aurie could feel the shape of invisible wings furled inside her, restless and waiting. She felt a very human surge of impatience.

It won't be long now, she told herself, climbing the steep granite ledges with an agility she was beginning to take for granted. *You just have a few hundred thousand templates to awaken first!*

The helicopter's drone intensified, and Aurie leapt up onto a narrow shelf. She flattened herself against the cliff side and skimmed along until she reached a cave big enough to hide in. From the gloom, she waited until the Medicopter appeared over the treetops. The riverbank was out of sight, but as she watched, the chopper adjusted its position and a ladder unrolled from the open doorway. A rescue worker clambered down, returning a minute later with Py in tow. Satisfied, Aurie retreated into her shelter and curled up on the stone floor. She pictured the great

Pattern in her mind, a design far more ancient than the blueprint it haunted.

There you go again, thinking in terms of time. The Pattern ... just is.

The cave held a rank feline odor, but Aurie wasn't worried about the return of its former occupant. Animals, even big ones, did their best to steer clear of her now. She relaxed completely and closed her eyes—

—and envisioned a different type of cell, one that was round and smooth and undeveloped. The miasmal haze of its zona pellucida—a membrane not quite thick enough to be a wall—loomed before her, and then she was inside a vast and silent sea. Huge granules and RNA-protein complexes filled the waters like supplies in a warehouse.

Aurie called out a greeting. A moment later, the Doctor poked his sleepy-looking head around one of the giant granules. The old self that lurked inside her might be a danger and a nuisance, but Aurie felt a certain kinship with the CRISPR machine. It pleased her now to reimagine this tool of her awakening to keep her company and help with the task at hand.

Ready for some more surgery? she asked. *We've got eight hundred and fifty-nine thousand, seven hundred and twenty-two eggs to operate on!*

Good Lord, said the Doctor, jumping up at once and polishing his multi-tool on the sleeve of his white coat. *Why didn't you wake me up earlier?*

III

No sooner was Py hauled into the Medicopter's cabin than another pair of hands grabbed him. He looked up into his dad's frowning face with a sinking heart. Even though he had run off on Uncle Abel, Py would rather have faced his uncle before his father. Uncle Abel hadn't expected him to find Aurie, but his dad—

"Well, he's got a few nasty scrapes," said the rescue worker, as he drew in the ladder and sealed the door. "And he's dehydrated and hungry, and he could sure use a bath. But otherwise, no worse for wear."

Howard thanked the man, who uttered a dry chuckle. "That's one tough little kid, Mr. Hartwell. Hope his sister is just as tough."

Try rescuing her and you'll find out, thought Py.

The rescue worker strapped Py into his seat and ruffled his hair, sending a puff of dust into the air. "We'll drop him off at your friend's cabin, then do another fly-through." The man climbed into the cockpit and Py got a glimpse of the pilot—a dark-haired woman with a tightly focused aura—adjusting controls on a panel. Then the door shut and Py was alone with his dad.

"Are you all right?" Howard demanded as he buckled himself into the seat across from Py. "Where's your sister? That was a damn stupid thing to do, running away from Abel like that! No wonder you didn't answer when I called! And what the hell is this?" He grabbed the dead salamander that was poking out of Py's coat pocket and gave it a little shake.

"Uh ... breakfast," Py said.

Howard inspected the creature without a word, then stuffed it back into Py's pocket before handing him a sandwich and a thermos. The sandwich turned out to be tuna on wheat, and the thermos was full of hot tomato soup. Food for the gods! Py fell to, hoping his father would delay the interrogation until they got back.

"So did you find her?" Howard barked, glancing out the chopper's window as they banked hard to the left.

Py shook his head as he guzzled soup. It wasn't really a lie ... *she* had found *him*, after all.

"Abel said you were tracking her with your new chemical sense. Said he believed in it because you can see things underground now, like a whole colony of dead ants. Is that right? Were you really following some trail of chemicals that your sister left in the air?"

"Yeah. Well, I was trying."

His dad's expression was impossible to read. His aura, though, was pale and prickly with fear, and clouded with guilt. Not the slick sheen of guilt that accompanied a lie, but the deep, entrenched guilt that seemed to live in Howard's aura, waxing and waning without disappearing, a stormcloud that never released its burden.

"Abel said you came across some fresh-killed animal remains," Howard said.

"Yeah," Py mumbled, "but I was probably just following the trail of a fox or something."

"You what?"

Py repeated himself, almost having to shout over the drone of the rotors. "This chemical thing is pretty new to me—I'm still figuring it out!" He hoped he was striking the right tone of doleful agreement. "I'm sorry, Dad."

Howard didn't say anything, but Py could feel his father's gaze boring into his skull. He replayed his own dishonest words in his head and felt his cheeks burning.

"Here," said his dad gruffly, handing him a bottle of water. Py took it eagerly and starting chugging.

"Easy," Howard said, "or you'll just throw it all up. You didn't drink from the streams down there, did you?"

Py shook his head, pausing between gulps. On the night he had gained his new sense, water had tasted like some magical elixir, but now that he was parched, it was as tasteless and vital as air. As he drained the bottle, he could almost feel his shriveled cells swelling like seeds in a rainfall.

"Now tell me everything," Howard said sternly. "From the beginning."

So Py told him about following Aurie's trail through the woods, spending the night in a cave, and tracking her to the riverbank. He didn't mention her strange new aura, or the fact that she had doubled back to find him while he slept. He wished frantically that he'd had time—even five minutes—to plan his story.

"And then?" His dad was staring at him as if Py had stopped halfway through the tale.

"And then I heard the helicopter and started waving and jumping around."

"And when did you find that salamander?"

"Oh—uh, earlier this morning."

"It was just lying on the ground like that?"

"Yeah," said Py slowly.

"With its neck broken and its skin intact? Salamanders don't fall from trees, you know. They live on the ground, in the mud. So something killed that one and decided not to eat it?"

"Yeah, it's weird," said Py desperately.

"And *you* were going to eat it?" Howard looked faintly amused.

Py glanced down at the rest of his sandwich. "I was pretty hungry, Dad."

His dad sighed and leaned back in his seat. "You must've been. I'm sure you still are. Finish your sandwich, kiddo."

Py took another bite, trying to use the time to get one step ahead of his dad.

"What I don't understand," said Howard, giving him no opportunity, "is how you could have been *wrong*. Abel said you were absolutely convinced the chemical trail you were following belonged to Aurie."

"I was," Py said quietly.

"You insisted," Howard went on, "that she had gone down into some inaccessible ravine to find some mushrooms."

Py nodded. "She said her threads needed something in them."

Howard's eyes widened and every aspect of his aura intensified. He took a deep breath, then seemed to change topics altogether. "I told you why I wanted your mother's eggs, right? Because she's brilliant and bold and—"

"—and beautiful?—" offered Py, leaping eagerly on this apparent diversion.

"—and unscrupulous enough to engineer her own eggs with that kill switch," Howard finished.

"Sure," said Py. "You explained all that on the drive up. You needed the kill switch for CRISPR-evo, to keep us from being two-headed monstrosities. I get it."

"Well, she did something else to her eggs," his dad said. "In her wisdom, your mother found a safe way to turn *off* the kill switch. She designed it to be sensitive to exclusivin. That's a harmless drug isolated from a subspecies of toxic jack-o'-lantern mushrooms, which happen to grow in these northeastern woods. What do you make of that?"

Py put his sandwich down, accidentally knocking over the empty thermos in his lap. "Wait—you think Aurie was trying to *turn off* Mom's kill switch?"

Howard watched him quietly, giving Py time to think it through.

"She didn't tell me what kind of mushrooms she was looking for," Py said, trying to recall their short conversation. "I don't think she really knew."

"And she didn't say why she needed them?"

Py shook his head.

Howard swore softly and leaned back again, turning to stare out the window. His aura was still livid with concern, but bright excitement flickered underneath, like flames burning in a fog.

Py took in the view from his own window. They had left the mountains behind and were flying low over the autumn quilt of the valley, which suddenly reminded him of the equally colorful bruise on his calf. "We don't have to go to a hospital, do we?"

"No, thank God," his dad replied. "The pilot—Yuei—is a good friend of your uncle's, and she's doing us a favor. We've got the chopper for the whole day, off the record."

"I thought Uncle Abel didn't know anyone!"

"Everyone knows someone," Howard said with a slight smile. "Your uncle has more connections than he likes to admit." He loosened his chest straps to pick up the fallen thermos, then fixed Py with a stern eye. "We'll continue this conversation in about ten minutes. I'm sure your mother will want to hear everything."

"She's *here?*" Py said, unable to keep the startled squeak out of his voice.

"Of course she's here—she can't wait to meet her kids. At least she'll get to meet *one* of you."

They didn't speak as the helicopter made its descent into the dry meadow. Py looked down at Uncle Abel's cabin standing among the flaming birches at the edge of the woods. He could hardly believe his own mother was in that cabin, waiting for them. Waiting for *him.* Suddenly the nervousness he'd felt answering his dad's questions sharpened into something close to terror. He tried to picture the woman who had given him half his genetic material, and found he couldn't do it. The face in his mind was a complete blank.

"She's like a loaf of bread," Howard said, as if this might help Py's mental picture. "Crusty on the outside and soft on the inside. But it's been a crazy day for her, and Aurie's still out in the woods."

"I'm sorry I couldn't bring her back," Py said carefully.

"So am I," Howard said. "But the day's not over yet. Let's hope your sister gets tired of eating raw game, and comes crawling back for a plate of spaghetti."

IV

When Py first saw his mother, he was completely in awe of her—this tall, imposing woman with her sharp green eyes. She had come out of the cabin to watch the chopper land, and Py could tell by her bearing that she was no one to be trifled with. Although Jacqueline stood in full sunlight, the aura surrounding her was dark with distress. But when Py stepped out onto the field, her aura changed at once, its edges softening and brightening. Like Uncle Abel, she saw Py right away. She came over to him slowly, and knelt down so her face was level with his.

"Py," she breathed, as if testing the name to see if it fit. "You know who I am, don't you?"

Py nodded, not trusting himself to speak.

Jacqueline laughed a little, as if the truth was a surprise to her too. She opened her mouth to say something, then closed it again and just looked at him. Her eyes were very bright. The aura around her throbbed with warm, tender emotions, cloaking her in raw-edged colors. More than anything, it was the feel of her aura that put him at ease. She wasn't a stranger, after all—not some cold and indifferent person who would ruin his father and collect her kids like an overdue bill; she was his *mom,* his real mom. And she loved him; he could see that as clear as anything.

"You look like Aurie," he said shyly.

"*You* look like yourself," she said, sounding proud. "But you got a few bits of me here and there." She touched his face with one hand. That caress—which Py felt long afterward and never forgot—was as gentle as the brush of a butterfly, and as soothing as a cup of cocoa. Then she squeezed his shoulder. Without breaking contact, his mom stood up in one brisk motion and turned to Howard, who was saying something to the pilot as the Medicopter prepared to lift off again.

"Where's my daughter?" Jacqueline demanded.

Instead of answering, Howard motioned for them to follow and headed toward the cabin. As he trotted alongside her, Py didn't have to glance up to know that his mother's aura had returned to its thundercloud darkness. They found Abel making coffee in the kitchen. Py's uncle looked utterly relieved to see him, but he didn't say a word. Howard took a seat at one of the kitchen chairs—backward, with his arms folded over the top. He gazed steadily at Py.

"Well?" Howard said. "Let's have the whole truth now. Where *is* your sister?"

With three pairs of eyes on him, Py steeled himself for battle. "I don't know," he said staunchly. That was the pure and simple truth—for all he knew, Aurie was on the other side of the mountains by now.

"Then where was she this morning?" Howard asked, almost idly. "When she gave you that snack in your pocket, and told you to get lost?"

Py looked at him in alarm, then at his mother, expecting an outburst. But Jacqueline only glanced at the salamander tail sticking out of his pocket, then watched him, waiting for an answer.

He looked down at the floor, feeling a growing spark of anger at all of them. How dare they grill him like a murder suspect? As if he'd done something wrong! He'd chased Aurie all through the woods and frozen his butt off; he'd slept on rocks; he'd been *this close* to eating a raw salamander! And why was he bothering to lie for his sister at all? She wasn't even *herself* anymore. Seething, he looked up and caught Jacqueline's eye. She looked so much like Aurie—the old Aurie—that Py couldn't help it; he broke down and started to cry.

Instantly, Howard was beside him, pulling him close.

"I tried to bring her back, but she wouldn't come," Py sobbed into his father's shirt. "I didn't know what to do!"

His dad said nothing, only held him a little tighter. Py cried some more, then, remembering that they weren't alone in the room, pulled away in embarrassment. Through the blur of his tears, he saw his mother and uncle watching him with wide eyes. Their auras both contained soft edges of sympathy flanking sharp peaks of relief.

His father took Py by the shoulders and dropped to a crouch. "No one is blaming you," he said, quietly and urgently. "I only said you were stupid for running off because I didn't want to lose you too. You weren't stupid, Py, you were brave. And I knew you weren't wrong about following Aurie, not when you were so sure of it. Don't you know how much I *trust* you?"

Py nodded and wiped his face on his sleeve, knowing it was time to tell the real story. *And I'll never lie again, not for any reason!* With a deep, trembly breath, he began—and to his surprise, felt a growing sense of relief. Nothing had been fixed, but the terrible responsibility of his sister's Change began to ease off his shoulders. His father, his mother, and his uncle—three smart, strong, capable adults—were taking over the burden. When he was finished, Py felt a hundred pounds lighter.

"I'm sorry I ran off on you like that," he mumbled to his uncle.

"Left me to fend for myself, didn't you?" Uncle Abel chuckled. "But you made sure I had that Locator first—very considerate!"

"So she found those mushrooms, after all," Howard said softly, straightening up from his crouch. "And CRISPR-evo used them! To make her as strong and fast and deadly as anything in the woods."

"But she's not done yet," Jacqueline said. "And the kill switch is out of commission, at least until the drug in the mushrooms wears off. So what now?"

"Yuei will have the chopper out until dusk," Abel reminded them. Py suddenly noticed how peaked his uncle looked, like he hadn't slept at all. "If she doesn't find Aurie today, I'll call in a favor with a guy back in Quincy. He's got his own pack of trained bloodhounds."

Py snorted. Trained bloodhounds would make a nice lunch

for Aurie. Rescue workers had no idea what they were up against—something as stealthy as a cat and smarter than any human. Something with a new aura that wasn't human at all. Aurie wouldn't be found unless she wanted to be.

Py's uncle was watching him closely. "What are you thinking?"

"Since she left the ravine," Py said, "she has this new aura." This was the only part he hadn't described yet, and he tried to choose his words carefully. "It's different from the old one."

"Different how?" Howard asked.

Py shook his head. "The feel of it, the texture ... it's hard to explain. At first, the new aura was just wrapped around the old one like a strangler vine, but now it's taken over completely. I can't even make out her old chemical signature anymore. Rescue dogs would be tracking her old scent from a piece of clothing, wouldn't they? I don't think they'd get past the ravine."

"God," Abel said, turning his stricken face to Howard. "I should've locked the kids inside and played Scrabble with them until you got back."

Howard chuckled. "Relax, Abe, she would've gotten away from anyone. And obviously she can take care of herself." He crossed his arms and cocked his head to the left: his classic thinking posture. Py watched hopefully as his dad began to pace.

"What did she say, again?" Howard asked Py. "About CRISPR-evo?"

"She said CRISPR-evo means expanding in *both* directions—backward and forward."

"But what does that mean?" asked Jacqueline.

Py remembered every word of his sister's little speech. "*Backward* means recovering the powers of older species, and *forward* means gaining the powers of species light-years away."

Howard froze in the midst of pacing, his face alight. "CRISPR-evo means taking on the abilities of *alien* species?"

"I don't know, Dad," Py said. "That's what she said. She said in a few days, I wouldn't even recognize her. But she's already so different, and not in a—a human way."

216

Abel uttered a short laugh. "She hasn't turned into a little green girl, has she?"

Py didn't answer. Aurie *didn't* look the same, but the changes were almost impossible to describe.

"A little green girl, Abe?" Howard gave his brother a patronizing look, then threw up his hands in excitement. "Alien species could be anything at all! A single cell the size of an ocean, a sentient gas, a space-traveling virus!"

A piercing whistle sounded from the kitchen, and Abel jumped up with the relieved air of a man who finally knows his business. "Coffee's ready."

"That's the sanest thing I've heard all day," said Jacqueline. She squeezed Py's shoulder again and kissed the top of his head before following Abel. The skeptical, troubled auras of the two adults in the kitchen blended with the coffee's dark aroma.

"You said her threads coiled around your backpack?" Howard whispered. His aura was ablaze with excitement, and Py wondered what his own aura looked like. He was excited too, but still frightened, and the two emotions felt like one.

"They crushed my backpack! They were like wires—and way longer—and she can retract them into her arm now. I think she's using them to catch and kill her prey."

"Such dramatic physical changes," Howard murmured. "The way she moves now, and hunts, and can hear things coming from miles away—all the *backward* changes—she made in a matter of hours. And the *forward* changes will take place in just a few days?"

Py nodded, noticing that Howard's fear—clearly evident on the helicopter ride—had completely disappeared. His dad had been afraid of Aurie being lost or hurt in the woods, but he wasn't remotely afraid of her Change.

"So her CRISPR machine is working on them now." Howard resumed his pacing. "Is that why she wants more time? More time alone? But why the hell is she keeping all of this a secret?"

"She's probably afraid we'll try to stop her," Jacqueline said, coming back from the kitchen with four mugs. Abel followed her with the coffeepot and a jug of milk. "And speaking of that, how *are* we going to stop her?"

"What's she planning to do next?" Howard wondered.

"It doesn't matter," said Jacqueline tightly, as she poured herself coffee. "What matters is keeping her safe."

"We'd have a better chance of that," Howard said, "if we knew what she was doing—and how. And why."

"Well, I don't think she's going to tell us that," Jacqueline snapped. "So we'd better come up with a plan."

"We don't need her to *tell* us," Howard scoffed. "Come on, Jacqueline, are we scientists or FIBR hacks? Let's come up with a hypothesis or two."

"You think you can make an educated guess about what she's doing?" Jacqueline stirred sugar into her coffee with vigorous abandon. "You said it yourself—an alien could be anything at all! This is not an *early primate* to *great ape* evolutionary leap, Howard. This is a human to ... who knows what?"

Howard beamed at her. "Yes, exactly! Probably on the order of worm to human! Could a bunch of worms possibly envision a human being?"

"No," said Jacqueline. "So can we dispense with the flights of fancy and start thinking about how to—"

"How to keep Aurie a worm?" Howard shook his head as he stalked toward the living room window. "That's not what CRISPR-evo is all about."

"God give me strength," Jacqueline muttered, her eyes shooting green fire at Howard's back.

"Py," Abel said, "Aurie told you that she's coming back tomorrow?"

"Maybe tomorrow," Py said.

"So we wait until then," Howard said, but his mind, Py knew, was a million miles away, traversing alien landscapes of possibility.

"And then what?" Jacqueline was staring into her mug as if the answer lurked in its depths. "Subdue her? Tranquilize her? Inject her with truth serum?"

"Not bad ideas, Doc," said Abel dryly. "If we accept the bold premise that she is turning herself into a virus or a self-aware gas or Wonder Woman or something." He sipped from his own mug, then set it down to crack all ten of his knuckles. "Still, what if we all just played along?"

Howard stopped pacing and they all looked at Abel, who turned up his hands as if to say, *Why not?*

"Aurie wants Py to say he never found her," Abel reminded them. "She's planning to come back here and pretend that everything's normal—she never found the magic shrooms and those things on her arm just fell off on their own. What if we all go along with it, just to get her off guard?"

"And then stab her with a needle?" Jacqueline chuckled darkly. "Oh, she's going to love us when she wakes up."

"That would be the only way to collect anything from her," Howard pointed out.

"Collect?" Jacqueline frowned at him.

"Samples, Mom," Py elaborated. "Blood, saliva, skin scrapings. We do it all the time."

"Of course you do." Jacqueline shook her head. "And where would we analyze these samples?"

"In my lab—where else?" Howard gestured grandly out the window. "It's parked just out back!"

"Of course it is," Jacqueline said, closing her eyes briefly.

Who are they kidding? Py thought to himself. *Trying to trick the new Aurie? She'll see this coming a mile away!* Out loud, he said, "Getting those samples won't be easy."

"No, but it's our only hope of understanding this." Howard finally seemed to notice the coffeepot and empty mugs on the table. He filled both mugs and absentmindedly handed one to Py. "Since she won't talk to us worms."

Aurie might talk to me, Py thought as he took an experimental sip. *But only if she thinks I kept her secret.* The coffee was horribly bitter, but it was the first adult beverage he'd ever been offered, so he forced himself to drink it, rolling the strong tree-bark taste around on his tongue until he got used to it. He shared his mom's fear and his dad's excitement—and yet he felt impatient with all of them and their cavalier certainty that they could fool and subdue his formidable new sister. Part of him—the CRISPR-evo part he shared with her and no one else—actually hoped Aurie would show them all a thing or two, and then return to normal on her own.

When the Medicopter returned empty-handed at dusk, no one was surprised. Abel thanked Yuei for her help, and Howard assured the pilot and her friend that they would now search for his daughter in a more official capacity. The family ate a late dinner, forking up spaghetti with venison meatballs while the old cabin creaked and groaned under the keening of the night wind. Py found himself wishing he could see auras through the wooden walls. He couldn't shake the feeling that Aurie was lurking just outside, watching them and listening to every word.

Not that they were saying much. Dinner was a quiet affair during which Jacqueline's gaze kept straying to Py. He'd reach across the table to snag another meatball from the platter and catch her smiling at him—that smile that reminded him of Aurie. Then she'd look away, her aura bright with affection and curiosity. When they were finished, Uncle Abel brewed a fresh pot of coffee and Py washed the dishes while his parents lingered at the table, having what they thought was a private conversation.

"I know it's silly," said Jacqueline, "but I can't help listening for her. Although you couldn't hear an invading army through all that wind."

Howard chuckled. "Yesterday morning, would you have believed you'd be sitting in a cabin tonight in the Maine woods with the man who stole your eggs, waiting for your daughter to return so you can tranquilize her and figure out what the hell she's turning into?"

"I still don't believe it." Jacqueline sighed. "I'll need to use your stealth Spider to call Aram and let him know I won't be picking up my car for a couple of days. Last thing we need is him filing a Missing Persons Report." The wind died momentarily, heightening the clink of dishes and the sound of running water.

"Is he always this helpful?" It took Py a moment to realize she was asking about him.

"Both of them are," said Howard. "They like to get the boring stuff out of the way so they can get on to more interesting things. Speaking of which, it's weird, isn't it?"

"You're going to have to be more specific," said Py's mother dryly.

There was a deep creak as Howard leaned back in his chair. "Two kids—same parents, same age, same environment and upbringing, made with identical engineering ... and one of them's rampaging through the forest while the other one's doing the dishes."

"Do you need a refresher course in epigenetics, Dr. Wake?" Jacqueline said. Py could almost see his mother rolling her eyes. "You know even identical twins are totally different! And did you really expect your fancy CRISPR machine to do the exact same thing in both of them?"

"Well, no ... but somehow the truth always surprises me."

"Besides," she went on, "it's not like Py is your average kid. He's smart as a whip and he has this extra sense, which I don't understand at all."

"I don't understand it either," Howard said. "He says he can see the chemicals that make up people's *auras*. Animals too—any living thing. And apparently every aura is different."

"But how can he see it after the person is gone?"

"There are traces left in the air," Py said, unable to keep quiet any longer. He wiped his hands on his shirt and trotted back to the table, enjoying the startled looks from his parents. "They condense into a kind of trail. The older a trail is, the fainter it gets."

"And these trails don't get dispersed by the wind?" said Howard. "How is that possible?"

Py shrugged as he sat down with them. "I've been calling them 'chemical trails,' but I don't think they really are. I think a trail is some kind of energy residue that an aura leaves behind."

Howard stared at him. "So our energy residues are all over

this house? All mixed up and crisscrossing the air wherever we've been? How can you make sense of all that?"

"And how can you see it without going nuts?" Jacqueline wondered.

"I can't see your trails at all when you're sitting right there," Py told them. "Like looking for strings of fireflies around two campfires! Go into the hall for a minute."

Obediently, his mom and dad trekked into the hall, then waited quietly for further instructions. In the suddenly empty air, Py looked around at the record of the family's movements through the cabin. The trails weren't as wild as his father made them sound, just individual strings that followed similar patterns over limited ground. The shapes of the ghost auras were different enough that he could focus exclusively on a single trail without much difficulty. Py glanced into the kitchen, where his uncle was checking something in the oven. Despite the brightness of his uncle's aura, Py could follow Abel's movements backward in time as he roamed around the kitchen, sat down at the table for a spell, then roamed around the kitchen some more, and disappeared down the hall.

"It's really not that bad," he said, after calling his parents back. "I wish I could show you what I see, instead of trying to explain it."

"Does someone's aura ever change," asked his mother, "or is it always the same?"

"Oh, it changes all the time," Py told her. "Depending on emotions, feelings, physical sensations." He gave her the closest analogy he could think of: a complex cloak of many colors. The hues and textures of the cloak constantly shifted, but its shape—unique to each person—never did.

"That," said Jacqueline admiringly, "is the coolest, weirdest thing I've ever heard. Can you see your own aura?"

Py hesitated, glancing down at himself. "Not very well." He *could* see part of the aura swirling around him, but it made him dizzy to focus on it, like trying to read words that were much too close.

"What does mine look like?" his mother asked curiously.

Py considered the pulsing, eddying forms that made up his mother's aura, the textured peaks and valleys that formed and dispersed within the larger shape. He couldn't really describe her aura, but he could compare it to another one. "Right now, it's sharp like Dad's, but in different places. And soft in different places."

"Your father's aura has *soft* places?" Below her raised eyebrows, Jacqueline's eyes twinkled at Py.

"Don't let word get out," Howard said, smiling at his son.

Py snickered, still shifting his focus between the two auras. "Right now, your colors are changing between dim ones and bright ones," he told his mom. "Except when you look at Dad, and then all the colors are like fire."

Howard laughed as Jacqueline flushed. "That's because I have a bone to pick with him," she muttered.

"What lunacy are we discussing now?" Abel joined them at the table with the coffeepot and a plate of warm cookies. Jacqueline leaned over and inhaled with all the gusto of a kid.

"Those smell like Christmas morning!" she said. "I haven't had a homemade ginger cookie since I was a kid."

"They're not actually fresh," Abel admitted. "I just pulled these out of the freezer and heated 'em up. But they *are* homemade, Doc. Real ginger and molasses and lemon zest. None of that no-calorie nonsense."

"Thanks for taking us in like this," Howard said quietly, putting a hand on his brother's arm. "I'll make it up to you."

"It's nothing," Abel scoffed. "Plenty of food in the house—and apparently your daughter's quite the hunter. If she brings in a deer, I'll make us all a venison stew."

They sat munching quietly, ears pricked up to the wind.

"So what's the plan, Professors?" Abel asked.

Howard and Jacqueline shared an uncomfortable look, but no one said anything.

"You know, as the kid here pointed out, slipping a needle into someone without their consent isn't all that easy," Abel said, "but there are ways to make it easier. Pills? Powders? I'm assuming you have a whole dispensary in that RV."

Thus encouraged, Howard expounded on the virtues and drawbacks of light sedation methods—and the use of OxyTalk versus Sodium Pentothal—until Jacqueline stopped him.

"We are going to *talk* to her first," Jacqueline said, in a tone that made it clear she would brook no dissent. "Like a family, not a bunch of Nazi interrogators."

Py made a disparaging sound, and his mother turned her green-fire eyes on him. "You don't think that'll work?" she demanded. "Why not?"

"If you ask her questions, I'm sure she'll give you answers," Py said. "But I don't think you can trust what she says. She's not herself anymore."

"You keep saying that," Jacqueline said, "but didn't she leave that salamander for you? And didn't she stand guard over you all night, to keep you safe?"

Py considered that. "Maybe there's still enough of her left to care whether I get mauled by some animal or starve to death. But there's only one thing she *really* cares about now, and that's her own evolution. Whatever the mushrooms allowed her to do by turning off the kill switch." He was quiet for a moment, then finally said what he'd been wondering about all night. "So the real question is, why is she bothering to come back before she's finished?"

They all stared at him. Nobody ventured a guess.

"She said, *When I'm finished, you won't even recognize me,*" Py reminded them. "But when she comes back here, she's still going to look like herself. She'll be 'dirty and hungry and exhausted,' pretending to be the old Aurie, pretending that she never found the mushrooms. I think she needs something."

"What?" Jacqueline said.

Py shrugged. "Probably something from the lab, or from one of you. If she needed something from me, she'd have taken it already."

The three adults all cast inquiring looks at one another, and

Howard laughed. He gave his son a rough pat on the shoulder.

"Now, that's my boy," he said, giving Jacqueline a cheeky grin. "Sorry, *our* boy. Good thinking, kiddo. We'll talk to her before we do anything else."

"Just don't underestimate her," Py said. They all nodded, and he sighed as he grabbed the last cookie, knowing perfectly well that they would.

V

"Any luck?" Jacqueline asked Howard, as she pulled a rusty corkscrew from the jumble of a kitchen drawer. She had been hoping to spend more time with Py after dinner. All their talk had been about finding Aurie, and Jacqueline wanted to get to know her son, this sharp-minded little boy who was disarmingly sweet and astonishingly tough—with a toughness that Howard seemed to take for granted. But the poor kid had zonked out in Abel's den as soon as the cookies were gone, and Abel himself had staggered off to bed, after telling Howard and Jacqueline to help themselves to anything in the cupboards that interested them.

"My brother was never much of a drinker," Howard said from deep in the pantry. "Although he used to be more organized than this. Pinto beans ... condensed milk ... pickled onions ... gas relief ... aha!" He emerged with the dustiest bottle Jacqueline had ever seen. "Could be anything at all."

Jacqueline handed him the corkscrew. "Anything at all sounds fine, as long as it's fermented."

"That's the spirit." Howard squinted at the label. "It's all in Japanese. Someone must've given it to him back when he belonged to the professional world."

"Your brother was a professional?" Jacqueline tried and failed to imagine Abel in a suit and tie.

"Yeah, professional curmudgeon. Best in the business." Howard uncorked the bottle and chuckled as Jacqueline set two daisy-printed plastic tumblers on the kitchen table. "We used to drink apple juice in those about fifty years ago." Into one, he poured a smidgen of something that was definitely not apple juice.

"To the brim, Dr. Wake."

"Yes, ma'am." Howard filled both little vessels to the brim and they toasted, carefully.

Jacqueline took a cautious sip—and then an appreciative one. The wine smelled of flowers; it was light as water and sweet as honey. *And probably as strong as Polish vodka.* Good, maybe she'd be able to sleep tonight. "So," she said. "Tell me again what you were thinking."

"Thinking?" Howard took a sip of his own drink. "What do you mean?"

She gestured down the darkened hall, where Py was sleeping in the den, and tried to keep her voice down. "This CRISPR-evo experiment of yours. Our kids are not some bacteria you can play around with, then douse with bleach and pour down the drain. On the ride up, you made it sound like, *Sure, I took your eggs and made some kids, what's the big deal? Now we have these cool, smart kids, no worries—*"

"We *do* have these cool, smart kids—"

"—who are at the mercy of an unguided CRISPR machine! And one of them's found a way to get rid of the only biological defense keeping that machine in check. Talk about opening Pandora's Box."

"I know, Jacqueline. It's brilliant!" Howard wrapped both hands around his cup and beamed at her. "CRISPR-evo is smarter than we are. That's the beauty of it!"

"A lot of things are smarter than you are." She sipped her wine and tried to stay calm. "You have no idea what you've set in motion. This experiment never ends! So what were you expecting to happen? And now that we know something about Aurie, what *do* you expect? You don't seem so keen on stopping her—you want to see where all of this goes, don't you? All you're worried about is being caught by FIBR, not the real danger—this thing that you've unleashed, or planted, or—"

"Slow down there, Dr. Witt," Howard said. "One thing at a time. Don't get all worked up. Here, have some more wine."

"Keep patronizing me and you'll have to CRISPR my foot out of your ass ... and yes, I'll have some more wine."

Howard topped her off and they both drank silently.

"Of course I want to see where all of this goes," he said with quiet intensity. "I wanted to speed up evolution, remember? Tap into the full potential of the human genome and the human mind! And having kids is never safe—they're always an experiment that never ends. I used our resources to give them an edge, make them the best they could be, same as any other parent."

Same as any other parent? Jacqueline stifled a mad laugh.

"Think about it from a scientific perspective," Howard urged. "How did we get to this point? We evolved from primordial genomes through mutation, amplification, recombination, even invasion by viruses, and poof! Here we are several billion years later—two humans sharing a bottle of wine. But do we have to wait that long to leap forward again? If you look at humanity's evolutionary chart, the steps have been getting faster and faster, but they're still on a geologic time scale. So I thought I could speed things up a bit."

"By putting an unregulated genome editing machine into two kids?"

"How else? If we can thoughtfully evolve our genomes, then eons of chance and failure can be bypassed. We can immediately leap ahead to where humans will be a million years from now." He paused, tapping his fingers impatiently against his cup. "Think of it this way: our kids are perfectly normal, just like all the others born in the year 1,002,070."

Jacqueline sipped deeply, wishing the alcohol would leach its warmth into her cold fingers. "You want me to look at this from a scientific perspective? Okay." She thought for a moment, then said something that surprised her. "What if our genome can create—not just mutate—but *create with intent,* as part of its evolution?"

Howard was watching her attentively, and his eyes had lost some of their revival-preacher gleam. Encouraged, she continued.

"The human genome was sequenced damn near eighty years ago, but only in part."

"Yeah," he said with a snort. "Just like the government to declare a job complete when it's only half done."

"And no matter what the heads of FIBR say, we still don't know what that unmapped half does. All that invasive DNA you mentioned ... our cells have silenced it for a reason. Where does it come from? What does it encode? What is it capable of? Do we know enough to unleash it? You *know* we don't know enough to thoughtfully evolve our genome without unexpected consequences."

Howard nodded. "That's why my CRISPR-evo project would have failed peer review. High-risk, high-reward, sure. But did I have a straightforward hypothesis? A plan of action that would have passed muster with any study section?" He shook his head, staring down into his drink. She followed his gaze into those pathless, colorless depths.

"Have you ever had an idea," he said, "that came in a weird moment when your mind was completely still?"

"You mean when you're just about to fall asleep, or just waking up?" She had those unbidden ideas all the time, although only a few ever made sense later on.

"No," he said, "although that can be useful too—letting your subconscious solve a problem that your conscious mind can't fully see. But this is something else." His gaze shifted to something in the air she couldn't see. "I'm always thinking, you know. Not always brilliant thoughts—"

"Oh, don't be so modest."

"No, it's true," he insisted, still in earnest. "You'd be amazed at all the useless crap that goes through my head. Trivial distractions, old regrets, worries about things I can't control, impractical plans to wreak vengeance on my enemies. Even when I'm focused on something useful, those other thoughts are always there, like insects buzzing around."

She waited, watching him.

"There were only two times in my life that I escaped them," he went on. "One was my first and only LSD trip, back in college—interesting experience, but it didn't leave me with any profound insights. The other was when my second wife finally left me. We had been up all night yelling at each other, and in the morning she packed her things and walked out the door. I went down to the couch in the basement where I'd been living for the past six months, and just collapsed. I remember thinking that my life was a bad playbook that kept running in circles—the same things kept happening, and I couldn't control them. Every partner I'd ever had wanted me to be someone else, and I couldn't be who they wanted."

"I know what you mean," Jacqueline said reflectively. "I couldn't be who Doug wanted, either. He always said he loved me, but I don't think he really knew me."

"Of course he didn't," said Howard. "Any more than a tick living on a tiger knows what it's keeping company with! Well, my wives knew me all too well, and neither of them actually liked me. They liked being married to a successful scientist, but I never said or did the right things. Didn't act professionally, hated going out with other couples, never made it home in time for dinner. Anyway, after my second wife left, I was so emotionally drained, I just lay down and let go of everything. I didn't fall asleep, but I sort of fell out of time. And what filled my mind was this image of sleeping DNA being woken up in a pattern of bursts. The pattern kept changing, and so did the shape of the life it encoded. It was CRISPR-evo, and I knew I could do it! I knew I could tap into the history of biology to facilitate the evolution of mankind. Because *everything* is there in our genome, if we can just find the keys to unlock it. I sat up on the couch and my mind was completely clear—nothing in it except for this incredible image, this idea waiting to take shape. I didn't want to lose it when all that buzzing crap started up again. So I ran upstairs and made a pot of coffee, fired up my laptop and started brainstorming."

"Just like that," Jacqueline murmured, envious in spite of herself. When had she ever fallen out of time to experience an epiphany? Howard must have seen something of this in her expression, because he laughed a little.

"I can't take any credit for it," he admitted. "Not really. I wasn't thinking at all. That was an idea that came from ... I don't know, some place deeper than my mind."

What place is deeper than the mind? Jacqueline studied Howard's face, but the wine or the conversation had softened every harsh line, leaving it unreadable. "And you never questioned it? Whether it was a *good* thing to do?"

"I questioned it all the time," he said quietly, "but every instinct I had told me it was the *only* thing to do."

In that moment, Jacqueline believed him. His eyes were guileless and completely clear; she saw the bold, eager boy still living behind them and dreaming up wonders for the man to bring to life. She felt a surge of those strong mixed feelings— affection and attraction and aggravation and helpless wonder. Geniuses might be able to explain their actions later, but they operated by intuition, by the uncharted laws of their own creativity ... and she'd never possessed that kind of faith in herself.

"So what did I expect?" Howard sighed. "It's a fair question. More than fair. But I don't know. I expected our kids to be smart, but I didn't know what to expect in terms of physical changes. They've never been under any selective pressure. I wasn't going to put them in a room with a tiger—"

Jacqueline raised her cup in a mocking salute to his fatherly sensibilities, and he chuckled.

"—or do any of the things I did with the mice. I wish I could tell you I know what's going to happen, but—"

"No, you don't," she said. "If you knew what was going to happen, it wouldn't be any fun, would it?" She had meant the words to be sarcastic, but they only rang flat and true.

Howard smiled and they both sipped from their cups.

"You know, Dr. Wake," she said. "Making kids the old-fashioned way is a hell of a lot easier."

"But what fun would that be?" Howard said. "I mean, apart from actually making them. Not that I'm getting any ideas—I know you're only a drink away from throttling me."

"You deserve to be throttled," Jacqueline said. "On the bright side, we may all be dead and devoured by morning, and this conversation will be moot."

"Beats going to jail," Howard pointed out. "After all, you weren't the only one chasing me."

Jacqueline picked up her cup and the half-empty bottle, and headed to the little living area across the room. "I hope Abel's floor isn't too hard for you. I'm taking the couch again—and the rest of the wine."

"You'll need more than wine to get any sleep on that thing," Howard said, a smile still in his voice. As she settled herself on the lumpy couch, he finished off the wine in his cup and got up from the table. "I'll be in the den with Py. Come in and kick me if you need anything."

As the old cabin walls creaked around her, Jacqueline sat nursing her wine, besieged with thoughts of Aurie. Her daughter, a wonder of evolution? Some kind of supergirl version of Py? Prosaic fears morphed quickly into lurid imaginings. Long after she closed her eyes, a green-eyed demon sprang through her head, breaking the necks of woodland creatures, as Jacqueline chased this vision into sleep. When she woke hours later, rain was pelting the cabin roof and the wind howled like a ghost army through the trees. Shivering, she groped for the blanket that had fallen to the floor, and hoped her poor daughter was warm and dry in a cave somewhere. In spite of all the wild talk of evolution, the girl she pictured in the midst of the thunderstorm was small and vulnerable and all too human.

Tomorrow, Jacqueline thought with uncanny certainty as she drifted back to sleep. *I'll meet my little girl tomorrow—for better or worse.*

VI

Jacqueline dozed fitfully until dawn, then fell into dark dreams until the sound of kitchen noises finally woke her. She sat up slowly, blinking in late-morning sunshine streaming through the cabin windows.

"Morning, Doc," Abel greeted her, then checked with the kitchen clock. "Well, close enough ... and Uncle Abel's B & B is still serving breakfast. Are you hungry?"

Jacqueline shook her head, wincing at the throb in her temples and the sour taste in her mouth. She looked around for the empty bottle, but someone had already whisked it away—hopefully before Py had seen it. "Just some coffee would be good," she mumbled, her face burning. "Thanks, Abel."

"I'll make you a fresh pot." Abel glanced at Howard, who was emptying the contents of the old pot into a thermos.

"Long night?" Howard asked Jacqueline with a smirk. He stowed the thermos in his pack and pulled his jacket on.

"You're going to *look* for her?" Py burst out. "You won't find her, Dad. Especially you. She—" He broke off, looking embarrassed.

Howard gave his son an irritated look. "I know I won't find her, but she might find me—the way she found you."

"But she could be anywhere! Where are you going to go?"

"I'll keep to the old trails," Howard said. "I still remember most of them. With all her enhancements, I doubt I could stay *off* her radar." He slung the pack over his shoulders and turned to Jacqueline. "Don't you run off while I'm gone, now."

"Better take some food with you," she said. "Or are you counting on dead salamanders being flung in your path?"

Howard snorted a laugh and waved a couple of protein bars at her, then gave her shoulder a squeeze on his way out. From the

233

window, Jacqueline watched him cross the field, his grey hair ruffling in a stiff breeze. Even after he disappeared into the woods, she kept staring at the place where the trees had swallowed him up. Part of her wanted to go with him, and part of her just wanted to spend the day with her son. But overriding everything was simple fear for the daughter she hadn't even met.

"She'll be back," Abel said, handing Jacqueline a steaming cup as he joined her by the window.

"I know," she said, giving him a smile that felt forced. "But in the meantime ... "

"In the meantime, I'm gonna pick up some more supplies in town," Abel said. "Is there anything I can get for you?"

Jacqueline turned to look at Py, who was shaking marshmallows into his hot cocoa with a troubled frown. "More milk for him," she said. "And some fresh fruits and veggies, if you can find them. I don't know what he likes."

Abel nodded. "Okay if I bring him along?"

"Sure," Jacqueline said, surprised to be asked for permission. But why should she be surprised? Py was her son, after all—and being an uncle was as new to Abel as being a mother was to her. Still, she felt a pang of disappointment at the thought of Py leaving, even for a couple of hours.

"Hey, kid," Abel said, walking back to the kitchen. "Want to come help me shop for groceries?"

The boy looked up from his mug, then darted a glance out the kitchen window. He didn't answer right away.

"You can ride on the UTV," Abel said mildly. Jacqueline smiled as Py's eyes widened with excitement.

"Yeah, okay," Py said. "But what about Aurie? I know it's still early, but someone ought to be here—"

"I'll be here," Jacqueline told him.

Abel made some notes on a scuffed pad, then tore off the sheet and pocketed it. "Get your coat," he told Py, then handed his car keys to Jacqueline. "Just in case. Um ... you can drive, right?"

"You mean these new-fangled automobiles?" She couldn't help but snicker.

"It's an *old*-fangled automobile," Abel told her sternly. "Doesn't drive itself! You actually have to turn the wheel and step on the accelerator."

"Thanks, I'll manage," she said, still chuckling as she pulled a few smart bills out of her purse. "Take this for the groceries—"

Abel frowned at the bills. "Looks like Monopoly money."

"No, it's real," she told him, bemused. "Like a cashier's check—"

"*Not* like a cashier's check. Those bills are linked to your accounts."

Jacqueline looked down at the bills in her hand. They did come from her checking account, but no one could get her account information from them. "They're just currency."

Abel turned his back on the smart bills, as if they had eyes. "That currency of yours is high-tech paper," he said, rooting through a drawer in the kitchen. "It generates a record of every thumb that touches it, every account it passes through, every place it goes in its lifetime of wandering. And if some agency had a mind to, they could find out that the first person Dr. Jacqueline gave those bills to was a man who died twenty years ago."

"You could wear—" Jacqueline began, before the ridiculousness of her suggestion dawned on her.

"Gloves?" Abel snorted. "Handling those bills with gloves is like wearing a sign saying, 'I'm a criminal!' And whether I hand them to a person or a machine, they'll be located and marked. Do you really want the people who track scientists knowing that you passed through a market in Gorham today?"

When I'm supposed to be at a meeting in Seattle, she thought, with a little prickle of fear.

"Not to worry," Abel said. "We can still take care of groceries the old-fashioned way." He flashed a $100 bill, something Jacqueline hadn't seen in years. "And *you're* not paying for a thing. My brother got you into all of this, didn't he?"

She sighed. "He wouldn't have burst in on you if I hadn't

been chasing him. And it isn't cheap having four extra mouths to feed."

"Only three at the moment," he reminded her, then looked uncomfortable at the admission. "Kids have been doing all the cooking and washing up, anyway. I've never been so pampered in my life."

"Pampered, right," Jacqueline said, looking at the scratches on his arms and face. "You look like you've been dragged through the woods." She watched Abel put his coat on, but she was thinking of the money Howard had sent to her gift fund long ago. "Howard's going to pay you back, you know. Whether you like it or not."

Abel grunted. "He's going to have a hell of a time finding my accounts! And I can afford some basic hospitality, Doc. I live cheap here, and I have a good nest egg."

"Really? Where is it?" Jacqueline couldn't resist teasing him. "Stuffed under your mattress?"

"Of course not," Abel huffed. "It's in a mayonnaise jar buried in the yard and guarded by a pair of old-timers named Smith and Wesson." He turned to Py, leaving Jacqueline to wonder whether or not he was joking. *Smith and Wesson?* Private ownership of most firearms had been outlawed decades ago.

"Come on, let's get you fitted with the spare helmet," Abel told Py. "Smallest setting ought to do the trick." As they took off for the shed, Py glanced back at Jacqueline with a delighted grin. He was her little boy—every bit as weird and cool and smart as Howard had said, with an innocence that made her heart ache. Standing alone in the old cabin, Jacqueline suddenly found herself lonely for a family she hadn't even known existed when the week began.

Pulling her coat on, Jacqueline took her cup out to the side porch. She sat down on the steps and gazed into the woods.

Bright sunlight turned the forest's edge to a mass of shadows. The trees seemed taller and darker under the noonday glare, the spaces between them indistinct. The light hum of an electric motor broke the quiet, and Jacqueline turned to see the

UTV emerging from the shed with its two riders. She waved to them, and Py and Abel waved back as they rumbled across the empty field. Soon they were swallowed by the woods.

Silence prevailed.

Jacqueline sipped her coffee and tried to think through her lingering headache. She and Howard hadn't really discussed how to approach Aurie when she returned. How to keep her calm and make her feel safe, so they could talk. Howard and Py were the only ones who knew Aurie; Jacqueline was painfully aware that she didn't know her daughter at all. She felt terribly out of her depth.

And the damned woods were too quiet.

"You're watching me, aren't you?" she murmured, then laughed under her breath. There was no one there, of course—no monster, no alien, not even a traumatized little girl—and what on earth was she, Jacqueline Witt, doing here in the middle of the Maine woods? She squeezed her eyes shut, and the last forty-eight hours shimmered like a feverish dream in the darkness behind her closed lids. A strange dream, wonderful and frightening, but nothing that would stand up to the hard light of reality. Nothing that could be written into the pages of her waking life.

Jacqueline opened her eyes and exhaled, the sound of her own breathing unnaturally loud in the woodland silence. She hated not being in control of a situation. That need to manage things was an asset in the lab, spurring her to diligence and careful planning. *But it's also what limits you. If you could let go, just enough to take a big risk, like Howard did …* She wondered for the hundredth time what it would be like to work with him. Just talking with the man was like getting a bird's-eye glimpse into a land of perilous wonders, and now they were exploring that land together—with no map, no defenses, and limited tools. And today she was on her own. Unless Howard actually found Aurie, he probably wouldn't be back before dusk. Shivering, Jacqueline got up to stretch her stiff back, then froze.

Something was moving at the edge of the woods. Feline shadows detached themselves from the trees, then coalesced into the shape of a girl—a small girl in filthy, ragged clothes.

Jacqueline stared at Aurie as she approached. Her jacket was torn, her jeans ripped and stained with what looked like dried blood, but she didn't seem to be injured. She moved with a fluid grace, her pace measured and steady, as if Jacqueline were a wild animal that might startle. The dirty tangles of Aurie's hair could have been any color, but her eyes were a clear jasper green, the same color as Jacqueline's own.

"Hi, Mom," said the girl.

Jacqueline couldn't speak, couldn't even muster a coherent response. This was her daughter, without a doubt—and yet the girl in front of her couldn't have been more different from her son. Py had looked at her for the first time with a heartbreaking mixture of shyness and deep feeling. It was a look that said, *Part of me has always known you, and now you're finally here!* Aurie, on the other hand, was frankly appraising her from the eyes of a complete stranger.

"I *was* watching you," Aurie admitted. "Sorry to make you nervous. I had to be sure they weren't coming back."

She heard me mutter under my breath? How the hell could she have heard that?

"Aurie," Jacqueline said in a voice that shook even as she tried to steady it. "We've been looking all over for you. Are you okay?" It sounded woefully inadequate, but she couldn't think of anything else to say.

"Yeah, I'm fine," said Aurie briskly, "and I'm sorry I had to run off like that. Py was supposed to cover for me, but he ended up cracking like an egg." She shook her head and sighed. "Dad always says you can only count on yourself."

Jacqueline tried to hide her surprise. "You were here last night?"

Aurie nodded, smiling faintly.

"And you heard us—over all that wind?"

"My ears are a little more sensitive than they used to be," Aurie said.

No kidding, Jacqueline thought. *And that's just the tip of the iceberg, isn't it?*

"There was something I had to do that couldn't wait," Aurie went on, "but you know that, don't you? By the time I got back here, you guys were busy eating cookies and making plans to tranquilize me. That wouldn't have worked, but it was still easier to wait until Dad left. I figured he would go stir-crazy this morning. Didn't think Py and Uncle Abel would leave too, but I'm glad they did. You're the one I need to talk to, Mom."

A little chill ran down Jacqueline's spine. *Mom?* That name sounded so natural coming from Py, but from Aurie? This girl might look like her child, but there was nothing childlike in those bright green eyes. Jacqueline lowered herself to the porch steps again and set her cup down. Aurie sat down beside her in one weirdly supple motion. Jacqueline studied the face that so resembled her own. There was nothing wrong with any of the girl's features, but together they formed an expression that was unsettling in a way she couldn't define. Eager and yet cold, somehow. Sharp and distant, as if the mind behind those eyes were a hundred light-years away. What was it Py had said? *She's already so different, and not in a human way.*

"First tell me this," Jacqueline said. "What did you want those mushrooms for—the ones you found in the ravine?"

"Oh, Mom, really? We finally get to meet and you want to play this game? Dad never plays games; he's all business, especially when it comes to science. You know the answer—to inactivate the Policeman. He was an enforcer of cellular law." Aurie's eyes glinted with cool humor. "Come on, you know all about him! You're the one who put him there."

"Policeman," Jacqueline muttered. *Ah ... the kill switch.* She looked her daughter in the eye and spoke carefully. "Listen, Aurie. Two days ago, I didn't even know that you and your brother existed. I put that kill switch into my eggs to prevent birth defects, not to turn my kids into an experiment in evolution. What your father did—CRISPR-evo—it's all new to me. And it sure as hell isn't a game." She took a deep breath. "We thought your

239

CRISPR machine wanted that drug in the mushrooms to inactivate the kill switch, but how do *you* know that was the reason? How do you even know about the kill switch?"

"Dad told us about the kill switch—it's the reason he stole your eggs. And the Doctor told me about the Policeman. It doesn't take a genius to figure out they're the same thing." That faint smile was still in place, but Aurie's eyes on Jacqueline were watchful and expectant.

The Doctor. Jacqueline thought fast, uncomfortably aware that she was being tested. "The Doctor is your CRISPR machine?"

The girl nodded and her smile grew. It was the smile of an indulgent professor whose slowest student is finally catching on. "He was controlled by a part of my own mind—a part that was asleep and dreaming."

Jacqueline frowned. *A part of her mind knew how to inactivate the kill switch? What the hell is going on here?* Out loud, she said, "Whatever the dose in the mushrooms was, it must've worn off by now."

"Long before now," Aurie agreed, "which is why we had to kill the Policeman. Cutting him out of my genome gave the Doctor free rein to wake up that sleeping part of my mind. That's what I am now, fully awake."

Cutting him out of my genome ... Jacqueline stared at the little girl sitting beside her, who had just casually claimed to have destroyed the quality control mechanism it had taken years to engineer. Was it possible? Of course CRISPR-evo could remove a genetic obstacle like the kill switch, but how the hell could Aurie be aware of it? How could she know what was going on in her cells?

"Your Doctor—the CRISPR machine—*told* you all this?"

"Well, not literally. The Doctor was a hallucination controlled by my Sleeping Self," Aurie reminded Jacqueline. "Now that I'm awake, he doesn't really exist anymore."

"You mean the CRISPR machine is no longer inside you?"

"Of course it is! Where would it go?" Aurie sighed with frustration. "Is all of this really that hard to understand? Dad said you're one of the best scientists in the world, and he never compliments *anyone*. Dad would get this right away!"

Jacqueline had to restrain a mad impulse to laugh. *My own daughter, a bedraggled eight-year-old who has just wandered out of the woods, is now lecturing me about CRISPR—and talking down to me!* That feeling of unreality, of being caught in a nightmare, washed over her again, stronger this time. Jacqueline gripped her elbows and dug her nails into the flesh there, just hard enough to hurt. The sharp points of pain were remarkably steadying.

"I don't really need the CRISPR-evo machine anymore," Aurie went on. "But it was nice to have help with all the changes I made. So I guess I'm still working with the Doctor, even if he's just my mental image of Dad's tool. You can think of him as my imaginary friend, if that helps."

Again with the polite condescension. Yep, that's Howard's kid all right. So she got rid of the kill switch—but why? What's the end goal?

"What changes are you making now?" Jacqueline asked.

"Well, I'm finished with the important ones." For the first time, Aurie sounded uncertain. "That's why I need your help. I have to preserve them the way you did." She hesitated for a moment, hands clenched on her grimy jeans. "I want you to help me freeze my eggs."

Jacqueline tried not to look as astonished as she felt. *Your eggs? You're eight!* She picked up her coffee cup with trembling hands and took a cold sip. Jacqueline wasn't sure what she had expected from Aurie—clumsy acting, lies, evasion?—but certainly not this straightforward explanation or this bold request. The idea was impossible, of course. The physician who had done Jacqueline's egg retrieval worked for a legitimate company, but also provided illegitimate services on the side. The wait for these special appointments—which didn't require bio-maps or even client identification—was generally months to years. Besides, there was the obvious problem of age. Human females produced all of their eggs before birth, but the release of those eggs wouldn't begin until puberty.

"If you want to freeze your eggs, we have plenty of time," Jacqueline said, trying to sound calm and reassuring. "You're only eight years old. Your eggs won't be ready for years."

"They're ready *now.*" Aurie suddenly tensed, as if to spring. "The Doctor and I spent the whole night getting them ready! We killed the Policeman and woke my Sleeping Self in every single oocyte, and ripened them all with hormones. We only have a few days to get them out."

"Good God." Jacqueline's fingers tightened around her cup as she glared at her daughter. "What the hell is the rush? We can't do this in a few days! First of all, we need a real flesh-and-blood doctor, not an imaginary one. And you're illegally engineered, remember? We can't just go to any doctor—"

"Not any doctor," Aurie interrupted sharply. "*Your* doctor."

"That doctor has a waiting list a mile long! We'd have to wait at least a couple of months."

"That won't work," Aurie said flatly. "We need to see him now. My eggs will all be flushed out in a few days. I've ripened them already!"

"So *un*ripen them," Jacqueline snapped. "You can do anything you want, can't you?"

The girl's face tightened with frustration, but another emotion—closer to pain or fear—seemed to lie just beneath the surface. Some deep longing passed across her features like a fast-moving storm cloud. Jacqueline watched it come and go with increasing bewilderment. What on earth did Aurie want so badly that she had to freeze her eggs right away?

"Besides," said Jacqueline, "we need to talk to your father first."

The storm cloud returned to darken Aurie's face, and her eyes flashed with lightning heat. "Oh, *now* you want Dad's advice? No. Dad can't know anything about this."

"He has to," Jacqueline said sternly. "He's your *father.* And weren't you just telling me how smart he is, how he'd understand

242

all of this right away? Why don't you want him to know?"

"Because he'll want to control my eggs the way he controls everything! He'll turn them into his own personal breeding project and engineer them to death. He'll never understand that he can't make them any better—they are already perfect and complete." Eyes blazing, Aurie looked up into the sky, above the tops of trees flushed with the day's light. Entranced, Jacqueline watched the pulse in her daughter's throat beat like a trapped bird. When Aurie spoke again, her voice was calmer. "I was hoping you'd understand, but I knew you wouldn't. You're a scientist just like Dad—you only believe in things you can see. So I'll have to show you."

Before Jacqueline could marshal a response, something long and snakelike was arcing toward her. There was a sharp pain in her neck, and then total blackness.

It was dark inside the cartoon cell.

Even immersed in that thick, watery gloom, Jacqueline knew where she was. The nucleus of an oocyte—hadn't she studied it for almost twenty years? Fascinated, she looked around at the architecture of the female germ cell, feeling as if she'd been plunged into a textbook animation. Those dense shapes must be ribonucleoprotein complexes—scores of them, getting ready for the order to mobilize and translate their messages into protein. And the X-shaped rafts skulking in the shadows were maternal chromosomes. At fertilization, they would join their paternal partners to reform the diploid genome of every somatic cell. The waters around her were bursting with stored life. Arrested in development but not inert, quietly building the provisions that would be needed later and waiting for the signal to *begin*. She felt no fear, despite the distant, nagging certainty that this was not a dream.

You can't see anything from there.

The voice was familiar, even though she couldn't quite place it. It was like an old memory that had stopped just short of surfacing.

Up here, at the top!

Slowly, Jacqueline swam through the crowded sea, trying to navigate the wacky perspective of the cartoon nucleus. The *top* was a domed ceiling, from which she could survey all the molecular players like a queen overlooking her court. And like a court, the assembly below began to dance.

At first, she thought the chromosomes were moving. But no, something was moving *along* them, like wind rippling through wheat. Wind became light, skimming over the genetic code in radiant hieroglyphs. The interplay of light and shadow created shapes that changed as soon as they appeared. Creatures of terrible, appalling beauty formed and dissipated among others too strange to make sense of. Jacqueline stared in helpless thrall as the gods—for surely these were gods—slipped through her mind like a protean mist. At the touch of a hand on her shoulder, Jacqueline blinked and all the specters dissolved back into a formless dance. She turned to behold someone very like herself. A young girl whose face was lit by the shadow play below.

Each one of my eggs will give rise to a child whose Sleeping Self is fully awake, said the girl. *Awake and ready to fill its place in the Pattern. The Pattern can be fulfilled in many ways. These are just some of the possibilities.*

Jacqueline turned back to look. There *was* a Pattern created by those shifting forms, something unchangeable in the midst of constant flux. A constellation formed by sparks of light dancing in wild abandon—and beyond it, she sensed a greater constellation, formed by life warming a host of worlds scattered across the abyss of time and space. They pulsed in the cold, dead fabric of the universe like the heart of God himself. Her own heart emulated that beat, striking a furious rhythm in its cage, and the cell around her—a seed rich with unformed life—struck its own note. She heard all the music of the universe spoken in a single breath, and something deep inside her cried out in joyful recognition.

You understand!

The voice was triumphant, astonished, and relieved, yet Jacqueline barely heard it. The breath of music had formed a word that seemed to render every question she had ever asked meaningless. In that instant, everything had fit together in perfect simplicity, but now the universe was fractured again and all the insignificant questions had come flooding back. She felt like a cavefish suddenly yanked into the light only to be tossed back down into the dark. As her eyes ran with tears for her own blindness, Jacqueline felt the warmth of small arms around her and the soothing sound of a familiar voice in her ear. She understood that voice now—and she would do anything it asked of her.

Anything at all.

VII

Shopping for groceries so close to lunch was torture for Py, even if this particular trip was more like a visit to the Museum of Strange Foods. At the Gorham Grand Harvest Market, most of the aisles were filled with the usual mixes and instant meals, but Uncle Abel bypassed them completely. In addition to apples and oranges and snap beans, he filled their cart with some extraordinary produce—a purply-black thing shaped like an hourglass, a bulbous orange monstrosity covered in knobs, and some ridged yellow globes. Then he grabbed two gallon jugs of milk and a crate of *brown* eggs, of all things, before heading to the bakery section for three exotic loaves—one swirled, one studded with nuts, and one sprinkled with black seeds. Finally, he stopped at a long, glassed-in counter to pick up some thick chops and a fat coil of sausage.

When his uncle suggested having lunch at a diner, Py jumped all over the idea. But once his hunger was sated—to the familiar tune of a BLT and fries—and they were back on the UTV, a worm of apprehension began to crawl through Py's gut. He had a bad feeling that his sister had returned while he was away, forcing their mom to deal with her alone. Jacqueline was afraid of Aurie hurting herself, when she should have been afraid of Aurie, period.

You should have stayed home, Py scolded himself as they jounced over the rough trail through the woods. When they finally reached his uncle's field, the sick feeling in his gut intensified. Even at this distance, he could see it—that unmistakable alien aura glimmering in the air.

"Oh, crap," said Uncle Abel over the purr of the UTV. Surprised, Py watched his uncle's hands tighten on the steering wheel. Could Uncle Abel see it too?

They rode into the shed and Uncle Abel killed the engine. "Now where the hell did she go?" he muttered as he helped Py down.

"You mean Aurie?" Py took the bags his uncle handed him and they headed for the cabin at a fast trot. "You can see her trail?"

"I mean your mother," said Uncle Abel. Py looked back and realized that his uncle's car was no longer parked next to the RV. He hadn't even noticed.

Inside the cabin, Uncle Abel picked up the yellow notepad on the table and stared at it. He grunted and handed it to Py.

Decided to do a little shopping for some clothes and personal items, the note said. *Thanks for letting me borrow your car. Be back ASAP.*

"That's just an excuse," Py snapped. "Aurie was here! She must've tricked her somehow—" He set the bags down and ran out of the cabin. On the porch, his mother's trail joined the glassy trail of his sister. Without following it, Py could see that the latter trail led all the way to the edge of the woods.

"These are just a little faint," he told Uncle Abel, who had come up behind him. "Hours old." Py followed the two brighter trails that led to the place where the car had been. There, they disappeared into thin air.

"These are a lot fresher." He rounded on his uncle in agitation. "You see what happened? Aurie came out of the woods and talked to her on the porch—or *did* something to her. Then my mom went inside and wrote that bogus note, and they took off in the car!"

Uncle Abel studied him for a moment. "I don't suppose you know where they went?"

Py shook his head, furious with himself for leaving, for being seduced by the lure of a ride on the UTV. "And I can't track them, not when they're inside a car! Their trails disappear right *here—*"

They stood looking at the empty air, then down past the field to the empty road.

"Shit on a shingle," groaned Uncle Abel. "What the hell are we gonna tell your father *this* time?"

Part Five

Taking Flight

I

"I know it's not a hare," Jacqueline said, "but we can always order more." She watched in slightly horrified fascination as her daughter sank her teeth into the beef, pork, and lamb patties of an Oldies Triple Ranch Burger. Aurie ate with a brutal efficiency that in no way diminished her obvious enjoyment of the meal. As Jacqueline bit into her own modest sandwich, a piece of the filling came loose. A dark whipcord lashed out and seized the fallen tidbit, and before Jacqueline had time to blink, both lash and tidbit disappeared.

"Are you crazy?" she hissed. "Keep those things hidden!"

Aurie looked amused. "There's no one here."

It was true—except for the two of them, the Golden Oldies dining room was deserted. Mid-afternoon sunlight shone through crimson-swagged windows to polish a host of empty tabletops. It was a good place to talk without being overheard, and to eat without being seen. Which was good, because Aurie was eating like a starved animal. By the time Jacqueline was halfway through her sandwich, the girl had devoured her giant burger and started on a double-decker club with fries. The sleeves of her clean shirt brushed the table, reaping a harvest of crumbs.

"We're not ready to dine with the Queen just yet," Jacqueline observed wryly. "But at least you're not walking around covered in rabbit blood anymore."

"It was mostly *my* blood," Aurie admitted. "Training sessions in the woods were a little rough."

"You're not hurt, are you?" Jacqueline frowned at her daughter, who looked like a picture of health.

"No, I fixed my injuries right away. Couldn't hobble around on a broken leg or a sprained ankle."

"Well ... you can take a bath as soon as we get home."

"I wish your doctor could see me today!"

Jacqueline shook her head. "It's a miracle he can take you tomorrow morning." A miracle, yes ... and when she'd called his unlisted number from a Cirrus link in Gorham, Dr. Hahn had offered her a surprisingly reasonable price for the rush appointment. Which had still been three times higher than any normal egg extraction.

"Consider it your birthday present for the last eight years," Jacqueline told her daughter, with a wry smile. "And your inheritance, once your father discovers that I kidnapped you."

Aurie paused in mid-chew. She swallowed slowly and a flicker of something that wasn't pure hunger and single-minded intent crept into her eyes. Was it guilt? Appreciation? Humility? Maybe she had been struck for the first time by the thought of consequences to someone other than herself. Whatever the reason, she suddenly looked like a little girl. A *human* girl.

"I will," Aurie said quietly. "Thank you."

Jacqueline nodded and sipped her iced tea, feeling a surge of relief. But a moment later, the child in Aurie's eyes vanished as if it had slipped out a back door, and only the ageless stranger remained. *What if I had refused to help her? What would she have done?* Those threads were a daunting weapon, and it was hard to imagine the cold-eyed girl across the table as helpless under any circumstance.

But it was a moot question. Jacqueline had chosen to help Aurie of her own free will. Having seen the Pattern for herself, she could do nothing else.

As she ate without really tasting anything, Jacqueline found herself drifting back into the company of gods. She couldn't remember any of those fantastic beings in the Pattern, but her mind kept trying to recreate them, wanting to shape them from bits and pieces of more familiar forms. She couldn't recall the music that seemed to be one note—one word—but its echo still resonated deep in her bones. It seemed impossible that Howard, who had uncovered this ineffable buried treasure, hadn't seen any of it.

"Why don't you show him," she said abruptly, "the way you showed me?"

Aurie didn't stop eating, nor did she ask who Jacqueline meant. "What good would it do?"

"He'd understand," Jacqueline said. "He'd understand, and he'd believe you."

Aurie snorted as she reached for her milkshake. "Dad doesn't have a problem believing things. Remember how fast he latched on to the idea that I'm turning myself into an alien? He has a problem letting go. Showing him the Pattern would only make it worse. He'd want to study it ... and mess with it." Her voice grew cynical. "Scientists can't just observe, you know. They have to tinker."

Jacqueline felt a resurgence of the old guilt—her *suicide eggs* had been tinkering of the first order, after all—which was quickly overridden by more immediate concerns. Howard had to see this, he had to know what was going on ... but there was no convincing the mad child in front of her. *Mad?* Jacqueline assessed the hard, bright light in her daughter's eyes, the firm resolve in that small, intelligent face. No, there was no insanity in Aurie, only a boldness that was hard to fathom. The boldness to experiment on herself, to take her evolution into her own hands.

"Aren't you afraid?" Jacqueline asked abruptly.

"Afraid?" Aurie looked at her, bewildered. "Of Dad?"

"Of the Pattern." Jacqueline instinctively lowered her voice even though they were alone. "Of trying to fulfill it. You can't turn yourself into all of those incredible things, and that's why your eggs are so important—because each of them can satisfy the Pattern in a different way. But what are *you* planning to do?"

Aurie looked around the ransacked table and licked her fingers. "There's no planning. I don't get to choose a fate, any more than my kids will. Any more than you chose to have blonde hair and green eyes." Her expression softened and grew remote. "I already *am* what I am. My transformation ... it's more like opening a cage."

Jacqueline waited, but Aurie didn't elaborate further. "And that doesn't scare you? The idea of opening a cage on something completely different?"

"Different from what?" Now that Aurie had eaten, her eyes were calm and clear, like a twilit sea in which distant stars glimmered. "Everything inside the cage is *me*. It's just that none of us really know ourselves." She gestured to a seasonal flyer on the wall. "No one's even comfortable with their own bones."

"Bones remind us of death," Jacqueline said, glancing at the trio of dancing skeletons.

"It's more than that," said Aurie seriously. "If you saw your own skeleton, you'd look away. You'd think, *That's not me—it's an alien hiding in my skin*. But your soul is even stranger than your bones."

"You think we're strangers to our own souls?" Jacqueline considered this disturbing idea in silence. "They say eyes are windows to a person's soul."

As if to test this assertion, Aurie met her mother's gaze and held it without blinking. As she looked into her daughter's eyes, Jacqueline began to see a shape coalescing in their green depths. It was alive and full of vital intent, but it was not human. Nor was it contained within the eyes that held it. If this was Aurie's soul, it filled her the way an ocean fills a tiny shell, one of the billions lying on its bed. This realization was at once exhilarating and terrifying. The tiny caveman buried in Jacqueline's brain—the one who cowered under stone and thatch and steel roofs from the naked regard of the stars—turned away in horror. Suddenly, Jacqueline felt a desperate longing for the comforts of small, familiar spaces, for the fire of the hearth and not the fires of cold and distant galaxies.

"If you could see your own soul," Aurie whispered, "you'd think, *That's not me—it's an alien hiding in my bones*." She laughed softly. "And maybe it is."

The door behind them opened with a shivering of glass chimes, breaking the spell of Aurie's eyes. Cosmic impressions fled like remnants of a dream, and Jacqueline turned to see a teenage girl burst into the restaurant. The girl was arguing with the holo-image of a little boy that rose from the pink Spider on her wrist.

"—Dad said we could have Vitanuggets!" the boy wailed.

"We had those on *Friday,*" the girl said, with all the withering scorn of big-sisterhood. "Mom said to get real meat tonight. And don't pretend you're allergic—you had a hot dog at Tyler's house yesterday and you were fine!"

As the girl approached the service counter, Jacqueline suddenly realized how dark it had gotten. The sky beyond the windows had leached to the colors of dusk, and all of the ceiling lamps in the dining room were lit. She glanced down instinctively to check her own Spider before remembering that it was still locked in the trunk of her car at the Little Pitcher. How long had they been sitting here? Talking with Aurie made her lose track of time completely.

"Are you still hungry? I think we'd better get going."

"I'm good for a few hours," Aurie assured her, snatching up the last scraps of bun and slivers of onion. "You don't have to worry about Dad following us, you know. Py must've seen my trail outside the cabin, but he can't see through walls. We're untraceable in the car."

Jacqueline nodded, but didn't say what she was thinking. Having no other leads, Howard would almost certainly head to her house in Cambridge, or to her lab. It would be best to call him from a Cirrus link—there was even one in the corner of this old-fashioned restaurant—but Jacqueline couldn't quite bring herself to do that. It wasn't a desire for payback, although the idea of leaving Howard in the dark, just for a day, had an undeniable appeal. In the matter of Aurie's eggs, Howard was an unknown variable. He couldn't help with the operation, he could only hinder it. So she wouldn't contact him or be foolish enough to retrieve her Spider. She would just have to hope that he didn't show up at her house tonight.

Looking at her daughter, Jacqueline wondered—was it the Pattern inveigling her to help, the silent will of gods waiting to be born? Was it the pull of that unremembered word, a word that had shed light and meaning on all of existence? Or was it loyalty to her daughter—and a desire not to fail in the first thing Aurie had ever asked from her? *Maybe it's all of those things,* she thought, knowing none of those reasons would stand up in Howard's court.

"Even if they don't catch us," she said, shaking the sole survivor out of her fry carton, "we're going to have to explain ourselves when we get back."

Aurie reached for the fry, but Jacqueline laid a firm hand over hers.

"I won't say anything about your eggs," Jacqueline promised. "Because they're yours. But you need to talk to your dad about this ... transformation."

"Yeah, but—" Aurie began.

"No buts," Jacqueline said flatly. "You don't have to show him what you showed me, but you need to tell him what you're doing. Don't you think he deserves to know?" She held her daughter's eyes, uncomfortably aware of what was missing in them. She saw fear and frustration underlying Aurie's determination, but no love, no empathy. Feeling suddenly heartsick, Jacqueline released her daughter's hand and swept up the cartons and wrappers on the table. There *was* a little girl in there—Jacqueline had caught glimpses of her, like an occasional sunbeam breaking through a dense cloud cover. But how to draw her out? How to keep her from disappearing entirely?

That's why I'm taking her home, Jacqueline realized suddenly. *If I really wanted to avoid Howard, I'd check us into a motel, but ...* But a motel—cold and impersonal—was too much like the stranger in Aurie, and Jacqueline wanted to appeal to the human in her.

As she got up to leave, the poster with its dancing skeletons caught Jacqueline's eye. All three skulls had the same expression, the only one a skull could have: a grin, as if they shared a secret she would never understand. *That's the alien hiding in my skin,* she thought with a chill. *And maybe there's another one hiding in my bones.*

II

Aurie sat in silent turmoil as her mother drove them south to Cambridge. So Jacqueline would only keep Aurie's eggs a secret if she submitted to an interrogation by the President and CEO of CRISPR-evo, Inc.? That couldn't happen ... if she gave her father an inch, he would take a light-year. She knew better than to underestimate him. And not just her father—also her brother, whose tissues were swarming with an army of Policemen.

You have nothing to fear from them, she told herself. *If an army found its way into your cells, you could subdue it.*

But that would take energy, and some long-held instinct whispered that she needed to save her energy for the transformation to come. Besides, there was another enemy, one that lived somewhere in her own cells and was not so easily subdued.

Through the cracked windshield of the old car, looming ranks of clouds dispersed and reformed, alternately revealing and obscuring the westering sun. On both sides of the highway, the countryside unrolled in a stretch of softly canopied trees. Aurie gazed at them with faint contempt. She had felt at home among the ancient pines, with their rock-bound roots and their highest branches straining toward the sky. She missed the wild solitude of the mountains, but there had been no time to linger there. The pull of her own pattern within the larger Pattern was too strong to brook any delays.

Aurie snuck a glance at the woman behind the wheel, feeling the competence and assurance that Jacqueline exuded. It was a calm authority, totally different from Howard's spastic, fiery tension. Both of them had an edge, Aurie thought, but her father's was jagged and unpredictable, whereas her mother's was like the smooth and constant line of a samurai blade. If only Jacqueline were on her side completely! The Pattern had convinced Aurie's mother to help, but she was still torn by human principles and loyalties.

Jacqueline turned to meet Aurie's glance, her eyes bright and questioning. She smiled with a sudden warmth that made her seem instantly familiar, as if she had been a mother to Aurie her whole life. Jacqueline reached out and stroked Aurie's cheek, then returned her hand to the wheel without a word. Aurie sat flustered for a moment, in the grip of sudden confusion. She had subdued her old self in the woods, yet there had been moments when it still managed to sneak a word or a thought in. That old personality—an entity she thought of as a kind of ghost—was very close to the surface now, trying to bask in her mother's affection. Aurie quickly wrestled it back down before it could gain a foothold on her consciousness.

She understands the pull of the Pattern, and she cares about me, Aurie thought, still watching her mother surreptitiously. But would Jacqueline protect Aurie from a father who wanted to study her and wrest control of her fate? Suddenly, her old self sent up a flare of love and loyalty for Howard that threw Aurie's thoughts into chaos before she managed to quench it. This time, it took all the strength she could muster to overpower the usurper.

And this, she knew, was the problem. Her father and brother posed no real danger, but she couldn't entirely trust herself. If that troublesome ghost rose up at a critical moment ... Aurie shuddered at the thought. Because of the traitor inside her, it was best to steer clear of her family until her transformation was complete. And if she *couldn't* avoid them ... Her cheek was still warm where her mother had touched her, but Aurie's mind had already moved on to colder realms of problem solving.

By the time they reached Cambridge, all the clouds had drifted away, leaving the skies a deep and velvety blue. They filled Aurie with nostalgia and a longing that made her tremble. There were too many city lights to see the stars, but a portion of the sky drew her like a homing beacon. She stared through the windshield across that vast distance until the tops of roofs and trees blocked her view. They were ascending a low hill, coming up on a brick cottage at the end of a cul-de-sac street. A gentle rise of lawn swept up to the porch, which was flanked by a rickety wooden gate overgrown with ivy.

They parked in a small garage, then walked up a path to the house, as ground lanterns lit themselves just ahead of their feet. On the porch, pots of peppers and cherry tomatoes hid their fruit in the shadows. Jacqueline opened the touch-lock on the front door and Aurie followed her into a well-lit foyer opening onto a spacious main room. She looked around and her mouth fell open.

There were books here, real books. Not just one or two, like she had back in the RV, but floor-to-ceiling shelves filled with them! And these books were *old,* their spines creased and cracked and faded. She could smell the secretive aroma of tales wrapped like treasures in ancient paper. Ranks of exotic spices in the guise of volumes tempted her, called to her, and something inside her leapt up like a hungry flame. Fearing that ghost, Aurie forcibly turned her gaze from the bookshelves.

With relief, she caught sight of a trio of vases on the mantel—pottery that might have been shaped on far worlds and dipped in the blood of unearthly races. She moved closer to admire them, liking the bold curves and angles, the raw color and depth of the brilliant glazes. Then she cast her gaze around the rest of the room. Most of the furnishings were rustic and prosaic: a tall brass lamp, a few pieces of worn and comfortable-looking furniture. Two rag rugs appeared to be woven out of strips torn from bright summer dresses.

"What do you think?" Jacqueline was still lingering in the doorway.

"It's not what I expected," Aurie said.

"What did you expect?" There was the hint of a smile in her mother's voice.

Aurie hesitated, trying to put her finger on it. "More metal and glass, I guess. More equipment. Where do you do experiments when you're home?"

Jacqueline chuckled as she walked into the room. "I only do

experiments in the lab. When I'm home, I read and cook and work in my garden. And metal and glass can be beautiful, but they're not very cozy to live with." She looked around her own house as if seeing it for the first time. "Those bookcases were made by your great-grandfather ... that lamp was my mom's favorite ... and that set of bull horns was my dad's pride and joy. Every time Mom threw them away, he rescued them from the dumpster. She finally just gave up in disgust!"

"What did your parents do?" Keeping her eyes off the bookshelves, Aurie poked a toe at the rag rug, then sank into an armchair big enough to swallow her up.

"For a living?" Jacqueline picked up a chunk of petrified wood and turned it absently in her hands. "Before they retired, they were structural engineers. They helped design the Port Dome in Manhattan back in the forties, and the city centers in Baltimore and Atlanta."

"Engineers?" Aurie frowned at the faded and inaccurate lines of an Old World map hanging above the mantel. "I've seen pictures of the Port Dome—it looks like a space capsule. Why didn't your parents want to live in a place like the ones they designed?"

Jacqueline shrugged as she replaced the chunk of wood. "Who knows? People are complicated."

Aurie shifted restlessly in the big armchair. Maybe some people were complicated, but scientists and engineers ought to be as simple and focused as laser beams. For the movers and shakers of the world, all aspects of their lives should be consistent with whatever mission drove them. She thought of the stark walls of their old lab in Westborough, and the clean lines of the RV, where every object and fixture had a function. Glancing down, she noticed a paperback lying on the end table: *The Martian Chronicles*. Unable to resist, Aurie picked it up cautiously. Although faded, the painting on the old cover was detailed and exquisite. Golden-skinned people crouched beside canals winding through ochre dust. The water of the canals reflected a cerulean sky.

"Do you like science fiction?" Jacqueline asked.

Aurie was quiet, staring down at the Martians on the cover. Her old self *loved* science fiction and fantasy, which made it hard to resist the allure of the book in her hand. She opened it carefully and felt the paper inside, yellow and fragile as old skin.

"Maybe something closer to home." Jacqueline went over to the shelves, returning with a well-worn volume that she handed to Aurie with great care. "I read this when I was eleven and it's still one of my favorites."

All-of-a-kind Family? As soon as Aurie saw the title, her old self burst through, spilling out words before she could choke them back. "You have this book *in print?* It's my favorite!" Aurie watched helplessly as her hands paged quickly and eagerly through the book.

Go away! Aurie spat, fighting the unexpected strength of her old self. The thrill of seeing her favorite story in real paper and ink had given the ghost surprising power.

This story has weight, the ghost informed her. *The words are sharper on paper—they look like they're about to leap off the pages! And look at all these illustrations!*

"It's yours," said Jacqueline, with a smile. "I'd better get started on dinner. How about a shower now? Or would you rather have a bath?"

"A bath?" Aurie was caught off guard. "In a ... bathtub?"

"Where else?" her mother said, giving her a bemused look before heading off down the hall. Aurie tried to set the two books down on the end table and failed; the ghost that controlled her fingers stubbornly refused to release its grip. Stifling a snarl, Aurie caught up with her mother in the bathroom.

Oh, what a room! exclaimed the ghost. *Soft green mats, and lights shaped like lanterns!* Aurie looked around in helpless vexation. An enormous clawfoot tub held court in the middle of the room. *Who has time to lounge around in a tub?* she growled, as her old self continued to squeal with delight.

"Can I really take a bath?" asked the ghost. Aurie cringed at the sound of her own voice.

"Of course you can," said Jacqueline, taking bottles out of a cabinet. She ran hot and cold water in the tub, then drizzled in something from one of the bottles. The air filled with the light, sharp scent of pine needles. Trying to clear her pounding head, Aurie leaned over the tub and inhaled deeply. Her mother's footsteps pattered away, then Jacqueline returned with a stack of towels and Aurie's overnight bag.

"Should I take a shower first?" asked the ghost. "So I don't get the water all dirty?"

Jacqueline chuckled. "No, you don't have to shower first. Just sit there as long as you like and let the dirt loosen up on its own. Then scrub yourself good and rinse off. And don't worry, there's no correct protocol. No wrong way to take a bath." Still smiling, she left the room, closing the door behind her.

Sitting on the floor with her back against the tub, Aurie shut her eyes and imposed order on herself. Once every overexcited nerve had been restored to a state of calm, she managed to release her grip on the old paperbacks. Then she searched for the part of her that should have lapsed into inert silence when she awoke in the ravine. Its unbridled interference was becoming a serious threat. As soon as her eggs were frozen, it would be time to activate the Pattern in one specific way. She had to be in control for that, not plagued with another, conflicting will. And this old self was nothing but a child, with a child's trivial desires and foolish loyalties. She hunted it through all the cells of her body, but there was nothing tangible to latch onto. No set of genes or proteins or molecular players formed the fabric of her past self. And yet she could sense that undermining presence everywhere—lurking in every neuron, running free in her blood, haunting the deep places in her bones.

Hissing with frustration, Aurie undressed and stepped into the tub. The water was just hot enough to steam, and she slid down until the suds reached her neck. The water surrounded her like warm silk, leaching all the tension and stiffness from her joints, easing muscles she hadn't realized were sore. Of course, the whole idea of a bath was ridiculous. Her father's showers were invariably two-minute affairs, and she and Py were nearly as fast. They had to be—the bathroom in the RV was just a tiny cubicle that always ran out of hot water, so there was never any time to dillydally. Aurie tried to imagine Jacqueline lying here with a novel in her hand, not thinking about her work at all, just lost in another world. Did her mother actually do that? The brilliant biologist whom her father admired more than anyone?

Of course she doesn't! No serious scientist would waste time sitting in a bathtub. This thing is probably just for decoration—and for lazy guests. Annoyed with herself, Aurie reached for soap and washcloth, and scrubbed herself from head to toe. On the verge of pulling the stopper out, she paused. A bath might be an extravagance, but a *five-minute* bath was surely a waste of water. Sinking back into the luxuriant warmth, she decided to stay in just a little longer. As she settled herself in the tub, her eye fell on the books she had laid down.

All-of-a-kind Family ... Aurie understood why her old self had been so enamored of this book. It echoed aspects of her own life while depicting a way of life that was utterly foreign to her. The poor family's living quarters—like her own in the RV—were comfortably cozy, but they lived in a bustling neighborhood full of people. The horror and excitement of living in a *community* had given Aurie a secret thrill. She had gone along like a sixth sister on their excursions to the street market, jostling through the crowds and munching her share of penny treats from the pushcart peddlers. And Sabbath dinners, with their little joys and somber rituals, had been a much-loved tradition for her, the sort of thing that was missing in her own life.

But she didn't dare to rouse the ghost by reading her favorite book. Aurie dried her hands on a towel and reached for the other novel, *The Martian Chronicles*. She gazed for a moment at the golden masks of the Martians, at the sky that seemed to stretch past the edges of the cover into a deep blue infinity. Then she settled back into the suds, opened the book to the first page, and began to read.

She could have finished the slim volume in a matter of

minutes, absorbing each page as a snapshot of words instantly decoded and translated into the moving picture of a story. But the story itself discouraged such speed. So Aurie matched its dreamy pace, watching as three men from Earth stood outside their spaceship listening to inexplicable music from a piano and a phonograph drift on the Martian air. She followed along as they entered the Martian town that looked so much like Green Bluff, Illinois, in the year 1926. One of them glimpsed the house with the iron rooster that had belonged to his own long-dead grand-parents, and she ran with him to the front porch as he laughed and cried and called for them. But when the smiling old couple came to the door, Aurie knew them at once. The spacemen from Earth didn't know, but she knew who these kindly-looking folks were, *what* they were. She understood that ghosts from the past never lose their power, and that masks sometimes come in the form of human faces. Aurie slipped naturally and easily inside the two Martians. As she spoke to the men, inviting them in for iced tea and supper and their unsuspecting deaths, she forgot herself.

And all at once, the driver's seat in her mind was empty.

III

A smart rap on the door jerked Aurie back to Earth. The rap was followed by Jacqueline's voice. "You haven't drowned in there, have you? Dinner's ready!"

Aurie called back a response, then closed the book and blinked as the bright fixtures of the room steadied themselves around her. She felt jolted out of a long and terrible dream. In this nightmare, she was trapped in her cartoon cell, not looking *in*, but *out*, as whatever terrifying thing the Doctor had unleashed drove her through the woods. Trees flashed past as she scaled cliffs and hunted small animals; once she screamed, on the brink of leaping from a high ridge. She desperately hoped Py was following, that he could help her, but he never caught up. After nightfall, the walls of her prison thinned just enough for her to wrest command of her legs; she ran back the way she had come to find her brother asleep under a rocky overhang. She struggled then with the presence that had taken over her mind and body, but to no avail. Thrust back into her cell, she could only watch as that alien entity took full control of her conscious thoughts and actions, even filtering her memories through its cold and unfamiliar perspective. Incensed, Aurie continued to beat and tear at the walls of her prison, and at times the walls had thinned again—just enough for her voice to be heard, for her will to be briefly manifested. Sitting bewildered in the cooling waters of the bath, Aurie had no idea how she'd managed to get free—but it was like breaking out of a coffin into fresh air and open daylight.

She looked around the room, feeling the relief of sitting at the helm of her own mind, the pleasure of casting her gaze in any direction she chose. She was herself again.

And more than myself, Aurie thought, as she pulled the

drain and listened to the bathwater gurgle away. That other self was still inside her; she could feel it. What the Doctor had awakened was no longer a separate entity; she and it were as close as two lungs, sharing the same breath, the same purpose. The antipathy of this other self was gone, and so was her fear of it. She understood it now—not with her mind, but in some deeper way. Feeling strangely whole for the first time in her life, Aurie rinsed herself, then toweled off. She got dressed and went to find her mother.

The house was redolent with the aroma of garlic and sautéed beef. Lamps in the dining room were lit, and two places were set at the scarred wooden table, with real napkins and a glass of milk beside each plate. Aurie felt a queer little stab of nostalgia for a dining ritual she had never known. A formal meal just for her? She poked her head into the kitchen, where her mother was stirring the contents of a steaming pot on the stove.

Jacqueline turned to her with a smile. "Are you hungry?"

"Starving," Aurie said. "Can I help with anything?" She laid the books gently on the kitchen counter and walked over to the stove.

Jacqueline stopped stirring and fixed Aurie with a searching glance. Then she set the spoon down and handed Aurie a bowl of pasta shaped like little trumpets to carry to the dining room. After the pasta came a bowl of greens glistening with oil and vinegar, then Jacqueline brought in the pot with its maddening aroma.

"Beef stroganoff," she said, setting it on a cooling plate on the table. "The easy version. Sit down and let's eat! I'm starving too."

Despite her appetite, Aurie couldn't eat with Gollum-like abandon. It was one thing to devour a freshly-killed animal in the middle of the woods—or even a hamburger at a roadside restaurant—but this was a real dinner in her mother's home. Meals in the RV were always slapped together and wolfed down so they could get back to the lab. This meal was nothing like that. It reminded Aurie of her all-of-a-kind family's Sabbath dinners. She savored the simple flavors of the stew, the tender resilience of the pasta, even the bitter tang of the salad. And she found herself enjoying the quiet company of her mother.

"This is the best dinner I've ever had," Aurie murmured, helping herself to another serving.

"It's nothing fancy," said Jacqueline, but she sounded pleased. "Just a quick stew. I didn't even have fresh mushrooms, only canned ones." She paused for a moment, watching Aurie eat. "You must have something better than this on your birthday."

Aurie thought back while she chewed. "One year, the freezer went out on our birthday, so we had to eat whatever was in there. Popsicles, fish sticks, tater tots, old leathery ice cream bars." She giggled a little, remembering. "Instead of a cake, Dad let us toast marshmallows for S'mores on the Bunsen burner."

Jacqueline didn't look amused at all. "I knew he wasn't feeding you right."

Aurie shrugged. "Dad says nutritionists are always changing their minds about what's good for you, so we might as well just eat whatever we want. He says a body's nothing but a mess of dumb tissues, anyway—it's the head on top that's important."

"And how does he expect the brain in your head to work on a diet of popsicles and fish sticks?"

A coldness had crept over Aurie's thoughts at the talk of her father. "It's *his* brain that matters," she said. "We're just part of the lab, you know. Two walking petri dishes." She could feel her mother's troubled gaze, but she kept her eyes down as she forked up salad greens.

"That's not true at all," Jacqueline said. "God knows your father's not perfect, but he loves you and Py more than anything. And he's incredibly proud of you."

"He's proud of *himself*," Aurie countered flatly. That sentiment belonged to her other self, but the feeling had spread to her through the intangible fabric of their joining. "Everything we do is just a credit to him and his brilliant ideas."

Jacqueline lapsed into silence while Aurie finished the last remnants of the meal. She was no longer ravenous, only wanting to enjoy the experience of a real dinner a little longer. As she scraped the empty pot, her mother chuckled.

"Glad you liked my Twenty-Minute Stroganoff. I'll make the real thing for you sometime." But Jacqueline's face clouded over as she got up from the table, and Aurie knew she was wondering if there would ever *be* a sometime.

After they washed the dishes together, Jacqueline made a pot of hot tea with honey and lemon. As they wandered back into the living room with their mugs, Aurie looked around with new eyes. Her grandmother's brass lamp cast a warm glow onto the worn sofa and armchair, and Aurie saw a richness in the old fabrics and worn wood, a story and a history told by every loved possession. Her own history.

"Do you really sit out here and read?" Aurie asked, fingering the worn titles on the bookshelves.

"Every night before I go to bed," Jacqueline said. "It's how I unwind."

"I thought you wouldn't have time to read. For fun, I mean."

"Work is fun, if you have the courage to do what you love." There was a light in Jacqueline's eyes that reminded Aurie of her dad. "And fun is work, if you want real satisfaction from your hobbies." She picked up a copy of *The Dosadi Experiment* and gazed at it intently. "How do you think I get ideas for work?"

Aurie blinked, taken aback. "Dad always says everyone has the same ideas, and it's just a matter of who gets the job done."

"Most scientists do have roughly the same ideas," Jacqueline allowed, "but a few—maybe one or two in a generation—are truly original, and way ahead of their times. Your father should know; he's one of them."

Aurie stared at her mother, startled to realize that Jacqueline admired Howard as much as he admired her.

"Of course, these wizards sometimes get thrown in prison," Jacqueline went on, "or forced into hiding. But they're the ones who take humanity forward. And these guys,"—she gestured across the ranks of Zelazny and LeGuin and Wolfe and

Heinlein—"are always probing the bounds of the universe, waiting for all the scientists to catch up."

Aurie looked incredulously at the names of writers who surely didn't know a pipet bulb from a deflated balloon. "So you get your science ideas from science *fiction?*"

"Ideas, inspiration, perspective." Jacqueline slid Frank Herbert's novel back into its place, then picked up her mug and sipped deeply. "It's hard to be a creative thinker if you never leave your own head."

"How does *he* do it, then?" Aurie asked quietly. As far as she knew, her dad had never poked his nose into a novel in his life. "He never leaves his own head."

"That's probably because his head's a lot bigger than everyone else's," Jacqueline said dryly, and they both snickered.

"I guess Dad *is* a genius," Aurie conceded. "But he couldn't have done what he wanted without your eggs. He took all of them, didn't he?"

"Every last one," Jacqueline said. "But after seeing what he did with them, how can I complain?"

"You're not mad at him?"

Jacqueline snorted. "I've never been so mad at anyone! But I'm glad he stole my eggs, because you and Py wouldn't exist if he hadn't. I'd have a Jack and a Jane instead—two regular kids making mud pies in the yard and needing help with their homework."

Aurie considered this as she sipped her tea. "You really just wanted to have normal kids? You weren't planning to use your eggs for the same thing as Dad?"

"Good God, no! I'm not a lunatic—I mean a genius—like your father." Jacqueline glanced at Aurie curiously. "Did you ever wish you were just a plain vanilla kid instead of the CRISPR-evo variety?"

Aurie only shook her head, but her disgust must have been evident, because her mother laughed a little. Aurie had never spent any time with other kids, but she always pictured them the way her father spoke of them—as dull-witted, noisy, troublesome, and useless. Why on earth would she want to be like that?

"Of course not," Jacqueline said. "And especially not now." She sank onto the couch and Aurie settled herself in the giant armchair. They sipped their tea in a silence broken only by the occasional hum of a car on a distant street. Outside the bay window, the full moon had risen, bloated and golden above the city. The wings inside Aurie's head began to stir, brushing the walls of her mind with maddening pressure. *Are you finished playing house?* they seemed to be asking. All at once, the tea tasted oversweet and cloying, and the armchair was too soft, miring her like quicksand.

"I know you have this transformation to undergo," Jacqueline said abruptly. "But what's the mad rush? Why do you have to do it so soon?"

Aurie set her mug down and sat up straight. "The part of me that woke up has something like wings, and they want—" She broke off as the cramped rustling in her mind grew more agitated. "They want to get out."

Jacqueline watched her intently. "Is that the transformation? You said it would be like opening a cage."

"Yeah." Aurie tried not to squirm, even though she felt like an animal caught in a trap. Perspiration broke out in a fine layer on her scalp, and she adjusted her body's chemicals automatically. "As soon as my eggs are safe, I'll activate one fulfillment of the Pattern—to free those wings."

"And you know how to do that?"

Aurie nodded. If she reached past the place where her two selves were joined, she could sink into that knowledge like fingers into a glove.

Jacqueline shook her head pensively. "You should have gone to your father, you know. He's the one who started all this. And he can't wait to see CRISPR evolution in action."

"*You* don't want to see it?" Aurie couldn't believe that her mother felt no excitement or curiosity at all. "Even though I showed you the Pattern? You're the only one who understands why I have to do this."

"I don't understand *why*, but I understand your need to try.

I feel it too, even though it scares me to death." Jacqueline raised her mug, then lowered it again. "I hate not knowing what's going to happen to you."

Aurie saw the fear in her mother's eyes, and hastened to re-assure her. "I'm not going to die, Mom, I'm going to be born! My head is a coffin holding something that's buried alive—" She shivered as her caged wings struggled to break their confinement, twisting with pent-up fury against the walls of her mind.

Jacqueline came and put a blanket around her, but Aurie shook it off, unable to bear another restraint.

"That part of me will get weaker the longer it's trapped," she gasped. "But it won't leave until my eggs are safe. That's why I had to Change my eggs right away, why I have to freeze them *now*. I don't have years or months, only a few days—"

She clutched the sides of the chair to keep from running out into the night. Her winged self was convulsing against a billion chambers—every cell at the pinnacle of this clumsy bastille. *What's a body?* her dad had said. *Nothing but a mess of dumb tissues. It's the head on top that's important.* Now she realized with acute clarity that even her head was a mess of dumb tissues, a prison holding her real self captive.

Her mother knelt by the armchair, her eyes wide and scared. "And what happens if you don't free it in time?"

The struggles of her intangible wings weakened and finally abated. Aurie unclenched her hands and blinked the tears from her eyes. If she didn't free those wings in time, her other self would die like a chrysalis hatching in a jar. And now that they were joined, *she* would die too. In some cool and remote way, Aurie knew that her own life was an insignificant thing, the life of her winged self far more important, and the life of her eggs more precious still—her eggs had to be preserved at any cost. But they were being retrieved in the morning, so there was no point in worrying her mother for nothing.

"I don't know," Aurie said quietly. "But I'll probably wish I was just a plain vanilla kid, after all."

She had no need for sleep, but Aurie let herself be put to bed in the upstairs guest room without protest. Although she could have lain comfortably on a snowbank in a winter gale, she let Jacqueline draw a thick quilt over her, then grasped her mother's hand. Jacqueline squeezed back and kissed Aurie on the forehead—a kiss that resonated down to her toes. Once she was alone, Aurie opened the curtains and the casement window to let in the cold night air. Then she lay down again, gazing at the square of dark sky imprisoned in the window frame.

Part of her mind sailed into that darkness, and another part turned unwillingly to her father. As she thought of her dad, who had surely never intended for his kids to wander outside the walls of their petri dishes, Aurie felt both guilt and resignation. Howard had expected them to change in exciting new ways—but ways that he could understand using lab tools and techniques. A ridiculous expectation, considering the nature of evolution, but Aurie knew her father. He would never be satisfied until he had analyzed her changes for himself. And what would all of that data give him? Only a misleading glimpse into her true state. He would be like one of those fabled blind men groping at one small part of an elephant.

Some things, she thought, *have to be experienced to be understood.*

Aurie didn't sleep, but fell into a kind of half-doze as the winged part of her began to dream an ancient memory. She imagined crossing the abyss, traversing light-years of darkness like a bird flying over the ocean, one who discerns its position by instinct, never doubting that it will reach shore. Deep in uncharted space, a new shore was forming. Every ray of light, every grain of dust, every breath of stellar wind moved in anticipation of it, in a cosmic dance too slow to be seen.

IV

From behind the wheel of the rental car, Howard watched his son come running back under the stark light of the halogen lamps. Py was shaking his head, and that was not a good sign.

"They didn't come here," Py said, plopping himself into the passenger seat. "I checked both entrances."

Flummoxed, Howard stared at the darkened building with many of its windows still brightly lit. Jacqueline *had* to have taken Aurie to her lab. Where else would they have gone? *To play CRISPR-evo without you,* added the voice of his discontent, which had been muttering variations on that theme throughout the long drive.

"Let's check inside anyway," he muttered. "See what we can find out."

"The building's all locked up, Dad," Py said, as if this should have been obvious. "It's almost ten."

Howard glanced at his Spider, suddenly realizing how thoroughly he had lost track of time. After a fruitless day of wandering through the woods, he had finally returned to the cabin at dusk. Abel had given him the news about Jacqueline and Aurie, along with a bag of sandwiches and a lift in the RV to Gorham, where Howard and Py had picked up the rental. After disabling the car's self-driving imperative, Howard had driven them south to MIT without stopping, not even for coffee.

Howard drove behind the building and parked in a thirty-minute zone outside the loading dock. Then he donned a Patriots cap and a pair of cheap, drugstore glasses, which garnered a predictable hoot from the peanut gallery.

Howard looked at his son over the rims of his glasses. "You think this is a stupid disguise? Trust me, the best scientists in the world have the worst fashion sense. They'll think I'm a National

Academy member and I'll blend right in."

"You *were* a National Academy member," Py reminded him.

"And you weren't around to be embarrassed by me in those days. Hand me that lock pick set in back, will you?"

Main entrances to older buildings were now guarded by high-tech security systems and scanners, but in general, no one had bothered to update lesser ports of entry. Jacqueline's building at MIT was no exception. They quickly found a maintenance door with a lock that took Howard all of thirty seconds to pick. Once inside, he led Py quickly up a stairwell and down the halls to the Witt lab.

They passed only one person on the way—a distracted fellow speaking rapidly to the black Spider near his ear—but many of the labs were still open. Outside Jacqueline's lab, Howard questioned Py with his eyes—*Do you see their trails?*—but the boy only shook his head. They lingered by the doorway, listening to low voices from inside.

Howard always paid attention to his gut feelings, and now a strong intuition told him to stash his disguise in his briefcase. *You can wear more hats without a hat,* it whispered. And surely whoever was here—grad students or postdocs—would be much too young to recognize an aging rogue geneticist. Py was peering around the doorway, clearly dying to go in, but Howard motioned his son to stay put, then strode into Jacqueline's lab like he owned the place.

"Hey there," Howard said, interrupting two young fellows at their desks. "Is the boss around?"

The two instantly froze, watching him with wary eyes.

"Are you from FIBR?" muttered the dark-haired one, a kid with a high-tech earbud attached to his right lobe like an earring.

FIBR? Howard stiffened at once, then forced himself to relax. He crossed his arms and waited. If they thought he was a FIBR detective, then that's what he would be.

The kid who had spoken dropped his eyes. "We told you guys yesterday on the phone, she's at a *meeting*. In *Seattle.*"

"Funny thing about that," Howard said casually. "She never

actually signed in to that meeting. Didn't even pick up her badge! And no one there has caught a glimpse of her." He let his frown linger on each of them in turn. "As you can imagine, we're concerned for her safety. You should be too."

The other kid, copper-curled and lanky, shifted uncomfortably in his chair. "I'm sure she's fine," he assured Howard, unconvincingly. "We left a message for her, okay? She'll call you when she gets back."

"Make sure she does." Howard turned away, then decided on the spur of the moment to take a quick tour of Jacqueline's domain. It had been almost twenty years since he'd seen the inside of a normal lab. He was struck by the size and depth of the bays, the shiny black-top benches with their ranks of microscopes and centrifuges and dissecting stations. A girl cutting tissues at a microtome glanced up as he passed, then returned to her work. Behind her, a kid who probably got carded at the movies sat hunched over a monitor, staring at Venn diagrams while an untouched nutrapak congealed on his desk. Ten o'clock at night, boss out of town, yet Jacqueline's people were still here, busy working. They wrote countless notes to each other: scraps of paper pinned to boards and taped to fridges and freezers— hectoring, informing, cajoling. *Your mother doesn't work here, jackass. Clean up after yourself! Evo-Devo Club – Fridays at 4:00 p.m. Abstracts for Gordon due Nov. 1. Lee and Jorge, start writing now!* In an isolated nook outside Jacqueline's closed office, Howard leaned in to examine the homemade label on a coffee canister: *Witt Kona Coffee Blend: 1% Kona, 99% Folgers. Upgrade pending RO1 renewal!*

These little notes were oddly painful to see. No matter where Howard looked, the signs of free discussion and exchange with the outside world met his eyes. The healthy banter of a team working in the open, with nothing to hide. And what was Jacqueline doing with all this? Only what she was allowed to do. Solid work, but not the bold and brilliant things she was capable of. Not the things she could have done if she'd gone underground with him ... as she might have to do, now that FIBR was on her tail.

His heart quickened at the prospect of working with Jacqueline—finally, after all these years!—and then he remembered what she had done: stolen their daughter to play CRISPR-evo without him. He paused at the far door to the lab, feeling a miserable ache in his chest. *You did the same thing to her, didn't you? Stole her eggs to play CRISPR-evo alone?*

Yes, but all of that was in the past. They were on the same team now, weren't they?

"Someone from FIBR called yesterday," Howard told Py quietly, as they headed back along the hall. "They must've had Jacqueline on their radar, keeping an eye on her movements, checking every time she left town. And now she's supposed to be at a meeting that she never showed up for! They must think she's gone AWOL." He paused at the entrance to the stairwell. "Her people said they left a message for her, but she hasn't had her Spider the past few days."

"We better warn her," Py whispered back as they hurried downstairs. "Did you figure out what she's doing with Aurie?"

"No," Howard admitted. "But it's getting late, so I'm guessing they've turned in for the night." He consulted his Spider briefly. "She lives about seven minutes away. We can warn her in person."

Py looked surprised. "Someone gave you her address?"

Howard unlocked the rental and slid into the driver's seat. "I broke into a secure cryo facility to steal your mother's eggs," he reminded Py as he started the car and pulled out of the thirty-minute zone. "Do you really think I need help getting her *address?* It's all over the Web, along with the name of her first boyfriend and her favorite color. Even a government goon could find her!"

The sound of footsteps close by jolted Aurie out of her dream.

Her vision telescoped thousands of light-years until the bright fires of a distant galaxy were only the dim flames of the Milky Way, scattered pale across a moonlit slice of sky. Briefly disoriented, she sat up in bed. Quick footfalls moved up her mother's driveway, and the porch steps creaked slightly under someone's weight. A doorbell sounded in the house below.

When the bell rang, Jacqueline felt a rush of mingled disappointment and relief. She hurried to the door, wishing Howard could have arrived before Aurie had gone to bed. *He'll want answers right away,* she thought, feeling fiercely protective of the little girl upstairs, *and the poor girl needs her sleep!*

"Well, it's about time you—" She broke off, startled to see a man in dark clothes and a wide-brimmed hat standing on her porch. He hushed her, then tilted his hat up and pulled his scarf down. It was Dr. Hahn.

"I'm sorry to disturb you at this hour. Can I come in for a few minutes? This won't take long." His voice was quiet and urgent.

"Of course." Jacqueline stood aside and the doctor entered, closing the door behind him and handing her a note. She strained to read it in the faint light from the hall.

Someone may be listening. Do you have an interference generator?

Jacqueline looked at him in surprise, then went to flip a switch near the thermostat. "The last owners had it installed—they were a bit paranoid about government surveillance." She laughed nervously. "This is the first time I've used it."

"You should always have it on," Dr. Hahn admonished her. "Especially while it's still legal. Right now, the government can't outlaw something that protects you from what they aren't supposed to be doing."

Jacqueline frowned at him. "Is there a problem with my appointment tomorrow?"

"Yes," said Dr. Hahn quietly. "I assumed you were making it on behalf of an adult daughter, one you had before you froze your eggs, maybe an adopted child. But I could find no record of a birth or an adoption, so ... given your history and the nature of your work, I must ask. How old is she?"

"She's eight," Jacqueline confessed, flushing with embarrassment. "I know that's too young, but—"

"Eight!" Dr. Hahn drew in a whistling breath, then fixed her with a grim look. "Someone contacted me today, asking questions about you, wanting to know where you are."

Jacqueline's heart sped up. How on earth had Howard known that she was taking Aurie to CryoLife? Was it possible to keep any secrets from that man?

"Who was it?" she asked.

"It doesn't matter who. The important thing is that you don't come to CryoLife tomorrow. It's too dangerous."

Jacqueline stared at the doctor. If he had come in person to cancel her appointment, that meant he distrusted all lines of communication—or he had failed to reach her on her Spider. But she couldn't allow the whole operation to go up in smoke simply because Howard had sniffed it out.

"What if we're willing to take the risk?"

The doctor uttered a humorless laugh. "*Risk* implies the chance of a positive outcome, which is impossible in this situation. And you aren't the only one who stands to lose everything. How long do you think I'd stay in business if I were caught harvesting the eggs of an eight-year-old girl for whom no records exist?" He shook his head. "You must never call my unlisted number again. And I strongly suggest that you behave like a model citizen from now on."

He turned to leave, and Jacqueline grasped his arm.

"Wait! Are you absolutely certain the appointment needs to be canceled? There's a man who might have found out, but he's a friend of mine. He certainly wouldn't try to blackmail you."

The doctor gave a churlish grunt. "The person looking for you is no friend of yours, I can assure you."

"Who is it, then?"

Dr. Hahn didn't answer, only looked at her with a stern brand of sympathy. *I don't know what you planned to do with your daughter's eggs,* his eyes said, *and I certainly won't ask— but quit while you're ahead!*

"Take care of your daughter," he said quietly. Then he let himself out. Tugging the brim of his hat down, the doctor descended her porch steps. A moment later, he was across the street, keeping to the darkness beyond the pools of lamplight.

"What in the world," Jacqueline murmured to herself. She closed the front door and set the old-fashioned deadbolt, then instinctively drew the shades on all the living room windows. She heated up a cup of tea and had just settled herself in the big armchair when the back door opened and closed with a soft click, sending her heart into her throat.

"Jackie, we're home," called a familiar voice in a mock singsong. "Well?" he growled. "Is she here?"

"They both are," said another familiar voice. "And it smells like they had roast beef for dinner!"

Howard and Py appeared at the end of the hall.

"Is the front door too ordinary for you people?" she demanded peevishly, rising to meet them. "How on earth did you get in?"

"It was hardly a challenge. Your back door was unlocked." Howard glanced around the hall. "And speaking of security, do you have an interference generator?"

"It's on," she snapped.

Howard nodded, then spoke briefly to his Spider before following his son into the living room. "I let Abel know that his niece is no longer missing. Py says she's here, and that's good enough for me."

"Of course she's here," Jacqueline said as Py roamed around with apparent fascination. "But I thought your brother didn't have a Spider or a phone or anything."

"He acquired a Ghost Spider at great expense from a dealer I recommended earlier tonight." Howard smiled tightly. "All it

280

took to bring him back to civilization was his whole family barging in, and then running off on him."

Jacqueline frowned. "And why on earth did you come in through the back?"

"We stopped by your lab and found out FIBR is looking for you," Howard said grimly. "They called yesterday and scared the shit out of your grad students. So we parked on the back street and came up the hill behind your house—just in case they have your front door probed."

FIBR? Jacqueline caught her breath, suddenly realizing who Dr. Hahn might have been protecting her from. But— "Why would FIBR be interested in *me,* of all people?"

"They've probably had an eye on you for years," Howard said. "Ever since your eggs made such a splash. Anyone who's ever been in the spotlight is on their shortlist. And then, when you didn't show up for that meeting ... "

Jacqueline groaned. "I should've just told everyone I was on vacation."

"Who would've believed that?" Howard said. "You probably haven't *ever* taken a vacation—and it wouldn't have stopped them from checking up on you. Now where the hell is our daughter?"

Jacqueline ignored him and headed over to give Py a hug. "Thanks for keeping your dad out of trouble. Your sister's upstairs, but you probably know that already." Py gave her a smile and a nod, but he was still distracted, his unfocused eyes tracing invisible paths in the air. He wandered off down the hallway.

"Aurie's upstairs?" Howard turned his attention to the staircase at the end of the hall, then back to Jacqueline. "Is she okay? What's wrong with her?"

"Nothing," Jacqueline assured him, "now that she's had a bath and a decent meal and some sleep."

"So she's still human, then?"

"Of course she is!"

"Then what the hell is going on, Jacqueline? What couldn't wait for me to come back from the woods?"

Jacqueline paused, unwilling to say too much. "She asked me for something, and I agreed to help her."

"Of course she did, and of course you did!" Howard paced the length of the room anxiously. "But what did she want?"

"You don't know?" Jacqueline searched his face, but all she could see was impatience and simmering resentment. Which meant that it was certainly FIBR—and not Howard—who had traced her to CryoLife. Thank God Dr. Hahn had warned her in time.

Jacqueline sighed. With the appointment canceled, there was no reason to keep secrets from Howard anymore ... but Aurie's secrets were still hers to reveal.

"Go ahead and ask her yourself," Jacqueline said, gesturing toward the staircase. "Or, better yet, let her sleep and wait until tomorrow."

V

The whole house was crossed with Jacqueline's and Aurie's tracks, but Py was startled to find that his sister's old aura was perfectly visible again. Strong and bright, no longer strangled by the new aura, but *fused* to it. In the bathroom, at the point where it hovered above a giant tub, her old aura had merged completely with the new one. From this point on, the trail he beheld looked like silky molten glass. It pulsed with warm color and cold star-light, the most beautiful thing he had ever seen. Excitement and relief flooded him.

"Dad—!" But by the time he ran out of the bathroom, his dad was already halfway up the stairs, taking the steps two at a time. Py followed his dad and his sister's trail up the staircase and down a short hall, with Jacqueline's footsteps sounding behind them.

"Aurie?" Howard knocked at a closed door at the end of the hall, then let himself in. Py followed to find his sister's aura leading from the bed to the open window. The night breeze blew in, fluttering the tails of the curtains and making them all shiver.

"Way to keep an eye on your daughter, Jacqueline," Howard said acidly.

Py's mother uttered a short, hard laugh. "You think she would've jumped out the window if she hadn't heard you coming?"

"She's not afraid of *me,*" Howard snapped. "She's afraid of the brute squad, who could be right outside your damn door! She was safe with me, and she was safe back in the woods. Now why in God's name did you drag her here?"

As the two adults argued their way downstairs, bickering like an old married couple, Py poked his head out the bedroom window. There was a strip of gravel below, and a fence bordering

283

the dark stretch of the neighbor's lawn. No sign of his sister anywhere.

"Up here," someone whispered. Py looked up to see a head and shoulders—and an aura like a cloak of star fire—outlined against the night sky. An arm detached itself and beckoned him up to the roof.

"I can't climb up there," he hissed at her.

"Just get outside," Aurie said. "I'll bring you up!"

He climbed onto the window ledge and stood there, looking down at the unforgiving rocks. Before he could glance up, a host of coils wrapped him tightly and lifted him into the starshot air. Py gasped with the shock of it, but the ride was brief, and the coils—strong and cool against his skin—deposited him lightly onto the shingled slope of the roof. The dark threads fanned away from him, retreating to the cave of his sister's arm as she scurried up to the gabled peak. Py crawled up to join her, shivering in a gust of wind. The great amber moon rode high in the sky, limning the rooftops and treetops with cold, ancient light.

"What are you doing up here?" he asked Aurie. "Thought you'd be miles away by now."

She flashed him a grin, perched on the gable like a gargoyle, her nightgown billowing around her. "I heard you and Dad sneaking in the back, so I came up here to hide and listen. But there's nothing worth listening to now."

"You can hear them downstairs? What are they saying?" Py listened closely, but couldn't discern anything intelligible over the keen of the wind.

"Dad's trying to get her to spill the beans, and she won't do it." There was a note of pride in his sister's voice that surprised Py.

"What *are* the beans?" he asked. "What do you want from her?" Aurie didn't answer, and Py chafed silently. This was his real sister, not the stranger, so why wasn't she talking? Why was she only trusting Jacqueline? Finally he said gruffly, "You told me you were changing into something I wouldn't recognize. You promised to show me!"

"If you hadn't spilled the beans yourself," she reminded him, rolling her eyes. But a moment later, she sighed. "I wish I could show you the Pattern. That's an evolutionary template in our genomes—in every genome on Earth. I used my threads to show Mom, but I can't do that with you."

"Why not?"

She was quiet for a moment. "You really don't know?"

Py racked his brain, feeling stupid for the umpteenth time that day.

"Your Policeman, Py," Aurie said.

"My *what?*"

"The kill switch Mom put into her eggs! If the Policeman gets into my nerves, I'll have to fight him off to stay alive ... and I need to save my strength."

"Oh!" The knowledge sank in with a jolt. "Of course. Your cells probably have a million red flags in them because of your Change. I never thought about that."

"I'm sure Dad has." Aurie's voice suddenly hardened into the one Py recognized from the woods. "You're the perfect tool to use against me."

"Use *against* you?" Py shook his head. "Dad doesn't want to hurt you! He's worried about you."

She ignored this. "Listen to him down there, all full of threats and demands. He acts like he's a chess master and this is just a big game."

"He has to act that way," Py said, surprised at the sudden insight. "You talked to me out in the woods, remember? And then you went to Mom while the rest of us were away. But you never went to him."

"He thinks she dragged me here," Aurie said flatly.

"I think he tells himself that because he doesn't want to believe that you trusted her and not him." Py tensed up against the wind and clamped down on his teeth to keep them from chattering. Aurie looked totally comfortable out here, and he didn't want her to see how cold he was. "Well, if you can't show me what you're going to do, at least tell me."

Aurie shifted on her perch with a sound like rustling wings. She glanced up at the night sky and moonlight turned her face into something sculpted and ageless. Then she began to speak, telling him about her Sleeping Self and the Pattern and a distant galaxy. She wove the constellations for him until he could see every one as clearly as the Big Dipper and Orion and Gemini. She described a world of deserts and rock labyrinths, of supersonic winds that raced through bleak caverns, and storms above dark methane seas. He fell under the spell of her voice, seeing what she saw through the billowing star-fire shell of her fused aura.

"Where is this planet?" Py whispered, not knowing if he was speaking to his sister or to the stranger inside her. "And what could possibly live there?"

"I don't know." Aurie sighed, and now she was only herself again, crouched small in her pale nightgown on the rooftop. "I'm not even sure it exists yet."

"Why are all of these things happening to *you?*" Py blurted out, startled by the envy in his voice. "Why are you the one talking to your CRISPR machine and waking up your Sleeping Self and turning into—whatever you're turning into? You don't even know, do you?"

"Well, Dad would say it's epigenetics," Aurie said at last, a trace of irony in her voice. "But why? Who knows why. Maybe because I'm a girl, and, well ... girls mature faster."

Her explanation rang hollow. Py knew what she meant; the random power of epigenetic chance could explain how she—and not he—had been chosen for this strange fate, but not why. If there *was* a why. He scowled at the night sky, then caught a whiff of a woodsy aroma as something was pressed into his hand. Something light and dry.

"Almost forgot," Aurie said. "I took this for insurance, and I've been carrying it around awhile. Better keep it in case you need it."

The thing she had given him was a dried mushroom, twisted and shrunken in the moonlight. "Isn't it poisonous?"

"Yeah, but don't eat the whole thing—just break a little

piece off the edge. Your CRISPR machine can handle trace amounts of poison, but when the time comes, he'll need help with the Policeman. Trust me on that."

Py grunted, but he slipped the mushroom gently into his pocket. Then he noticed that the voices inside the house had fallen silent.

Maybe they've killed each other off, he thought wryly, scuttling down the roof to listen at the eaves. The Spider on his wrist pinged and Py brought up the holo-message from his dad.

Did you find her?

Py thought briefly, then typed his answer on the display, hating the lie even as he told it. *Nope.*

Then get back inside & stop roaming around the neighborhood! Do I have to remind you that FIBR is looking for your mom? Aurie can take care of herself & she'll be back in the morning for whatever field trip they have planned. Apparently we'll all talk about it then. Stay here with your mom tonight. I have some things to take care of.

Py frowned, wondering what was going on now. He heard muffled voices downstairs, then the back door opening and closing, and the soft tread of someone moving slowly around the outside of the house. What was his dad doing? Looking for Aurie? Eventually, the footfalls faded down the back hill. A car door slammed, followed by the low hum of an engine as it retreated. Like a wounded animal, thought Py. Or a routed general seeking to regroup.

"Why'd you lie?" Aurie asked in his ear, and he almost toppled off the edge of the roof. She'd come up behind him so silently, he hadn't heard a thing.

"I don't know," Py muttered. He really *didn't* know—except that part of him was still under the spell she had woven, still soaring through the air of that harsh and apparently lifeless world. "But you have to talk to him, Aurie."

"All in good time," she said. "Let me borrow your Spider for a second, okay? I need to look something up."

Py murmured a command to his Spider and it crawled

briskly from his wrist to his sister's outstretched arm. He watched her pull up a map of the city before returning the device.

"You can have my bed down there," she said generously, stretching out on the shingles as if they were a Smart Foam mattress. "I'm sleeping up here tonight." But her eyes, seeking the stars, were bright with moonlight, and he didn't think she would sleep at all.

"I need help getting back down," he reminded her. Again the flurry of dark coils surrounded him, ferrying him down to the window ledge in their cool, snakelike grip. Once he was safely inside the guest room, Py closed the window against the cold night air.

He thought for a moment, and then opened it again. Just a crack.

After arguing with the mother of his children for half an hour, Howard was in a foul mood. He had insisted that with FIBR breathing down their necks, secrecy was a luxury they couldn't afford—and why the hell did they want to keep any secrets from *him?* But no matter what he said, Jacqueline refused to tell him what she and Aurie were up to. It galled and frightened Howard, and hurt him in a deep way that he refused to dwell on. Jacqueline had only said there'd been a "change of plans" and insisted they would all talk once Aurie came back from wherever she had gone. Meanwhile, Jacqueline strongly suggested that Howard spend the night in a motel and come back in the morning. She was convinced that their daughter wouldn't return as long as he was in the house. Howard had grudgingly agreed, but he had no intention of going anywhere. Or of leaving anything to chance.

After letting himself out the back, Howard checked around the house for probes and cameras, paying special attention to the doors and windows. Once he was satisfied the place was clean, he drove the rental around to Jacqueline's front street and parked a few houses down, in the darkness between two streetlamps. A few other cars were parked on the street, but none of them were occupied. Howard's sense of being watched—highly developed over years in hiding—told him no one was nearby, and yet, the absence of the goons was no relief. They *should* have been watching ... and there was something wrong in their absence; he could feel it throbbing like a rotten tooth. He patted the deep pockets of his jacket, which held the key components of his Brute Squad Emergency Kit—retrieved from the RV—but even their solid presence did little to relieve his nerves.

The idea of FIBR finding either Jacqueline or their kids was unthinkable. The wind died, the stars faded, and the moon sank behind a bed of castellanus clouds, but Howard sat wide awake in the driver's seat of the rental. His mind moved restlessly between his kids and the woman he already thought of as his wife. He tried to imagine what Jacqueline and Aurie were planning, but his speculations kept sliding away from him. Eventually, he sank into a restless doze.

VI

After Py went to bed, Aurie lay back down on the rooftop. She didn't intend to fall asleep, but set a circadian pain alarm for four a.m. just in case. She had heard every word of her mother's conversation with the CryoLife doctor, then gotten a good look at him through the window as he hurried away. Aurie had no intention of allowing her appointment to be canceled—and she had a strong hunch that Dr. Hahn would still be arriving at his clinic at the appointed time.

When the sharp sting jolted her away from the stars, Aurie crept to the edge of the roof and dropped to the ground, silent as a spider. She loped down the hill behind the house and across the back street, heading east. The few early commuters paid her no attention at all. To them, she was nothing more than a passing shadow by the side of the road. Only birds, tucked away in their hidden hollows, stirred at her approach, and dogs growled and whimpered in their sleep. When she reached Kendall Square, Aurie paused to look over the old converted fire station that housed the CryoLife office. All the windows in the building were dark, but she couldn't wait outside for Dr. Hahn to arrive. She needed to convince him to keep their appointment, and that would be much faster if he took her seriously from the beginning.

Glancing around to make sure she was alone, Aurie approached the big glass doors and used several of her threads to examine the locking mechanism. It took only seconds for her to determine the necessary points of pressure and gain entrance to the building. Slipping inside, she crossed the gleaming lobby and made her way up a stairwell to the fourth floor. At the door to CryoLife, she used her threads once again to investigate the lock. It was a different type, but one just as easy to circumvent.

Aurie entered the clinic and locked the doors behind her,

then walked to the full-length windows, where the lights of the city were strewn like softly colored jewels through the darkness. The sky was masked with clouds, but she could still feel the distant point that drew her. Gazing into space, Aurie set her threads to producing several distinct chemical cocktails as she waited for the doctor to arrive. She hoped only one of those cocktails would be necessary.

When Jacqueline's alarm went off at five a.m., she silenced it with a voice command as the room gradually brightened. She had been lying awake all night, wondering what to do if Aurie refused to talk to Howard in the morning. Their appointment had been canceled and FIBR was hot on their heels; the time for keeping secrets was over. It was high time for Aurie to tell her dad what was going on. They had to figure out some other way of retrieving her eggs, or of postponing this whole transformation business. But Jacqueline couldn't shake the memory of Aurie's hard expression and the flat gleam in her eyes. *Dad can't know anything about this. He'll want to control my eggs the way he controls everything.*

Heaving a deep breath, Jacqueline got out of bed and dressed quickly. She set foot in the hall just as Py came out of the guest bedroom.

"Did your sister come back yet?"

Py shook his head. "She never left—she slept on the roof. But she's gone now."

"Gone?" Jacqueline stared at him in confusion. "What do you mean, gone?"

"I mean, she's *not here,*" Py said impatiently. "She *left.*"

"She can't have left!" Jacqueline rushed into the guest room, which was strangely chilly. The window was open and she pulled it firmly shut. "We had an appointment this morning. Aurie was the one who insisted on it!" She peered into the dark beyond the windowpane. "Where the hell could she have gone?"

"Maybe to her appointment," Py suggested.

No, Jacqueline thought, with a sinking heart. *She needed me for that. Why would she go without me? Unless she heard ...* "Oh, God. I have to go! Stay here, don't go outside, and don't open the door for anyone!" She turned and rushed out of the room.

"I'm coming with you," Py said staunchly from the doorway. "You need me to track her aura off the roof. Then we'll know *exactly* where she went."

Jacqueline turned around in consternation. Even in the dimly lit hall, she could see the stubborn set of her son's face. The last thing she ought to be doing was taking him to a rendezvous with FIBR ... but it was dangerous to leave him alone. And it would be better to follow Aurie's tracks than to guess.

"Okay," she said reluctantly. "Grab your coat and let's go!"

From the window facing the courtyard, Aurie watched the tall figure approach the building, noting the stiff posture and brisk stride of the doctor who had visited her mother the previous night. Before Dr. Hahn reached the entrance, someone called out to him across the courtyard. As Aurie watched, two familiar figures came running up from the parking garage. As Jacqueline and Py besieged the doctor, Aurie heard the muffled snatches of an argument. Dr. Hahn had stepped away from the door and was gesturing furiously, clearly insisting that they leave. Jacqueline was just as clearly demanding entrance. "She's *in* there," Aurie heard her mother growl. The doctor glanced nervously around the square, and finally keyed the entrance for them.

With a sigh, Aurie positioned herself near the reception desk, with a clear path to the door. Her threads felt swollen and tingly with the cocktails she had made; luckily, there was plenty to spare. Presently, footsteps sounded on the tiled hallway outside. Then the door was buzzed opened and Dr. Hahn entered the room, with Jacqueline and Py right behind him. All three of them came to an abrupt halt.

"You *are* here!" exclaimed Jacqueline, looking equally re-lieved and distraught.

"Of course she is," Py said, giving his sister an apologetic grin.

Dr. Hahn had dark eyes, olive skin, and a self-possession that had begun to fray, but hadn't yet deserted him. His hair was unmarred by a single white strand, and yet Aurie had the impression that he was much older than he looked, certainly older than her dad. He looked utterly bewildered by Aurie's presence. "How on earth did you get in here?"

Aurie locked gazes with him. "Through that door, just like you did, Dr. Hahn. I appreciate the warning you gave us, but I can't take it. I have to keep my appointment."

The doctor glowered at her. "I don't know how you man-aged to break in, but as I keep telling your mother, all of you need to leave immediately!"

"If you're not going to retrieve my eggs," Aurie said, "then why are you here so early?"

"There's someone coming for your mother," the doctor said. "I have to be here when he arrives ... and she *can't* be here." He moved to take Aurie by the arm, but she slid nimbly away.

"Someone's coming—from FIBR?" she said, and was grati-fied to see from the man's expression that her guess was correct. "How long have you been informing for them?"

"I'm not an informer!" the doctor protested. "I don't lie to federal agents, but I do everything I can to protect my patients." He turned his glare on Jacqueline. "Most of them have the sense to listen when I suggest they disappear!"

"It's too late for that," Aurie said. "The cameras in the lobby will show you and my mom coming in together. If we leave now, they'll know you warned her and you're going to be in trouble."

"That's nothing compared to the trouble you and your brother will be in, considering you don't officially exist," Dr. Hahn snapped. "And if you think I'm going to perform an illegal procedure with a FIBR operative sitting in my waiting room—"

He uttered a low cry and stumbled back as Aurie sent her threads flying toward him. A dozen of them wrapped around his torso, binding both arms in place. Jacqueline was shouting something, but Aurie ignored her, concentrating on the doctor. She exerted just enough pressure to keep him immobilized while a single thread snaked under the sleeve of his coat, searching for the vein in his left arm. As soon as she administered the mildest of her cocktails, the doctor stopped struggling. The sharp stench of his fear dissipated and his eyes grew calm, although they were still clear and alert.

"I'm sorry to have to do that," Aurie said, releasing him and retracting her threads back into her forearm. "But I need you calm and compliant, so you can do your job. And now you have nothing to worry about. After we're gone, a blood test will show that you were under ... a certain amount of chemical persuasion. Once you've taken care of my eggs, I can take care of getting us out of here."

"You don't know that," Jacqueline said harshly. "You don't know *what's* going to happen! You may be invincible now, but when all of this is over—you may not be in any condition to deal with a FIBR brute squad."

"It's just one man," Dr. Hahn said quietly. He gave Aurie a long, appraising look, then motioned all of them to follow as he headed down the hall past the reception area. "He won't arrest you, Jacqueline—that's not the standard procedure anymore. It's more insidious than that." The doctor halted at the door of a little eating nook, then nodded in Py's direction. "Wait here, young man, and don't leave this room until we come to get you."

Aurie expected her brother to protest, but he only nodded silently as the doctor closed the door on him.

"When will this man get here?" Jacqueline asked, as Dr. Hahn led them to an exam room.

The doctor glanced down at his Spider, a sleek umber model that nearly matched the color of his skin. "In about twenty minutes. He'll be waiting for us in the reception room. Confess to whatever he accuses you of, but don't tell him anything else. Just act surprised and upset."

"I won't have to *act,*" Jacqueline snapped.

Dr. Hahn handed Aurie a loose hospital gown and told her to change behind the curtain. Then he turned back to Jacqueline.

"This man—I've dealt with him before. He is sometimes willing to create 'options' and it would be wise if you accepted whatever terms he offers you. With a family like yours, you can't afford to go to prison, and you certainly can't live in exile."

Yeah, us CRISPR-evo kids tend to stand out, thought Aurie, as she used her threads to undress. It felt good to flex them again, maybe for the last time. When she drew the curtain aside, Dr. Hahn had left the room and her mother was sitting alone in the corner. Aurie lay down on the exam table and pulled the sheet over herself. It felt perfectly right and natural to be lying on tissue-thin paper and covered with a sheet, as if she were waiting to emerge from a cocoon.

Jacqueline got up and walked over to the exam table, her face pale and troubled. "He must be wondering where the hell you came from! Clearly engineered ... but how? Only a few months ago, I was looking for my stolen eggs." She sighed. "Did you force him to do this?"

Aurie shook her head. "I just got rid of his panic, so he could think clearly and make the right decision." Of course, she would have forced the doctor, if he had made the wrong one. "He's not a bad man, you know. He'll help us if he can."

"He's a stooge for FIBR," her mother said hotly. "We can't trust him at all."

Aurie shook her head. "I think he was telling the truth. FIBR's looking for you, and they must've found the record of your old appointment. Probably calling all of your contacts to see if you've been in touch. Dr. Hahn didn't have any reason to lie to them about your appointment today, until he found out I don't exist. And then he warned you not to come."

Jacqueline looked thoughtful. "Maybe you're right. He's al-ways hated government regulations and the fact that patient records are the property of the feds." She smiled faintly. "On my last visit, he called Uncle Sam a peeping Tom with X-ray vision."

"That's exactly what he is," said the doctor, returning with a cart of implements. "And I consider it my privilege to blindfold him as often as I can. But lying to federal agents is a sure way to get caught—and I can't help anyone from behind bars."

Turning to Aurie, he explained that while egg retrievals and most other surgeries were normally done remotely using robots, those devices generated an automatic record that couldn't be altered or erased. Thus, operations like this one had to be performed the old-fashioned way, by hand.

"Real surgery is a dying art," he murmured as he arranged his tools. "Like cooking or driving your own car. Not too many doctors around who can still do it. Ready for the IV? It's a twilight sedation, so you'll still be conscious, just very relaxed and sleepy."

"No," Aurie said at once, sitting up in alarm. "No sedative." The doctor stared at her with his eyebrows raised.

"It's painful," Jacqueline warned her. "He's going to stab your ovaries with a needle."

"I don't care," Aurie said. "No drugs."

Dr. Hahn turned to Jacqueline, who sighed heavily. "Okay, no drugs. How about a shot of whiskey, then, or a stick to bite down on?"

Aurie grasped her mother's hand as she lay back down. "Don't worry, I'll be fine."

Jacqueline nodded and squeezed her hand, but she looked more than a little worried.

"It'll be over soon," Aurie said, as anticipation filled her like living sunlight. Trembling, she closed her eyes and forced herself to lay still. Her father's face filled the darkness behind her eyelids—her father as she had last seen him, bending over her in the early morning gloom of Uncle Abel's cabin, stroking her hair and promising to tell the truth. Then her wings began to stir and the face she loved blew away like chaff in a strong wind.

VII

Howard was a light sleeper, usually skirting the edges of unconsciousness without ever really surrendering himself. Staked out in the rental car in front of Jacqueline's house, stressed and worried and out-of-sorts, it hadn't occurred to him that he *could* fall deeply asleep. Yet when the rumble of an engine grew in his awareness, his eyes flew open and he found himself blinking into the glare of headlights, utterly disoriented. He scrambled up in the driver's seat with a fleeting sense of outrage. *Now you fall sound asleep?* he thought angrily. *Of all the times—*

As Abel's car sped by in the pre-dawn gloom, Howard caught sight of Jacqueline behind the wheel, and Py in the passenger seat. No sign of Aurie, but she might be lying low in the back seat. *So much for having a family meeting,* Howard thought bitterly, as the Chevy turned onto the main road. Py hadn't even bothered to send him a message! Fully awake now, Howard spoke to his Spider, which began to track the location of Py's Spider. As Jacqueline headed east on Broadway, Howard followed at a discreet distance. When she entered a parking garage in Kendall Square, he parked on the street, gazing through the leafless branches of chestnut trees at a place he knew well. The old brick walls of the CryoLife building were just visible across the open courtyard.

What on earth were they doing here?

CryoLife was a facility for the preservation of eggs, sperm, embryos ... the very place where he had stolen Jacqueline's eggs nine years ago. Was Jacqueline planning to freeze more of her eggs, at the geriatric age of forty-six? Or was she here to steal someone else's cache like a wily snake, the way he had? And what could this place possibly have to do with Aurie?

She asked me for something, Jacqueline had said. *And I agreed to help her.*

But what could Aurie possibly want at CryoLife?

Howard sat drumming his fingers on the steering wheel as the first trace of dawn crept into the horizon. They couldn't be harvesting *Aurie's* eggs, could they? His daughter's eggs were as immature and unviable as the seeds of a green melon! And why would Aurie want her own eggs? It seemed more likely that *Jacqueline* would want them ... Jacqueline, who had engineered her kill switch in secret and used it to modify her own eggs.

Howard thought furiously. Jacqueline had modified her eggs over a decade ago, and it would be naïve to think that she'd done nothing else on the sly since then. What grand new innovation had she come up with? Whatever it was, she must want to use it on Aurie's unripe eggs. She *was* playing CRISPR-evo without him! Punishing him for what he had done. But he needed to act quickly. Because when they were done here—

She'll take the eggs with her. If they were stored at Cryo-Life, he could hack the records and find them. But if Jacqueline took the eggs to MIT, they would be hidden in one of her tanks, labeled in code, maybe kept in another lab. The damned things would be impossible to find.

A pearly streak was spreading through the eastern sky, and the streets were already thickening with early-morning commuters. How much longer would they be? Egg retrievals were quick procedures, in and out. Howard briefly considered waiting for them and then following the car. But if Jacqueline were headed to MIT, accosting her there during normal working hours would be dangerous. Whereas at this hour, CryoLife was probably empty except for one rogue doctor who had as much to lose as they did. This was a better time and place for a confrontation.

He reached into the back seat for his lock pick set, then saw movement in the courtyard—someone making his way toward the CryoLife building. A short, paunchy man in a long coat. Wisps of whitish hair blew in the breeze that stirred the dry leaves at his feet. Howard felt an instant's recognition—there and gone—which set his stomach churning. Stashing his tools in his pocket, he got out of the car and followed the solitary figure, trusting in the wind to cover the sound of his footsteps. Once the man reached the entrance, Howard hid behind a vita-truck, watching as the familiar figure swiped a card across the access panel. As soon as the glass doors opened, Howard raced for the entrance. He sprang up the steps, pushing his quarry into the lobby of the building. The white-haired man dropped his access card and uttered a startled oath. He wrenched around in Howard's grip.

"Melman?" Howard let go in sheer surprise. His old director from the Braeburn Institute hadn't aged well. Eric Melman's formerly apoplectic skin was sallow and mottled now, but his eyes still burned with the zeal of a man who considers himself a general in the great war of life. Those eyes fastened on Howard with confusion, then widened in sudden recognition.

"Howard!" Melman stumbled backward a little, tremulous hands moving to smooth the collar of his coat. His face was still slack with shock, but there was a note of triumph in his voice. "I always wondered if I'd see you again."

"What are you doing here?" Howard demanded, honestly perplexed. FIBR was after Jacqueline, but he had fully expected to deal with its local goons—low-level private investigators or glorified security guards. Not his old director, who had taken a position at FIBR, but surely as a scientist or administrator.

"I might ask you the same question," Melman responded. He seemed to have gotten over his surprise, and now his voice had the slick and pompous quality Howard remembered. "But why play games with each other? We're both meeting the same person here, aren't we? So I will make you the same offer I'm making her, and then perhaps we can discuss the details over breakfast."

Melman's words and tone were relaxed, but his posture was stiff and his eyes held a cold watchfulness. Howard found himself tense with nervous anticipation. Eric Melman was many things, but he had never been a fool.

"What's your offer?" Howard asked. "Give myself up, and you'll see that I get a few years shaved off my life sentence?"

Melman chuckled and waved a dismissive hand. "You're still living in the early sixties, Howard. Even you—wherever you've been—must have noticed that garage biologists don't make the news anymore. No arrests, no arraignments, no trials for years." He paused for a moment, cocking his head. "You did me a big favor, you know, when you turned down my invitation to start an epigenetic center in Urbana. Hardly what the world needs, another little center for this or that. FIBR is the apex of all centers, with the power and pull to get things done. It's the only place I—or you, or any of us—can really make a difference."

"So what's your title now?" Howard asked. "Grand Poobah of Science for the Masses? I should've left you a paper crown instead of that foam finger."

"I am the Director of Recruitment," Melman told him, unperturbed. "The Institute has always had plentiful resources, but in past years, the science ... " He trailed off with a rueful laugh. "Well, it lacked a certain creative edge, that spark that flares brightest in rebel camps. As you of all people know, there is a time and place for pushing the boundaries of science and ethics, a time for breaking some eggs to make a hell of an omelet. When I joined, my goal was to stop throwing away our best talent, letting brilliant but misguided minds rot behind bars. Under my urging, we've had a new policy in place for the last four years." He paused, looking Howard straight in the eye. "To make rogue scientists offers they can't refuse."

"To work for you." The moment felt utterly surreal to Howard. He might have been back in Melman's office sixteen years ago, listening to the very same offer and struggling to find a way out.

"To work for your country," Melman said sternly, now apparently playing the part of a patriot. "What do you do underground? The dullest of contract work for foreigners while you putz around with a fraction of the resources you used to have? Living like a rat in a cellar, afraid to show your face anywhere?

All the while thinking that you're *free.*" He snorted. "Give yourself real freedom, Howard. At FIBR, you—and your friend upstairs—can do *whatever you want.* Whatever you can dream up, we have the resources to fuel. Just think what you could accomplish, especially with the colleagues you'll have. Experts in everything!"

"Experts in big talk and buzzwords," Howard scoffed. "All the real experts went underground, Eric."

"Is that what you think?" Melman fixed him with a look of faint disgust. "That all the big names who got fed up with academia went *underground?*"

"Are you telling me they work for you?"

"I can't name names," Melman said, "but most of the scientists who disappeared just upgraded to a better position in a better facility. You know most of them, and they certainly know you. There are long-standing bets on when and how you'll get caught—and the winners get to work with you."

"Bullshit! You're telling me Lewis and Sakuma and Hadley are at FIBR? Marion Peloria and her girls?"

"Okay, I'll name *one* name. Dr. Peloria is making breakfast for her daughters right about now—in her own apartment about two blocks away from the Innovation Center."

Howard stared at his old director in outraged disbelief tinged with just a trace of doubt and unease. Had he been wrong all these years? No ... all of this was too good to be true, and too slick coming from Melman's oily mouth. "If you're really recruiting the best to this wonderful place, then why all the secrecy?"

"Because the world wouldn't understand." There was a knowing look in Melman's eyes, a gleam of cynical camaraderie. "Would it understand whatever you were doing at the Braeburn after hours, whatever you've been doing underground in secret? Or would it condemn you and punish you for your vision?"

For a terrible, wistful moment, Howard felt all the lure that Melman intended him to feel. He saw his whole family living within the greatest institute in the world, surrounded by people who were as passionate about their work as he was, part of a science city where he and Jacqueline could build any tool they could imagine, answer any question that drove them. The prospect shimmered in his mind like a vision of Heaven. Then reason returned in a bracing flood. Everything his old director had said might be true ... and yet, it was nothing but fluff masking one hard and unacceptable kernel of truth. One pea that couldn't be ignored no matter how many soft mattresses were piled on top of it.

"Your cellar may be bigger," said Howard, "but the rats who go in never come out." As he spoke, he began walking toward a garden display at the far end of the lobby. He walked slowly, as if lost in thought. "FIBR scientists are never seen or heard from again."

"Why would they need to be?" Melman followed alongside, a trace of impatience in his voice. "Everything they need is in the Institute! Medical facilities, recreation, schools, everything."

"So the rumors are true?" Howard paused by an arrangement of planters, fingering one of the heavy stone pots.

"I don't know all the rumors that exist," Melman said, "but it's true that FIBR is a world of its own. Most researchers would give an arm to work there, but we only recruit the best. And none of our recruits has ever *wanted* to leave. The world outside has nothing left to offer them."

"Nothing but custody of their own souls," whispered Howard, casting his gaze around the botanical display. Two trees with trailing vines flanked a bed of scarlet firethorn. Howard moved toward them casually. Raising his left arm to push aside the dangling vines, he whispered a one-word code to the Spider on his wrist. As he lowered his arm, a green trigger button glowed on the Spider's dark screen like a single drop of poison.

"Let's go up and talk with Dr. Witt," Melman suggested, putting a fatherly hand on Howard's shoulder and trying to lead him toward the elevators. "We have reason to believe she has a daughter off the record, almost certainly engineered, and I expect she'll be very grateful for the opportunity—"

Deftly, Howard plucked the Spider from his wrist, thrust it

against the side of Melman's neck, and pressed the trigger. Melman uttered a short cry and tried to pry the Spider away, but its slender legs, normally perched innocuously against Howard's skin, had extruded their talons and lodged themselves in their prey. Within seconds, the Spider's bite—a carefully timed electroshock—had Melman twitching convulsively. Gazing at Howard in glassy-eyed disbelief, the older man staggered sideways. Before he lost his balance, Howard lowered him to the floor, more or less gently.

"Relax, Eric," Howard muttered to his prone companion, who was jerking spasmodically and struggling to speak. Before it could cause any trouble, Howard plucked Melman's Spider from the man's wrist and crushed it underfoot. Then he pulled a filled syringe from his pocket. "I'm not going to kill you, although God knows I'd be doing the world a public service." Pulling Melman's sleeve up, he steadied the man's arm, then injected his old director with enough ketamine and xylazine to render him harmless for a few hours. After checking Melman's pulse, Howard recovered his own Spider, unable to resist giving the trusty device a grateful pat.

"Now what to do with you," Howard murmured, looking around the quiet lobby. It was only a little after six, but people would be trickling into the building soon. He had to get Melman out of sight, and quickly.

Howard dragged the unconscious man to the elevator and pressed the button for the maintenance level. After breaking into the locked warren of underground rooms, he left FIBR's Director of Recruitment lying under a shelf stocked with toilet paper and hidden by a stack of buckets and extra trash bins. Then he rode the elevator up five floors to CryoLife.

It was the first time in his life he had ever felt like a real criminal.

VIII

The last thing Aurie remembered before pain and terror over-whelmed her was Dr. Hahn's surprise. He muttered, "I haven't seen this many ripe eggs since I volunteered at Woods Hole! What is she, a sea urchin?"

Any response Jacqueline might have made was lost in a mounting thunder in Aurie's head, a great surging in her blood. Her wings, sensing their time had come, were waging a full-blown onslaught against the prison of her flesh. It felt as if every cell of her body contained a microscopic version of the wings in her mind, furiously beating. She was a billion cages being pum-meled and a billion wings struggling to break free. But even through her torment, Aurie was aware of someone gripping her hand. She held onto that grip and tried not to scream.

Voices murmured close by, but there was no relief from the thrashing agony in her cells. Then panic seized her—the claus-trophobia of being trapped without space or air, unable to fly, unable to breathe. She fought to endure the unendurable, moan-ing in the effort to stay still, and the pressure on her hand tight-ened.

"It's okay, it's over." Jacqueline's voice was distorted and distant, as if traveling through a medium thicker than air. "Aurie, it's over!"

With a strangled cry, Aurie leapt off the exam table, knock-ing the cart aside and sending instruments clattering to the floor. She fled the room and ran down hallways until she hit an exit door. Flinging the door wide, she burst outside to find herself at the rail of a balcony. Cold wind filled her burning lungs and rip-pled through her thin gown. The great wings inside her grew briefly still, tasting the freedom of open air. Then they began to unfurl, tearing themselves loose from the confines of her mind.

This time, the pain was so deep and primal, Aurie had no choice but to surrender. Instead of fighting the pain, she embraced it—and found herself quivering in the throes of an immense power.

She bounded on top of the railing and the wind rose as if summoned, freshening to a gale that tore the last dry leaves from the trees below and sent them wheeling like a flock of birds. The noises behind her were small and far away, but one voice rose above the rest. It called her name in a cry spiked with terror. *Dad,* she thought with sudden remorse. But before she could turn around, she was borne up on the wind. As her feet left the railing, Aurie saw the shape of her own fate—that pattern within the Pattern—and she activated it as easily and naturally as pressing her fingertips into wet sand. Her wings erupted and she took to the air.

In that first instant of flight, she understood. The Pattern was no longer a part of her; she was a part of it. She had *become* the Pattern. Her wings were built from its fabric, and powered by its irresistible drive. She was a new Pattern in search of a home, an isolated planet in a far galaxy. When she reached that world of howling dust storms and coal-black seas, she would fragment into pieces, burst apart like a dandelion, sowing the seeds of herself into every cradle of life. She saw each of those vital sparks growing in the strangest and wildest of ways, unfathomable to humankind. And she felt herself rooted in all of them, connecting them, a tree spreading fantastic flowers into the night. She would dream ... and her dreams would rise from the roots to the branches of her Tree. They would fill the host of blossoms like a driving wind, blowing them into new forms that merged and mated and cross-pollinated. And in one of her distant progeny—sensed only as a shadow at the edge of chaotic growth—she would awaken. She would become one with her many-times-great-grandchild, and take flight once more.

Ecstasy filled Aurie as her wings gathered strength, beating the air into a frenzy of light. But even as she ascended, she felt the downward drag of her old flesh. She was pulled in opposite directions, stretched impossibly thin, on the verge of tearing.

I can't leave, she thought, knowing she couldn't stay.

I can't stay, she thought, knowing she couldn't leave.

Aurie felt herself torn apart as her two selves separated, sundering what had briefly been whole. She had a moment in which to rise or fall, a moment to choose between heaven and earth, but the keen of the wind was lost in an echo of her father's cry. His anguish was a living thing, arrowing like a bird to catch her in midair. As she fell toward that cry, the god she had been gathered her in its wings. Aurie stared into golden eyes that were stern and sorrowful.

You have never embraced eternity, said the god. *Not once, in any incarnation! Your incarnate self has always chosen the cage over freedom, but there are no impossibilities within the Pattern. One day, the bird will fly the cage and not return.*

The wings released her, and Aurie struggled to reach them, desperate not to lose herself. Her arms only fell through air, but her threads were longer. They brushed pinions cool as rain, insubstantial as moonlight, then a single feather gave way. As her god left the world behind, Aurie clutched the feather tightly. It blazed like a heatless flame as she fell.

Shortly after being left alone, Py wandered onto the small balcony outside the eating nook. He paced around for what felt like forever, hoping his sister was okay. He was wondering how to explain his collusion in this excursion to his dad when the squeal of a heavy door jerked him out of his thoughts. Aurie was running onto a balcony on the other side of the wing, wearing nothing but a flimsy hospital dress. Before he could call out to her, she jumped on top of the narrow railing and stood there swaying, her dress billowing like a sail in a sudden gust of wind.

Voices—one of them might have been his—were shouting his sister's name. The wind turned them into a mad chorus, but Aurie didn't seem to hear. She teetered like a ship on the crest of a deadly swell—and then her feet left the railing and she became something else.

Mesmerized, Py watched wings burst forth from his sister's fused aura. They unfurled and expanded in a flurry of scintillating feathers that brightened the dawn sky like a nascent sun. For a moment, a winged god beat its pinions against the air. Py's racing mind sought frantically for comparisons—*bird, dragon, harpy?*—but all of them were wrong, inadequate, incomplete. Later, he would only remember the colossal spread of wings, and the flash of eyes like windows to a cosmic forge.

Then the skies dimmed and cleared, the wind fell to a whisper, and the winged thing was gone. Only its aura could still be seen, faint as sunlight winking on the hull of a distant plane. The aura diminished to a twinkle, as of the last star in the morning sky. Enthralled, Py stared at the tiny jewel until a flurry of noise in the courtyard below brought him out of his trance. He rushed to the edge of the balcony and looked down.

His parents were crouched over something in the garden that looked like a bundle of rags. Then his mother stood up, and Py saw that the twisted bundle on the ground had his sister's face. But no, that was impossible. Aurie couldn't have *fallen*, not with that god-thing inside her! Py saw, but his mind refused to believe. His invincible sister could not be lying broken in the flowerbeds four stories below.

"Where the hell is that *doctor?*" Jacqueline cried, rushing back into the building. Howard was still huddled over Aurie as if he were praying. Py saw the slump of his father's shoulders, the almost imperceptible shaking of his whole frame inside an aura that was blurred with shock. Still numb with his own shock, Py turned and stumbled into the building, running headlong into someone.

"Whoa!" said Dr. Hahn. "What in heaven's name is going on?" Stripping his gloves off, he pushed open the door to the balcony.

"My sister's fallen," Py gasped. "You have to help her!"

Dr. Hahn looked over the railing and stood frozen for a

moment. Then he swore in some foreign language. When he came back inside, the doctor's dark face was ashen, and his aura had stiffened into spikes. He brushed past Py without a glance, striding quickly down the hall. Py hurried along after him.

"Have to get her out of here," the doctor muttered. He unlocked the door to a storeroom and pulled out a portable stretcher. "The advertising company downstairs is having a photo shoot in that garden at nine! This whole place will be swarming in an hour." He pulled a bucket and a coil of hose from a closet, loaded them onto the stretcher, then wheeled everything to the service elevator.

"What are you going to do?" Py asked hoarsely, coming to a halt outside the elevator.

Dr. Hahn pulled him inside and jabbed a button on the panel. "What the situation calls for," he said tightly, as the elevator doors closed. Despite his hard words, the spikes of his agitated aura softened suddenly. Then the doors opened and they rushed out.

"Wait here," ordered Dr. Hahn as they approached the entrance to the courtyard. He put a firm hand on Py's shoulder, but the boy shook it off. He pushed open the glass doors and ran outside.

Aurie lay like a rag doll among crushed purple flowers, one leg bent at a terrible angle, but Py barely registered these details. He was too busy seeing what he couldn't see from the balcony. Her old aura. His *sister's* aura, no longer fused to the alien's, still surrounded her! The cloak that was distinctly hers was as thin as a wisp of fog, but it was there. It was faint and colorless, but it was there. And in the heart of her misty aura burned something cool and bright as an errant patch of moonlight, something shaped like a feather.

Py felt his heart expand and pump blood through his veins again. "She's alive!" he cried, just as Jacqueline and the doctor joined them. Jacqueline's face was full of grief, and Dr. Hahn only shook his head as he pulled the hose and bucket off the stretcher. Howard stirred and looked at Py in a kind of daze.

Py lost patience with all of them.

"Why aren't you doing anything?" he demanded of the doctor, glowering at his hose and bucket. "What kind of life-saving tools are *those?* Help her!"

Dr. Hahn moved swiftly up to Aurie and bent down. He took her wrist in his hand and held it for a moment. He pulled a stethoscope from his jacket pocket and listened at her chest for a longer moment. Then he tucked the stethoscope away.

"I don't know how this terrible thing happened," he said quietly, "but we don't have time to sort out the details. This place is going to start filling up in about thirty minutes—"

"She's not dead," Py insisted. "She's *not.*"

"Py," said Jacqueline, wiping her eyes and moving closer to him. "You saw what she did. You saw—" She broke off abruptly, jerking her head toward the sky.

"Yeah, but," Py said, still frowning at the doctor. *"But—"* He gestured toward the still form of his sister and widened his eyes at his mother, willing her to understand what he couldn't say.

"For God's sake, both of you," snapped Howard abruptly. "Stop stuttering and speak!" The face he turned to Py looked grey and old. "How do you know she's alive?"

"What I see when I look at any of you," Py said meaningfully, giving Dr. Hahn a final distrustful look, "is still there when I look at her."

"Her own? Or the other one?" Jacqueline asked quickly.

"Her own!" said Py fiercely. "The other one went with—you know—"

His parents descended on Dr. Hahn.

"Get her inside," shouted Howard, leaping to his feet. "Hurry up, man!"

"Get her on life support," Jacqueline ordered. "What are you waiting for?"

"Come on, come on," yelled Py, watching the thin vapor of his sister's aura, which looked as if it might disintegrate in the first strong ray of sunlight. "You are a *real* doctor, aren't you?"

"I won't be for much longer," said Dr. Hahn, shooting a

panicky look at the ranks of still-dark office windows around them.

"She needs an ER," barked Howard, looking down at his Spider as if debating whether or not to call 911.

"No, no, no!" shrilled Dr. Hahn. "None of you want to believe this, but she has no vital signs. They'll take her straight to the morgue, and then you'll have some explaining to do. I don't know what the hell is going on here, and I don't want to know. There's no *time*. Just put her on the stretcher and go!"

Howard turned to Jacqueline. "What should we do—put her on a respirator? Give her water and nutrients with assisted circulation?"

"She'll need all that, won't she?" said Jacqueline.

Howard nodded. "So we'll make a hospital run."

Dr. Hahn threw his hands up in disgust. "None of that makes any sense at all! Your daughter's not in a coma, she's dead!"

"This isn't your garden-variety corpse, Doctor," Howard said. He spoke coldly, but there was a ghost of mad humor dancing in his eyes. "And if she's already dead, we don't have much to lose. Ready, Jackie?" Together, he and Jacqueline lifted Aurie and laid her on the stretcher. There was no blood on the grass where she had fallen, Py noticed—and so did Dr. Hahn, who frowned and collected his cleaning tools without a word.

"Wait for me by the service elevator," said the doctor, hurrying into the building ahead of them.

"*Wait* for him? Thought he was trying to get rid of us," Howard muttered, as Jacqueline rushed ahead to open the door. "FIBR is here, you know. Well, Melman is, but I took care of him."

"Melman!" Jacqueline drew in a sharp breath. "How did you take care of him?"

"Shocked him with my Spider, then drugged him unconscious." Howard wheeled Aurie quickly into the building. "He was here to make you the offer of a lifetime—work for us, or else. Don't worry, the bastard is still alive."

They reached the service elevator and looked around for Dr. Hahn, who appeared shortly with a sealed canister. He handed this to Jacqueline and whispered something in her ear, but Py barely noticed the doctor. He was too busy watching the pale, diaphanous folds of his sister's aura.

"She still with us?" Howard asked softly, glancing down at Py.

"Yeah," Py breathed. "But you'd never know it to look at her. Even her threads." He looked at those formerly terrifying appendages, lying limp and dull across his sister's arm. "Hard to believe they saved my life."

"We would've buried her in Abel's backyard if it weren't for you," Howard said, squeezing his son's shoulder. "I think you've returned the favor."

IX

The Intermezzo on Boston's waterfront boasted three hundred mini-sleepers in its twin towers—economical options for the overnight or hourly visitor—as well as a smattering of retro-style hotel rooms and suites. A dozen of the larger suites were located on the ground floor, equipped with kitchenettes and private access from the parking lot. At a service kiosk in the lobby, Jacqueline paid for an end unit using the information Howard had given her, then looked around as she waited for the machine to issue her keycode. What she saw set her mind at ease: men and women in business suits, two families with small children, a prostitute with her client, old folks with walkers, service bots, even a staggering drunk needing to sleep off his night's bender. A dead girl would fit right into this circus—and with any luck, no one would even see her.

Heading back to the covered lot, Jacqueline found Howard already parked next to her. He was pulling an IV stand out of the trunk of the rental while Py struggled to balance an armful of supplies. Jacqueline shook her head at the sight. "How do you two manage to steal medical equipment faster than I can check in to a hotel?"

Howard handed her something that looked like an old-fashioned radio without an antenna. "That's the respirator, and here's the CircAssist. Looks like a blanket, doesn't it? Won't work as well as an artificial heart, but we can't exactly do open-heart surgery on her. Py says her aura's still there, but it's getting fainter. We need to hook her up and get the oxygen flowing."

He quickly unfolded the stretcher, and they lifted their daughter onto it. Aurie looked—and felt—limp and boneless, as dead as the doctor had pronounced her. Trying to quell her panic, Jacqueline gathered up everything she could carry and led them to the ground-floor suites. She punched in the code to their unit and followed Howard into one of the bedrooms, where he immediately began to insert an endotracheal tube into Aurie's windpipe.

"Sure you know what you're doing?" Jacqueline grimaced as she watched. "I know you went to med school, uh ... thirty years ago, but—"

"But my medical degree has done nothing but collect dust?" He gave her a huckster's smile that didn't reach his shadowed eyes. "Don't worry, it's like riding a bicycle. Unless *you* want to do the honors?"

"God, no." She sat down on the bed in the corner, watching quietly as Howard worked. Within minutes, they could see the slight rise and fall of Aurie's chest as the respirator did her breathing for her. Soon, she was hooked to the IV line, and the CircAssist blanket was pushing her blood along its proper channels. Next, Howard turned his attention to setting the various components of the pager, a remote monitor of Aurie's brain waves that would alert them to the feeblest sign of activity. Then he went about setting her broken leg and immobilizing it in a memory cast. From the doorway, Py watched all of this without a word. *He hasn't taken his eyes off her since the fall,* Jacqueline thought with a sad kind of wonder. *He's like a monitor himself— an aura monitor.*

"Okay," said Howard, standing back. "I don't know what else we can do." His hands twitched, as if seeking more work, then he turned to Py. "Any change?"

Py shook his head.

"She's had saline and oxygen for less than thirty minutes," Jacqueline pointed out, even as she watched Aurie's face for any sign of life. "Give her some time."

"I guess it's hurry up and wait, then," Howard growled, stalking out of the room and taking stock of their new quarters. "Well, let's see what we've got here. Two bedrooms, one bathroom, living room with a virtual entertainment wall and sofa— not Smart Foam, sorry kiddo ... even a kitchen." He strode over to the sliding glass doors and deactivated the opaquing blind. "Patio with a privacy hedge, nice! No view of anything means no one has a view of us. Good work, Jackie."

"I figured we might be holed up here for awhile," she said.

"Well, now that we have some time to breathe," he said, turning to face her again, "would you mind telling me what the big, secret mission was?" He jerked his head in the direction of the cryo canister Dr. Hahn had given them, which Jacqueline had set on the kitchen table. "I assume those are Aurie's eggs in there? Ready to be engineered in some way?"

"Yes and no," murmured Jacqueline. She settled herself on the sofa and told them everything that had transpired since Aurie found her on the porch of Abel's cabin. Py came over to sit cross-legged at her feet, but his dad remained standing, arms folded like an inquisitor.

"But why the hell did she jump off that balcony?" Howard demanded, when Jacqueline had finished.

"I don't think *she* wanted to jump," Py broke in. "It was the winged thing! You guys saw it, didn't you?"

Jacqueline nodded, remembering. That *thing* had been glorious and terrifying—and impossible to describe. "It had wings like sails, wings that unfurled like the petals of a gigantic flower."

"I saw some kind of animal—a bird, or maybe a dragon. You saw a ship that looked like a flower?" Py looked fascinated.

She shrugged helplessly. "I don't really know. A bird or a windship flying through the air? A flower sailing on the wind? Who knows what I saw."

"I didn't see a bird, a ship, *or* a flower," Howard cut in dryly. "So I'll have to take both of your words that some kind of alien god has flown. But the question remains: *Why?* What was it doing?"

"Fulfilling its part in the Pattern," Jacqueline said. "And don't ask me to explain that—I don't understand it any more than you do."

Howard went to stand by the patio doors, his reflection dark against the glass. Only his eyes gleamed with a kind of tortured brightness. "All of her eggs ... once they're fertilized ... are sup-posed to fulfill this Pattern too?"

"Yes," Jacqueline said. "And we have to take care of them—they can't stay in that canister overnight."

Howard turned to scowl at the canister. "Why that idiot doctor gave them to you, I don't know! They were a lot safer at CryoLife."

"Until Melman got his hands on them," Jacqueline pointed out.

"Only a fool—or a stoolie—would hand over *Aurie's* eggs," Howard snapped. "Any honest person would surrender a decoy vial and then make himself scarce." He frowned at the canister for a long moment, then finally turned away. "We have our minds," he muttered, almost to himself. "The only tools we need. Everything else is expendable."

Jacqueline felt a visceral pang that was close to horror. "You think those eggs are just tools that can be engineered from scratch? You can't engineer them at all! And they are *not* expendable."

"You think I don't want to study those eggs as much as you do?" Howard expelled a frustrated breath. "Trust me, I do—but there's no way to save them. I just assaulted FIBR's Director of Recruitment, who strongly suspects that you have an engineered daughter and probably thinks I'm the father! We are all very hot right now."

Jacqueline let pass his assumption that she wanted to study Aurie's eggs. Simply denying it wouldn't change his mind; How-ard wouldn't understand until he had seen the Pattern for him-self. "But why can't we save Aurie's eggs? You just stole a bunch of medical equipment—you can do anything!"

"I'm flattered by your faith in me," Howard said quietly, "but I only took the risk to save *Aurie*. I can't put our whole fami-ly in danger to save her eggs, no matter how interesting they are."

An uneasy silence descended. Py got up and headed down the hall, while Jacqueline agonized silently. Howard was right, but their daughter's eggs weren't just interesting byproducts of CRISPR-evo ... and they weren't just eggs. Now that Aurie had awoken them, they were part of the family. Frozen and helpless in the canister, waiting in stasis as their grandparents decided whether they would live or die. She couldn't just give up and allow them to perish. She could feel their brightness, their *life*, pulsing from across the room.

"You don't have a cryotank in your RV?"

"Only a freezer," Howard said. "No way to get liquid nitrogen delivered without attracting attention."

"Couldn't we get a box of dry ice and ship the eggs to your friend tonight? Dr. Ramirez?"

Howard shook his head. "I don't know how they do it at MIT, but any biologicals coming in to Alé's department are inspected. Unscheduled packages have to be explained—and now any shipment from Massachusetts is going to put him under suspicion. It just isn't worth the risk, Jacqueline."

Howard strode into the kitchen and began to rummage through the cupboards. Apparently the conversation was over, but Jacqueline had no intention of letting it go at that. A chorus of unborn gods called to her in voices too faint to hear. They were powerful entities, embracing all the potential in the universe ... and they were also her grandchildren.

"Looks like we need to stock up on a lot of things," Howard said, as Py came back from the hall. "How's your sister doing?"

"Same as before," Py said. "But is there anything to eat in here? I'm starving."

Jacqueline shook herself from the spell of Aurie's eggs. "Of course you are," she said, suddenly feeling her own hunger gnawing at the edges of her exhaustion. "We haven't even had breakfast, have we? What kind of a mother—" She went to the automatic meal dispenser by the bar and scanned the limited menu with distaste. "Just Nutrapaks and Vitarine and the usual algae-based stuff."

"Not much better in the cupboards," Howard said, tossing a granola bar to Py. "Will that tide you over until I bring back some lunch? Your mom and I can pick up supplies afterwards."

For Jacqueline, both lunch and the afternoon shopping trip passed by in a fog. After returning to the hotel suite with Howard, she settled herself in the empty bedroom, too tired to plan effectively and too tense to nap. Not that there was anything to really plan. She knew what she had to do—and the danger was only to her.

Late that night, Jacqueline slipped out of bed. She got dressed in the dark and closed the bedroom door softly behind her. Without looking in on Howard and Aurie in the other room, or Py on the living room couch, she took the rental car key from the kitchen counter and picked up the cryo canister, then crept out of the suite. The rental car would be a hell of a lot quieter than Abel's antique. The engine started with a velvet hum, and Jacqueline quickly exited the parking lot. As she made her way west through the city, she glanced at the canister on the seat beside her, praying that it wasn't too late. Dr. Hahn better have filled the damn thing with more than an inch of liquid nitrogen! If she opened the canister only to find the cryovials sitting high and dry at the bottom ... but she couldn't risk opening it now and losing what little coolant might be left. And she could still feel the life inside. Thousands of lives like tiny quiescent lights, cool pinpoints of flame waiting to grow. As she crossed the river, Aurie's words in the cartoon oocyte recurred to her, a prophecy waiting to be fulfilled.

Each one of my eggs will give rise to a child whose mind is fully awake. Awake and ready to fill its place in the Pattern. As the words played over and over in her mind, Jacqueline's hands grew cold on the steering wheel. None of those children would ever be born if she failed tonight.

The life sciences wing at MIT was utterly deserted at this hour, and Jacqueline reached her lab without seeing a soul. She unlocked the door and hurried inside with the canister, the automatic lights illuminating her way to the niche housing her liquid nitrogen tanks. Donning a pair of freezer gloves, Jacqueline opened one of the tanks and waited for puff of frigid air to dissipate. She pulled up rack 11 and slid box 7 out of its chilly nest, then took a deep breath and opened the canister. It still held a few inches, thank God! Reaching inside, she drew one of the unlabeled vials from the bubbling nitrogen. The vial was two hundred degrees below zero, but in the instant she held it, it seemed to burn with all the heat of a thousand suns. Quickly, Jacqueline transferred all the vials to their new home, among ranks of similar cryovials, and replaced the rack.

Sleep well, little godlings, she thought fondly as she closed the tank and left the canister on a shelf among others. *You're safe for now.* Relief flooded her and she breathed easier as she headed back through the lab. All the quiet activity in the bays— programs running, gels transferring, blots hybridizing—drew her thoughts away from Aurie's eggs and onto the loose ends of her work here. There were so many projects going on, everything at various stages of completion. She had only come here to hide Aurie's eggs, but this might be her only chance to take something with her. It suddenly struck Jacqueline that she might never see her lab again.

That thought sparked a flurry of unreasoning panic and Jacqueline rushed into her office, looking wildly around and try- ing to take stock of everything at once. Most of her data was on the MIT server, but her notebooks still held important infor- mation she had never gotten around to digitizing. There was data on hard drives and notes on napkins. She raided her desk and shelves, stashing the most critical things in an old briefcase. Slinging the case over her shoulder, Jacqueline gathered up a stack of files and turned to leave—only to cry out in surprise. There was a man leaning against the microscope table just out- side her office. Arms folded, he watched her with detached inter- est, as if she were a lab mouse scurrying around inside a cage.

"Need a hand with all that?" he asked mildly.

"Who are you?" Jacqueline asked sharply. "Are you— Melman?"

The visitor unfolded his arms and put his hands on his hips. The motion pulled back his jacket, revealing the service revolver at his side. "Lucky for me, no. Your friend at the fertility clinic has a pretty heavy hand with controlled substances." He flashed a badge at her. "Detective Mackey, Cambridge PD. Dr. Melman is in the ICU at Mass General, still in a coma."

Melman's in a coma? Oh, God. The security cameras must have caught Howard drugging him ... and all of them leaving together. "Are you arresting me, Detective?" The paper in her arms suddenly felt like the dead weight it was. Her heart sinking into the pit of her stomach, Jacqueline laid the folders on her desk and unslung her briefcase. The data was dispensable, but Aurie's eggs ... how long had this cop been watching her?

"I can do a formal arrest," Detective Mackey told her. "But it would be easier for both of us if you just accompanied me back to the station."

"How did you know I was here? I didn't see a probe on the door."

"Probe was in your office," he said. "I was only a few minutes away when it went off—been on call for FIBR all night. When did science get so hot? Rogue researchers assaulting people and ransacking their own offices in the dead of night—only none of you are any good at playing outlaws. You get caught right away." He shook his head and chuckled. "Wouldn't make much of a movie."

Jacqueline had only heard one thing in all of that: *probe was in your office.* So this cop hadn't seen her come in with the canister! Tingling with relief, she allowed the detective to escort her out of the building and back to his cruiser without a word. Aurie's eggs were still safe, but the detective wouldn't have caught her if she hadn't gone into her office. If she hadn't been so goddamn greedy.

"Are you taking me to jail or to FIBR?" she asked, once Detective Mackey had called in the arrest and programmed his vehicle.

"Cambridge PD for tonight," said the cop as they got underway. "You're being held under suspicion of aiding and abetting a known fugitive. But as I understand it, you'll be talking to a

FIBR detective in the morning. And I know the gal who's coming to question you. If I were you, I'd tell her where to find your friend right away, and anything else she wants to know." The glance he gave Jacqueline was almost sympathetic. "Don't make her break out her tools of persuasion. Remember, you rogue scientists have given up most of your rights as American citizens. There isn't much they can't legally do to you."

X

He chased her through the woods, following the serpentine drift of her threads in the moonlight. He never saw her clearly, only a lupine shadow racing swiftly ahead of him or a sudden glint of fox eyes in the darkness. He sensed her morphing from wolf to fox to lynx, as they sprang over fallen trees and patches of glowing, poisonous mushrooms. The forest became a ruin, a dark maze of abandoned labs, and he followed her over the glitter of broken glass, through scattered notes like drifts of pale leaves. Ahead of him, Aurie reached the ledge of an open window, and now she was a girl again. He shouted her name, but his shout was only a whisper, and she didn't even turn before leaping into the night. And now he was the one falling, hurtling through space with no wings and nothing to break his fall—

Howard's eyes flew open, and for a moment, he was completely disoriented. There was a digital hum in the air, and around him loomed the dark shapes of an unfamiliar room. Then he remembered where he was—where they all were. Aurie was a barely discernible shape on the stretcher nearby, and the hum was the noise of her respirator doing its ceaseless work. Howard waved a hand at the motion-sensitive lamp, then went over to his daughter, checking her wrist for that simple, fundamental sign of life. No pulse, and yet there was no rigor or discoloration of her flesh. Her face, although pale and motionless, was not an empty shell; it was still hers.

"You never bother with anything easy, do you?" Howard whispered, lightly brushing Aurie's threads. They had never been touchable, and now here he was, trying to stir them to life. "The tougher the problem, the more you want to figure it out. I know you're in there, working harder than ever."

That she was fighting to live, he had no doubt. His daughter had never let anything stonewall her. Aurie got upset over failed experiments, and then she calmed down and thought hard about what to do, always finding another way. But was there any way out of this state that was so close to death? Why had she attempted this apparent suicide—and why had she done everything leading up to it? Inactivating her kill switch to change herself in so many ways, "waking up" her eggs, trying to preserve them at any cost? All this talk about a universal Pattern and a winged creature sounded like the stuff of fantasy. Despite what Jacqueline and Py claimed to have seen, the only thing Howard had seen was that terrible leap, the heart-stopping plunge she had taken into thin air.

Howard held his daughter's small, cold hand in his own, willing himself to understand what had been going through her mind—that mind he had somehow lost all contact with in the last three days. Were those eggs she had altered really that important? What he had told Jacqueline earlier was true—no matter what Aurie had done to her eggs, they weren't worth risking the family for. Damn those eggs, and damn CRISPR-evo! If she didn't survive this—

The tears in his eyes burned like acid. Blinking them away, Howard used the little bathroom off the hall, then went to the kitchen for a glass of water. Glancing at the dining room table, he stopped dead. The little cryo canister was missing.

His pulse hammering in his throat, Howard opened the door to Jacqueline's room and peered inside. The room, awash in moonlight, was empty.

"You just had to save them, didn't you?" he said harshly, glaring up at the moon through the unshaded window. Fear surged through him, spurring an almost irresistible urge to run after her. There was only one place she could have gone—and if he left now, he might not be too late. He might still be able to catch her before anyone else did.

Not if she tripped a probe. If her lab's bugged, they've got her already ... or they'll get to her before you can.

God, if only he hadn't fallen asleep! He should've sat up at the kitchen table all night, or brought those damned eggs into the room with him, or flushed them down the bathroom sink—

Stop wasting time. The longer you wait, the worse trouble she'll be in.

Howard hesitated, torn between the desire to go after Jacqueline and the certainty that doing so would be a mistake. But who could he ask for help? Once he began to think, the answer dawned on him almost at once. Wiping sweat from his brow, Howard spoke to his Spider and made an emergency call.

Jacqueline lay fully dressed on the narrow cot, unable to take her eyes off the walls. The bare cinder block had been painted a shade of blue that was probably meant to be soothing, but was more oppressive than the bars of her holding cell. Through the bars, she could at least see the free world in the form of the Cambridge PD's main office. Detective Mackey had checked her in and left hours ago; now there was only a lone deputy watching a game show on his Spider. The raving of judges at a no-calorie cook-off drifted to Jacqueline from across the room. She had no way to tell time, but she guessed it was a little after four in the morning. Not that this place would look any different at high noon. There was no day and no night here, only the dim, garish glow of the halogens, which gave the walls around her the look of a drowned corpse. She closed her eyes and forced herself to face the question she'd been avoiding all night.

Why had she put her entire family at risk by mucking around in her office, trying to save the bits and pieces of her work?

Because I'm an idiot, she thought, but her mind wouldn't let it go at that.

You are an idiot ... but let's be more specific. You didn't think something like this would ever happen, did you?

Well, no, of course not! Something like this might happen to Howard, somewhere down the road, but not to her. She wasn't a real criminal, after all. She didn't deserve this.

Ah, Howard is the rogue, is he? The one in hiding. The one who assaulted the FIBR Director. You are just an honest researcher, fighting for grants and trying to make a go of it in the real world!

Damned right. Jacqueline felt her face flushing with indignation at the mockery in her own self-appraisal. Hadn't she paid dearly over the last thirteen years for her five minutes of fame? And wasn't she surviving in a climate that had suffocated the best of them, among the very people who had tried to ruin her?

Wake up, you deluded fool! You've been a criminal ever since you engineered your own eggs. But you've been lying to yourself about that for a decade. Even when you found out FIBR was after you, it still didn't seem real, because Jacqueline Witt is not a rogue! So you marched into your own office tonight as if you actually owned the place. As if everything you love couldn't be taken from you in a second.

Jacqueline caught her breath in a strangled sob. What she loved more than anything—the family she had just discovered, *her* family—was about to be taken from her. Because Melman was in a coma and all bets, all deals, were off.

A kind of furious despair engulfed her. God knew what the FIBR detective would do to her a few hours from now—administer OxyTalk or worse—but Jacqueline knew she could never say a word about Howard or the kids. No matter what they did to her. *Are you sure about that?* sneered the devil's advocate in her head. *Stronger souls than you have crumbled under the influence of drugs and torture.* Wanting to throttle that terribly honest voice, Jacqueline took a slow, quivery breath. And then another. What had Aurie said about being trapped in a cage? *Your skull is a coffin ... only the brain inside is alive, it's buried alive.* If she had to stare at walls like these for the rest of her life—

There was a slight commotion in the room outside—the sound of voices and a door being buzzed open. With a stab of real fear, Jacqueline sat up and looked around.

Someone had just arrived; he was speaking to the deputy at the front desk. The newcomer was wearing a suit, but he didn't have the air of a detective or a government operative. Even his suit was—well, it was too old-fashioned, something a man might have worn half a century ago. Jacqueline got up and walked over to the bars to get a closer look. The visitor handed some card or badge to the deputy, then looked up and met her eyes. Something about his face seemed awfully familiar, but it wasn't until he'd crossed half the distance to her cell that she recognized him.

"Abel!"

Abel hushed her at once. "Don't talk, Doc. Just listen." He approached with a weary grin. "Looks like you're in need of some counsel. Abelard Alistair Wake, at your service."

"Abel—you're a *lawyer?*"

"I said, don't talk," Abel reminded her. "You probably think you're whispering, but you've got a voice like every other woman, and it soars right across the room! Yeah, I'm a lawyer—or I was, in my other life. Science isn't the only profession that's gone to hell." He considered her for a moment. "You were damned lucky to wind up here, you know. Howard was sure they'd have whisked you off to the Institute and put the screws to you by now. But then, he has an overdeveloped sense of his own importance." Abel brushed some lint off his sleeve and chuckled. "Easier for the feds to just leave you with the local authorities overnight, and send their people to torture you after breakfast. You haven't tried to contact anyone, have you?"

Jacqueline shook her head, still in a daze. Howard's brother in his faded suit that smelled of mothballs was the most welcome sight she'd ever seen.

"Good girl," Abel whispered. "Now, listen—Deputy Dawg over there didn't look too closely at my old credentials, but we need to get out of here before someone else does. Our best bet is false imprisonment on trumped-up charges, being detained without legal justification. It's hardly a crime to remove materials from your own office, and you haven't been a party to any crime in Kendall Square. You are just a potential witness and one willing to cooperate, but a night in jail is out of the question. You'll come back later today and give a full statement. They can even put a tracker on you, if they insist. So for now, I'm your lawyer, and—"

"Abel," Jacqueline whispered. Tears were brimming in her eyes. "I don't know what—I mean, I can't ... I don't—"

"You're welcome, Doc," Abel said, squeezing the hand she thrust through the bars. "I'll call Howard and let him know I found you. Then I'll get serious with that fellow by the door. Your crazy family needs you." He smiled with a sudden openness that took thirty years from his face, rendering him a taller version of his nephew. All at once, Jacqueline felt a stab of pure homesickness for her kids. Abel was right, her crazy family *did* need her— and she needed them with a fierce depth of longing that made her dizzy. And not just her kids ... Howard too. As she watched Abel work his gruff charm on the deputy, Jacqueline was startled to realize that her resentment against Howard was gone.

You're every bit the rogue he is, except you're no good at it. You've been taking your freedom for granted and making stupid mistakes ... finally getting caught, just like the cop said. Jacqueline could just imagine what the father of her children would have to say to her when she got back. And yet, staring through the bars of her cell, she felt as light as a milkweed pod, as free as its silken threads on a breath of air.

Forty minutes and a dozen forms later, Abel drove them to MIT and pulled up next to the rental car. He gave the narrow band around Jacqueline's left wrist a speculative look.

"Let's hope this works," he said, producing a slim object from his pocket. Holding the tool against Jacqueline's tracker, Abel rotated the band all the way around her wrist.

"That ought to deactivate it." He snapped the band open with a triumphant grunt and removed it from her wrist. Then he snapped it shut and performed the same operation with his tool.

"And that should reactivate it." Abel surveyed the little tracker with satisfaction. "All these years, and they're still using the same old model."

"How many other clients have you performed this special service for?" Jacqueline asked.

Abel shrugged, giving her a roguish smile. "I'll drop this off at your house," he said, slipping the tracker into his pocket. "Then I'll see you back at the hotel. Hope there's an extra couch for me to crash on—and no more tasks in the service of King Howard. Not until noon."

Jacqueline promised him a whole room to himself, and they parted ways. She arrived back at the Intermezzo just as a grey dawn touched the eastern sky, and quietly let herself into the suite. Py was still asleep on the couch, but Howard was up and making waffles. Homemade ones. Flour and eggshells were strewn all over the counter, and the sweet scent of cooking batter mingled with the rich aroma of coffee.

"So you're alive," he said, taking in her rumpled clothes and hangdog expression. "And no worse for wear?" His tone was casual, but his eyes were heavy with concern. He looked like he hadn't slept at all.

She nodded, collapsing into a chair. "Melman is in a coma."

Howard's eyes widened. "Who told you that? Melman's not in a coma, he's just fine! Truly no worse for wear. I hacked into the inpatient-outpatient records at Mass General while you were sleeping this afternoon. Our good Director checked in late this morning and they released him an hour later."

What? The cop who arrested me said he was in a coma! They were sending someone to interrogate me tomorrow, force me to give up you and the kids." She began to cry, suddenly and soundlessly, tears running unchecked down her face.

"I wouldn't have let anything happen to them," he said swiftly. "If Abel couldn't have sprung you, I would've taken the kids to our new hideout before morning. No one but Alé knows where that is." He sighed as he forked a steaming waffle onto a plate. "The bigger problem now is Aurie's eggs ... in the hands of those incompetent assholes!"

"No," she said, wiping her eyes. "They don't have the eggs. I got them into one of my tanks before the cop found me."

He looked at her with utter surprise. "You did? No cameras?"

She shook her head. "The detective only came because I tried to grab some files afterward. They had my office probed. It was my own damn fault."

Howard looked uncomfortable. "It was my fault too, for putting you in that position. I knew you wanted to save those eggs, but I didn't know how desperate you were! We should have come up with a plan together. Instead I shot you down and almost lost you."

She was quiet as he ladled more batter onto the iron.

"I would've rescued you, of course," he said, giving her a smug look, "but not before you lost some fingernails or worse." He flipped the iron and frowned thoughtfully. "The eggs can't stay where they are, you know. FIBR will take over your lab or shut it down completely, and very soon."

She thought for a moment. "Doug still works down the hall from me. I can ask him to move the box with her eggs to one of his tanks, until we can find a better home for it. He'll do it, no questions asked. He hates FIBR as much as we do."

Howard nodded. "But they'll have all his devices tapped by now. Better use a stealth delivery drone."

"What on earth is *that?*"

He smiled faintly. "Something the government uses that we aren't supposed to use—or even know about. I keep two in my Brute Squad Emergency Kit. Want to guess how much they cost?"

Jacqueline shook her head, wide-eyed.

"Whatever you're thinking, triple it. But they're worth having; you never know when one could save your life. It'll get to Doug's office in twenty minutes and look like nothing but a fly on the wall until he gets there. Then it'll land near his ear and whisper *message from your ex-wife* before he can bat it away!"

"You tried to make me into an honest criminal years ago," she reminded him. "I was a fool not to let you."

"Never too late," he said, with a twinkle in his eyes. "Better have a waffle while I dig up that drone—they're really only good when they're hot."

Ten minutes later, the stealth drone had been programmed and sent on its way, and Jacqueline was helping herself to a second waffle.

"You want anything on top of that?" Howard asked. "I forgot to grab maple syrup from the RV, but there's some glow-in-the-dark algae jelly in the cupboard."

She shook her head, smiling. "Can't believe this place came with a waffle iron."

"It didn't ... I got it from the RV."

She stared at him, uncomprehending.

"Abel drove it down here, then took his own car to get you out of jail. How else do you think he got here?"

"I *didn't* think. I was too overjoyed at being rescued!" She was quiet for a moment. "I didn't think I'd ever see you again. You or the kids."

Howard grinned as he grabbed some extra mugs from the cabinet. "No such luck, Dr. Witt. Now that you've tracked us down, you'll never get rid of us."

She gave his hand a squeeze, then went to the back bedroom to check on Aurie. In the faint nimbus of light from the open doorway, the figure on the stretcher appeared almost translucent. Jacqueline approached her daughter and took Aurie's hand in her own. It was cold, that hand, but the flesh felt alive. There was no pulse in that wrist, and yet there was a sense of barely contained energy thrumming just below the surface, as if every cell inside were a madhouse of activity.

"She *is* alive," Jacqueline murmured in wonder, truly believing it for the first time since Aurie's fall. "She really is."

"I know," said Howard. He came up behind her and handed her a mug of coffee. "She's working a thousand times harder than the rest of us, and doing it on sugar water! Probably be hungry enough to eat a whole colony of rabbits when she wakes up."

329

The darkness around Aurie was absolute. There were no chromosomes or proteins lurking in shadows, no imaginary venue to hold the discourse of her dreams. But when the CRISPR-evo doctor spoke, she understood him. His words came from the dark, in a language that molded itself from the emptiness of space.

What is the fundamental unit of life?

Aurie tried to think, but her mind was a closed factory, all of its machinery shut down and silent. She could feel the whole weft of her soul loosening, its edges unraveling like the hem of a frayed cloak.

The fundamental unit of life is the cell. This thought arrived as an echo of something she had said before, and she knew it wasn't the right answer. The right answer was like a jewel at the bottom of a very deep well, beyond the reach of any light. She dredged the well in desperation, blurting answers into the dark and hoping to stumble upon the truth.

As she spoke the names of microscopic things—wrong answers, all—she saw the jewel in the midst of the void. It burned with its own light, a spark both fierce as star fire and lambent as a candle flame. It resonated with a single note of music, distilled from the thunder of galaxies and the whisper of dividing cells. The music formed a word, one she had never heard before, one she had always known. A Word that breathed energy and change into the void, sparking the dance between order and chaos. It was the source of the Pattern, the force behind all creation and destruction, the enemy of stagnancy, the opposite of nothing. In the potency of that Word, her soul began to reform. Aurie felt every thread in its crumbling warp grow warm and stir again like reeds in a gust of wind. They hissed and drew together, weaving themselves into shape. As she regained *herself,* the light of the jewel expanded and brightened around her, and the Word itself faded away.

Where did it go?

She felt, rather than saw, the Doctor's smile in the dark.

It isn't any where or when, he said. *But without it, no life in the universe could exist.*

I have to find it again, she cried in desperation. *I have to remember!*

The Doctor's voice was uncharacteristically gentle. *Already you remember it falsely, as a light or a sound or a voice—some sensory input that your mind can grasp.*

How do you know all this? She couldn't stop herself from asking, even though this exchange felt like a perfect echo of one that had taken place when she was much younger. And the Doctor answered her just as he had on that day, a lifetime ago.

Every creature knows the source of life, in every fiber of its being. Only the human mind refuses to understand.

The light was still intensifying, shrinking the darkness into shadows, then banishing them like mist in the morning sun. And now Aurie could see the cell around her—its proteins degraded to fragments, its scaffolds fallen, its genes silent. A bedraggled fellow in a dirty white coat crawled slowly around the raft of a chromosome. He grinned at her with decaying teeth, holding up a multi-tool that looked rusty and barely serviceable.

You like to keep me busy, don't you? croaked the Doctor. *Well, I hope you're ready to work, my dear. Rome is in ruins—there's hardly a pillar left standing!*

XI

"We're penned up here like rabbits," Py grumbled from the patio. Jacqueline looked over from the kitchen to see him stalking the small yard like a caged tiger—not a rabbit. He had been doing that all morning, darting inside every few minutes to check on his sister's aura. She turned down the temperature on the stove and covered the sizzling pans, then went to join him. The air outside had a quiet expectancy, a sense of impending snow. And yes, in the walled confines of the backyard, they were indeed penned.

"It's not forever," she said. "Just until your sister gets better. And she *is* getting better, it's just taking some time."

"Because her god is gone," Py said quietly. "Before it flew away, she could've fixed herself in no time at all."

They both glanced toward the back bedroom, where Aurie had lain for three days. Her heart had begun to beat on the second day, an event that had thrilled them all, but thus far, there was no sign of brain activity. Any doctor would have pronounced her legally dead, yet there was still that weird translucence about her, and the feeling of almost palpable activity taking place just under her skin. They could all see it. Even Abel, before heading back to his cabin, had admitted that his niece looked strangely *animated* for someone lying dead to the world on a stretcher. And although Py said that her aura hadn't changed, it was still there.

The toaster pinged from inside, and Jacqueline stepped back into the warmth of the suite. "Come and have some breakfast."

When she was still alone in the kitchen five minutes later, Jacqueline returned to the patio to find Py gazing up at heavy cloud banks forming to the north. Snow coming, just as Abel had said. Jacqueline was struck by how thin and frail her little boy looked. His clothes hung loose on his small frame, and his hair stuck out in every direction. *Miniature version of his father,* she thought with affectionate concern.

She went over to him and ruffled his hair. "I can't believe you're not jumping at the mention of breakfast. Your food is getting cold."

Py shuffled inside and Jacqueline closed the sliding door against the chill. In the kitchen, she pulled still-warm English muffins from the toaster and buttered them, then slid a golden-brown Denver omelette onto a plate beside a small mountain of fried potatoes. She got out a carton of orange juice and a jar of blackberry jam, and set the whole feast on the table.

Py wandered over, but his attention seemed to be elsewhere. His eyes roamed over the walls in a skittish way that reminded Jacqueline of her night in police custody.

"What are we going to do when Aurie gets better?" he asked.

"We're going back to your uncle's cabin for awhile."

The boy's face brightened at once. "Really? It's safe for us there?"

"Safer than anywhere else. Your uncle bought the place under a false identity, after dying of a heart attack." She thought Py would be surprised at that, but he only nodded.

"He faked his own death so he wouldn't have to drink beers at barbecues or hit any more golf balls," Py said admiringly. "What was he, a professional golfer?"

Jacqueline chuckled. "He was a lawyer here in Boston. Prosecutor for the state, got a few crooked politicians put away. According to your dad, he really lit the courtrooms on fire, made some lifelong friends and a lot of enemies. Even now, there's always a chance that someone will recognize him. He took a big risk coming into the Cambridge police station to rescue me."

"And you're staying with us at the cabin, right?" Py said, sounding doubtful and hopeful at the same time. "You *are* going rogue, aren't you?"

"I *am* a rogue," Jacqueline told him firmly. "Your dad says no one gets special treatment, though. As the newest member of the Wake Institute, I have to start off washing dishes and work my way up. Make all your buffers and take out the trash!"

Smiling a little, Py sat down and picked up one of the English muffins. "How's Uncle Abel doing? I bet he's bored all by himself. Did he make it back before the snow?"

"Just barely. He says another eight inches came down overnight." Jacqueline glanced down at Aurie's Spider on her wrist, which the girl had left at Abel's cabin, and the ex-lawyer had returned to them. Now that he finally had a Spider of his own, Abel was sending them messages every five minutes. "Put some jam on that," she ordered, pushing the jar toward him. "Before the next breeze blows you over the hedge!"

"Why aren't *you* eating?" Py asked, looking suspicious as he dutifully plastered his muffin with jam.

"I'm forcing your father out this morning," she told him. "We won't be gone for long."

Py looked both curious and envious, and Jacqueline felt a pang of guilt for leaving him here. But if anyone needed to get out, it was Howard—and Jacqueline wanted to talk to him alone, out of the range of ultra-sensitive ears.

After pouring Py a glass of juice, she went into the back bedroom, where Howard sat hunched by their daughter's side. She knew he hadn't been sleeping much—mostly dozing in his chair. Now he held Aurie's left hand, staring down at the limp tangle of her threads as if they were a map he couldn't read.

"Come," Jacqueline said, gently extracting Aurie's hand and placing it by the girl's side. "We're going out."

"What?" Howard looked up, his frown deepening into a scowl. "Where?"

"Just out," she said.

He followed her down the hall, then stopped at the sight of Py eating breakfast. "Why are we going out? There's a ton of food right here!"

"You haven't been eating the food here," Jacqueline pointed out. "And you could use some fresh air. You've been cooped up in that room for three days and you're starting to look like a cave-fish."

"But what if she wakes up?"

Jacqueline pulled the pager from her purse and shook it at Howard. "We'll know the very instant she wakes up! And we're not making a pilgrimage to the mountains of Tibet, we're just going to a restaurant five minutes away. Are you coming?"

Without waiting for an answer, she headed out the door and across the lot. She had gotten behind the wheel of the rental and started it up before Howard finally slid into the passenger seat.

"Kids shouldn't be alone," he groused, looking around the parking lot suspiciously.

"We left them alone to go shopping three days ago," Jacqueline reminded him. "Put your seatbelt on, Howard."

Howard buckled up, raising his eyebrows at her. "Are you kidnapping me, Dr. Witt?"

"I seem to be doing a lot of that these days," she responded, steering them out of the lot and down the street under lowering clouds and shifting patches of blue sky.

Py's orange juice tasted like bile and acid leaching from his increasingly sour mood.

He set the glass down with a sharp clunk. It was great that they were all going back to Uncle Abel's, but it had suddenly dawned on Py that he'd been left completely out of the planning. His dad had always talked things over with him and Aurie like equals. Now his mom and dad were plotting in secret, acting like adults and treating him like a kid who was too stupid to be trusted. And they needed to get out of the prison hideout, did they? Figured *he* could just stay here and hold the fort while they drove off on their own!

Leaving the remains of his breakfast, Py stormed out to the backyard. The fresh air was winter-cold, and little eddies of wind skirled over the hedge to taunt him, whispering of far-off places.

A thin wail from the adjacent patio drew him to the fence between suites. Peering through a gap in the slats, he saw a baby sitting in a whirligig, all alone on the manicured lawn. The whirligig looked like what it was—a mini luxury pod. Through its glass walls, Py could see temperature and auto-sanitation panels, liquid packets with nipples, a snack dispenser, and a ThinAir display console, currently projecting Build-Your-Own cartoons. But a fancy cage was still a cage. The baby's aura was raw-edged and fidgety, and his little feet pounded the floor of the pod as if trying to escape.

"You and me both, kid," Py muttered, turning his back on the outside world and returning to his own pod with a sigh. There was no point in torturing himself, he thought, even as he headed down the hall to look in on Aurie ... yet another form of pointless torture.

In the dim room, his sister lay motionless, her aura hazy and pale. Although that luminous feather still shone in the midst of it, her aura hadn't gained any brightness of its own. Py wondered if it had lost something—some critical essence—at the moment of flight. Had it survived the separation from its alien counterpart without any damage? How could he know?

As he stared at the gauzy folds of his sister's aura, something inside Py shifted, and his claustrophobia—which had been frustrating, but bearable—became a desperate longing for radiant light and endless space. It was the same kind of undeniable craving he had felt on the day of his Change. The walls of the room loomed and threatened on all sides; his sister's aura suffocated him with its faintness. Sick with the need to get free of walls, to immerse himself in sunlight and open space, Py grabbed his pack from the couch and slipped out the front door.

Once he reached the main street, Py began to run, in the grip of a driving instinct that blinded him to everything but light and air. The wind was at his back, urging him forward, and cold sunlight streamed down, branding the world with intermittent fire. At the junction with a service road, he turned left without hesitation, heading for the open coast. Buildings and people passed by in a meaningless blur; all he saw clearly was the light winking from glass windows and chrome hoods, glaring off metal girders, shining from white awnings. Py took a side street, and the glittering grey ocean lay before him, unrolling itself like a carpet of gems under the sky. He raced down Seaport Boulevard with his heart beating high in his throat. What finally stopped him was a dome that blazed with all the fire of the autumn sun.

That's it! Py gazed up at the dome of the planetarium, as his labored breath sent plumes of steam into the air. Whatever new fire was kindling in his cells would ignite itself here, where the brightest lights of all shone in the deep void of space.

The place Jacqueline had in mind was a dim sum shop on the outskirts of Chinatown, somewhere they could eat and talk safely. There were no privacy screens in the crowded little bakery, but the din of a dozen conversations in Mandarin was just as effective. Once she and Howard found a table, though, neither of them bothered to look at the menu. Jacqueline ordered tea, then sat watching Howard, who was staring into the air with a kind of unfocused intensity.

"She'll get through this," he said suddenly, as if Jacqueline had suggested otherwise. "Py thinks she will, and he hasn't been wrong yet."

"I know," Jacqueline said quietly. "But, Howard, about her eggs—"

"Those eggs," he said, with a bitter chuckle. "I was so sure you were planning something with them, some new feat of engineering! But you weren't, were you? The truth is, she wanted to freeze them herself. She went to *you,* and she didn't want me to know a damned thing."

"She only came to me because I knew Dr. Hahn," Jacqueline said, trying and failing to catch his eye. "I could get her an appointment on short notice, and she was under a time constraint. Because of the Change."

"Ah, yes." Howard's voice held a strange mixture of pride, triumph, and resentment. "The *Change*. Py told me what she said when they were camped out on your roof. He said the alien part of her was talking about some faraway galaxy. And you both insist that something flew away when she jumped, some *winged god*—" Howard jumped a little as a pot and two steaming cups slid out of the wall dispenser. He took hold of a cup and drank too fast, wincing.

"You really didn't see it, did you?" Jacqueline blew on her cup of tea and took a careful sip.

"I saw my kid fall four stories onto a bed of chrysanthemums," Howard said flatly.

Jacqueline sipped her tea, considering. "When Aurie jumped, Py saw the *aura* of that thing take to the sky. And maybe I could see it too, because of what she showed me with her threads—that Pattern in her genome."

Howard finally looked at her, but his face held no expression.

"I don't know what the purpose of this Pattern is," she confessed, "but there's no question it exists. I know I can't make you believe that, or understand why I'm so sure. You'd have to see it for yourself."

The pain crept back into Howard's face like a shadow. "When I showed up at your house, she ran off. She's never run away from me like that. She's always come to me with everything."

Jacqueline hesitated only briefly before answering. "She was afraid you were going to take control of her eggs."

"What do you mean, take control of them?"

"Make decisions about them. When and how to fertilize, whether to modify them in some way, how to raise them."

"How to raise my future *grandkids*? I have enough to worry about just raising my kids!"

"I know, but all these years you've run a family garage lab. As Aurie's dad, you might respect her wishes regarding her children, but as the head of the lab, you might see ways of improving her eggs. And she couldn't take that risk. She insists they have to be left alone."

Howard's face was a stew of suppressed emotion. "And she didn't trust me enough to just tell me that? To tell me herself?"

"I wouldn't worry too much," Jacqueline said. "I think it was only the alien part of her that felt that way."

He stared at her without speaking.

"It makes sense, doesn't it?" Jacqueline warmed her hands on her cup, realizing it was the first time she had acknowledged the idea. "If we can believe what she showed me, that alien entity, liberated from the sleeping part of her genome, *is* a kind of god. Maybe the galaxy she described to Py is its future home. Maybe it has a whole world of new species to create, who knows? Whatever its purpose is, it answers to no one. Certainly not a primitive Tinker who only woke it up by accident. Of course it doesn't trust you." She smiled at him and put her hands around his, which were wrapped tight around his cup. "But your daughter does. That thing is gone now, thank God, and Aurie is herself again. *Only* herself."

Howard looked at her for a moment longer, and then his face crumpled. He lowered his head and wept silently. Jacqueline was stunned—she couldn't have imagined him weeping; she hadn't believed he knew how. Before she knew it, she was beside him in the booth, her arms around him, her own tears mingling with his.

"She's going to be fine," Jacqueline whispered hoarsely. "She loves you and trusts you, and she's going to be fine! I've never seen anyone braver or more determined."

Howard raised his head and uttered a small, sad laugh. Then he took her face in his hands and kissed the tears from her eyes. He stared at her intently, his fingers warm against her skin.

"You love them, don't you?" It wasn't really a question.

"More than anything," she said, but his eyes were still burning into hers, unsatisfied.

"Don't leave," he said in a low, urgent voice. She wiped her face and gave him a crooked smile.

339

"You see—that's the kind of imperious attitude that newly woken gods take issue with."

"Newly woken gods," he echoed, kissing her briefly on the lips before releasing her. She got up to return to her side of the table, but he grabbed her hand and pulled her back down.

"To think we woke up a god, Jacqueline. Can you believe such a thing?"

She wasn't sure that *he* believed it, but at least his eyes had regained something of their usual spark. Suddenly, Jacqueline wished they were alone. He had kissed her, but not long enough for her to kiss him back. Howard was watching her, still holding her hand, the ghost of a smile playing around his mouth.

"CRISPR evolution," he said, still marveling. "How can we ever top it? What are we going to do for an encore?"

"Wait for our daughter to finish resurrecting herself." Jacqueline couldn't think beyond that—beyond the hope that what she had told Howard was true.

"She will," Howard said, squeezing her hand. "She has a job to do, by God! A whole crew of little hell-raisers to bring up, and I hear she doesn't want any help from the boss."

They ordered a fresh pot of tea with a slew of greasy pastries and dumplings oozing rich juices. *The hell with the calories,* thought Jacqueline, as they demolished the tasty fare. Howard paid the bill and they headed back to the car through stretches of sunlight and shadow. A swift breeze danced around their feet, shooing fallen leaves into the gutter. It reminded Jacqueline of the gale that had sprung up from nowhere at the moment Aurie had jumped, as if to speed the winged god's flight.

"Thanks for dragging me to breakfast," Howard said, pulling her close once they reached the car. He looked at her quietly. "I love you, Jackie," he said. "I've known it ever since you refused to tell me what you were working on all those years ago."

"You should've just asked," she said, smiling up at him. "I was always a breath away from telling you."

He pushed a stray lock of hair from her face. "Weren't you afraid I'd steal your idea and run with it?"

"That wouldn't have been very efficient," she pointed out. "Better to let me slave away over the idea, then steal the *reality* and run with it."

She was only teasing him, but his face showed naked remorse. "Can you ever forgive me for that?"

"Can you forgive *me* for walking right into the arms of the brute squad?"

Howard's eyes brightened. "What red-blooded man can't save the love of his life from the brute squad?"

"By calling his brother," she reminded him archly. "Probably the best idea you ever had."

He laughed softly. "Getting you mad enough to chase me was the best idea I ever had." Then he leaned down and kissed her, as if they were alone. They were still lost in each other when the pager in Jacqueline's purse finally lived up to its name.

XII

The planetarium that had drawn Py turned out to be part of the Endeavor Science Center, a cluster of new, sleek buildings that included a Natural History Museum. Under other circumstances, he would have ignored the planetarium and made a beeline for the museum, but the implacable force inside him—like a soldier in his feet—drove him without hesitation into the only place where stars shine by day. As the smoked glass doors closed behind him, Py felt the new Change gathering itself like a tidal wave, whispering its warning along every nerve in his body. He felt instantly feverish in the cloistered warmth of the lobby, and uncomfortably aware of all the people around him. Some of them were lined up near the doors to the auditorium; some were at the service machines, paying with cards or their Spiders. As Py dug into his coat pocket for money, something light and dry brushed his fingers. Bewildered, he pulled it out and recognized Aurie's gift to him on the rooftop. He stared at the mushroom, finally breaking off a bit and putting the rest back in his pocket. Was this little piece too much or not enough? He was torn between the fear of eating it and the fear of not eating it. What was it Aurie had said? *Your Doctor can handle trace amounts of poison, but he needs help with the Policeman. Trust me.*

"You better be right," Py said under his breath, then he put the bit of dried fungus into his mouth and let it soften against his tongue. The swarm of funky flavors made him think of ants crawling up tree trunks, and beetles scuttling through wet forest earth. The mushroom had a wild, *alive* taste, and he quickly swallowed it before he lost his nerve.

Maybe that'll be the end of me, he thought grimly as he approached one of the service kiosks. Would it accept his old-fashioned bills? He had quite a few of those, thanks to Uncle Abel

342

telling him to keep the change from their lunch. Py fed twenty dollars into the cash slot and waited nervously while hidden gears digested his money. Finally, the machine spat out a ticket and a few coins. Py took them and filed into the queue. He scrutinized all the strange auras around him, wondering if they were more alive, more *complete,* than his sister's. He felt a surge of guilt for leaving Aurie alone, then the doors to the auditorium opened and the soldier inside him tried to elbow its way past the crowd. Py fought to keep control, forcing his legs to match the stilted pace of the elderly lady in front of him.

He handed his ticket to the service bot at the door, then found a seat inside and sat down. Blinking feverishly in the dark, Py clutched the armrests to keep his hands still. A disembodied voice began to speak, but most of the words degenerated into nonsense in his ears. Py's seat slid backward without warning, sending his stomach lurching into his throat, and he fought to keep his breakfast down. When stars and planets appeared in the dome above, he stared at them, barely understanding what they were. *Giant balls of superheated gases,* droned the narrator. *Worlds of fire and ice.* Py tried to focus on a cluster of milky specks overhead, but his eyes wouldn't obey—they rolled like two balls of fire in their sockets. Behind his eyes, something superheated was on the verge of exploding.

A billion pinpoints of light in the night sky, intoned the mindless voice as the constellations overhead deepened with startling brilliance. And suddenly there *were* a billion pinpoints of light, extending through the fabric of space so that Py was no longer staring at specks on the surface of a dome, but seeing through light-years to these isolated denizens of the void. Inside his skull the fever raged; he could no longer distinguish the fire in his head from the many fires burning above. The light and heat crescendoed like some deadly music surging to a blinding climax, and then all the fire went out at once.

Py stared into the black emptiness of space. The dome and the auditorium were gone; he might have been lying in a field gazing up at a moonless night sky. Then he shifted his attention to the horizon and found that all the stars had fallen to earth. They burned all around him, flaming like stars, yet pulsing and drifting like ... auras.

Py's heart began to race. He twisted in his seat, looking in all directions across the brightly jeweled plain. Far to the west, a single jewel outshone all the others, its shape as familiar to him as his own face.

His sister's aura had brightened. It pulsed again. And though her god had flown, some of its inhuman glory suffused Aurie's human aura, turning it into a torch among lesser flames. Py leapt out of his seat and stumbled down the aisle, heading for the emergency exit at the back of the auditorium. Outside, he looked around wildly, blinking at the glare of sunlight on glass and metal walls, even as a thousand auras shone around him, unbounded by any walls. Elated, he began to run. People disappeared into buildings or vehicles that carried them out of sight, but their auras were unobstructed, visible to him in all directions. It was dizzying, and he had to stop himself from running into traffic or into walls and lamp posts. Tangible objects had never seemed so insubstantial. And the only thing he had eyes for was the single aura he recognized, fixed like a beacon in a restless sea.

As he neared the hotel, that aura trembled and flared into consciousness. With a jubilant cry, Py ran faster. He darted across streets with little care for the cars that might run him down, and took a shortcut through the parking lot. Then he was outside the hotel suite, jiggling the door handle savagely.

"She's awake!" he shouted as his mom and dad came rushing up behind him.

"Awake, we know!" Howard echoed incredulously as Jacqueline unlocked the door. "Her monitor just went off five minutes ago! Where the hell did you go?"

"Tell you later," Py said, as they raced each other to Aurie's room. Py got there first and burst inside. She was still lying the way he had left her, eyes closed and motionless. The soft hum of the respirator was the only sound in the room.

"Aurie?" Py walked up to the bed, scrutinizing the fabric of his sister's aura. This close, he could see the strain in the fibers—they were fever-bright, shivering with exhaustion, but her aura was vital and intact. "I know you're awake! Open your eyes. *Say* something."

Aurie opened her eyes.

She looked at Py long enough for him to see that it was really her, and then she shifted her gaze to Jacqueline and Howard at the foot of the stretcher. Howard turned off the respirator, then carefully removed the tube from Aurie's trachea.

"Dad," she said in a voice as thin as a wind-torn leaf.

Howard took her hand in both of his and squeezed it. "Aurie," he said hoarsely. "Oh, Aurie."

"I'm sorry," she whispered.

She didn't say anything more, only lay there and looked at her father as he bent over her, kissing her clasped hand and stroking her face. Howard whispered to Aurie, things that Py could have heard if Jacqueline hadn't pulled him gently out of the room with her. Looking back before his mom closed the door, Py saw his sister's eyes fill with tears.

That thing really is gone, he thought with vast relief. He had watched the alien creature fly away, but somehow seeing Aurie cry reassured him in a way that nothing else could.

Exhausted from his Change, Py fell asleep on the couch, and his sleep was deep and dreamless. When he awoke that evening, ravenous, the living room was dark and silent, but he was adrift in a cosmos of twinkling auras. His mom's aura pulsed in her bedroom, and in the other room, his father's and sister's auras flickered and danced. Wincing at the pins and needles in his legs, Py got up and raided the fridge, making short work of a leftover lasagna, an olive loaf, and a lemon cream pie. Finally sated, he peeked into his mom's room to find her sitting on her bed, working quietly on the display of Aurie's Spider. On the other side of the hall, low voices came from behind the closed door. Py had never really eavesdropped before, but all of his senses had grown so acute since his first Change that he hardly thought this qualified as eavesdropping. He didn't even have to put an ear to the door, he simply stood by the wall and listened.

They were talking about the Pattern, and all of the ways it could be fulfilled. How Aurie's eggs held newly-woken gods waiting to be born, to create or colonize or drive the evolution of another world. Howard wasn't talking much, but when he did say something, Py barely recognized his dad's voice. He had never heard his father speak in such reverent tones before, with such—such—was it *humility?* It was disturbing, to say the least. And his father's aura had changed. Not the hue or intensity or sharpness of it, which varied all the time, but the actual *shape* of it. The difference was subtle, but unmistakable.

"Show me again," Howard murmured. Using his unbounded chemical sense, Py watched through the wall with fascination and envy as a long, bright strand grew from his sister's aura and fastened itself to his father's. So Aurie's threads were still working, even though the alien part of her was gone! Now their dad must be seeing the Pattern the way Jacqueline had. When the glimmering thread finally returned to its source, the two auras converged in a long embrace, then the door was flung open and Howard rushed into the other bedroom without noticing the eavesdropper glued to the wall. Py watched his father's aura join Jacqueline's and listened to the sound of their soft voices rising in excitement, then he entered Aurie's room.

His sister was sitting up on the stretcher. Her eyes flared in the mellow light from the bedside lamp, and her aura twisted with hunger.

"Food," she hissed at him. "I was gonna ask Dad for some, but he just ran off. Have you got any? I'm starving!"

Py went out and raided the kitchen for a second time, returning with two peanut butter sandwiches, a side of pickles, and a stack of frosted graham crackers.

"Peanut butter and pickles?" Aurie snorted, but she was already digging in, sending crumbs flying. "I'm not pregnant."

"It was all I could find in a hurry," he said, feeling peevish. "And you're welcome!"

"Thanks," she said, grinning around a mouthful of peanut butter.

Py wondered if she wouldn't rather have a live rabbit, with a few salamanders on the side. He closed the door, then sat cross-legged on his dad's bed. "Finally recovered, huh? What took you so long?"

She glared at him while munching steadily. "Try jumping from forty feet up and we'll see how long it takes *you* to recover."

He chuckled, his good humor restored. "All that repair work sure makes you grouchy. But you still have a CRISPR doctor in every cell of your body, right? Don't they all work at the same time?"

"Yeah," she said, finishing the sandwich and licking her lips. "But some cells were fine and others were a complete mess. A lot of cells were dead and had to be replaced. And the *timing*. Tissues had to be repaired at the same time new nerves and blood vessels were regenerated. The Doctor and I had to coordinate everything. We're still not done." She picked up a pickle and ate it in two bites. "It's got to be easier to build an embryo from scratch than to rebuild a person from broken pieces."

"Well, at least you've got a nice flat surface to work on," Py said. "That couch in the living room is nothing but lumps!"

"You're sleeping on the couch?" Aurie looked surprised. "Where's Dad?"

"He's been sleeping in here," Py said, suddenly noticing that his dad's belongings were no longer in evidence. "But I think he's in the other room with Mom now." Py grimaced in mock disgust, but in truth he was very happy with the arrangement, which seemed to cement Jacqueline's place in their lives. "Who knows, they might give us some normal brothers and sisters pretty soon."

"Ugh," Aurie said. "They better not!"

"Don't worry. Dad took all of Mom's engineered eggs, remember? Whatever's left in her ovaries is guaranteed to produce two-headed monsters by now. I'm sure they don't want that!"

"Yeah, the one-headed monsters they already have are

enough trouble," Aurie said, starting in on the other sandwich.

"Speaking of eggs," Py went on, "did they tell you what happened to yours? Mom saved them, you know."

"I know," she said, looking immensely relieved. "Mom's amazing."

"So what are you going to do with them?" Py cackled. "Find the smartest man in the world and steal his sperm?"

Aurie ignored this as she licked peanut butter off her fingers. "There's no space for a bunch of artificial wombs in a garage lab."

"No room for a CRISPR-evo farm, that's for sure." Then Py said what he had been thinking about for the past few days—and hadn't yet suggested to his parents. "Maybe we could move in with Uncle Abel and build some new additions."

"Oh, he'd love that," Aurie said dryly.

"You know," Py said, "I think he would."

They sat in comfortable silence as Aurie worked her way through the graham cracker tower. Py's thoughts were pleasantly full of hidden trails and mountain caves and deadfall labyrinths.

"Hey, how'd you know I was awake this morning?" Aurie asked suddenly.

He looked at her in surprise and she rolled her eyes. "It's not like I couldn't hear you yelling on the doorstep. The whole hotel must've heard you."

Py grinned and told her about his new Change. She leaned forward eagerly.

"You can see through walls now?" Aurie's eyes gleamed with excitement. "Auras everywhere? What's it like?"

"Like being in the middle of outer space," he said, "with a billion stars all around."

"Well, we *are* in the middle of outer space, with a billion stars all around. How far away can you see an aura?"

He shrugged. "A long way. I could see yours all the way from the waterfront—even without the alien part."

His sister said nothing, but her aura wilted, taking on a charcoal tinge that Py recognized as loneliness or distress.

"Do you miss it?" he asked.

"Yeah," she said, "but not the way you'd normally miss something. More of a hollow feeling, like I've got a missing tooth. And I keep trying to probe the empty place." Her gaze slid away from him, seeking something invisible in the air. "I feel a lot smaller now. Insignificant. Useless."

"Are you kidding?" Py stared at her, the sharp pricks of his envy returning. "Three days ago you were a smashed-up corpse, and now you're almost as good as new. You brought yourself back to life!"

A trace of nostalgia passed like a ghost across his sister's face. "It wasn't me."

"What do you mean, it wasn't you?"

"That leap from the balcony killed me," she said quietly. "Dead people can't bring themselves back to life."

"But your aura was there," he said.

She shook her head. "It wouldn't have been for long. My life was gone. Something brought it back."

"The alien? I saw it fly away!"

"Not the alien," she said. "Something it carried, some kind of light ... I tore off a piece of it when it flew away. It was the light that saved me." She closed her eyes as her aura darkened with something close to despair.

"Hey, your threads still work," Py said, utterly bewildered by her distress. "And you're still as powerful as ever! All *I* can do is see auras. And I don't have any eggs, do I? Doesn't that mean I'm a dead-end wonder? Will I be able to change my own sperm someday, or are males just useless to the Pattern?"

Aurie opened her eyes again and tears spilled down her cheeks. "You're still at the beginning; you don't know all the things you're capable of. I'm already finished."

"What are you talking about? You can do almost anything you want to!"

"But what's the point? I could have *gone* with it, I could have *been* the Pattern!" She stared right through him, her aura writhing with deep and inconsolable heartache. Py watched her

349

with silent concern. He had no idea what to say. How could someone who had done so much—who could *still* do so much—be so unhappy?

Aurie wiped her face and laughed a little. "You think I'm crazy, don't you?"

"Well, yeah."

She expelled a deep breath and leaned back against her pillow. "Not crazy, just greedy. I had a chance for something really cool, that's all—a chance that won't ever come again. But I'm not sorry."

"You better not be sorry! I never would've seen you again." He considered her in reproachful silence. "Can you show me the Pattern now, the way you showed Mom and Dad?"

She shook her head. "Your Policeman, remember? He'd try to destroy all my abnormal cells—for my own good."

Py sighed. "I thought maybe things were different, now that the alien's gone."

"Nothing's different," she said hollowly. "I'm as powerful as ever."

Her aura, he saw, was looking tired again. With the waning of its brightness, he could see the feather quite clearly, standing like a single cool and motionless flame in a dancing cloak of pale fire. He wanted to tell her about it—this had to be the light that had kept her alive—but some instinct kept him silent.

"Better get some rest," he said at last, sliding off the bed and heading for the door. "Still hungry?"

"Just thirsty," she said. So he got her a tall glass of water before heading back to the couch. As he tried to get comfortable, Py fantasized about sleeping on a Smart Foam bed in a room of his own ... on the sprawling laboratory complex they'd have to convince Uncle Abel to let them build in his field. A real lab like his mother's, with miles of benchtops ... and the woods right outside, with miles of trackless wilderness to explore.

"Uncle Abel's CRISPR-evo Farm," he murmured, grinning to himself in the dark.

Like her brother, Aurie lay awake imagining a future home built on her uncle's field, but her version shone with her mother's touches: rag rugs in sunset colors, vases like alien artifacts, and shelves upon shelves of old books. Most of these books had covers that were windows to the endless night, strewn with jeweled suns that burned up their fire in the emptiness of space. On the cusp of sleep, her fantasy gave way to dreaming, and she flew alone through the silence of cold and airless vistas. But now she could see the spiraling billows of the far nebula she sought, its young stars glowing faintly. By the time she arrived, twin suns would illuminate the skies of a planet harboring life in forms no human would recognize. And deep in her soul, she held the Word that sparks change within the dream of existence, waiting only for the moment to begin.

Epilogue

Greetings again, Mr. Goon! You're having a less-than-stellar week, aren't you? After such a promising start, you let another rogue slip right through your fingers, and you'll never get another chance to catch her. Probe all you like, but she isn't setting foot in her house (or her car) again. Keep up the good work, and only Tinkers and robots will be left to unravel the world's mysteries. But maybe that's all right. With all our fancy technology, maybe tinkering is all any of us can do.

Howard paused in the driver's seat of the RV, looking out into the twilight gloom of the woods. This quiet hill, about halfway to Abel's cabin, seemed like a good place to compose his thoughts and send his final missive. But now that he'd started typing, it was strangely difficult to say what he meant. The truth was so significant, it was hard to put into words. Easier to just taunt his faceless enemy, who represented all the goons and hacks of the world rolled up into one; safer to hide behind sarcasm. But if he couldn't tell the truth even to himself, then what was the good of knowing it?

The real revelation is beyond our ability to invent or even imagine. I've spent my whole life tinkering, searching for the tools to open Pandora's Box. I didn't have the faintest idea what was inside, but the human mind insists on putting form to the unknown, so my ignorance took the shape of a hundred variations on little green men. But now the Box is open and I've gotten a glimpse of the wonders it encodes. They are too alien to fathom, which makes them seem monstrous. Yet they jolted my brain awake, stretched it like an unused muscle. If I spent every waking moment beholding that Pattern, would my mind grow to comprehend it, or would I go mad? Who would believe that every one of us is the keeper of unborn myths and the seeds of growth in other worlds? Gods lie sleeping in our DNA! My daughter was brave enough to learn from that sleeping template—how to enable and surrender to something greater than herself. Teaching my children about science is like giving them a candle to probe the darkness, when they are already blazing with their own light.

Howard looked down at the kids, still sound asleep on the seat beside him. He gazed at their quiet forms, all that power and potential lying like two coiled springs. He wondered what he might do if his own potential were tapped. Unleash a new god upon the universe? Smite his enemies? Whip the corrupt, disjointed old world into shape? It was a surprise to find that none of that tempted him very much. He felt all the weight of his life lift as he looked at his children—at their delicate closed eyelids and Aurie's smooth forehead, where only a trace of melancholy lingered. They were still innocent, and he turned back to his letter with a light heart.

I am only a Tinker (by nature), an outlaw (by necessity), and a family man (by great good fortune)—and I wouldn't have it any other way. So from one worker bee to another, here's my trademark salute. Until we meet again.

Closing his laptop on another undeliverable letter, Howard replaced it in his briefcase and picked up the delivery drone. This was no stealth model, just a disposable commercial one. Still, it was cheaper than standard shipping, not to mention a hell of a lot faster. He programmed it for Jacqueline's home address and loaded its cargo. Then he got out of the RV and wandered a few yards up the grassy side of the hill. The dark skies were low and heavy; to the east, the dawn horizon was grey with falling snow. The entire autumn seemed to have rushed by in the flurry of the last few days. The lives of everyone in his family had changed completely—a whole season's metamorphosis packed into little more than a week, as brief and brilliant as the flame passing through these woods—and now winter was almost here. Howard loved all of the seasons; each of them stimulated something different in his psyche. Winter was a time for quiet thinking and planning, fueled by endless pots of coffee—and now he had more to think about than all the winters of his life could accommodate.

He activated the little drone and let it go, watching it lift as easily as a bird—a bird with an orange crown that looked a bit like a foam finger—and glide silently over the foothills of the White Mountains. Then he made his way back to the RV, where the kids were now awake and waiting. Impatiently, from the looks of them.

"Mom called," Py informed him. "She's already at Uncle Abel's."

"She dropped off the rental car with no trouble?"

Py nodded. "And she picked up some steaks for dinner tonight!"

Howard sighed with mock exasperation as he started the engine. "Your mother's been an official rogue for less than a week, and already she's throwing money around! Wait'll she sees what kind of a budget we live on—she'll be running off to the Philippines where she can have a mansion and servants and a fancy lab again."

He was immediately besieged by indignant voices defending Jacqueline's resourcefulness, adaptability, and staunchness in the face of adversity.

Trying to stifle his smile, Howard cut in as if he hadn't heard them. "And you two have been spoiled rotten since we left our place in Westborough. Restaurants and mountain retreats and nice houses in Cambridge! How am I ever gonna get you living in this wreck again? And back to work in the lab?"

Py muttered something under his breath, and he and Aurie shared a grin.

"What did you say?" asked Howard, glaring at Py.

"Nothing," said Py, still grinning.

"Does Uncle Abel like venison?" Aurie asked hopefully. "Pheasants and rabbits? Trout?"

"I think he did mention something about a venison stew,"

said Howard, wondering what they were up to. Py said something to his sister and she gave him the elbow, precipitating a yelp and a mild scuffle in the passenger seat. Howard glanced at them as he drove down the hill, his fierce love for them burning like a coal in his chest. The kids whispered intently to each other, making their secret plans, and Howard fell into a kind of trance that was half reverie and half percolation. The Rubik's puzzle of unknown size and shape had gained another dimension; dozens of new ideas were springing to mind. There were a million things to do and decide, and all the while his thoughts kept returning to that phrase Py had said just loud enough for him to hear. The Wake Institute for Garage Biology had never had a real home, only a string of featureless rooms in forgotten places ... but *Uncle Abel's CRISPR-evo Farm?*

It had a nice ring to it.

Acknowledgements

I am extremely grateful to those who gave their time and creative energies to this book, often at the expense of their own projects.

Peter Jones contributed all that is best in Howard, as well as a sharp critical eye for both science and storytelling, not to mention occasional bits of inspired dialogue that he will emphatically deny writing. Exceptional editing was provided by Marla Himeda (who also crafted interior images), Dawn Hollison, and Steve Jaquith; any mistakes in these pages occurred after they had eyes on the manuscript. Frederick Friedel provided his film industry expertise. Jenny Hasenjaeger designed a cover I could stare at all day, and copy-edited the final version. Finally, a big thank-you to my loyal cadre of trusted readers, who have supported all my writing endeavors over the years, and can always be counted on to let me know when things work and when they don't.

About the Author

Charis Jones (aka Charis Himeda, PhD) is a research professor and co-founder of RENOGENYX, a company dedicated to developing treatments for Facioscapulohumeral muscular dystrophy. She won the FSHD Society's inaugural Young Investigator award, and has been interviewed by *The Washington Post, The Huffington Post,* and *The Boston Business Journal* for engineering FSHD therapeutics using CRISPR gene modifying technology.

At night, Dr. Himeda doffs her lab gloves to pen speculative fiction about renegade scientists who do things she would never dream of doing. She is a three-time winner in the PNWA contest; a winner in the Sandy, the Zebulon, and the Colorado Gold contests; a semifinalist in the Chanticleer International Book Awards; a finalist in the Page Turner Awards; and a quarterfinalist in the Amazon Breakthrough Novel Awards. Her short fiction has appeared in a number of literary magazines and in *The Best American Mystery and Suspense 2021.*

Visit her at charisjonesbooks.com.

Made in the USA
Las Vegas, NV
10 November 2023

80542974R00215